Orcblood Legacy: Madness

BERNARD BERTRAM

Book Two of the Orcblood Legacy Series:

-Honor-
-Madness-
-Book Three Coming Soon-

Acknowledgements:
Todor Hristov (Cover Art Illustrator)
Jaclyn Schickling (Map Illustrator)

1st Edition

ISBN: 1-7327607-5-6
ISBN-13: 978-1-7327607-5-2

Please visit https://bernardbertram.com for additional stories regarding the champions of Orcblood Legacy, updates, contests, and much more!

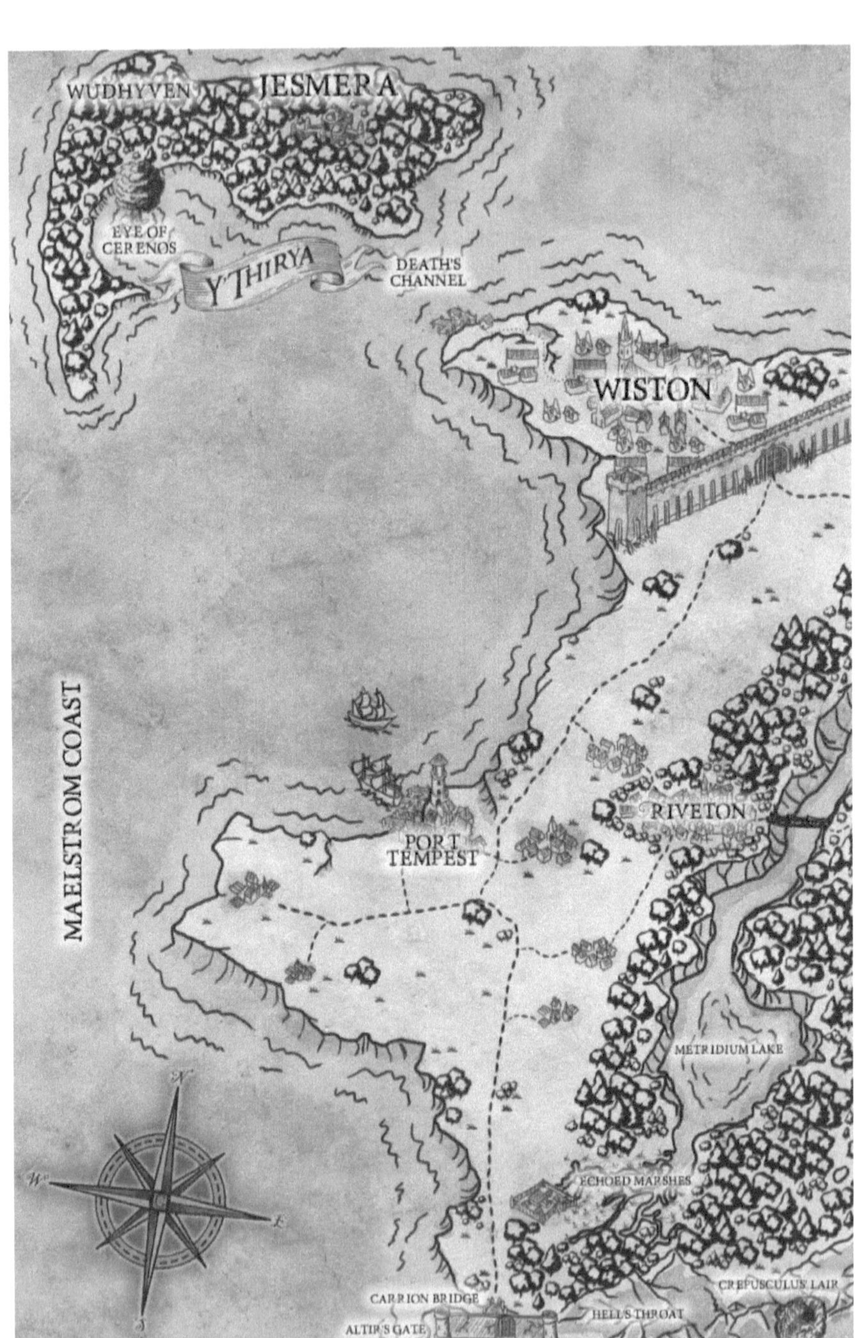
WUDHYVEN
JESMERA
EYE OF
CERENOS
Y'THIRYA
DEATH'S
CHANNEL
WISTON
MAELSTROM COAST
PORT
TEMPEST
RIVETON
METRIDIUM LAKE
ECHOED MARSHES
CARRION BRIDGE
ALTIR'S GATE
HELL'S THROAT
CREPUSCULUS' LAIR

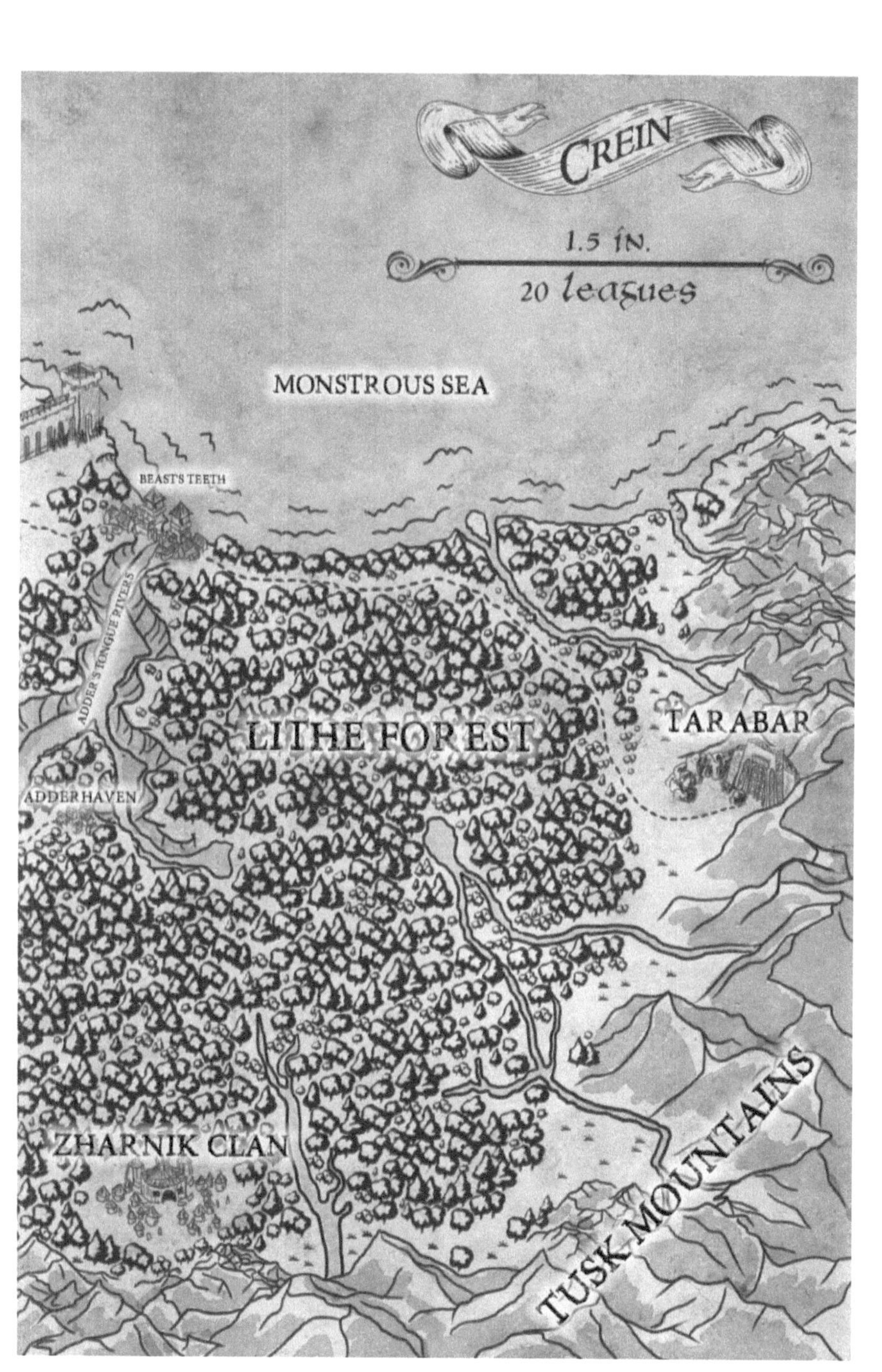
CREIN
1.5 in.
20 leagues
MONSTROUS SEA
BEAST'S TEETH
ADDER'S TONGUE PIVERS
LITHE FOREST
TARABAR
ADDERHAVEN
ZHARNIK CLAN
TUSK MOUNTAINS

DEDICATION

To my daughter, for giving me a reason to explore my dreams, so that one day I can guide you in yours.

PROLOGUE

"Elethain, why are we hunting a dragon, exactly?"

"Because, Rotheilan, I am going to enslave it. Our people would benefit greatly from such an asset."

"As would you, no doubt." The elf cast a smug look to his older brother, who only smirked in reply.

Eithas, the more skeptical twin of Rotheilan, leaned closer to better hear the conversation. "How are you even going to enslave it?" He was convinced their task would fail yet refused to allow his three brothers to continue without him. Despite Eithas' unshakable loyalty, he never failed to question their eldest sibling.

Elethain sighed as he halted his march through the thick brush. Silently, the necromancer stared out through the screen of purplish-blue leaves that restricted most of his view. He could still see the sparkling light reflecting from the surface of the water far below. Their climb up the Eye of Cerenos, the ancient tree near their homeland, Y'thirya, had been more treacherous than expected. Elethain looked to his brothers, each beginning to wither from exhaustion due to traversing the enormous magical growth. Even Idérys, their youngest kin, who was often so full of youthful energy at just a mere two-hundred years old, could be seen dripping with sweat. Elethain had requested they join him in his quest—for the future of their people, supposedly.

Elves had been living on Y'thirya for countless millennia, typically in harmony. However, the elders spoke of a foreboding future. Though they held no mystical knowledge, they believed a great war was fated in the years to come. The date and its cast were unknown, yet they were confident the act would occur. Elethain wasn't one to believe such prophecies but found opportunity in their ramblings. He had heard a myriad of tales of a dragon who rested atop the Eye of Cerenos. As a necromancer, the elf possessed the capability to enslave beings within his domination, to be used as he commanded. In truth, a dragon *could* aid in their future endeavors. But Elethain's goal wasn't to provide an advantage to his people—only himself—and enslaving the beast was no simple task.

Elethain turned back to his kin. "Well, we have to kill it first. From there, I should possess the ability to trap it within the Undying Realm where it will answer my call."

"*Should*?!" Eithas blurted in surprise. "You mean you are not certain?!"

"Should," Elethain repeated with a smile. "Once it is dead, I do not expect it to be a problem. However, I have never done so before, of course. The ritual itself is not so difficult, it seems. The struggle lies thereafter."

"What do you mean?" Rotheilan asked as he casually cut one of the thousands of luscious apples dangling from branches twisted around them with one of his swords. His second sword chopped down another just above Eithas' head, plopping it on his twin's noggin with a dull thud and bringing a smile to each of their faces.

"Once it is trapped within the Undying Realm, it is no longer dead. It would be reanimated and with a constant will of its own. I must maintain control by sheer domination of will. That is how the link is created, master to slave. It can take years—dozens, even *hundreds*—to ensure complete control. During that time, I cannot risk summoning it to the Living Realm, or it could break the link."

Idérys pressed further in eagerness, possessing only a lust for excitement and adventure. "What happens if it breaks the link?"

Their youngest brother's curiosity brought a smile to Elethain's face. "If the link breaks I can either attempt to maintain a semblance of it in order to reel the slave back under my control, or I can relinquish it, which would simply eliminate the reanimated corpse."

Each of Elethain's brothers had nothing left to say, being far out of the realm of their knowledge—or interest. Unlike their eldest kin, they were warriors of the blade. The twins each favored a pair of swords to strike at their foes while Idérys preferred a shield and spear. The band rested easily against thick branches as they ate their apples, pondering their task ahead. Elethain had assured his family the task could be completed, though he remained secretly unconvinced. Very few dragons had ever been conquered in the past, let alone reanimated to be the slave of a necromancer. However, he couldn't deny himself the chance of such a claim. His pursuit of power pushed him to heights others, even those who greatly surpassed his thousand-years of age, dared not risk. The elf bit into his apple, hoping he could achieve all he desired.

* * * * *

"Elethain!" Idérys called out, his eyes full of terror in the moment the golden dragon's massive clawed talon swiped at him.

The necromancer watched in horror as his youngest brother was torn apart in a burst of purple blood by the razor-sharp claw. Elethain looked on, trembling, as

Idérys' entrails spilled onto the floor made of purplish-blue leaves. His brother's hollow eyes remained open but unseeing.

Elethain broke from his distracted state as Rotheilan and Eithas bellowed in unison at the fate of their kin. The twins each stood atop the horns of the drake and swatted pitifully at its eyes with their negligible steel. The dragon roared in annoyance and shook its head violently, throwing them to the ground. Elethain could only watch as the godlike beast turned and retracted its tail, aiming to smash the twins against the floor.

As the monstrous appendage came plummeting toward the pair, Elethain conjured a wall of black magic over top of his brothers. Rotheilan and Eithas stared blankly from their prone position as the massive, mace-like tail smashed into the barrier. They cheered to their eldest sibling for saving them. In their excitement, they failed to notice the giant, golden tail whooshing through the air once more before slamming into the barrier above. This time they didn't cheer, as large cracks appeared in the magical shield.

"Elethain!" Rotheilan called, looking toward his brother who was struggling with all his might to maintain the forcefield.

Beads of sweat poured down the necromancer's face as he attempted to gather the strength to fortify the shield that prevented his brothers from certain death. "Get up, you fools!"

As if they had forgotten their position, the twins quickly attempted to rise. They managed to turn around and nearly escape before the beast's tail came crashing down again—through the barrier.

Elethain watched as the twins faded from view beneath the heavy limb. He couldn't avert his gaze as the appendage peeled away and revealed the crushed elven warriors adhered to the armored scales. Their once pale skin resembled a massive bruise with blood being pressed through each pore and bones protruded from their bodies. Elethain's mouth wavered in a feeble attempt to form words.

While words were impossible, noise was not. The elf screamed as loud as he could, pressing all his emotion into a single outcry. Flashes of his brothers' destroyed forms raced through his mind as he continued to scream. His eyes grew wide in his maniacal state of pain. Elethain reached out to each side with his hands and conjured a dozen large spear-like manifestations of black magic, all pointing to the monster that had eliminated his family.

With another cry of rage and sorrow, Elethain launched every magical spear toward his enemy. They crashed against the dragon's scales, though couldn't pierce its hide. The monster started running toward Elethain, its mountainous form shaking the thick branches beneath its feet, determined to eliminate the last of its intruders. As it approached, the necromancer only grew more maniacal. Deep inside, he knew the fate of his kin was his own fault, though he refused to accept such knowledge. To him, the dragon charging toward him was the cause. He held no regard for himself demanding they wake the slumbering beast. To threaten it within its home when all it hoped for was peace and solitude. There was only the conviction that the dragon was the assassin to press the blade, not he.

Elethain roared in denial and forcefully extended his left hand high into the air. As he did so, an enormous, magical hand appeared in front of the drake. As the elf clasped his own hand shut, the magical formation followed suit, clamping tightly around the beast's neck. The dragon roared in anger as it thrashed wildly, snapping with its jaws and swinging its tail. But Elethain kept his hand clenched tightly to keep his prey immobilized while his other shook harshly in the air. To the side of the monster's exposed neck, a large spear began to form. The shape matched Idérys' spear, driving Elethain's pain more. But he needed it. His anguish turned to strength as he felt every emotion running deep through his veins. His body felt empty yet so full of life due to the sorrow.

The necromancer struggled to maintain control of the dragon while also building up a tremendous amount of energy needed for his weapon. Just a bit more . . ..

Then, the creature stopped thrashing. Elethain's confusion nearly broke his concentration. The mythical beast stared directly into his frenzied eyes, seeing the pain behind them. The passion, the power, the lust. The golden drake simply maintained eye contact as the spear was launched toward its neck at blinding speed. It never blinked as it telepathically spoke to Elethain. *I forgive you.*

Elethain's eyes widened in surprise and quickly turned to sadness as he watched the spear pierce through the dragon's exposed neck, just behind the jaw and into the drake's brain. Tears welled up in his eyes and he fell to his knees. The tormented elf cried out in pain as the dragon's eyes slowly slid closed with a final low exhale. He sobbed uncontrollably as the shining, golden scales that encompassed its body turned to a dull gray, one by one. His painful throbs of woe only grew as he made eye contact with Idérys' ripped corpse a short distance away. During his channeling, Elethain failed to notice that the dragon's thrashing caused the twins to be thrown to the side in a shattered heap.

He continued to weep for what seemed an eternity. His brothers had fallen in *his* quest. *His* pursuit of power. For a purpose they cared naught. Their only concern had been for Elethain's safety. His guilt was immense in that moment as the realization struck him hard. Never before had he felt such agonizing pain as his mind assaulted itself in guilt. After many grieving moments, the necromancer finally stood from his huddled-over position and walked over to the dragon.

In the presence of his target, all thoughts of Elethain's guilt faded immediately. He was too drawn to the power at hand. His mind shut out considerations of consequence as he produced the transparent orb in his necklace. Eyes wide with lust, Elethain began channeling the magic needed to absorb the dragon's faded corpse, trapping it in the Undying Realm and within his pendant. The ritual didn't take long. The beast's corpse turned to a trail of energy and soared toward the orb. Once gone from the Living Realm, the godlike drake could be seen peering around from inside the small globe, fully reanimated. The orb emitted a bright golden light that resembled its captive.

Elethain pulled the pendant to his face and stared at his slave with a grin. "Hello, Aurum." The dragon gave no response other than a deep sigh of hopelessness. Not at its own fate, but its captor's. The irritated necromancer tucked the necklace away and looked to where its corpse had been. All that remained were the trample marks of its previous existence atop the Eye of Cerenos and the mutilated husks of his brothers. He walked to the center of the platform between each of his sibling's corpses. With little effort, Elethain called upon each of them to heed his call.

The elven warriors began to rise.

CHAPTER ONE
DESCENT

The black tide spread like a plague in the distance. While unable to see much, it appeared that the enemy had already traversed half of the Orclands. Fangdarr felt a shiver run up his spine. He didn't know if his people had joined the masses or fought back. Which did he prefer? If the Zharnik orcs posed as resistance, there was no doubt they would have been wiped out with ease. It seemed unlikely that the bloodthirsty orcs would turn away a chance for war, especially one in which the odds were in their favor. However, an odd realization struck the stressed chieftain. His concerns didn't last long for his clan, rather for the people inhabiting the Lithe Forest and the coast. *Humans.* The irony made Fangdarr uncomfortable.

"What we do?" Fangdarr asked in order to stifle the puzzling thoughts.

His friends seemed at a loss. What could they do? Luckily, someone spoke out. "You may do as you wish. *We*," Elethain began before grabbing Aesthéa by the wrist, "shall return to Jesmera."

The elf retracted her hand in shock. "Do you not feel for the fate of those who would be lost to the wave of shadow?"

Elethain's expression remained unmoved, fixed in its negligence. "My thoughts are with them," he stated half-heartedly. "But this is between them and their gods now."

"We have to aid them!" Bitrayuul blurted out in frustration. The half-orc and Cormac could hardly peel their eyes from the spectacle. They hoped for the safety of their homeland, Tarabar. Unfortunately, it was impossible to see more than a sliver of the enemy between the gaps of the mountains in their path.

Cormac turned to the group. "Aye, the lad be right. This war will change everything. If we don't pitch in, there might not be a home left," the dwarf added. He lifted his eye patch and rubbed his eyes with dry, calloused hands in weariness.

Elethain began to grow irritated with the group's resistance to him. "We *did* aid them. Crepusculus formulated this plan! The dragon is no more. What fate do you think the pathetic humans would suffer had we not conquered it? I can assure you, there would be more pillars of smoke than you see now!"

None of the companions could argue with that. After all, they *did* eliminate the largest threat. But what chance did the humans have against a nearly limitless horde of enemies?

Fangdarr watched as his friends began bickering back and forth over the plan. To aid or flee, to hunt or hide. He grew tired of the turmoil. With a brief roar to demand silence, the chieftain spoke with undeniable command. "We go to Wiston. Inform humans of cause for war. Crepusculus gone but revealed information that could benefit them. *Then*," he turned to Elethain and Aesthéa, "we go to Jesmera."

"*We*? Hah! An orc in Jesmera? The king would never allo—" the necromancer began refuting before being shot an angry glare by the elven druid.

"Fangdarr *will* be welcome in Jesmera, or you shall return home without me." Her tone left no room for argument. Aesthéa watched her uncle's advisor turn to disgust as her slender hand slid into the orc's.

Before the bile forming in Elethain's stomach at the sight of Aesthéa and Fangdarr clasped in harmony could be formed into harsh words, Cormac stepped in. "Lad, I got no qualms with that plan. But we best get there fast." His gaze turned back toward the growing rolls of smoke billowing higher into the sky.

The necromancer sighed and threw his hands up in hopelessness. The proud elf wasn't accustomed to being without a voice and disregarded in favor of those he considered his lesser. "Fine. What is our next action, then?"

Bitrayuul offered the strategy. Due to his military experience with the Dwarven Regime, the half-orc felt confident he could formulate a plan of success. "We go back down to the west, through Hell's Throat. It will take a day to reach the bunovir's lair. We should rest there. I expect we will not be ambushed with all the enemy around the corner. From there, assuming the army will continue to the coast, we will need to go with haste to attempt to get in front. They should be slowed by the marshes. If we can get far enough ahead, we may be able to follow the road north all the way to Wiston. We can inform the king of the events we have seen and request a ship take you to Jesmera."

Elethain remained silent for a moment, pondering the suggestion. "What happens if we do not reach the coast before the enemy?"

"I suppose ye'll get yer wish of killing some lowly orcs and trolls," Cormac responded with a lash of distaste.

That seemed to satisfy the elf, though he attempted to hide it. The conceited necromancer simply nodded and turned westward to begin their descent. Shortly after, he was followed by the remaining members of the group. There were no high spirits to add a skip in their step, only thoughts of the doom that waited for them on the other side of the Tusks.

It was past nightfall by the time they had reached the filthy cesspool that marked the bunovir's lair in Hell's Throat. They had expected the descent to be much swifter, but the constant risk of slipping had proven a more treacherous trek than considered.

Cormac threw his pack down, caring naught for the pile of bones it had disrupted, before crashing down himself in an exaggerated heap. "Ye see, Fang, this be why dwarves stay *under* mountains."

The orc chuckled at his friend's ever-present humor. Fangdarr looked to the north above the mountains. Even near the end of the mountain range he could hardly see anything above the tall peaks. Though, the faint glow of fires that spread through the Lithe illuminated the darkened sky enough to know the army had progressed through the day.

"We be safe here, Bit?" Fangdarr asked.

Bitrayuul halted setting up a spot to lie down in order to gage the army's position from the radiance of flames. "We should be fine. It's tomorrow that concerns me. The enemy is around the corner, but we need to rest in order to cont—." His words were interrupted by Cormac's loud snores. The half-orc shook his head in disbelief that rest could come to the dwarf so easily at such a time. He turned back to Fangdarr. "Armies are slow. And one so vast needs food and supplies. My hope is that they will delay long enough for us to sleep half a night and slip ahead."

"You are too accustomed to skirmishes," Elethain scoffed. He took the half-orc's confused stare as enough reason to elaborate. "You said an army so vast needs food. That army is primarily *trolls*. Trolls do not need to eat often. In addition to their regenerative capabilities, they have adapted to living in desolate solitude in the mountains. It is not as if the Tusks are crawling with an abundance of nutrients; the race has evolved to go without food for months. Their magical regeneration serves as a way for their bodies to continue without sustenance or to even disregard exhaustion. This war will not end by attrition—at least not on our enemy's end."

Bitrayuul's jaw went slack. He could hardly believe it. He and his recently deceased father, Tormag, had fought hundreds of trolls together in the defense of Tarabar. How could he not know that capability? Better yet, how had no dwarves passed that information to him when even the elves knew it as commonplace? The half-orc had served as a general in the Dwarven Regime under Tormag for a few years. Though his service was short, he had slain more than his fair share of trolls. Could it be that even the dwarves were not aware? His curiosity forced him to press for more information. "Elethain, when was the last war with trolls and dwarves?"

The elf let out an annoyed exhale. "If I recall, dwarves have not been a part of an all-out war for thousands of years. Crein has remained relatively peaceful in terms of open war. The region is small, meaning it is more subjective to skirmishes, as you have often been a part of, as opposed to full-scale wars. It also helps that each race is only one 'clan', so to speak."

"What do you mean?"

"The orcs are the Zharnik clan, the humans are of the same people, the Tarabar dwarves, all of them. Each originates from a single group. Wars are not always fought over differing races. Most are from the same race, but multiple clans. The Zharnik orcs, for example, were once a part of three clans, five hundred years ago. However, due to an internal war for dominance, the Zharnik clan was all that remained. It had consumed the other tribes and formed a single banner—for power, not peace. The humans have a similar story from a thousand years past. Though that was in pursuit of harmony, which is why the elves actually offered aid."

Bitrayuul looked shocked. "The elves aided humans?"

The elf scoffed. "Don't look so surprised. Elves do not meddle in other's business, as we expect the same. However, when it is within the pursuit of peace, we consider joining an effort. Wiston was once one of two prominent human settlements. The other was actually in Ifildé—the Hollowed Vale in your tongue."

"So, there is a human settlement past the mountains?"

"There used to be," Elethain laughed wryly. "Humans are emotional, frail creatures. Wiston originally wished for peace. Then their king was assassinated, and they eradicated their opponents in retaliation. After wiping the other city from existence, they put up the wall just south of Carrion Bridge, a short distance from here. It is named 'Altir's Gate' in honor of their fallen king."

"I thought the gate was to keep out the monsters that traversed the Hollowed Vale?"

"It does. The other settlement used to serve as a defense against the numerous enemies in that region. Once the humans of Wiston destroyed their opponents, they needed a way to keep everything out—including the last remaining survivors of the other city. Enough questions. The road ahead is long." Elethain rolled to his side away from Bitrayuul, tired of the conversation and ready to catch up on rest in order to begin their urgent journey.

Seeing the elf turn away, Bitrayuul politely acted in kind so as not to disturb him any longer. His mind was racing with the new historical information he had never heard previously. After a short moment of restlessness, he couldn't help but ask the resting necromancer one final question. "The humans did not let survivors into Crein?"

Elethain let out a heavy sigh. "As I said, humans are emotional."

CHAPTER TWO
PILLAGE

Sweat glistened on Fangdarr's furrowed brow as he slept. His mind couldn't remove the vision of Malice's bloated face staring back at him from the boiling acid within Crepusculus' stomach. His hands clawed away at the slippery passage to flee from her gaze, but he couldn't. All attempts to rid himself of the guilt of causing her fate seemed for naught. Instead, the normally fearless orc wiggled in discomfort as he was forced to watch her skin blister. From all directions within the nightmare, he could hear its voice. That tantalizing voice. Taunting him. Beckoning.

Your army awaits. Soon they shall be pounding at the gates, ready for your command to eradicate your opponents. You shall sit atop the throne of Crein, then the world. Fangdarr, the World-Chieftain.

The orc's nightmare changed in an instant, replaced with spectacles of war, death, and chaos. The land in flames, thousands of humans, dwarves, and elves lay dead at his feet. An army of unfathomable scale bowing in obedience. Fangdarr couldn't deny the surge of pride at such a sight. Then, as soon as it came, the scene was replaced by yet another—an illusion of his friends being ripped apart in gory anguish. His eyes shut in horror but were forced open against his will. Fangdarr didn't fail to notice the scene took place in their current location.

Though he didn't command it, his legs propelled him to stand over each illusory corpse and inspect them in detail. The orc couldn't contain his tears as he looked upon the sundered form of Aesthéa, a smile of love still on her face. Or the disappointed expression frozen on his brother's decapitated head. Each terrible image felt like a dagger being pressed deeper into his gut. Deep, wide cleaves had cut down his friends. It was obvious the wounds inflicted resembled those of his greataxe, Driktarr. As he looked down, his hands felt the familiar weight of the large weapon he so cherished, blood still dripping from its edge.

He woke with a gasp and heaving labored breaths. His elf companion rose with the orc's sudden jolt and slid her small hands over his chest as it rose and fell with each desperate inhale. Fangdarr turned to her, concern and fear clear in his visage.

"Hush now, it was only a dream, Fangdarr." Aesthéa's hand continued to run gently over the orc's chest. "Do you wish to recall it?"

Fangdarr shook his head. "No, painful." He was worried she would press for more, though his companion only held him tightly. Being only half his height and less than a quarter of his weight, he smiled at the slight squeeze she offered. Joy overcame the dwindling recollections as the druid rested her head on him, scooting closer into his embrace. The orc responded with a gentle squeeze of his own, careful not to crush her beneath his bulging physique. "We should rise. Need to get on road," Fangdarr reasoned, though it was the last thing he wanted to do.

Aesthéa shared his reluctance. The orc's words only made her snuggle in tighter, drawing a small chuckle from the orc. With a yawn, the elf stretched her aching limbs. In one quick motion, the nimble druid gave Fangdarr a kiss on the nose and rolled to her feet.

Groaning as he rose, Fangdarr got his legs beneath him and strode over to his lover. He looked down at and picked her up from the ground. Her giggles tickled his heart as he pulled her close to him. "I love you, Bear," he said softly while staring into her eyes.

The elf simply kissed his nose once more. "And I, you, Fangdarr."

"Oye, get yerself a cave, why don't ye?" Cormac called out jokingly, still laying on the ground and staring into the sky. "Bothain's beard, just give me some stone to sleep on. That's all I ask. These damned things . . .," the dwarf complained as he pulled a skull from under his back, followed by a few random bones. With a grunt of frustration, he rolled to his side. "Should've slept in the rotten corpse of the bunovir."

By then, Bitrayuul and Elethain had stirred from the commotion. The half-orc immediately began packing his supplies for the journey. Contrarily, the elf stared in disgust as Fangdarr and Aesthéa were in each other's embrace in plain view. Elethain forced his eyes away, hoping his king would put an end to her abhorrent behavior.

The group packed quickly and set back on the road. It wasn't long before they had managed to put the mountains to their backs. The smoke rising from the forest could be seen closer than before their rest, darkening the midnight sky. They continued directly west along the outer edge of the Lithe until reaching the road that would lead to Wiston.

Bitrayuul looked southward at Altir's Gate, this time in a different perspective. It seemed almost evil in purpose now. All this time, he had expected it to serve only as a defense to the beasts that dwelled in the wastelands beyond. Instead, it had trapped those who couldn't defend themselves, leaving them to die. Bitrayuul pulled his eyes away and began walking north. Despite the past, Wiston needed aid now. He wouldn't turn his back.

The sun was already past its midpoint by the time the southernmost village came into view. They had made good time and had been hopeful that the army would be at their heels. Instead, they all froze in their tracks at the scene that unfolded ahead. A few hundred trolls, ogres, and even orcs could be seen cutting down the helpless citizens. Fangdarr's suspicions were confirmed as he watched orcs—*his* orcs—running down women and children before cutting them down from behind. The unmistakable screams of agony echoed loud enough to reach Fangdarr and his friends.

Fangdarr was about to start running but Bitrayuul held him back. The chieftain's look of surprise lashed back harshly. "You leave them to die?!"

"I do not wish to, but we cannot take on that many. There are hundreds, Fangdarr."

"We not just watch!"

Elethain approached, his brother's lifeless corpses close behind. "We could possibly kill that many. But," he paused to emphasize the importance of his next statement to the eager orc, "do not think the remaining army is not there as well, hidden in the forest."

Bitrayuul was caught off-guard at the elf's reasoning to keep Fangdarr alive. Unfortunately, it wasn't enough to quell the fire burning in his brother. The orc's honor demanded he come to the aid of those who couldn't hope to survive, even at the cost of his own life. Bitrayuul felt a sense of inferiority well up inside him.

"Lad," Cormac started softly while clasping a rough hand on Fangdarr's hip, "ye got more than just yerself to consider now, don't ye doubt." The dwarf's eyes motioned toward Aesthéa, who simply remained at the ready in silence, waiting to follow Fangdarr with whatever path he chose.

Fangdarr looked to his lover. He knew without a doubt that she would follow him into the heart of the enemy without a second thought, and most likely die by his side. Such a fact brought him insurmountable joy but also a deep sadness. He nodded thankfully to Cormac. With a sigh, the orc relaxed and turned to Bitrayuul. "What we do?"

"We can try to slip past now or wait until nightfall. In either case, the enemy is in our path. We need to get ahead of them or find another way to Wiston." Bitrayuul looked to each of his companions. "Any ideas?"

Everyone remained quiet as they pondered alternatives. After a while, Cormac proposed an option. "That village be on the coast. It'd be likely they'll have a fishing boat; one that might fit all [illegible] eight of us, assuming the lads can't swim." He pointed to the elven ghouls at Elethain's side.

The group waited for the necromancer to confirm or deny the animated corpses' capabilities, but none came. "Right, so eight it is," Cormac added. "We can try to slip by now. Trolls and ogres can't swim, most likely. The longer we wait, the more chance they burn any boats that might be there."

"Or there may be no boats at all," Bitrayuul chimed in.

"Aye, that too."

Fangdarr drowned out most of their continued conversation. He could hardly hear them over the constant screams of the nearby villagers. Babies could be heard screaming after being ripped from their loving embrace, only to be silenced shortly after and followed by the mother's soul-piercing screeches. Fangdarr couldn't help but feel their pain deeply, knowing he had once been the cause of such screams. Once more, he felt Aesthéa's supporting hand slip into his. Swallowing his desires, he forced out the sounds of the village and returned to the task at hand.

"Ye mean ye can do that?!" Cormac shouted, drawing concerned looks from his companions as the dwarf drew too much attention. He shrank back after having forgotten the enemy was only a short distance away. His voice quieted to an awed whisper. "Ye can actually do that?"

Elethain smirked. "Yes, though it is not so simple. Necromancy is not just a spell to cast. It involves the will. The will of the subject, the will of myself. For example, my brothers," he pointed to his ever-loyal ghouls, "allowed me to dominate their will without resistance. Once a subject's will has been dominated, it is lost forever. Until then, they are free to fight back and resist. That is why it takes so long to command a dragon. Their will is vastly superior to most beings. It must be chipped away, piece by piece, until it is finally broken. Resurrecting a fallen subject immediately, without breaking its will, requires that I maintain the link through a channel, which is extremely difficult, or fatal if I cannot maintain it."

Bitrayuul was riveted. He had never learned much about magic, as dwarves were largely prejudiced against such practices. The only magic dwarves used were those of healing and enchanting, which they considered to be usable only in the favor of their god, Bothain. As a result, magic such as necromancy was regarded as blasphemous and couldn't be discussed or researched.

"So, ye can command an animal like a bird or squirrel and see through their eyes?" Cormac pressed.

"If I have complete domination of their will, yes. Once their will has been squashed, they are essentially an empty shell; just a tool or weapon to be used. They are held together by magic, though the energy it takes me to keep a subject under command and animated after its will has been removed is much less than prior. With my brothers, I have grown accustomed to the energy required to keep them animated permanently. Though, they have been under my command for over two hundred years. I can control an animal easily enough. Their will is weak but still requires energy to break. A single critter is a small task, a hundred not so easy."

"Let's find a bird," Bitrayuul insisted.

CHAPTER THREE
NECROMANCY

Elethain groaned in disgust as Cormac held out a bloody white-winged sparrow that had chosen the wrong area to soar. As the dwarf was about to hand the animal over, he remembered the arrow protruding from the bird and extracted the missile with a squelching of guts.

Aesthéa was forced to look away in grief at the animal's fate. As a druid, her link to nature as a druid was profound; preserving life was the largest principle undertaken by those who were chosen by Cerenos. She had always been deeply fond of animals, even before becoming a druid in her adolescence. Unlike Elethain, who was born with the capability of magic, her abilities had been gifted by her deity.

"Not much one for blood, I'm thinkin'," Cormac mentioned as Elethain tenderly pinched the bird's wing between his fingertips.

The necromancer gave him a look of disgust as a drop of blood fell onto his white, silk robe. Elethain gave up and simply dropped the creature to the earth with a *thud.* The members of the group all watched eagerly, save for Fangdarr who couldn't break his stare at the brutality of the nearby village.

"Step back," Elethain requested.

Everyone complied without hesitation. Immediately, the living magic tattooed under the elf's skin began to crawl and swirl around his body. His exposed torso visibly flexed as he strained to direct the current of magical energy inside him as it fed off his life force. A novice necromancer would surely become exhausted almost instantly on the channeling of the ritual due to lack of conditioning. But Elethain had devoted his life to his craft and a task such as this would hardly cause him to break a sweat. In short time, the black forms beneath his skin had been forced into his forearms, leaving his torso entirely bare from its previous markings.

Bitrayuul watched in wonder as a pair of tangible clawed hands were produced from the elf's extended arms. The large, black extremities clasped tightly around the lifeless animal as if clenching the life out of it. A dark, pulsating shadow burst from inside Elethain's necromantic claws, nearly indistinguishable from beneath the entombing digits.

Elethain took a breath and steadied himself, relinquishing the magic. His eyes closed as he felt the dark markings under his skin travel from his forearms back to his torso. He couldn't hide his prideful grin as Bitrayuul and Cormac audibly gasped at the sight.

After the blackness cleared, the bird which had just been a bloodied mass was up on its feet and bouncing about curiously. A blue light could be seen in its eyes as it stared at those surrounding it.

"The light within its eyes is what remains of its will," Elethain stated. "Now, watch." In complete silence, the creature turned to regard the elf. Unblinking, the necromancer simply stared back, commanding it mentally with enough power to subdue the small bird. The light in its eyes slowly dwindled before vanishing entirely, leaving naught but a void-like abyss. The elf smiled and said, "There. Now he is mine."

Cormac, like most dwarves, wasn't fond of magic but seemed awestruck, nonetheless. He nearly jumped up and down in enthusiasm for the elf's capabilities. "Bothain's beard, elf! That was some fine work!"

Likewise, Bitrayuul couldn't help but be astonished. Not only at Elethain's spell, but also at just how vast a world magic must be. He was keenly jealous that there was a whole world he would never be able to explore first-hand. Nevertheless, the half-orc made the silent vow to himself to learn as much as he could about all kinds of magic if the future allowed it.

Elethain relished in the praise—especially from a dwarf and a half-orc. It felt right to him that members of those races would be commending his abilities. He pivoted to see Aesthéa turned away, sniffling quietly. In his moment of pride, Elethain had forgotten the druid's feelings as she felt the bird's spirit being obliterated. The necromancer put his hand on her shoulder, though she shrugged him off harshly.

"So, what now, elf?" the dwarf called to Elethain, breaking his distraction.

He flustered for a moment, getting his mind back to the task at hand after a final glance toward his distraught friend. "Now we scout." As he spoke, the bird rose into the air and took off for the village. It didn't take long to reach the terrible scene that was dwindling. As his enslaved minion flew, Elethain watched through its eyes and relayed the details to the party. "The villagers are mostly dead. The enemy is looting corpses and houses." His face contorted in repulsion at the sight of the monstrous races walking about with ease. Some carried the corpses of their prey; others brutalized the remaining victims—alive or dead.

Bitrayuul shifted impatiently. "How many? Any boats?"

"Patience, orcblood," Elethain shot back. "Most of the raiders are heading back to the main army, which is about a league to the east. Hundreds of thousands, at least. The forest is being replaced by a sea of black-skinned foes. Now, back to the coast to find a way around . . .."

After many moments in silence, the elf began reporting the scene once more. "It is unlikely there is a boat. The town is far enough from the coast and the cliff is steep. Wait, I see something."

"What is it, lad?" Cormac urged, though the elf ignored him as he concentrated his will on the bird.

"I'm sending the bird closer, but it is getting too far out. I cannot command something so far, eventually the link will break. But . . . I can see . . .," the elf trailed off, increasing the group's suspense. "Aha! It's a boat. A small one, but we may be able to fit all eight of us. There is a problem, though."

They all waited for the necromancer to continue as he simultaneously expected them to beg for more details. He frowned at their lack of response. "There are humans in the boat, hiding from the enemy. It is out of sight, luckily, but we will need to remove them if we hope to use the vessel."

"*Remove* them?" Bitrayuul asked curiously.

Elethain nodded. "Either leave them on the coast or kill them, I care naught. But that boat is our only hope of reaching Wiston before the enemy and they are in the way. We can leave them on the coast, they should be safe until the army passes."

"We can't just leave 'em, lad," the old dwarf piped up.

The elf simply shrugged. "Then we abandon our quest."

"There must be another way!" Bitrayuul yelled a bit too loudly.

Elethain sighed as he broke the link from the bird, letting it crumble to dust in the air. "There is not. Not in time. It is not like we are condemning them to death. They are hiding *in* the boat right now, but it is out of sight in any case. They can simply hide *next* to it. The boat is beyond the cliff, on a small beach. The enemy is already returning to their army. You would risk the failure of our quest to let them keep their hiding spot?" The elf's frustration at the weakness of a good conscience was clear. It seemed illogical to him that they would sacrifice everything for something so small.

Bitrayuul and Cormac looked to each other. They pondered in silence before the half-orc turned to address his brother. "Fangdarr, what do y—" He paused and looked around. "Fangdarr?"

Upon the half-orc's confusion, Cormac and Aesthéa scanned the area for the orc to no avail. "He's gone," the dwarf stated.

"Oh no . . .," Bitrayuul started, knowing where his kin had gone. He turned his eyes to the smoldering village.

CHAPTER FOUR
REFORMED

Fangdarr walked cautiously into the village. He felt so out of place among the remaining orcs and trolls, despite being one of them. None of the invaders still inhabiting the razed town paid him any heed, however, and continued their looting and destruction. Fangdarr could hardly believe this was something he would have relished—the chaos and thrill of chasing down helpless villagers. Not even a full cycle of the seasons had passed since he was orchestrating his own raids, a small party of blood-thirsty orcs at his back. He couldn't help but see his actions from a new perspective as he glanced over the mutilated and scorched corpses littered on the ground.

The chieftain—if he could even call himself that anymore—was pulled from his stupor as a woman's piercing shrieks filled his ears. He watched, immobilized in his conflicted state, as one of the few remaining orcs dragged the poor girl by her hair toward a shack. One of *his* orcs.

Fangdarr found himself taking a step toward the structure, then another. His yellow eyes glowed with a fire burning deep inside, fixated on that shack and the screams within.

Stop. Do you not wish for conquest? For blood and glory? Are you an orc or some feeble human, destined to allow your own weakness to rule you? Fangdarr paused as the familiar voice pummeled in his mind. Anger dripped from every word like a corrosive ichor. Before he could think, it continued the stream of silver-tongued persuasion. *You are Fangdarr Blood-drinker, are you not? The Roaring One? The destined leader of my army; An army so large the forest breaks and the ground quakes. We are the scourge that will finally wipe the weakness of the oppressing races from existence. All you must do is join the cause. Direct the current. Take the mantle. Sit atop your rightful throne made from the bones of your enemies, drinking the blood of their descendants from their skulls. Join. Ravage. Show them that Fangdarr is the commander of the world!*

Fangdarr was frozen in his tracks. Each coercion came equipped with a vivid scene illustrating the future possibilities. He watched them play out, seeing himself dominating all who opposed him and sitting at a corrupted throne in Wiston as the city turned to ash. Interrupting the delusions were the woman's wails of horror and pain. Fangdarr took a step toward the door, expecting another mental assault from the remnants of the shadow dragon that poisoned his mind. None came.

Ducking low, the chieftain entered the human-sized doorway of the small shack. His enormous stature extended to full height after passing the threshold. Immediately, Fangdarr's attention was directed to the orc and its victim. Upon seeing its chieftain again, the vicious orc spread a gleeful grin on its face as it plunged deeper into the woman. Fangdarr watched as her horrified eyes turned to sheer terror upon his arrival. Could she not see he was there to aid her? No. She only saw an orc. Another savage beast to bring a fate worse than death.

The girl couldn't have seen more than twenty winters, yet she was experiencing the worst horror she could imagine. Though her eyes were pressed together tightly, blocking any vision of her fate, they weren't needed. She could feel the intense pain as the monstrous being forced himself into her continuously. The orc's horrendous breath came in an uneven mix of pants and snarls as it had its way with her. At first, she had attempted to resist. But each feeble offer of defense was met with aggression returned tenfold. Her face glistened from tears running over the swollen bruises the orc had inflicted. She had succumbed to her fate and wished for naught but death.

Fangdarr strode forward, careful not to hit his head as it nearly scraped the ceiling. He felt an immense sense of guilt for the girl. He knew what it was to be the assailant, caring only for your own selfish desires as your victim begged for it to end. How often had he ignored those whimpers and screams for help to fulfil his own animalistic need? As he reached the small table where the pair were entwined, Fangdarr could see just how savage an orc could be. Blood painted the end of the table and even the floor beneath. Too much blood. Though, he could see that the crimson liquid that spilled from the helpless girl only spurred the orc more. "Stop," he commanded.

The orc stared at him in confusion but continued to hammer away with thrusts.

"Stop!" Fangdarr repeated viciously, his lips curling into a feral snarl.

The opposing orc groaned in frustration. "Your turn soon."

Fangdarr grabbed the orc by the neck and pulled it harshly away from the girl, caring little for the erect appendage that was exposed and covered in blood. He continued to grip the monstrous beast by the throat and squeezed with all his might with a single hand. His muscles surged with energy as he lifted the orc into the air. This was the first time he had used his newly acquired strength from drinking the dragon's blood. He couldn't believe how much power rushed through his veins.

Fangdarr had already been abnormally strong before, but now he felt immensely powerful. The orc in his hand was thick and heavy, yet he held it above ground.

Kicking and struggling, the withering orc tried to break free of Fangdarr's hold. Its eyes turned from golden yellow to a blackened red as the blood in its head was trapped under intense pressure.

Nearly unable to move or see, the woman tried to slide off the table in order to escape. She thought Fangdarr was simply removing competition and would be the next to assault her. Judging by his size, the terrified girl quickly determined that risking her luck outside would be the safer route. However, her weakened form crumbled to the floor as she rolled from the table. She cried in horror as her body was too debilitated to escape.

Fangdarr considered offering the woman his axe to use against her assailant, both to heal her and as a form of retribution, but he decided against it. She was too weak to handle the weapon anyway, as it was more than likely heavier than her. Not to mention, he figured she would try to use it against him instead. His attention shifted to the orc dying in his grasp. Its final kick came, leaving the corpse suspended in the air. Fangdarr continued to squeeze for a moment longer before tossing the orc aside. He crouched down to the girl who shuddered at his gaze, thinking he intended worse for her.

"Hush, girl. Won't harm you."

She hid her face and continued to try to scurry away, slipping on the blood that had exited her body.

Careful not to cause her more concern, Fangdarr simply remained where he was in silence. After a few moments, he watched as she peeked through her fingers at him.

Her fearful eyes darted in every direction as if some invisible winged creatures were floating around the room. She quivered her lip and let her sobs come as the realization of what had occurred set in.

"I must go. You hide here. Army returning to forest. Cannot take you with me. Must go north to Wiston, help fight enemy." He realized that he didn't specify which 'enemy'. "I not with *them*. Here to help you."

She looked at him in shock and confusion. Such a contradiction was too much to process. An orc had just assaulted her despite her cries of pain. Yet, another had saved her and even spared her from further torment. All the girl could do was cry. It was too much to swallow, and the pain was too severe.

Fangdarr sighed. He hated the thought of leaving her alone while raiders remained in the area. Nevertheless, he had to. "Going to move you. More hidden, okay?" The girl visibly retracted at his outstretched arms. For many moments, he simply waited.

After the girl's fears had subsided, she turned back to Fangdarr slowly and nodded. She gasped and shrank back in fear upon feeling Fangdarr's arms slide gently beneath her before lifting her off the ground. Her breathing hastened as she started to regret her agreement.

Seeing her discomfort, Fangdarr pulled the girl closer to his chest. He took in a steady breath and let exhaled slowly. After a few more soothing breaths, the orc felt her lightly press herself against his chest, clinging to his protective form. "You be alright. You strong. Pain temporary. Body will heal." He set her down in the corner behind a handful of crates, hidden from view. "Do not worry," he offered, "you safe here, I promise." Fangdarr felt a wave of sorrow as her eyes lit up ever so slightly at his confirmation, knowing her ability to trust may have been shattered. With that, he exited the shack.

As he stepped outside, Fangdarr noticed the number of enemies had reduced even further—about fifty remained. He started to head south to return to his allies, passing by the creatures mostly unnoticed. After a while, he returned to the group where he was met with disapproving stares. "What?" he asked innocently.

"You know '*what*', Fangdarr," Bitrayuul answered with a glare. "You could have been killed, or us. We were about to go in looking for you. When will you learn you cannot just act on impulse?"

"He's right, lad. Ye need to think with yer head, not always yer heart," Cormac added.

Fangdarr scoffed at their words. "I'm fine. Needed to help."

"And did you?" Aesthéa tenderly questioned as she approached. Her hands wiped the blood crusted on his arms, flaking pieces to the ground. She stared intently at his face as Fangdarr nodded silently. With his response, she wrapped her arms as far around his waist as they could go. "Then I am proud of you, Fangdarr."

Elethain cut in, eager to postpone the inevitable lover's reunion that he knew would ensue. "We still need to get to the boat before it is discovered. There are not that many enemies left, we could either fight our way through or wait for nightfall and hope for the best."

"We cannot fight. There are still many waiting in the forest near the village. They would hear the commotion and shift the odds even further from our favor," Bitrayuul reasoned. "The boat has survived this long. It may go unnoticed. However, if the humans hiding there attempt to come out, it will most likely lead to discovery of them *and* the boat."

"Do you have an alternative?" Elethain shot back.

Everyone pondered quietly for a moment, weighing the best course of action. As they waited, the sound of flames igniting could be heard from the village. They turned to see an ogre setting each building on fire with a large torch. Most of the group turned back to the discussion amongst each other, however Fangdarr couldn't.

The orc took Aesthéa's face in his hands and smiled while pleading with his eyes. The elf returned his smile knowingly and kissed his hand. She watched as Fangdarr took off running toward the village once more before following.

Bitrayuul, Cormac, and Elethain all groaned in frustration as their orc companion was sprinting toward the host of enemies. They were uncertain as to why Fangdarr would charge back in after just being told keep his impulsive behavior in check. Nevertheless, they all looked to each other in annoyance—save for Aesthéa and Elethain's lifeless brothers—before taking off after Fangdarr.

Sprinting desperately ahead, Fangdarr watched as the ogre set the next building on fire. He willed his legs to move faster, knowing the shack in which the woman was hiding was next in line.

CHAPTER FIVE

RESCUE

Whoosh! The thatched roof of the shack immediately ignited as the ogre held the blazing torch beneath the overhang. Ravenously, the flames consumed the dry hay, spreading rapidly until the building resembled a large torch itself. Confident that its work was complete, the ogre trampled on in search of the next building.

Fangdarr, still a hundred bounding strides away, watching in fear. His heart pounded in his chest. *I should have tried to save her before! Why did I leave her there?!* The thunderous stomps of his heavy footfalls started to gather the attention of the onlooking invaders. Though, those watching him were more curious than concerned. Until they saw that he was being hounded by a group of dissimilar beings, that is.

The nearest group of trolls drew their weapons and advanced to intercept Aesthéa as if they were coming to Fangdarr's aid. They became even more baffled as the orc trampled past them toward the burning shack. Nevertheless, their attention turned once more to the elf who was secluded from her allies.

Aesthéa looked to Fangdarr who continued to sprint as she was cut off by approaching enemies. Had she not understood her lover's desperation she might have been emotionally scarred in that moment. But she knew his purpose and chose to follow him willingly. Her gaze steeled as the enemies approached. The elf took a quick count—four trolls and two orcs, each brandishing a crude weapon.

* * * * *

Fangdarr was almost to the shack, panic setting in as the flames had already moved to the walls. He was nearly there! But then it came—the shrieking. Inside, the young woman cried out in a mix of fear and pain as the inferno lashed at her skin. Her outcries caught the attention of the torch-wielding ogre who had stumbled away. It returned to the shack, blocking Fangdarr's path as it stood dumbfounded and looking at the doorway, wondering how a building could scream. As Fangdarr closed the distance, he withdrew his axe and let out a primal roar.

* * * * *

The pair of orcs came first, eager to taste elven blood for the first time. The druid was prepared and capable, though she didn't look it. Aside from her leather garb, she held no weapon to threaten her attackers with. Instead, Aesthéa magically called to the roots beneath her enemies, commanding them to rise. Each orc yelped in surprise as the thick cord-like growths exploded through the dirt and ensnared them. It started at their legs, then crept and twisted up their thighs, before finally twisting around their entire bodies. With another mental command, her magical grip on the roots squeezed impossibly tight. The orcs fought with all the strength they could muster, but their restrained form offered no defense. Each had their mouth gaping wide in an inaudible scream. Then, both burst into sprays of gore as the crushing roots shattered their bodies. The elf stared down the four remaining trolls as they looked to each other uncomfortably.

* * * * *

Too confused to catch on, the ogre turned its head to regard Fangdarr just before Driktarr's blade became embedded in its skull nearly to the hilt. Its eyes rolled into the back of its head, its life extinguished, before collapsing against the door of the shack.

Fangdarr cursed his own stupidity for allowing the monster to fall into the doorway, blocking it further. His urgency increased as the woman's piercing wails continued to haunt him. He considered which to be the better course of action: smash through the wall or remove the ogre. His new level of strength could probably lift the ogre out of the way, though he wasn't certain. It was at least twice his body weight and seemed tenfold in its lifeless form. However, if he chose to cut through the wall, what if the girl was on the other side? He couldn't risk it. Fangdarr ripped his axe from the beat's skull and slung it over his shoulder, then bent to wrap his arms around the ogre's neck. He pulled with all he had, not needing to lift the ogre overhead, simply to get it out of the way. Its body squished into itself as he pulled. Eventually, rather than moving, the ogre's head began tearing at the neck with a squelching sound. Fangdarr groaned in frustration at the time he was wasting and removed his axe once more.

* * * * *

After watching the two orcs suffer tremendously painful deaths, the four trolls in front of Aesthéa were cowered hesitantly. But their confidence was renewed as another dozen trolls fell in behind them.

Severely outnumbered, the elf's concern began to show. She could see that Fangdarr was still occupied, so Aesthéa raised her arms, ready to fight.

As if on cue, Bitrayuul came into view, trailed by Elethain and finally Cormac. The half-orc ran forward, seeing Aesthéa surrounded by foes. As he ran, Bitrayuul unslung Kwip, his great-bow, from his shoulder and let loose a quick arrow shot. With luck, it managed to clip the nearest troll in the shoulder. The missile wasn't meant to kill, rather to draw the group's attention to the oncoming aid in the hopes it would prevent them from attacking the lone druid all at once. It appeared to work as the troll retreated a few steps along with a few others, baring their teeth in hateful hisses.

Bitrayuul fired another arrow for good measure, though it missed the mark. He placed the bow back over his shoulder as he closed the distance. His armor gleamed in the sunlight, each bladed thorn reflecting a small sparkle from the sharpened edges. Despite being covered head-to-toe in thick steel plates, his enchanted gauntlets rendered his armor weightless. He looked to Aesthéa in confirmation. Once she nodded in reply, he immediately charged into the nearest troll.

The monster was caught by surprise at the half-orc's method of attack. It cried out as a bladed gauntlet cut deep into its torso. But the real pain came after. It continued to howl in agony as it was pressed against Bitrayuul's armor in a tight embrace. As it was held in place by the warrior's powerful arms, the half-orc began grinding the creature against the protruding spines of his weaponized armor, rending its flesh. Blood poured freely from a multitude of wounds. In short time, the creature was released and fell to the ground gurgling as it choked on its own blood. Its chest, neck, and arms were shredded beyond recognition. The trolls nearby could only gaze at their companion in horror.

Distracted by the grisly sight, two other trolls were impaled by magical spears. A dozen paces behind, Elethain launched black missiles around the battlefield, scattering foes.

Delayed thanks to his stubby legs, Cormac charged in while yelling at the nearest pair of trolls. They seemed much more eager to take on the dwarf due to his small stature than the other opponents. However, that underestimation would cost them dearly. Raising his thick, angled shields, Cormac blocked the attacks from both trolls with ease. Before the first could react, the dwarf shifted and plunged deep into its abdomen with the blade protruding from the shield. In one quick motion, Cormac ripped the blade out horizontally, cutting through the monster's stomach and kidney. As it fell to its knees, he kicked it hard with his steel boot, sending it flying into the nearby wall of a burning building. The troll's oily skin ignited, cauterizing the wounds to prevent its regeneration and burning it alive.

"Oye, don't ye forget the fire, lad!" Cormac called to Bitrayuul as he blocked another troll's lunging attack.

Bitrayuul sighed at his own stupidity as the troll he had torn apart had already begun healing to its normal form. Every cut had been completely restored as if he had never even touched the foul beast. With a silent curse, he raised his gauntlets at the troll's grinning face once more.

Next to the half-orc, Aesthéa watched as the pair Elethain had skewered were already healed and running in his direction as well. The only source of fire nearby was the burning buildings, far from the necromancer's position. She pulled another root from the ground between her and the nearest torched structure. Using the root as an immensely long arm, she wrapped a few flaming pieces of wood in the growth and flung them toward Elethain. Her distraction was short-lived, however, as she was almost cut down by an opportunistic troll. Thinking quickly, rather than relinquish her control of the plant, she allowed it to catch fire from the burning building. As the flames enveloped the root, a wave of pain seared through Aesthéa. It felt as if her own body was on fire, but she managed to maintain focus. With the root hosting its own flames, she quickly retracted it and entwined the troll as it was about to launch another attack. It screamed in pain as the fire instantly spread over its entire body, boiling its skin.

Thankful for the flaming planks his friend had provided, Elethain waited calmly as the pair of trolls rushed toward him. Once they were close enough, he stretched his hand and called upon a giant magical claw, which then crushed the pair together. He lifted both into the air and held them over the small pile of burning wood. As the trolls immolated, Elethain watched them with wicked glee while they squirmed beneath his magical grasp. The screams that came from the helpless creatures only rang as a sweet tune to his ears.

The remaining dozen trolls witnessed their allies being annihilated and took to caution. Bitrayuul and Aesthéa joined Cormac near the burning building and waited for the enemy to strike. However, no attack came for fear of the flames. Elethain approached them, walking calmly, wielding a burning piece of wood. He planted it easily in the ground before standing by his allies. All was silent except for the roar of fire and dwindling screams of the woman trapped in the shack.

* * * * *

Fangdarr had already launched a few desperate strikes into the thick wood. He was too frantic to make strategic cuts that would allow quicker entry, instead opting to simply smash the wall as many times as possible in any way he could. He managed to chip away enough to break a small hole through. The moment the portion fell away, the surge of oxygen reinvigorated the flames within the building, causing them to dance with life. A pang of guilt and horror washed over him as the girl inside screamed. He peeked through the opening but could only see the bright inferno and swirling black smoke. Suddenly, Fangdarr felt a sharp pain in his side as an unnoticed troll plunged a dagger deep into him.

With a wide grin etched upon its face, the troll retracted the dagger thinking its opponent crippled by the wound. It had no way of knowing Fangdarr's rage only increased exponentially at the creature's attempt to slow him down.

Without a thought, Fangdarr grabbed the troll by the hair and smashed its face into the burning wall harshly. He didn't even bother to watch it die as its skull ignited. Instead, his attention returned to the wall as his axe continued to bash against it.

* * * * *

Fangdarr's companions glanced at him from behind the circle of enemies, wondering what he was doing. Unfortunately, their current concerns were the trolls that remained. They needed to hurry, as they were certain more enemies would swarm them soon enough.

Elethain used magic walls to round up and trap the trolls into a tight bunch. Once the enemy was grouped and immobilized, Cormac and Bitrayuul started using burning wood to ignite them one by one. By the time they were done with the first six, the remaining trolls had already caught fire due to the neighboring troll's engulfing flames. The walls kept them packed tightly while the bundle of monsters died slowly. Once they were certain each troll was dead, they all took off running toward Fangdarr.

* * * * *

Finally, choking back tears, Fangdarr had broken through with a large enough hole to fit himself through. He put his hand over his face as the flames stung his skin. Crashing through the inferno, the orc ignored the searing of his flesh as he desperately searched for the girl. Eyes closed to avoid the scalding smoke, Fangdarr felt his way to the small cubby where he had told the young woman to wait, and his heart sank. There she was, huddled in the corner, where he had promised she would be safe—a charred and smoldering statue of her former self. The twisting in his stomach from the guilt of seeing her scorched body was nearly unbearable. He tenderly lifted her into his arms, despite her cooked skin scalding his own. The smell of her rotten flesh carried deep in his nose. Such a vile smell to come from such an innocent creature, reeking of the pungent odor of painful suffering and death.

Fangdarr's friends approached just as he exited the shack through the hole in the wall, carrying the girl's shrunken form. Tears ran down his cheeks, stinging the burns on his face. Falling to his knees, the orc let out a sorrowful wail at his failure. He looked down to the girl's smoldering carcass and ran a hand over her face—or what was left of it—committing the feeling of her cracked features to memory. With care, he laid her against the ground, knowing there was nothing left he could do for her with enemies gathering to the east. Heartbroken, Fangdarr watched as her dried out corpse shrunk from view as they sprinted toward the coast, a dwindling reminder of his failure. It was a sight he would never forget.

CHAPTER SIX

WOUNDS

The group skidded to a halt as they neared the cliff, staring over the edge. Behind them, hundreds of trolls and orc were hollering and roaring with glee at the expected slaughter to come.

"Find the way down!" Elethain shouted as he scanned the cliff. The words were unnecessary, as everyone was already frantically scouring the edge for some sort of escape route.

The ground trembled as their enemies drew near.

After a moment, Bitrayuul beckoned, "Here! Quick!" Without hesitation, each of his companions rushed toward him.

"Will it hold?" Aesthéa asked, caution in her voice as she eyed the crudely carved set of stairs the half-orc had found along the cliff's face. It was a steep climb, though the depressions of constant traffic gave evidence of its stability.

Without taking the time to respond, Bitrayuul stepped down onto the first stair. He let out a quick sigh of relief as the stone held his weight and proceeded to the next step. Before the half-orc had reached the third, Cormac started his descent, having no trouble navigating the treacherous stone.

Aesthéa waited for Fangdarr, who trailed behind clutching the wound in his side. His burns oozed with every laborious step. How he wished there were a lone troll nearby to claim with his axe. As he approached, Elethain began making his way down the steep cliff, not wishing to get stuck behind the wounded orc.

After reaching the fourth step, the necromancer commanded his brothers to stay at the ledge to delay the enemy. The lifeless ghouls noiselessly formed a defensive line facing the approaching horde with impossible stillness.

Bitrayuul looked back up at the edge as he hopped to the sandy beach. Concern etched onto his face as he watched Fangdarr move with dreadful sluggishness over the small stones. Quickly returning to reality, Bitrayuul remembered the humans that were hiding in the boat along the shore. "Cormac, with me," he requested before taking off for the vessel. As he and the dwarf approached, the pair of humans hiding within yelped in surprise.

"Please, don't kill us!" the older of the two shouted. It must have been the father, as he wrapped his arms protectively around the boy, who couldn't have seen more than fifteen winters. The fear on the young man's face mimicked his father's at the sight of the unlikely pair.

"We ain't gonna kill ye, lad," Cormac responded quickly. "But we need yer boat."

The man seemed puzzled for a moment before his eyes grew wide in horror. "Y-you . . . you brought them here?"

Bitrayuul could feel his conscience scream at him as he watched the blood drain from the man's face. "I'm sorry, we had no choice." His head hung in shame, knowing he was condemning the men to death for his own safety. He considered the possibility of bringing them along, but upon closer inspection of the boat, it was already unlikely to hold all eight of his party.

Bitrayuul could see the man's lips quiver as he was about to form words of debate, grasping for any chance of survival for him and his son. But before he could speak the pair were wrapped in a large, black hand. He watched the man's face turn white as the demonic conjuration lifted them from the boat and tossed them harshly onto the sand.

Cormac, aware of the necessity, stowed away his guilt and pulled the half-orc into the boat. Careful to avoid tripping over his long robe, Elethain nimbly hopped the lip and sat adjacent the dwarf. He looked back to the stair where Aesthéa and Fangdarr still were a quarter from the bottom.

"The fool will get her killed!" Elethain growled angrily. It appeared as if he was about to leave the boat to kill Fangdarr himself before Bitrayuul gripped his wrist.

"They will make it!"

Elethain shot a glare back at the half-orc, his disgust evident at being touched. Though he chose not to make an unfavorable situation worse with conflict. Groaning in frustration, the elf recalled his magical hand to the boat and used it to scrape through the sand, pushing the vessel toward the remaining party members.

The elf called out mentally to his loyal kin who had been stomped to fragments as the overwhelming horde had thundered past them. The ghouls instantly reanimated and leapt from the cliff onto the beach far below. They hardly even slowed as they crashed to the earth, shattering on impact and repairing themselves without pause. Trolls along the edge followed suit and plummeted from the cliff to smash against the rough grain and stone, just behind the ghouls. Each growled in pain as their bones splintered within their bodies but soon began to mend quickly. The remaining enemies lining the cliff above watched in confusion as Elethain's creations rushed toward the boat while trolls who continued to pour themselves over the edge.

Finally off the cliff, Aesthéa panted, weary from assisting the heavy orc down the steps. She watched the boat approach, shortening the distance. Her thankfulness was short-lived, however, as the sound of the trolls plummeting into the ground behind them started to multiply. First it had only been a single splat. But it was followed by another, then another. By the time she had pulled the orc off the final step and onto the sand, over a hundred trolls had fallen to the ground below.

Struggling to press on, Fangdarr was nearly drained of energy. Though, his eyes opened in curiosity as he felt his feet hit the coarse grain. He had never felt sand before. The tickling sensation as it slipped through his toes nearly brought him to laughter. His half-opened eyes looked to the horizon where the sun was high above the sea, reflecting its light over the small ripples in the distance. How serene it seemed to the orc. A stark contrast to the current moment's danger. His trance was interrupted as he heard Aesthéa call out to him once more.

"Fangdarr!"

The orc's mind returned to the present, now feeling the pair of crude spears in his back. Aesthéa pulled him toward the boat that waited only a few paces away. There was no plant life around to utilize. She could only hope to get Fangdarr in the boat as quickly as possible to escape. Trolls continued to launch themselves from the cliff as orcs slowly scaled the stair. Their lust for blood wouldn't allow a simple obstacle to deny them the chance for a kill. Even then, a few dozen of the sinister trolls were already up and limping toward them as their bodies still stitched together. Sharpened wooden spears from those remaining on the cliff above rained down around the pair and the boat, digging deep into the sand.

"Fangdarr, hurry!" Aesthéa called out, though he couldn't hear.

Fangdarr's pain was nearly unbearable. The sand and salty water scraped and stung the burns on his feet in a way he had never felt before. His breathing came ragged, still not free of the smoke that clung to his lungs. He could still smell the charred corpse of the girl he left behind. Each time he closed his eyes he could see her hardened form frozen in a lasting image of pain.

The orc didn't realize he was already at the edge of the boat, watching motionless as the others beckoned him with frustration. Barely conscious, Fangdarr rolled in over the edge, breaking the shafts of the spears in his back and nearly tipping the small vessel in the process.

At the back of the boat, the pair of humans were desperately trying to climb in unnoticed. Unfortunately, the vessel lifted too high as Fangdarr rolled in at the same moment, knocking them both back. "Help us!" the man shouted with immense fear in his voice. The boy wept openly as he attempted to crawl into the boat once more. Both Bitrayuul and Cormac started reaching over the edge to pull them out.

Seeing his companions trying to aid the family, Elethain immediately sunk the enormous, black fingers into the water and sand to push off from shore. The surge forward nearly flung Bitrayuul and Cormac into the water, but the man and his son weren't so fortunate. As the boat surged forward, the humans fell back into the water and cried out in dismay as it fell out of reach.

The half-orc and dwarf watched in horror as the trolls continued to approach by the dozen. Nearly a hundred had regenerated and were sprinting with vicious salivation at their prey's helplessness. The man tried to lift his son and stride further out to sea, hoping against all hope that the predators would be afraid to enter the water. His assumption proved false, however, and the sound of the trolls splashing through the shallows was all he could hear.

Bitrayuul was forced to look away as he heard the pair scream in pain as vile weapons plunged into their bodies, dyeing the water red.

Cormac watched it all, taking in every action that occurred and knowing he was partially to blame. He refused to shy away from their fate as Bitrayuul had. Instead, the dwarf watched with tears in his eyes as the young boy reminded him of his own loss. He watched as dozens of trolls swarmed the pair and listened as their screams didn't stop even after the monstrous beasts began feasting on their flesh.

He watched until the shoreline faded from view. And he listened until only the sound of the sea remained.

CHAPTER SEVEN

DELIRIUM

"Why did you do that!?" Bitrayuul roared to Elethain. "We could have saved them!"

The elf frowned. "You know we could not. Even if they had made it into the boat, what room do we have? This is no afternoon sail. It will take us *days* to reach Wiston, perhaps even a week. We have almost no food or water and a single oar. I cannot sustain magic for the entire day, and we will need to sleep." His arms stretched wide to each side. "Do you see any room for us to sleep as it is?"

Bitrayuul retracted at the rationality but still held his scowl. As he looked around, hardly any of the boat's interior could be seen between the group's overlapping forms. Even worse, the small vessel floated dangerously close above the surface. While Bitrayuul's enchanted gauntlets made his armor act weightless to him, it was still a tangible, heavy suit of steel. In addition, Fangdarr's enormous size was comparable in weight to even Cormac and Bitrayuul's metal armor and his injuries made it difficult for him to move. The half-orc's eyes fell upon his brother, struggling to breathe, and let his anger deflate.

"Will he be alright?" Bitrayuul asked Aesthéa. The distraught look on her face served as an adequate response. Bitrayuul moved closer, careful to avoid capsizing the vessel. As he peered at the excessive wounds on his brother's body, he couldn't help but audibly voice his thoughts. "Bothain's beard . . .. Was it worth it?"

Fangdarr immediately turned his head, wincing in pain. "Al-always, Bit." The orc groaned in agony as his burns scraped together and the deep wound in his torso tore open. Aesthéa quickly tore a piece of cloth from her leggings and bunched it into the gash. Within moments, it turned to black as it absorbed blood until it was fully engorged. Fangdarr gave a helpless smile to his lover and gazed upon her with the only eye not closed in a grimace.

Aesthéa leaned forward and kissed the orc on the forehead, as if that single act would let him know all would be well in the end. "I'm proud of you, Fangdarr."

The chieftain nearly chuckled in irony, though meant no offense. "Why? I failed. She is dead. My fault." His eyes closed as he relived the memory. The putrid stench of burning flesh that had filled his nose. The suffocating smog that had been trapped in his lungs. Even the look of horror on her face from their first encounter. Fangdarr remembered it all in painful detail. She had served as his final fork in the road to morality, choosing between prosperous harmony and lustful destruction. And he had chosen her over his kind in the fatal blow of his mental struggle. Fangdarr was confident he had made the right choice. For he shed tears for the lone girl rather than the trolls and orcs that they had killed—that *he* had killed. Still, that did little to numb his grief.

Cormac, who would typically be glad to offer consult in Fangdarr's time of mental struggle, sat at the rear, still looking toward the shore even though all that could be seen was the horizon and distant cliffs. Lost in his own battle, the dwarf knew he would prove to be ineffective for one needing comfort in that moment.

* * * * *

The day dragged on with only the sound of Elethain's large magical hands plunging into the ocean and propelling them forward to be heard. The sun had almost faded from view, coating the water in a beautiful pink and orange color—sa magnificent contrast to the devastation along the coast. As the sun continued to disappear beyond the horizon, they traced the cliffs with steady but slow progress. They looked to the east where blooming trails of smoke smothered the glow of flames in the darkened sky. The war was keeping pace with them as they headed north, a constant reminder of the horrors to come.

Completely exhausted from the day's travel, Elethain finally released his magic. By then, only Aesthéa remained awake, sitting by Fangdarr's side with unwavering care. There was nothing she could do for the orc's wounds, but still she remained. Elethain, too weary to even form a scowl of disgust, leaned against his brothers and passed swiftly into slumber.

* * * * *

At dawn, Cormac and Bitrayuul woke first, bumping into each other in the tight quarters. "Easy, lad, them thorns be sharp," the dwarf grumbled groggily as he noticed a bead of blood on his leg.

Bitrayuul apologized, though there wasn't much he could do to prevent it from occurring again. He watched as the dwarf stood up carefully and scanned their surroundings.

"Bah, looks like we must've drifted south a bit during the night," Cormac grumbled, noticing the same landmarks directly to the east as when he had fallen asleep. "Well, we lost some progress. Time to get to work." The dwarf scooped up the only oar—a battered thing that seemed it would snap at the first stiff breeze. He slid it into the water with care and paddled slowly. "Damned thing won't last." As he placed the instrument in the water a third time, despite doing so with care, it cracked within his hands. He yelped in surprise as the head of the oar floated away tauntingly. "GAH! By the stones, lad, our luck is worse than a dwarf beddin' a gnome from the tavern!"

Bitrayuul, equally distraught at the fate of their only paddle, tried desperately to contain his laughter but failed miserably. He bellowed loudly, waking the others. They nearly toppled the boat as they assumed defensive stances, only to see Cormac and Bitrayuul in boisterous merriment. Wiping away tears of joy, the half-orc tried to settle. The dwarf's humor was a wonderful reminder of Bitrayuul's adoptive dwarven father, Tormag, who had fallen a few days prior on their quest. In the severity of recent events, he had hardly made a conscious thought to remember the dwarf who had served as his role model for years.

"What's going on?" Elethain asked through gritted teeth.

Between gasping breaths and dwindling laughter, Bitrayuul and Cormac looked to the other to explain, only to lose control once more. Finally, Cormac managed to steady himself enough to speak with only a few chuckles seeping through. "We, uh, broke the oar." He raised the haft of the disintegrated wood for all to see.

"You what?!" Elethain blurted, his eyes bursting with anger. "You stupid dwarf! Do you mean to kill us out here?"

Cormac didn't take well to the insult. "*Stupid?* It ain't my fault ye picked the one boat that had a half-eaten oar, ye pointy-eared pixie!"

Seething, Elethain prepared to launch a burst of black magic into the dwarf but was halted by Aesthéa's hand gripping his wrist. He stared at her for a moment, considering whether to shove her aside and continue with the assault at the proud dwarf who stood with his chest puffed, bracing for the attack. Instead, he relaxed and spoke slowly, enunciating each word. "You still need to row."

Cormac huffed at the elf and his demands, though knew the words rang true. With a string of curses mumbled under his breath, he sat down heavily, splashing water into the boat and onto Fangdarr, who whimpered softly. The dwarf immediately sobered his anger and apologized profusely. Reeling with guilt, he put his arm in the water and began to paddle.

Bitrayuul felt uneasy as he watched the tension between the pair. Thankful he had avoided conflict, the half-orc sat next to Cormac before also dipping his arm into the water on the opposing side. Though dreadfully slow, they managed to push the boat forward.

Seeing her friends make an effort to prevent more conflict, Aesthéa, too, began to paddle—her free hand still clutching Fangdarr's. With his much-needed slumber disturbed and eager to be off the infernal vessel, Elethain conjured the large pair of hands and began rowing as well. In addition, he willed his brothers to join the others, though most of the water slipped through their skinless appendages.

As the day continued and the sun made its ascent, the vibrant orb's rays stung their exposed skin. It wasn't long before redness had formed on their exposed flesh, threatening to blister. Fangdarr was suffering tremendously due to his burns being further irritated by the constant sunlight, causing him to writhe in pain constantly.

Bitrayuul extracted his right arm from the water. They had been paddling for so long that the pain became unbearable. "How much food and water do we have left?"

The others each took a moment to relax as well, rubbing their sore shoulders. Cormac fumbled through the supplies. Within, he found a waterskin and shook it, listening for splashing. None came. Then another the same. "No water," he said with a dry exhale before reaching back into the sack. After more digging, he produced a small piece of stale bread. "This be the last of the food." Without question, he broke it into five equal sized pieces and shared them with the group, handing Fangdarr's to Aesthéa. They each chomped down on the single bite of sustenance, salivating at the thought of more.

"We won't last long without water, especially Fangdarr," Aesthéa mentioned as she pushed the piece of food into the orc's mouth. He chewed slowly with almost no energy behind the crunches of his jaw. The elf took a moment to inspect his wounds. The gnarly gash in his side had begun to fester with pus. Additionally, the two spearheads they had left in his back had been pushed deeper. "His side is infected. The spearheads seem to have stopped the bleeding, but they need to be removed before the wound closes around them."

"Should we remove them now?" Bitrayuul questioned.

The druid shook her head. "It is hard to say. If I thought we might get to a healer, or encounter something to use his axe against, it would not matter. But I suspect neither will occur soon."

Cormac looked to the east, where the fires had now surpassed them to the north by more than a league. "We can go to shore."

Everyone knew what that meant. Though none needed to voice it, Elethain didn't hesitate to add his opinion. "We should leave him. Roll him into the water and let him drown, or kill him yourself first, it does not matter. He will not survive the journey."

The other three companions couldn't speak as they were too awestruck by the necromancer's audacity. Elethain looked at their unfavorable expressions and rolled his eyes. "Oh, please. Do not think he will. We are at least five days from Wiston with no food or water. His added weight only slows us down. We could most likely make it in four if he is tossed."

Aesthéa was infuriated. She rose to her feet and stomped the short distance to the elf, showing no care for the rocking of the boat. Elethain's expression turned to mocking laughter as he looked at her with his eyebrow raised. However, his face contorted in pain as Aesthéa landed a heavy punch squarely against his temple.

Cormac and Bitrayuul immediately stood to break up the fight that was sure to follow. But Elethain's anger quickly rose and he subdued all three companions with black magic. He lifted them off the boat and watched as they struggled to break free. The amount of energy Elethain was wasting was noticeable due to his lack of nutrition; yet, to him, it was worth it.

As the trio was suspended, Elethain moved them over the water. "You dare threaten *me*? *I* am our sole chance of survival. Know that my *only* concern is returning Aesthéa to Jesmera, as my king has commanded. Were it up to me, I would dump the rest of you into the ocean without a thought. Even now, you are alive by my grace alone. I could eliminate your precious orc at any time yet have not done so. Why, I cannot be certain. There is nothing I wish more than to end that beast's life for the disgust he brings me. For the sight of you two together, Aesthéa. Yet, I have not! Something in me calls out in his favor." As Elethain's state of hysteria grew, his voice escalated and the essence that bound his companions tightened. His eyes grew wide as the poisonous magic raced through his body vigorously. The clash between the lack of energy and the surge of power from the magic trapped within him affected his judgment. Tighter and tighter they were squeezed, gasping in agony, though still Elethain refused to relent.

"The orc is naught but a blackened monster like the rest of his kind. Do not let his tricks fool you! He would carve out your heart and eat it while you slept! Yet, I cannot kill him! Why? WHY!? Why can I not end the life of the demon that haunts me? Why does he cling to life even now when he should simply wither? More so, why do you all care for him?! He ca—" Elethain's frantic shouting halted as he felt something cling to his leg. Looking down, he saw Fangdarr's fingers wrapped around his shin. Elethain's face twisted in disgust at first, then shifted to sorrow. The necromancer pulled the dangling companions back into the boat and released his hold on them, ignoring their gasps for air. Tears lined Elethain's eyes as he looked at Fangdarr's pained face. Within moments, the elf wept openly, the first real display of emotion that wasn't anger or hatred any had seen from him.

Elethain desperately tried to pull the orc's fingers from his leg. But he didn't have the strength, mentally or physically, to pry away those begging digits. The hand that belonged to the being Elethain hated most was the voice of clarity ringing in his mind, pleading that he free their friends and spare them the pain he was inflicting. He looked to Fangdarr once more and saw the orc smile weakly in gratitude. The elf wept once more and banged his hands on his knees in frustration. The inner turmoil was raging within him. His words were true; all he wanted was to be rid of the abhorrent orc. To throw Fangdarr into the sea where he would fade from existence. Yet, a strong chord stuck in his mind at every turn. For each time he wished for Fangdarr's death, an equally opposing voice objected with irrefutable demand.

Elethain pulled at his hair, hoping the pain would break him from the maelstrom in his head. "Why? Why, why, *why*!?" the necromancer shouted to himself. None of the others came to comfort him after being threatened to be tossed into the endless void of the ocean. "Why must I feel this way?" Elethain pried again weakly at Fangdarr's grip but couldn't break it. "Why are you stronger than me!?" His eyes connected with the orc's half-open gaze once more, breaking the elf's resolve. "Why . . .? Why did you try to save her?"

CHAPTER EIGHT
VULNERABLE

Elethain continued to weep softly, locked in his impossible struggle. He had given up on removing Fangdarr's grasp. In truth, it almost seemed the elf welcomed the touch.

Hesitantly, Aesthéa began to shift toward the distraught elf. He didn't refute her as she sat next to him and placed a comforting hand on his shoulder.

Looking up at her, tears glistening on his reddened face, Elethain could hardly form words. How could he put his feelings into words that made sense? He could only sob helplessly. Even Aesthéa, who had known him her whole life, had never seen him so emotional. Elethain had always remained vigilant and stoic, no matter the situation. But this was different.

Finally, the necromancer manager to whisper, "I'm sorry."

Aesthéa squeezed his shoulder lightly in response.

Elethain sighed, knowing he had to continue and let his emotions flow into the open and break free. He hated the vulnerability of revealing his most intimate thoughts. "I cannot make sense of it," he continued. His eyes were cast downward, refusing to meet the gaze of the others. "I wish for nothing but to eliminate the orc, yet . . . I don't *want* to. I see him and his morality and it angers me. It infuriates me that, despite being a brute, he is morally superior to myself. He cares more for the fate of others. He goes against everything I expect of him in the selfless pursuit of only what is right and nothing more. My hate for him becomes unwarranted and yet it burns brighter. As if I expect this to be some sort of trick. But it is my own deception at work. My eyes see what my mind does not wish to.

"Dark magic is a dangerous and fickle tool. It comes at great cost, even greater as one's power grows. I lost myself along the way. I believe the common races would refer to it as 'humanity'. My pursuit of power cost me my conscience, and perhaps even more. I . . .," Elethain paused, fighting back the bile building in his throat. He looked to his brothers. Motionless. Loyal. Neither living nor dead. "I brought my brothers to their doom for my own gain. Even then, I did not blame myself. Anyone, *everyone*, but myself. This gift is a poison." The elf looked at the blackness resting under his skin. "I am filled with hatred for many, this orc in particular. Yet, as much as I wish to cut into his heart or cast him aside, I cannot. A piece of me clings to him, for he is my final hope. He has broken the mold of his race. Every road in his path urged for war and violence, and yet, here he sits nearly fading from existence all at the chance to save a girl who could not be saved. How arrogant!" Elethain felt Aesthéa's hand clench more tightly on his shoulder as his anger rose once more. He calmed quickly with an exasperated breath.

The necromancer lifted his visage and turned to the orc latched to his leg. "He is my only chance at restoring my morality. To cleanse my body of the noxious venom that courses through it, purging any thoughts of remorse or consequence. I watched my brothers die as a result of my selfish desires and hardly flinched. When I look to Fangdarr, I see a monstrosity due to the color of his skin, though it is *I* who is the monster. No longer do I wish to be an unfeeling wretch who only dreams of more power. When does it end? What cost is too high? I fear the answer to that question above all."

Elethain lifted his eyes and gasped in surprise. Fangdarr's yellow orbs stared back at him with a small, wry smile, as if he had waited for this moment to come. *Arrogant!* Elethain's first instinct was to react with hate, but he held back with ease this time. He nearly laughed aloud at the absurdity of it all—the thought of him being guided back to morality by an orc. An *orc!*

"I cannot promise success, Fangdarr," the elf whispered gently as he put a hand on the large digits holding his leg. It was the first time Elethain didn't feel disgusted to touch the black-skinned orc. "I can promise I will try. Bear with me and be the unwavering mountain I must look up to in the hopes that I may find myself once more. You *must* survive. I need you. It is *you*, Fangdarr, who will be the pinnacle I must learn from so that I may break free of my own chains. Can you do that? Can you guide me?"

Everyone watched in tense silence, waiting for something to come. For what, they couldn't be sure. But they felt it—the thickness in the air as the entire struggle climaxed into this single moment. It was as if they expected Fangdarr to immediately be reinvigorated and leap to his feet to proclaim his acceptance of Elethain's vulnerable plea.

Still, they waited.

Finally, they watched as Fangdarr's hand slipped away from the elf's thin leg and moved to his pale hand. Though twice the size, the orc clasped his hand lightly around Elethain's and gave a small smile that couldn't hope to match the elf's before closing his eyes.

CHAPTER NINE

TEMPEST

Bitrayuul and Cormac watched as Fangdarr and Elethain formed a bond, an act they never expected to occur. And still with a hand on each, Aesthéa beamed with pride.

Clearing his throat to break the awkwardness, Elethain stood. "Well, that is that. Now, we must reach our destination quickly, for Fangdarr's sake." He smiled down at the prone orc who rested uneasily under the sun. It had only been a day since their departure with much more to come. His wounds were already inflamed and festering, desperately in need of attention. "It should take us about four days to reach Wiston. We have no food, no water, and little energy. But we must try to make haste. Let's just hope the Maelstrom Coast isn't named such for a reason!"

Nodding in agreement, Bitrayuul and Cormac switched sides to use their other arms, placing their hands back in the water before starting to row. They surged forward as Elethain plunged not two, but *four*, conjured hands through the water's surface.

"Brothers!" Elethain called out audibly over the constant splashing and rushing water's roars. "It's time for a swim!" Immediately, all three rushed to the rear of the vessel, past Cormac and Bitrayuul. They clutched the lip of the boat and threw their legs overboard into the water. The spectating dwarf and half-orc were confused as to what their purpose was, until they saw their legs move. Each lifeless creature kicked their limbs rapidly, incapable of fatigue, through the water. Elethain let out a hearty laugh, the first in a long time. He was eager for the future and refused to let Fangdarr die.

Aesthéa joined in the laughter, followed by Cormac and Bitrayuul. Their speed was tremendous! Spirits were high as they dashed through the water, feeling the wind whip past them. All knew the pace couldn't be maintained for long, already worn out from the day prior. But they would utilize their optimism and rush of adrenaline for as long as they could.

For a long while, their quick pace held, making excellent progress. Once the sun fell below the horizon and their bodies were depleted to exhaustion, they stopped to rest. Cormac and Bitrayuul's arms ached tremendously, even after switching positions back and forth. However, the worst was Elethain, whose magic took a major toll, though he did his best to hide it. He sat beside Fangdarr and Aesthéa, huffing with fatigue. Beads of sweat lined his weary face, stinging his sunburnt skin. But if the necromancer cared at all, he didn't show it—all his attention was on the orc.

Their haste had caught them up to the host of enemies once more. They anxiously looked on and listened as screams could be heard in the distance where the fires of war illuminated the sky. Shrieks of women and children were drowned out by the guttural roars of brutish invaders and carried out over the water.

"I don't miss the sound of that," Cormac stated.

"This is my first war," Bitrayuul added with a drop of fear. Though he was a high-ranking officer in the Dwarven Regime under his late father, the half-orc had only been involved in skirmishes with trolls near their homeland in the Tusks.

The dwarf kept his gaze fixated on the blooming pillars of smoke above the human settlements. "Me as well, technically." Cormac continued, seeing Bitrayuul's surprise. "I be only a bit over half a century, lad. I ain't never seen a war like this. The last we dwarves fought in was long before me time. But the sounds have filled me ears before, don't ye doubt."

Elethain caught wind of their conversation. "I have. The last great war was over a thousand years ago, the one I told you about previously, Bitrayuul. Wiston eradicated the other human settlement in the Hollowed Vale. But Cormac is right, you never forget the screams."

Bitrayuul shuddered at the thought. His nights were already filled with nightmares. His sister, mother, and father's deaths all haunted him relentlessly. So much death had occurred since he had left Tarabar less than a moon cycle ago. Now, war was on their doorstep and thousands were being slaughtered as the scourge trampled toward Wiston. His gaze was drawn to land, where fires continued to sprout, followed by more screams. It all seemed so surreal.

Their exhaustion didn't allow them to remain awake for long and they were eager to shut out their daunting thoughts. The ghouls continued to paddle through the night to avoid losing any more progress. In fact, by the time the group rose the next morning, they had traveled even farther north along the coast.

Even after a night's rest, the group's exhaustion persisted. But they forced themselves to carry on, with their mouths dry and bellies empty. They just needed to reach their destination, then all would be well. Wiston was a few days away still. It seemed impossible to last that long, but they had to try. Progress was much slower than the day prior as everyone able paddled half-heartedly.

As they rounded the corner of a peninsula to the east, Elethain called out, "I can see Port Tempest. There's a ship!"

Bitrayuul and Cormac rushed to the front of the boat, as if the few added paces would improve their vision of the vessel resting at port in the distance. Cormac clapped happily. "Bothain's beard! Right ye are, elf!" The dwarf's excitement carried on with loud cheers, even going so far as to clasp a hand on Elethain's shoulder.

While his comrades expressed their merriment, Bitrayuul remained staring intently at Port Tempest. His eyes narrowed in scrutiny. "It's a trap."

Cormac almost immediately halted his dance. "Eh? How are ye sure?"

"Look," the half-orc pointed to the docks, "all the ships are burnt, save the one."

Upon closer inspection, Cormac determined Bitrayuul was correct. "Bah, yer overthinkin' it. There be no smoke comin' from the other ships, looks like they were burnt at least a day ago. The beasts are probably gone, by the looks of it. Besides, ye see that flag hoisted high above the city?"

"The gray one?" Bitrayuul asked, though only one flag could be seen sitting atop a tall tower.

"Aye, the gray one. That means the city be locked down, ye know, for defense. Must've gotten attacked yesterday and are still on lockdown to be safe."

The evidence didn't seem to convince Bitrayuul. How he wished Elethain had access to a bird in that moment. He looked to Fangdarr, who held on by a mere thread. It was obvious the large orc wouldn't survive the remaining two days to Wiston. He sighed heavily. They had no choice but to risk it.

It took them longer than anticipated to reach Port Tempest. Elethain was still downtrodden with fatigue from the previous day's rush, and Bitrayuul and Cormac wanted to save their arms in case of danger, leaving only the undead ghouls to slowly kick toward the town. As they paddled closer to the dock, Bitrayuul inspected more closely.

There appeared to be no enemies in sight, though the heavy foot traffic of hundreds or thousands of troll-shaped feet could be seen, most likely from the previous attack, as far as Bitrayuul could tell. His eyes shifted to the city walls. He could make out a handful of guards. As they continued to get closer, though still out of earshot, a pair of the sentries waved at them.

As if he was able to read the question on his companions' minds, Elethain stated, "We cannot stop. We need to get on the ship and depart immediately. There should be food and supplies stored on the ship. Once we secure the area, we will transport Fangdarr. We need to leave him on the shore until then."

"Alone?" Aesthéa asked with concern. Elethain looked at her sternly and nodded in response. She didn't argue. There was little that could be done for the orc in any case. The more swiftly they could secure the ship and transfer Fangdarr, the better off he would be.

"What of the guards?" Bitrayuul questioned. "What if they come down? What if they need the ship to escape? Fangdarr would not want to abandon them."

Elethain sighed. He didn't disagree with the half-orc, though his concern lay only with their group. "I do not believe they will come down. The only reason the city is still standing is due to being tight in its defense. They will cling to the walls that have spared them. I see no enemies. If they wished to flee, they could have done so previously."

None could dispute the necromancer's logic. Bitrayuul continued to watch as the guards lined along the wall simply continued their endless waving. The half-orc looked away, unable to bear the knowledge that they may be taking the townspeople's only means of escape.

The boat pushed through the sand on the shoreline before coming to a halt. Unfortunately, there was no rope to tie it down, so they couldn't leave the boat near the ship at the dock for fear of Fangdarr drifting away with the tide. Making sure the orc's vessel was secure on the beach, Fangdarr's allies took off for the docks.

Once they were close, the smell of the burnt wood was much more noticeable. It clung to their noses, mixing the smothering thickness of smoke and scent of charred wood. Bitrayuul examined his surroundings at every turn. It seemed odd that nothing was here. No bodies, no blood, nothing. *Had the enemy truly destroyed the ships, then retreated? Why leave one? Perhaps to simply torture those sheltered behind the walls, as if freedom waited just out of reach?* He scanned the cliffs to each side of Port Tempest, expecting to see a horde of enemies lying in wait.

Elethain, followed by his brothers and Cormac, climbed the wide plank leading to the deck of the last remaining ship. Bitrayuul and Aesthéa remained on the dock, searching the area for any signs of a threat. Many moments seemed to creep by while the pair on the ship secured the interior. As they waited, Aesthéa remained still, listening and watching. She clutched Bitrayuul's forearm—nearly cutting her hand in the process—concern written on her face.

Bitrayuul just stared at her curiously, waiting for some sort of explanation. Then, he felt it.

CHAPTER TEN

ENDLESS

"Bothain's beard . . .," Bitrayuul whispered under his breath as the vibrations rumbled beneath his feet. At first, they were hardly noticeable. But the tremors rapidly grew exponentially. No enemies could be seen, yet the water below the dock shook violently.

Cormac popped his head over the rail of the ship. "Bah! Can't catch a break, eh?" The moment his words ended, he stuffed a large bite of potato in his mouth before throwing one to each of his friends below. Despite the coming danger, they, too, took bites of the meager sustenance. The short-lived ecstasy that came with the first chomp of food in days was hardly enough to sate their lasting hunger, but they would need all the strength they could.

"Where is Elethain?" Aesthéa asked through a mouthful of food.

The dwarf simply shrugged, taking another enormous bite. "I'm not for knowin'. But," he paused to look at the wave of enemies that had just appeared around the walls of the city, "I'm thinkin' we need to get movin'."

Bitrayuul and Aesthéa turned to follow the dwarf's gaze. It seemed that most had stopped to assault the town, though a hundred rushed toward them, eager for the quick kill. Aesthéa gasped when she realized they would see Fangdarr.

Cormac ran down the plank and onto the dock to follow Bitrayuul and Aesthéa, who had already begun sprinting toward Fangdarr's boat on the shore. There was no chance they would make it before the oncoming invaders. The druid shifted to her bestial form and charged forward on all fours, outpacing her friends. Bitrayuul called out, cautioning her recklessness, but it didn't matter. She only saw her companion about to be overtaken.

* * * * *

The horde rampaged forward viciously, approaching Fangdarr's boat. However, nearly all had simply run past him as they crossed the shoreline toward the docks, oblivious to his presence and eager to claim the victims of their trap.

Though most ran toward the dock to eliminate those foolish enough to fall for their ruse, a small group paused at the abandoned craft. They looked down to see Fangdarr, on the very brink of death. Between the burns oozing all over his body, the cracking of his lips, and his low wheezing, the curious creatures that had stopped to investigate assumed he had been tortured by the ragtag band, who now sought to escape. Enraged, the orcs and trolls worked together to lift Fangdarr from the boat and get him to his feet.

* * * * *

Aesthéa tried to follow the fate of her lover through the oncoming swarm but lost sight quickly. As Fangdarr faded from her view, she felt an intense feeling of despair. She roared loudly at the first troll in her path before raking open its abdomen with a single swipe of her claw. Within an instant, she became surrounded and was slashed and stabbed at with crude weapons. She winced in pain as a blade slipped through her thick fur and pierced her flesh, drawing blood.

Bitrayuul caught up and immediately launched himself into the nearest orc that screamed in agony as dozens of bladed spines cut into its body. Its wails silenced quickly, however, as Bitrayuul slid the blade of a gauntlet into its heart. Before he even retracted the weapon from the orc fading into oblivion, Bitrayuul lunged forward with his free hand to impale a troll ferociously releasing a flurry of slashes at Aesthéa. Crying out in pain, the creature turned its attention to the half-orc, sinister cruelty burning in its eyes. The deep cut the troll suffered was already mending even while Bitrayuul's gauntlet blade was still deep in its chest.

Laughing wildly, the troll clutched the half-orc's arm tightly, preventing him from retracting the blade. With a sharpened stone dagger raised, its monstrous expression contorted in glee as it plunged the weapon toward Bitrayuul's shoulder.

Bitrayuul instinctively tensed for the blow. His awkward angle had prevented him from pulling his other arm free from the orc he had stabbed. The half-orc cursed his foolishness; he should have ripped his weapon free before redirecting to the troll. Now, he remained immobilized as the dagger in the troll's three-fingered hand whistled toward his collarbone.

Clang! The creature's face shifted from grim satisfaction to confusion as the inferior stone fractured against the hardened carapace. Not wasting the opportunity, Bitrayuul smashed forward with his head, burying the giant blade at the forehead of his helmet deep into the troll's face. As its face split in half, exposing bone, brains, and all between, the troll released its grip on Bitrayuul's arm. With a hard tug, the half-orc pulled his other arm free. Unencumbered, he kicked at the beast, sending it rolling away, its face already stitching itself back together.

Cormac, finally present, jumped into the air over the rolling troll's form with a yelp of surprise. "Oye! Don't be throwin' no trolls, Bit! Bahaha!"

Seeing a troll about to swing for Aesthéa, the dwarf launched himself into the creature with his shields tucked tightly against his stout frame. Growling from the heavy bash, the troll was thrown to the ground. In a heartbeat, Cormac was over top of the monster, stabbing downward into its eyes. He didn't hesitate to move to the next foe in line as the piercing shrieks from the beast beneath him shook the air.

As Cormac squared off against the next troll, he was met with three more. He cast a quick glance to Aesthéa, worried she would soon fall to the overwhelming weight of enemies crashing against her. Though they seemed minor, the elf was bleeding from a dozen wounds beneath her fur. Her protective coat was the only thing that stood between the countless blades cutting away and death, but it wouldn't shield her forever. With each wicked slash against her, Aesthéa's fur lost a few more strands.

"We need to leave!" Cormac shouted, seeing numerous enemies still charging down the hill toward them. Severely outnumbered, there was no chance of victory. To make matters worse, their adrenaline was beginning to wane, leaving them with only the withered energy of their malnourished bodies.

Aesthéa could only roar to the dwarf in response as she continued to swat away enemies with heavy strikes—growing slower with each swipe. The front of her body was covered entirely in blue and black blood and gore clung to her claws and teeth. She couldn't even stop to think about the vile taste in her mouth as her jaws clamped down on troll after troll, only to watch it heal miraculously. They had no time to make a fire, allowing every troll they culled to rise moments later, always with that same wicked grin.

"Where is Fan—" the dwarf captain started before feeling a sharp pain in his arm. He immediately turned around to see the troll he had hopped over before brandishing its broken dagger, blood dripping down the fragmented stone. "Bahaha! Right, forgot about ye!" Cormac laughed—luckily the shard had only made a shallow cut. The troll looked at him in confusion. Without a second thought, the dwarf stabbed the troll in the groin and shoved it away with a quick smack of his shield. As it rolled away for the second time, Cormac commented to himself more than anyone, "Best remember he'll be back!" As he finished, his other shield clanged in sturdy protest as the enemies at his rear slashed at the curved steel.

A few paces away, Bitrayuul disposed of another orc before being met by a pair of trolls. He was becoming frustrated at the beast's absurd healing capabilities. He had fought countless trolls in small skirmishes where their small numbers often didn't matter—not to mention fire always being available. But this was a whole new challenge altogether. Numbers of this scale with no access to their sole weakness made a menial task seem impossible.

As the trio continued to fight, they finally managed to get into a more defensive formation side-by-side. The relentless horde didn't halt their aggressive tactics and continued to charge in with abandon. Ordinally, such tactics held little merit to seasoned warriors, but with such an overwhelming advantage even the trained fighters were desperately struggling to survive. Slowly, the allies were driven back. With each step they were forced closer to the ship at the docks but further and further from Fangdarr.

* * * * *

Near the small vessel he had been found in, Fangdarr could feel the orcs lifting him to his feet. On instinct, his grip held tightly to the shaft of his axe, dragging it through the sand. He opened his eyes as much he could to see the orcs supporting him as they walked forward, ever slowly. *Am I home?* he wondered as he hazily stared at his fellow orcs taking care of him. However, as the sounds of crashing blades met with wails of pain and the guttural sounds of death, he quickly realized he was on a battlefield. The chieftain forced his eyes open and tried to focus. For just a single moment, Fangdarr could make out enough of the scene ahead. Up the shore, he could see Bitrayuul, Cormac, and Aesthéa fending off a tide of black that threatened to stomp them out—and losing ground.

Fangdarr's eyes closed on their own, though he urged them not to. His strength was faltering, and he felt himself slipping in and out of consciousness. Picking up a few words at a time, he could hear the orc's discussing what to do with him. One stated they should protect and heal him, while the other argued they should let him die and take his weapon. It seemed they recognized him as their chieftain, despite his change in physique and being covered in severe burns. Fangdarr most likely resembled an ogre more than the orc they knew, but Driktarr was all the confirmation they needed.

Suffering from malnourishment and his grievous wounds, Fangdarr's mind was muddied to the point of uselessness. He couldn't remember the scene he had just witnessed, though he knew there was a gravely important aspect to it. He tried to focus his strength and open his eyes again, but they wouldn't listen to his commands. All he could hear was the continued debate between the orcs at each of his sides as they supported him. After a few more slow steps, they finally had enough of each other. One removed himself from under Fangdarr's arm and turned to the other, who nearly collapsed under the sheer weight of the large chieftain.

Knowing the other orc was about to confront him, the remaining orc slid out from under Fangdarr's arm, letting him drop to the ground. Immediately the two orcs were at each other's throats and trading blows. Fangdarr simply lay on the ground, feeling the sand scrape against his back, staring up at the sky. The sun was at its peak, shining down brightly and stinging his burns.

Then, Fangdarr felt a surge of energy course through his depleted body. It shook him to his core as it revitalized him. How good that felt! The chieftain's eyes managed to regain their clarity as his wounds began healing. His pus-filled burns were expunging the infectious liquid that had festered, leaving patches of discoloration all over his black skin, tucked behind his countless scars. Fangdarr looked to the left, still laying on his back in the sand. The orc who fought to save him lay dead next to him with Driktarr embedded deep in his back from being shoved by his opponent. Fangdarr felt a pang of guilt for the deceased orc's fate, knowing the victim fought only to keep the chieftain alive. He rose to his feet with his greataxe in hand—orc still attached—and stared down the other orc.

Immediately, the creature fell to its knees, pleading for its life. It spit endless comments about it being an accident and never really wishing to take Fangdarr's weapon. But the chieftain heard none of it as he strode forward and raised his axe high overhead. The limp orc stuck to Driktarr's head flailed wildly in the air, then smashed into the kneeling orc. The sheer force of the blow caused the axe to cut through both the attached creature and the begging grunt.

Fangdarr lifted his arms and rolled his eyes back in ecstasy as he felt vitality rush through his veins, renewing the last of his wounds. Seeing his friends up the shoreline struggling to hold back the wave of enemies that continued to pour in from the east, the orc walked toward the horde.

CHAPTER ELEVEN

ESCAPE

As Fangdarr pressed through the tightly packed array of monstrous creatures, he wasn't met with threats or blows. Instead, the orcs of his clan and the trolls he once swore an allegiance to stared at him in awe—their chieftain had returned. Within moments, Fangdarr no longer needed to push his way through those in his path. Instead, each of his subordinates moved apart, making room for him. He towered above the inferior beasts, only adding to their admiration. The horde began cheering and hollering victoriously once Fangdarr was halfway through the pack, expecting him to put an end to the stubborn warriors who refused to submit.

Aesthéa, Bitrayuul, and Cormac all stared in amazement as the horde stopped attacking and allowed Fangdarr to pass unharmed. The trio quickly caught on that their enemies believed the chieftain would be the doom of the party.

Fangdarr reached the end of the procession and made eye contact with his friends. All was still and silent for many tense moments. Even the guttural cheering stopped as the beasts waited for the chieftain to initiate. Fangdarr nodded slightly to each of his companions, too subtle for those at his back to see. Then, the orc raised Driktarr, pointing it at them. Not at *them*, his friends realized, but to the ship behind them.

The chieftain roared mightily, bringing back the cheer of the beasts who anxiously waited for the slaughter to come. Fangdarr gripped his greataxe tightly with both hands and, with blazing speed, planted his foot into the sand and spun around to cleave the nearest orc from shoulder to hip. Before the creatures had time to react, Fangdarr easily chopped through an adjacent troll—blood spraying into his face and painting him with its odd blue tint. By then, the chieftain's allies were already sprinting full speed to the boat, taking advantage of Fangdarr's distraction.

The horde of enemies turned in retreat at their chieftain's betrayal, tripping over each other in the sudden shift of position. When the chaotic mass finally stopped to reorganize their defense—after all, it was just one orc against a hundred—rather than being met with Fangdarr's devastating axe, they witnessed him dashing along the beach and toward the dock. The invaders growled in rage, charging forward as they watched Fangdarr sprint along the shore to catch up to the group.

Looking back and seeing Fangdarr running along the deck, Aesthéa shifted back to her elven form and quickly dashed up the plank to the ship's deck, followed by Cormac. Bitrayuul and Fangdarr remained on the dock, pushing against the bow with all their strength. They nervously glanced back at the small army closing in with haste. There was little time and the number of invaders only continued to grow. Turning his eyes to the city walls, Bitrayuul could see the same guards from earlier kneeling. He could hardly make them out, but it seemed as if they despaired as their only means of escape started to drift away from the dock.

The brothers groaned with effort as the boat was pushed as far as their arms could reach. They cursed their foolishness as the boarding plank fell into the water with a taunting splash. Knowing their fate had been sealed, Fangdarr and Bitrayuul looked to their friends on the deck one final time in farewell before turning to the approaching raiders. The kin nodded to each other in acceptance—knowing their companions could escape was a worthy enough cause for their doom. They prepared themselves as the beasts reached the dock, feeling the boards shake beneath their feet.

Fangdarr and Bitrayuul raised their weapons in grim silence.

Then, as soon as their enemies were upon them, the pair could feel a cold embrace lift them off their feet. They surged through the air the short distance to the boat and were dropped on the deck by the large, demonic hands Elethain had summoned. Fangdarr looked to the necromancer, who immediately transformed the conjurations into a wall between themselves and the dock. A moment later, crudely crafted spears struck the barrier, wiggling from the impact as if taunting their narrow escape.

"Good thing the beasts favor blades and not bows, else they might've shot us down a long time ago," Cormac stated, thankful that orc's savagery lusted for the feeling of sinking a blade into an opponent and smelling their blood as it leaked out.

Bitrayuul managed an awkward chuckle, still in disbelief at avoiding the fate he had resigned himself to. "True, but I could do without the trolls and their damned spears."

As the ship sailed farther out to sea, Elethain maintained the wall for as long as he could before collapsing from exhaustion.

Cormac and Aesthéa quickly pulled him to his rear. As they did so, the dwarf's hand was coated in purple-tinted blood. Surprised, Cormac lifted his hand to see the viscous liquid before shifting Elethain's robes, revealing a gnarly wound on the elf's thigh. Thankfully, it didn't cut too deep into the muscle. Fangdarr knelt beside his allies and questioned the dwarf with his eyes.

"It's a nasty one, sure as stones, but missed the artery. He should heal fine." Cormac clasped a hand on Elethain's slender shoulder. "How'd ye get this?"

The necromancer winced in pain as Aesthéa poked at the gash to ensure there was no debris. "I'm fine. There were only three. Just get me some food, I'm starving." In truth, Elethain was angered that the cut had slipped past the mystical tattoos swimming around his skin. He couldn't react fast enough to direct the magical markings to intersect the blow, allowing his skin to be cut.

Fangdarr chuckled at the persistent commanding presence of his friend before rising to his feet in search of food. He headed down the hatch to the lower levels in search of the storeroom. Entirely unfamiliar with ships, the orc wandered aimlessly, not knowing which direction to look. After traversing the deck below, he found himself in a luxurious room—the captain's quarters. Fangdarr wasn't fond of the small cabin that seemed so marvelously extravagant, filled with plush furniture and silk tapestries. He shook his head and returned to the main area. After searching the whole level and coming up short, the large orc struggled with climbing down the ladder to the next floor. Though much more open, Fangdarr didn't see any food or storage, so he proceeded to the next.

As the orc's feet hit the planks, he could immediately smell blood. Following his nose, Fangdarr turned to the rooms to the left, weapon at the ready. He continued through the threshold to see three orcs piled together, blood still pouring from the wounds they had suffered. One had a large hole blasted through its chest, while the other two appeared to have been squeezed to the point of bursting. Fangdarr's foot clanged against a crude iron sword from one of the deceased orcs, elven blood still on the blade's tip. Fangdarr eyed the scene once more, his respect for the elf only growing. Being caught unaware by three orcs in such close quarters and walking away with only a single minor wound was no small feat.

He turned back to the room he was in and was startled as Cormac poked his head down the ladder. "Oye! What're ye up to, Fang? The potatoes be up here!"

Before Fangdarr had a chance to respond the dwarf disappeared. Quickly, the orc peeked into the other room to see a large crate of food and other supplies. He palmed a handful of apples and threw them into a sac hanging on the wall before heading back up to rejoin his friends. Once on the deck, Fangdarr held up an apple to his brother. Oblivious, Bitrayuul remained fixed at the rail, staring at the chaos ensuing at Port Tempest.

"Bit," Fangdarr said, waving the fruit and drawing the half-orc from his trance. Bitrayuul turned to his brother and removed his helmet. There was no smile on his face as he took the apple, only pain. His eyes returned to the city as it slowly shrank behind them.

The brothers watched in silence as thousands of invaders crashed against the walls. Bitrayuul gasped as two ogres at the rear of the city finally managed to break through.

In moments, the black tide of monstrous creatures flooded like a river breaking through a dam, pushing over each other with blind bloodlust.

It wasn't long before the piercing screams made it to their ship—the ship that Bitrayuul knew was the townspeople's only glimmer of hope. The one that they took for themselves, damning those within the city. That was the second time they had condemned innocent lives to preserve their own since this war had started only a few days prior. Bitrayuul could only stare on in his own pain, knowing it was a mere fraction of what those left behind would feel. *When would it end?*

Feeling Fangdarr's hand on his shoulder, Bitrayuul looked to his brother and tried to force a smile. But his eyes couldn't help but stray back to the city. The screams had only grown with each passing moment as the horde surged through the streets like a creeping plague, killing and maiming all in their path. His eyes clenched shut each time a child's high screeches could be picked out among the sepulchral choir. *What unfathomable horrors did that child endure?* Bitrayuul trembled at the thought.

Cormac approached from Bitrayuul's right, hoping to offer comfort. He could see the half-orc's hands tightly clenched around the craft's rail. The wood had cracked and buckled under his strength, threatening to shatter at any moment. "Come, lad, ye need to eat somethin'." He tugged at Bitrayuul's arm lightly, but it remained in place. The dwarf looked to Fangdarr for assistance but was only met with a shrug.

As the pair started to walk away, leaving the half-orc to his torment, they heard him say, "This was our fault."

Cormac turned around. "Eh? How do ye figure, Bit?"

Bitrayuul spun to face the dwarf, lashing out in anger with his words. "How do I figure?! This is the *second* time we have sailed away as the humans are left to die in our place! We could have helped in some way—even if only a few. Where is our honor?"

Elethain strode closer to the group, Aesthéa by his side, growing frustrated with Bitrayuul's comments. "*Honor*? Orcblood, you are young. You will learn there are those with honor and those who survive. If you wish to die with honor, then you may do so. But *our* goal," the elf said, his hand sweeping the other members of their band, "is survival. That aside, there is nothing that could be done. The city would have fallen whether we arrived yesterday or tomorrow. Just be happy a ship was left, even if with malicious intent, or we would have died at sea."

Flabbergasted and overwhelmed by the nonchalance of his allies—his *friends*—Bitrayuul seemed at the edge of his patience. "We should have done something. *Anything*!" His eyes had shifted from rage to sorrow as the continuous sounds of carnage were his only response. The half-orc fell to his knees in anguish. *Why am I always so helpless?* Memories of the final moments of those he had so recently lost joined the current turmoil, only increasing his pain.

Too weary to bother arguing—and knowing no words would bring Bitrayuul comfort—the others went about their own ways while the half-orc continued to lament on the deck as Port Tempest faded from view.

CHAPTER TWELVE
THERAPY

Three decks below, Fangdarr and Aesthéa rested in the crew's quarters after cleaning the numerous minor cuts she had suffered. The large orc had too difficult a time squeezing into the tight bunk, causing him to destroy the bed above for more room. Aesthéa's laughter at his barbarism toward the inanimate object brought a smile to Fangdarr's face. The pair embraced for a moment, happy to be together and alive, before drifting to a deep slumber.

Cormac couldn't help but peek in on them from time to time as he worked to drag the three orc corpses from the cabin where Elethain had been ambushed. The old captain could hardly contain his own excitement that his dearest friend had found someone who truly accepted him—*loved* him. Though the relationship was unusual, to say the least, it mattered not to the dwarf. His smiled never faded, even as he forced the heavy orcs that were twice his size through the hatches above each ladder leading to the deck above. It was arduous work, to be sure, but it all felt worth it as he rolled the first and second bestial creature over the rail to the depths below.

Elethain watched the dwarf from the captain's cabin, his prejudice demanding he poke fun and insult the stout creature who cleaned the elf's mess. Yet, he didn't. It irked him more than a little that his distaste for orcs and dwarves was fast fading as his time with Cormac and Fangdarr continued. It was so much easier to hate blindly. There was no fuss, no gray area. There was simply the rejection. The necromancer lay back in the lush silks that covered the soft cushion. "Ah, this is more like home," he mumbled to the empty room. Exhaling in comfort, in only a short while he too had fallen asleep.

As Cormac was about to roll the third and final orc over the rail, huffing and puffing with exhaustion, he looked to Bitrayuul. The half-orc had stopped his weeping though remained immobilized and stared at the wooden planks beneath him, lost in thought. The dwarf slowly padded over. "How ye doin', lad?"

No response came at first, only an awkward silence that left Cormac uncomfortable. He threw his hands in the air and turned back toward the rail. Before he could push the corpse into the water, he heard his friend whisper, "I'm not sure."

"Well," the dwarf started, still at the rail, "come over here, son. I want ye to see somethin'." To Cormac's surprise, Bitrayuul rose and trudged closer, his eyes still glued to the floor. The dwarf disregarded the half-orc's gaze and continued. "Ye see this orc? I want ye to take a good look at it. What do ye see?"

Bitrayuul sighed as he gave a quick glance-over of the deceased creature. "I don't know. I see a dead orc."

"Right ye are, son. Dead." Bitrayuul just looked at him with confusion, missing his point. Cormac shook away his frustration, it wasn't the time to make an outburst at his distraught companion. "It's *dead*, lad. This be the third I'll be tossin' over, all dead. They're not some invincible creature. We can beat them, sure as stones. But we can't do so if *we're* dead. This war, like all, will be treacherous. Yer mettle will be tested, don't ye doubt. But we've got to succeed, or all be lost. No sense in dyin' in a lost battle. They've got the numbers; we can't beat 'em outright. It'll take strategy, time, and friends. Lots of friends. But . . . we can do it, I think."

Bitrayuul smiled at the dwarf. The words did little to help his mood, in truth, though he appreciated the attempt.

Cormac returned the smile and was about to plunge the orc into the sea but paused. "Say, why don't ye do this one, Bit?"

The half-orc didn't know what to think. He knew the dwarf offered the sentiment deliberately. As if lashing out against the corpse could help dissipate his pent-up hatred and turmoil. Yet, Bitrayuul considered himself more refined than to slip into the realm of barbarism.

As he was about to refute, he felt Cormac place his hand on the orc's body, causing him to almost jump back in surprise. He wanted to plunge his blades into the stiff form, to put every emotion he was suffering from deep into the beast. The urge was so intense. It would be so easy to let his anger take hold and drive him to viciousness . . .. Bitrayuul looked directly into the lifeless face of the orc before casting it into the sea. The dwarf put an approving hand on the half-orc's arm as they both watched the black form sink below the surface.

Bitrayuul descended the ladder behind Cormac to the first level. It surprised him just how much stress he felt had been lifted from his shoulders after pushing the corpse overboard. He watched Cormac as they slowly crept past the snoozing Elethain, thankful for what the dwarf had done for him.

The floorboards creaked beneath their heavy footsteps, though the elf remained undisturbed. They continued to the next level where a series of unchecked storage rooms sat at the back of the ship. Cormac kicked away a rat as he approached the door, frowning at the vermin as if scolding it for its naughtiness.

"Damned rats, bahaha!" Cormac quietly laughed to Bitrayuul. He pulled the cold, iron latch on the door. "Well, at least ye know there be fo—. Bothain's beard . . .."

CHAPTER THIRTEEN

RELENTLESS

Bitrayuul followed the dwarf's gaze forward. Beneath a gory display of six dissected rats and a man, strung up by their intestines as if a make-shift chandelier, sat Chakal. The elf rested easily on a crate on his back with his legs up the wall as he stared at the disgusting structure sway with the ship's motion over his face. As the assassin heard the door open, he turned upright, wiping away the drops of blood that had fallen on his face and showing a deviously friendly smile.

"Two targets in one day?" the elf said with an exaggerated look of surprise to one of the suspended rats as he kicked the dangling man—his first target—into a spin. "Ugh, where's the thrill of the hunt?"

Cormac and Bitrayuul were immediately on the defensive. Instinctively, the dwarf slammed the door shut as the half-orc pushed a heavy crate in front of the barrier for reinforcement, trapping the elf inside. Without hesitation, Cormac called out to his companions resting on the higher decks, pausing to hear their frantic footsteps overhead.

The others slid down the ladder hastily, confused as to what was occurring. But the grim look on Cormac and Bitrayuul's faces was all the evidence they needed to know the severity of the situation.

"What is it?" Elethain asked in a whisper.

"Chakal," Bitrayuul responded.

"*Here*? Now? Why?"

Before Bitrayuul could answer, Chakal called out calmly from behind the door. "Are you finished?"

All went silent.

"Will you let me out now, please? The stench is rather pungent in here." When no response came, the trapped elf let out a drawn-out sigh.

"Where is Malice?" The assassin asked through the door, his voice growing more agitated. "It would be a cruel irony for fate to land us in the same boat and she not continue our adventure. Please don't tell me I've sat on this ship, playing with rats," he chuckled, "for nothing." Within the small closet, Chakal eyed the sailor from Port Tempest that he had killed and laughed wickedly. "Well, not for *nothing*."

Bitrayuul finally decided to respond, hoping to give the elf a reason to leave. "Malice is gone. She . . . She did not survive the dragon." The somber tone of his voice gave Chakal enough reason to believe he was telling the truth. However, it didn't prevent their captive from immediately kicking a large hole through the thick, wooden door that separated them.

"What!? That miserable, pathetic, impudent, insufferable wench was killed by Crepusculus!?" His rage was insurmountable, and his visage formed the most violent anger he could muster. "She was *mine*! MINE!" Chakal groaned and screamed in intense frustration. "And she— but— then how— Ugh!"

The group watched in bewilderment through the gap as the lethal assassin spun himself in circles, literally ripping hairs from his head. The elf continued spouting incoherent nonsense before contorting his expression to a sinister grin. "No matter," Chakal started with eerie calmness. "You're the next on my list, half-blood."

Each of the companions prepared themselves as the assassin jumped through the slight opening in the splintered wooden door with ease. Cormac quickly charged first, thick shields leading, hoping to press the elf back into the small cabin. It was a pointless attempt, Chakal was too nimble, too quick. By the time the stampeding captain closed the distance, the assassin had already taken three full strides away from the door, heading for Bitrayuul.

"Do not interfere, dwarf!" Chakal roared with utter contempt.

Cormac ignored the command. "Careful, lads, he's a slippery one!"

Though only Bitrayuul had encountered the threatening fiend before, the others heard enough of his exploits as to not underestimate their opponent. Fangdarr strode forward, Driktarr in hand, and with Bitrayuul at his side. Behind them, Elethain remained with Aesthéa.

"An orc? The 'Great' Elethain walks by the side of an *orc*?" Chakal taunted, causing his oncoming foes to halt. As one, Fangdarr and Bitrayuul turned to Elethain, careful to keep an eye on their opponent.

Bitrayuul eyed the necromancer with curiosity. "How does he know your name?"

Elethain scoffed. "There are no large number of elves, half-blood. We are all known to each other, in one way or another."

Chakal chuckled maniacally in response. "And . . .?"

The elven necromancer groaned as he attempted to appear distracted by straightening his robes. After the stares continued to press, he sighed heavily. "*And* he *was* my friend." As his words ended, the tension in the room thickened immensely.

Elethain could instantly see the suspicious glares he was being cast. Aesthéa seemed to accept the news without much concern, as if she understood Elethain's hesitation.

"You see? This is merely a reunion between friends and me killing the half-blood. There is no reason to fuss. Let me kill the whelp, and I will be on my way," Chakal offered nonchalantly.

Fangdarr tightened his grip on the large greataxe in his hands, eager to put an end to the confident killer that had threatened his brother. Bitrayuul was still looking to Elethain, who remained unfazed.

"Will you aid us, Elethain?" the half-orc asked.

The necromancer didn't hesitate in his response. "If you recall, I told you how to beat him. But, no, I will not fight him."

"Ye what?" Cormac intervened. "This madman is goin' to kill yer friends and ye plan to sit back and watch?" The dwarf's eyes were wide with shock. "Where be your honor, elf?"

Elethain merely shrugged in response, as if that was all the response necessary. No matter the reason, he seemed adamant that his involvement wasn't a possibility. Though, none of his companions understood his moral dilemma. Elethain expected them to believe it was due to his past bond with the monster that stayed his hand. Unfortunately, it wasn't. The necromancer had sacrificed his own brothers for his goals, one he hardly considered a friend would be of little concern. No, it was his doubt that halted him. He strongly believed that Chakal could kill all of them with ease, right then and there. Elethain knew the assassin's mind, however, and that their foe cared little for those not his prey.

Surprisingly, Fangdarr was handling Elethain's attitude the best. He didn't mind that the elf refused to be dragged into Bitrayuul's fate, and why should he? The chieftain knew Elethain held no love for Bitrayuul. Nevertheless, Fangdarr did; he wouldn't allow the assassin to have his wish. The orc took another step forward.

"You too, orc?" Chakal questioned with a lax tone as if another target would be of no consequence.

Bitrayuul and Cormac readied themselves once more and joined Fangdarr in closing in on the assassin. Their elven companions—even Aesthéa—remained firmly rooted in place.

Chakal spread a wide grin on his face, ready for the challenge to come. His sinister smile refused to part, even as Fangdarr brought his axe down in a heavy blow toward his shoulder. With a quick flick of his curved shortsword, the elf deflected it easily.

Incredulous, Fangdarr watched as his enormous axe fell harmlessly to the side at the coercion of the slight weapon's push. *What sort of wondrous strength did this elf possess?* Chakal was muscular, yet slim. *How could he possibly possess such strength?* Before the chieftain could continue the dozens of questions racing through his mind, he was forced to parry a deft thrust of his foe's dagger, headed straight for his heart. As he parried, Fangdarr could hardly believe that the elf was on the offensive, even while squared against three opponents. It seemed Bitrayuul hadn't exaggerated the assassin's skills.

Bitrayuul and Cormac attacked simultaneously on each flank, four pointed blades seeking different targets. Meanwhile, Fangdarr's axe came from underneath and upward, hoping to cleave the elf from groin to neck. Such a coordinated attack would fell any foe, no matter how skilled. Yet, their confidence dwindled to nothingness as they witnessed their devilish opponent prevent every attack in a whirl of steel. Chakal backflipped in time with the devastating axe, preceding its path upward to avoid making contact, while each of his blades swept out to the side, deflecting both weapons from the half-orc and dwarf on his flanks.

The trio knew they couldn't relent—even with the knowledge that their foe may be greater than them all.

Taking advantage of their minor pause of awe, Chakal went back on the offensive. He danced around the field of battle, dipping and dodging, tucking and twisting, all to disorient the companions. Chakal's sword slashed toward Cormac at his left, forcing the captain to raise a shield in defense.

While the thickened plate was raised, Chakal leapt forward and ran up the shield in two quick steps, kicking with his feet as he went. Cormac rocked back on his heels, attempting to push the elf off, but he was too slow. By then, Chakal was already over his head in a somersault. On pure instinct alone, Cormac started to duck—just in time. Chakal's dagger reached down and cut a gash on the dwarf's bald head, producing a line of blood. Had the dwarf not ducked, the blade surely would have cut deep into his skull.

Chakal landed on his feet behind the dwarf and out of range of the orcish brothers. He retracted his shortsword as Cormac was falling backwards toward the elf from the blow to his head. The blade was lined up perfectly to pierce through the captain's heart. The grin that never left Chakal's face had only grown wider as he watched the dwarf continue to fall toward the poised weapon.

Fangdarr and Bitrayuul reached forward, hoping to grab Cormac's shield, belt, *anything* to spare him. It was no use; he was just a finger-length out of reach. They watched with eyes wide in horror at the expected outcome.

Distracted by the thought of the dwarf sliding over his blade, the assassin failed to notice the black, demonic hand form from nothingness at his rear before clutching him. "No!" Chakal screamed in rage, eyes flashing with such vigorous malice towards Elethain. His violent expression pushed to the extreme as the dwarf fell harmlessly to the floorboards. "For a dwarf!? A *dwarf*, Elethain!"

No response came from the somber necromancer. His reaction surprised even himself. He knew, then, that they must kill Chakal at any cost, or he would come to regret his involvement for the rest of his days—however short they may be.

Bitrayuul grasped Cormac's arm and quickly lifted him away from the elf while Fangdarr charged in, weapon raised. Fangdarr wasn't fond of attacking a defenseless enemy, but, in this case, he cast morality aside and his greataxe came down through the air.

Looking up at the axe, the grin from Chakal's face was replaced with sheer anger. He struggled from within the large hand and roared in outrage. He wouldn't die trapped like a rat! The elf's teeth grit as he pressed with all his might. Then, to Elethain's shock and fear, the assassin burst free from the magical prison just in time. By then, it was impossible for Chakal to get his weapons in line to parry Fangdarr's axe. So, as soon as he was free, his hands clapped together over the blade of the heavy weapon, stopping it a hair's breadth from his forehead.

If Fangdarr was surprised by the impossible feat he had just witnessed, he didn't show it. Instead, the orc seemed to almost expect it. As soon as the elf's hands clasped the blade, Fangdarr relinquished his grip on his beloved weapon and threw his arms around the assassin. Due to his hulking form, the chieftain could easily suppress his foe with a single arm, throwing his axe aside with the other. Fangdarr's other arm joined the first, squeezing tightly around Chakal. Additionally, the orc's legs wrapped around the slim elf's lower limbs, securing him in place.

Chakal screamed in rage at being so easily overpowered by the large orc. "Release me, behemoth! Fight me if you dare, for you know you cannot hope to defeat me!"

Fangdarr rose to his feet, shifting his grip to have both wrists in one hand and both ankles in the other. He carried the elf up the tight ladder with difficulty to the first level. Then again to the deck. It was still dark out, with only the moon and collected stars casting light over the ship. Fangdarr didn't bother waiting for his friends, who were close on his heels anyway, curious of his intentions. The orc strode to the rail with Chakal still spouting curses.

As the chieftain retracted his arms above his head to build tension in his muscles, the others had all reached the main deck and watched him hurl the assassin over the rail and into the sea.

The companions watched from the vessel as the assassin's head could be seen bobbing up and down with the gentle ripple of water. Their eyes shifted between Chakal and Fangdarr, who stood silently waving to the assassin.

Chakal sputtered a mouthful of salty seawater back into the ocean as he watched the ship sail away. The anger that was previously on his face had vanished, overwritten by his customary grin. "Oh, this will be fun," he said to himself with vicious glee as he started swimming east toward land, eager for the hunt to resume.

CHAPTER FOURTEEN

NOBILITY

"Bothain's beard . . . what happened?" Cormac asked, breaking from his daze.

Fangdarr gently lifted the dwarf's head from the floor, inspecting the wound after wiping the blood away. "Chakal cut you. Not deep. But need to stitch."

"Bah, damned elf. Ah, well, at least he didn't get me other eye, bahaha!" He sobered quickly as his fingers traced the new wound. "Did we get him, Fang?"

The chieftain nodded proudly. "He gone. Threw him into water."

Cormac returned the nod, though he wasn't as convinced they were rid of the assassin. Nevertheless, Cormac wasn't about to spoil the mood. They were safe . . . for now. The wound on his head pulsed under the strain as he pulled himself to his rear. "What about everyone else? They all okay?"

Fangdarr smiled in response before lifting Cormac from his seated position. Together, the pair climbed up the ladder to where their companions were sitting in the captain's chambers. As they walked closer, they could make out Elethain's voice. ". . . stupid. I should never have gotten involved—now we are *all* doomed."

"How's that, elf?" Cormac asked as he entered, startling those in the room. When no response came, the dwarf spoke once more. "I'm not knowin' how the rest of that fight turned out, don't ye doubt, but I know if ye got involved then it must've been needed. So, I thank ye."

"At what cost, dwarf?!" Elethain's harshness rocked Cormac back on his heels. The elf turned toward Fangdarr and scolded, "We should have *killed* him, not tossed him into the sea!"

Fangdarr looked out at the endless expanse of ocean that surrounded them, confused as to how anyone could possibly make it back to land. The orc shrugged in response as if it was all the same, resulting in another angry outburst from the necromancer. "You ignorant fool! He can *swim*!"

"Enough, Elethain. What's done is done." Aesthéa stepped over to Fangdarr and took his hand, signaling her acceptance of his actions. That was enough for the orc.

The necromancer rubbed his temple in frustration. "Why was Chakal even on the ship?"

"I'm guessin' it had to do with that man he strung up," Cormac replied. "Seems we ain't the only ones that pushed the elf's buttons."

Elethain laughed. "Oh, no. I can assure you Chakal's list is nearly endless."

Bitrayuul shifted uncomfortably, waiting to ask the question that had been nagging him. "Elethain, you said he was your friend. Why did you not mention that? What happened?"

All eyes turned to the elf as he let out a sharp scoff. Elethain groaned in frustration as Aesthéa stared at him expectantly. "Fine. Not that my history is of any concern to you all. Chakal and I are about the same age, leading to us spending our youth together. As elves live such long lives, it is not frequent that there are children born around the same time. Even when my twin brothers were born two centuries later, they always had each other. I remained by Chakal's side even after I became an advisor to the royal family." Elethain fell back into a lush, velvet chair and rubbed his eyes, already weary of the conversation.

"Before you ask, yes, Chakal has always been this way. Even in his youth, he was vicious, proud, and *deadly*. There was no tragic accident, nor any form of abuse that he had suffered to breed his nature. He is not the byproduct of some wrongful action. Some are just born rotten, even elves. Nevertheless, he was my friend. We were dreadfully competitive with each other, pushing the other to new heights that made us the powerful forces we are today."

Before the elf could continue, Bitrayuul interrupted, "Do you think Chakal being so close to you is what caused you to become the way you are?"

Elethain's eyes narrowed dangerously in response. "Yes, half-blood, the thought has crossed my mind before. Though, there is no sense in dwelling on the past." Despite granting Bitrayuul an answer, the elf didn't hide his disdain. "In any case, we went separate ways."

Each of the companions waited for Elethain to elaborate, though he simply leaned back in his chair and closed his eyes. After a moment, Bitrayuul pressed for more. The necromancer groaned, making sure they knew of his disapproval before continuing. "After I had just become an advisor, the king's son had insulted Chakal. I tried to convince the prince to avoid taunting him at all costs, but royalty tends to be arrogant. The prince thought that I was siding with my friend and threatened to remove me from my position—one I had worked strenuously for. So, instead, I tried to reason with Chakal. Unfortunately, you are well aware of his compulsion. Once he has deemed an opponent deserving, there is no stopping him. I begged and pleaded, for both his sake and my own, for him to simply move on.

"At first, Chakal seemed to do so. I was intensely proud of him, I cannot lie. However, the prince continued with his insults, goading Chakal further. Chakal challenged him to a duel, which was refused. The prince laughed in my friend's face for thinking one of noble birth could be challenged by one without status. Instead, the snob chose to continue his horrendous behavior, knowing Chakal could do nothing about it." Elethain shifted uneasily in his seat.

"Once, I told you that the best way to 'defeat' Chakal is to simply ignore him. That remains true. It will torment him for eternity, but you will stay alive. However, as with your friend Malice, he will find ways to tempt you into action—even if it means attacking those who have not wronged him. It is an odd line he draws; some sort of deranged validation, in his mind."

"Is that what he did, then?" Bitrayuul asked.

Elethain paused. The tale was known by almost all elves yet was held close to the chest due to its nature. Elethain chuckled at how absurd the notion seemed now that Chakal hunted them.

"Yes," the elf continued, "he did. Chakal started killing the prince's friends—any who were not nobility—and pushing him into a corner. The prince could either continue letting Chakal kill his friends and be seen by his people as someone who cares little for anyone of a lower social class or answer the assassin's call. He chose the latter."

Fully riveted like the rest of his companions, Fangdarr leaned forward in eagerness. "What happen next?"

"Chakal killed him; in his most brutal and wicked manner. One morning, the prince was found strapped naked to a makeshift rack in the center of the city. His entire body had been cut open, though every artery was avoided to prolong his death. His tongue was removed, then a molten blade was forced into his mouth, ensuring the prince could not yell out while he was tortured through the night. Chakal left his eyes, so he could witness himself being flayed. It was a gruesome death, deserved by none." Elethain took a steadying breath as he reminisced on the scene.

"The queen took her own life that same morning after witnessing her only child suffer such horror. And my king has never been the same since though he hides it well. His bloodline ended with his son, so the throne will fall to Aesthéa's father next, followed by her older brother."

Fangdarr turned to Aesthéa with the news of her having a brother and being in line for the throne. She shrugged at him as if none of it was relevant, so the orc turned back to Elethain. "Bear be queen?"

Elethain nearly laughed at the question. "No, Aesthéa will not be queen. Not only are her father and older brother next in line for the throne, her brother has a son as well. Even if something happened to all of them, Aesthéa cannot become queen."

"Why not? Because Bear girl?"

Aesthéa chimed in, "Because druids of Cerenos cannot hold positions of power."

Elethain nodded. "One of our many ancient laws restricts any druid from holding the throne. Additionally, the druids swear an oath to not pursue such things either. They believe it is not the will of Cerenos to rule over others, rather to simply be a part of the whole."

Fangdarr just blinked in reply, realizing how truly little he knew about Aesthéa and her culture.

"What about the elf?" Cormac asked, getting back on topic.

Elethain sighed once more. "Chakal was exiled, as expected. First, the king demanded I hunt him down and kill him, but I refused. I explained that it was the prince who provoked such an action, despite warnings against it. Normally, such insubordination would result in my death. But the king cherished my honesty, and still does. There is a reason I follow my king's orders without question. I have a deep respect for him and know he does not allow his emotions to make decisions. With my request, he did not send any elves after Chakal. Not because I cared for the survival of my friend—on the contrary, Chakal nearly cost me all I had worked for—but because I believed that those sent after him would be killed outright. Thankfully, the king did not wish to send others to their doom due to his son's arrogance."

Cormac was flabbergasted. "Whew, lad. A good king."

Elethain smiled at the dwarf's compliment. "Indeed. In any case, Chakal has not returned to Jesmera, as far as I am aware. He would be executed without hesitation. Our travels may take us to Wiston first, but then I must continue with Aesthéa to our home, especially with Chakal on our trail. Though she is not to be queen, she is still a part of the royal family."

"Right. Well, we got about a day's travel to Wiston, by me guess," Cormac said, peeking through a window in the cabin. The sun was nearly to the horizon, painting the sky in its lovely orange hue. "We best get some rest and eat up. The war be waitin' for us once we land, don't ye doubt." The dwarf's reminder sobered the group. Between the encounter with Chakal and Elethain's tale, they had almost forgotten that the humans were being eradicated.

Almost.

CHAPTER FIFTEEN

DREAM

Fangdarr rolled in the small bed in discomfort, attempting to not stir Aesthéa. He groaned in frustration, though settled quickly as his eyes scanned his lover's face. In the brief moments of sleep he had, Fangdarr had dreamed that she was the queen of Jesmera. The illusion had started with simple, tranquil scenes of Aesthéa sitting on a flowered throne in an elegant dress, discussing matters of the city with Elethain standing vigilant by her side. Though, the vision quickly turned sour as he witnessed himself being dragged to her, bound in chains, while elven guards whipped at him like a beast. Even as his skin was lacerated by the lashes, the pain was nothing compared to the sight of the disgust on Aesthéa's face as she sentenced Fangdarr to be executed. Now, lying awake next her to relaxed visage, the orc could hardly remember that lethal scowl from his nightmare.

Fangdarr watched his fingers disappear beneath the elf's black, disheveled locks. He loved sliding the cool strands between his fingers. After a few brushes, the elf started to wake.

Fangdarr cursed himself, but he couldn't help it. His nightmare left him yearning for her, even if just for a moment. He watched as Aesthéa blinked open her eyes before yawning sweetly. She stared at him and smiled. Fangdarr ran his fingers through her hair again. "Sorry. Not mean to wake you. Bad dream."

"It's alright," Aesthéa said before yawning. "Do you want to talk about it?"

Fangdarr paused. Luckily, Cormac and Bitrayuul appeared to be fast asleep in the cots nearby—with Elethain residing in the luscious bed of the captain's cabin out of earshot. "No, dream is gone."

Smiling at him once more, the elf planted a kiss against her companion's chest as her eyes started to droop again.

Stress built within the orc's stomach. "I ask something?"

Aesthéa's eyes fluttered open softly, still fighting the rest they so desired. "Mm?"

"What happen if elves turn me away? Or they refuse us?" Fangdarr felt badly about asking such difficult questions while Aesthéa tried to rest, but he couldn't help himself. These were the questions that drove away his sleep and made his heart pound—not the war ahead or the assassin on their trail. It was being denied that made the great orc anxious.

Unfortunately, his questions would remain unanswered, as they fell on deaf ears. He sighed and kissed his snoozing companion before wrapping his arm around her and he stared at the blank wall in silence.

CHAPTER SIXTEEN
WISTON

Morning came with the sound of distant clamor. The companions all rushed to the deck and their jaws nearly dropped. Hundreds of thousands of trolls—with a sprinkle of orcs and the rare ogre—lined the coast as far as their eyes could see. They looked north where Wiston's large wall held off the masses. Countless fires were lit, though no tents were visible; the monsters slept right on the ground.

"Bothain's beard . . .," Bitrayuul stated in awe. "How can such a horde exist?"

"What's worse," Elethain began with his usual stoic attitude, "is that if they are here, everything behind them has fallen." Their eyes all turned southward. Small wisps of smoke could still be seen, though no longer were there pillars rising into the air as the towns and villages had been stamped from existence.

"Bothain's beard . . .," Cormac mimicked, as he was struck by the realization that over half of the human population had already been eradicated.

Bitrayuul couldn't peel his eyes from the tide of black. "Our plight is impossible! How are we to defeat such a number?" In that moment, he was thankful the dwarves had the foresight to dig deep into the mountain. Though the half-orc's question wasn't rhetorical, none could answer.

Elethain straightened his robes. "We will be arriving at the docks before mid-day. We should prepare. Gather any food and supplies we may need from the ship. You will need to request an audience with the king. I have met him, once, King Dariel. He is a stern leader, but otherwise bland. He leads his people well and with pride, though I loathe to admit it. You know how fond I am of humans, after all." Elethain ended with a smirk before heading down the ladder to the lower levels. Without a word, his ghoulish brothers all followed.

Cormac and Aesthéa followed suit to start looking for supplies. Remaining on the deck, Fangdarr approached Bitrayuul, who still stood motionless at the rail. The half-orc just watched as the enemies along the coast had spotted their ship and had started to taunt and howl at them from the cliff's edge. They could never reach the vessel, of course, but it didn't stop the intimidation rushing through Bitrayuul as he felt their countless eyes upon them.

"Bit," Fangdarr said, not for the first time, drawing his brother from his trance. The half-orc looked at Fangdarr with concern written all over his face. The orc smiled in encouragement. "We find a way."

Returning the smile half-heartedly, Bitrayuul clasped a hand over his brother's shoulder before descending to join the rest of his friends, leaving Fangdarr alone on the deck. The orc stared at the spectacle for a moment before an all-too-familiar voice crept into his head.

Witness your army, Fangdarr. See the insatiable wave of darkness consume all in its path. The humans wait in their hole behind the wall, delaying the inevitable. Join your legion, O' Roaring One. Take command as glory is brought to you. Crush the humans beneath the blade of your axe. Wipe them from history and claim Crein in your name. Force the ver—

Fangdarr clutched his head in agony as the shadow dragon's words screamed through his mind. Growling, the orc shook himself free, ending the tantalizing words and regaining control. He looked to the horde once more, afraid it would incite another dialogue from the essence of Crepusculus trapped in his head. Thankfully, none came. With fleeting illusions of seeing himself on a throne in Wiston, the orc shrugged it away and climbed down the ladder.

After the preparations were complete, the companions stood at the rail as the ship approached the docks at the rear of the city. Within moments, a dozen guards ran toward the dock and were standing at the ready. Elethain commanded his minions to steer the vessel and bring it into the wooden pier.

The ship neatly approached before the anchor was released to lock the craft in place. Cormac slid the wide plank to the dock before exiting the ship. Upon seeing a dwarf, the guards relaxed a bit, and more so at the sight of the pair of elves who came next—even though Elethain had crumbled his brothers to fragments that now clung to his body partially hidden beneath his robe. However, their trepidation rose as Bitrayuul, fully hidden beneath his armor, strode down the plank. He seemed questionably large for a human, though too small to be an orc. Nevertheless, the guards didn't take action.

As Fangdarr took his first step onto the plank, shouts immediately were called out, followed by the guards lowering their pikes. Despite the orc's hands raising in the air and his friend's pleas to the guards about his innocence, the men closed in on him quickly. With spear tips poking into his back, the orc was disarmed and pressed toward the city by six guards. Fangdarr never said a word as the soldiers forcibly escorted him, trailed closely by his friends, still shouting in protest.

They reached the large steel door and passed into the city's Trade District. The few civilians that still walked the streets began cursing and shouting at Fangdarr, some even electing to throw stones at him. Forced to comply, the orc endured it all. His shoulders slumped in despair as the people of Wiston treated him like a plague. In part, the chieftain understood—there were thousands of orcs, *his* orcs, pounding on their walls even now. But the rationalization did little to numb the sting.

Once through the Trade District, the guards pushed Fangdarr through a small pathway to the next sector. Despite the circumstances, Fangdarr marveled at the defensiveness of the city. Even if the enemy ever managed to break through the thick outer wall, they would then need to pass through the interior barriers all the same. The orc felt a jab in his back, breaking his attention and forcing him to keep pace.

They moved to what appeared to be the royal courtyard. Ahead stood the castle, skirted by beautiful gardens, fountains, and luscious trees that seemed too green to be real. Astonished by the beauty, Fangdarr turned to his friends to gage their reactions before remembering that perhaps all had already been to Wiston before.

After realizing their words were hopeless, Fangdarr's companions quieted themselves. It wasn't until the guards opened the door at the rear of the castle leading into a dimly lit dungeon below that they raised their arguments once more.

Three men held back Fangdarr's friends outside the small corridor as the remaining three continued to prod the large orc forward. In the tight quarters, Fangdarr's head nearly scraped along the ceiling and his arms brushed against each cell lining the walls. It would have been nearly impossible for him to fight back, even if he wanted to.

The orc was forced to wait as the guard in front fumbled with the lock, fearful the orc would attack while he was distracted. Fingers still trembling, the man opened the door and roughly pushed his prisoner through the threshold. Once Fangdarr was inside, the guard clicked the lock in place and shook it vigorously to ensure the orc couldn't escape.

Fangdarr's eyes scanned the cell. Naught but a single bench of stone and a bucket were present. The immoral characteristics surprised him. In truth, the cell was no different than those kept by orcs for their own captives. The familiarity was little comfort.

The guards retreated down the corridor to join the others while Fangdarr remained staring from the cage. He could hear his friends calling out to him, offering reassurances for his release, and insults launched at the men who had trapped him. It brought a smile to his face, knowing he was cared for so deeply. However, there was little else he could do besides sit and wait.

Meanwhile, Bitrayuul, Cormac, and Aesthéa were outside continuing their protest. Elethain remained silent, however, refusing to put any risk on the perception his king—even for a friend.

"What do ye mean he can't be released?" Cormac asked with a flabbergasted look. "Are ye dense!? Ye got the damned key!" His fury had only grown on their short journey from the docks to the dungeons.

"This isn't your concern, dwarf. If you have a complaint you will have t—" the guard started before Cormac strode up to the man and pushed a stubby finger into his tunic.

"Oh, I got yer complaint! Right here, lad." The dwarf slammed his shields together.

The group of guards eventually seemed to realize that they were severely outmatched by the four companions who were growing more and more irritated. Finally, one angrily responded, "There is nothing we can do!"

Bitrayuul put a hand on Cormac to calm him, though it did little. The half-orc looked at the man and smoothly said, "Sir, we wish to have an audience with your king. We have important information of the enemy that can aid in this war. Will you help us?"

At that, the man slightly relaxed, though he still seemed suspicious. The guard that was addressed turned to his allies who nodded in agreement before he spoke. "We can take you to the king, though no weapons may enter the royal chamber." One of the guards in the rear was drenched in sweat from carrying Driktarr and happily passed the weapon to Bitrayuul with a hefty sigh of relief.

Bitrayuul looked to Cormac, as the elves didn't possess any weapons. The dwarf sighed but agreed without issue. The half-orc looked back to the guard. "Take us to the king."

CHAPTER SEVENTEEN

LUCIEN

Fangdarr sat against the cold, wet stone in silence. The only light within the dungeon was a dull glow from a single torch at each end of the long line of cells. He had called out in the hopes another was there but was only met with his own echo. Then, the sound of a door latch could be heard, followed by slow creaking as it drifted open. Fangdarr sat up, anxious but curious, hoping his friends had returned. The door gently closed. "Who there?"

Nothing.

"Hello?" the orc called out once more.

More silence. Finally, Fangdarr could hear light shuffling. On instinct, the orc reached for his axe before remembering the guards removed it.

The steps grew closer.

Fangdarr put his back against the wall, getting as far from the grated iron bars as he could. A young man stopped outside of Fangdarr's cell and stared inward. The unknown figure said nothing for many moments—just stared in silence. Fangdarr remained defensive, though there was little he could do from within his cage. The orc watched as the man laid his back against the bars on the cell opposite of Fangdarr's and slid to his rear. Curious, the chieftain relaxed his pose and took a seat on the floor as well.

"Hello," the man said with a smile. "What are you doing down here?"

Fangdarr furrowed his brow—as if the answer should have been obvious. "Orc. Why you?"

"I like to walk through here from time to time. There's usually no one down here, so it's a quiet place for me to think or relax."

The orc looked around at the slimy, damp walls of the darkened dungeon, clearly puzzled. "Why?"

"I don't know."

A prolonged and awkward silence followed. "Who are you?" Fangdarr asked, unable to bear the discomfort any longer.

"My name is Lucien. What is yours?"

"Fangdarr."

"Hello, Fangdarr. How long have you been in here?"

The orc shrugged. "Not long." Before the visitor could respond, he added, "Why you here?"

A genuine and kind smile was still etched on Lucien's youthful face. "Curiosity, I suppose."

Fangdarr started to grow irritated with the man's lack of elaborate responses. "Curious about what?"

"You, Fangdarr. You are the first orc I have seen who is not trying to smash and kill everyone around them. You're calm, collected, even respectful. Very different from a typical orc, as I am sure you know." Lucien's smile turned to intrigue as he eyed the lattice of iron containing the orc. "You could easily break out of here, yet you have not. Why?"

Fangdarr sighed. "You right. I different. Chieftain of orcs outside wall." The orc was a bit trepidatious to inform the man of his status, though felt compelled to remain honest. "I was away. Hunting shadow dragon to prevent war. We too late. Kill dragon, but war already started. We come to tell king what happened. Help end war. If I break out, humans think I monster. Need them to listen. So, I wait."

Lucien's grew even more interested. "You seek to *end* the war?"

The chieftain nodded. "I love battle. But don't want to hurt people. On journey I met good humans. Good dwarves. And elves. Show me I fight wrong battles. First, I hunt dragon as distraction. My clan wanted war. Needed way to buy time. If I kill dragon, clan never question me. I would be god. But Crepusculus planning war all along. Dragon recruit trolls and ogres. Even my clan. They killed many humans. Must end."

Lucien couldn't believe the orc's strength—turning against his own nature for the sake of others. He could hardly form words as his respect and admiration of Fangdarr clogged his throat. Rising to his feet, Lucien stepped closer, his face pressed against the bars. "I must go. I shall return."

Confused, Fangdarr watched him hurry away, listening to his quick footsteps fading down the corridor, and leaving the orc alone once more.

CHAPTER EIGHTEEN

PLEA

"Weapons here," the guard stated firmly.

Bitrayuul and Cormac started to remove their weapons, placing them on the ground within the small room past the castle's doors. The dwarf removed both shields, followed by a dagger tucked within his belt, and turned to watch Bitrayuul struggle to remove nearly every piece of equipment on his person.

Tapping his foot impatiently, the guard watched as the half-orc removed his gauntlets, greaves, bracers, boots, and breastplate, careful not to poke the other soldiers as he handed the sharpened equipment over. The men backed away as the putrid scent of old sweat filled their noses, nearly driving them to vomit. After carefully removing Tormag's hammers from his waist, all that remained on Bitrayuul's body was his helmet and soiled linens.

The guards stood waiting expectantly with their noses scrunched in disgust. "Your helmet, sir."

Bitrayuul exhaled slowly as he pulled the steel case from his head, revealing tan skin and a small pair of fangs. He knew what was coming. Almost immediately the guards were upon him. They gripped his sweat-covered tunic tightly, ignoring their nose's begs for mercy, and dragged Bitrayuul deeper into the castle. Cormac and the elves followed behind, once again forced to watch as a friend was mistreated.

Fortunately, the men didn't drag Bitrayuul all the way to the dungeon to join his kin. Instead, he was pulled along the red woven carpet to the throne room, where King Dariel slumped in his large, golden chair. Once in front of Dariel's throne, the Bitrayuul was shoved to the floor before the guards lowered their spears to his neck.

The leading soldier turned his head to the king. "Your grace, this half-orc entered the city, as well as an orc."

Bitrayuul raised his eyes to the throne, expecting to see a man intent on his doom. Instead, the king remained lax in his nonchalance. "And where is the orc?"

"The dungeon, sir."

King Dariel's nod was emotionless. He seemed disinterested, even as the loud, angry dwarf and pair of elves strode closer to the golden throne. "And they are . . .?"

The soldier craned his neck to the visitors and stammered, "T-the orcs friends, sir."

Dariel lifted an eyebrow. "Friends? A dwarf and a pair of elves came to my city with a half-breed and an orc? Do you jest?"

Before the guard could speak, Cormac pushed forward. "Yer highness, the words be true," he started, ignoring the guards shifting their spears in his direction for speaking out of term. "The orc be with us, as be this one here. They be our friends and we got important news of the war. We kindly request an audience."

Everyone remained silent while the king pondered on his throne, shifting his gaze between each of the guests. As his eyes fell upon Elethain, a flicker of recognition flashed through the man. "Elethain?"

The necromancer held back his discomfort and forced a polite smile. He wanted no part of this, only to return to Jesmera in haste. Nonetheless, Elethain stepped forward. "Indeed, King Dariel. It has been some time."

Dariel's face brightened at recognizing a known acquaintance among the group—someone he knew would never be a spy for the enemy. "Truly, it has. Does this dwarf speak the truth? Are you here on behalf of your king?"

"His words are true, your grace. Though, we are not here on behalf of King Nelthalius." Elethain paused, hoping he could end there, but the king's expectant look pressed the elf further. "The orc in your dungeon embarked on a quest to cull Crepusculus, a shadow dragon that had been terrorizing Crein for centuries, do you know of it?"

The king sat up straight in his chair. "Yes, I am aware of the dragon's existence. This orc set off *alone* to eradicate the beast?"

Elethain nodded. "At first, your grace. This half-orc is a General of the Dwarven Regime, and the orc's kin. The orc requested aid, though was initially rejected. Cormac, this dwarf," he said with a hand extended to Cormac, "was the first to join the orc's quest. Aesthéa and I joined as well, though that is a story for another time. We found the drake and eliminated it. However, we discovered that Crepusculus had been assembling an army—the one now pounding on your walls. Unfortunately, even with the dragon gone, they persist. You can have no doubt this war would have been over already had Crepusculus not been slain. Its breath could melt stone and even your great walls would have fallen to ruin."

Dariel leaned back in his chair. "That is quite a tale. What is it you request of me?"

Determined to end the conversation as quickly as possible, Elethain replied, "I would ask that you release the orcs—they only mean to aid you in this war—and allow Aesthéa and I swift return to Jesmera."

As soon as the words left the necromancer's mouth, Aesthéa chimed in. "No, Elethain! I will not leave these people to their fate!" Elethain scowled at her, though held his tongue for fear of shaming himself in front of a king.

Dariel raised a hand to demand silence. "My lady, I appreciate the sentiment. Dark days are ahead of us, there can be no doubt." His eyes fell to the floor and his head hung in shame. "I shall release the orc, as you request. After all, what is one more compared to the million at my door? All I care for will be destroyed. More than half of my people have already been killed, every village and town has been razed. This enemy seems beyond us. I appreciate your bravery, my dear. But I would not subject you to our fate. What can one elf do against such an enemy?"

Aesthéa stepped forward, pushing through the guards to stand an arm's length from the king and look him in the eye. "I will request the aid of the elves. I will not stand idle and watch as Crein is turned into a wasteland."

Dariel did his best to remain stoic though his eyes welled with tears. "Bless you, my lady. With the elves' help, we may yet survive this war!"

Elethain couldn't hide his furious glare as he listened to Aesthéa offer the aid of the elves. That was for his king to decide, not her. But it had already been said. Revoking such a statement now would only reflect negatively on elves. *Traitorous*, they would be called. All due to a single statement of a naïve young elf.

With a smile on her face, Aesthéa walked away from the throne and returned to her friends. Prompted by their ruler, the guards lifted their spears and a pair was sent to retrieve Fangdarr. Bitrayuul rose to his feet, glad to finally be free of the sharpened iron that had been poked into his skin.

Cormac stepped forward and addressed the king. "So, ye got a military commander, yer grace?"

Dariel raised an eyebrow in curiosity but nodded in reply.

"Right, ought to send for him too."

CHAPTER NINETEEN

OBEDIENCE

Fangdarr perked his head up as the sound of the door at the far end of the murky corridor creaked open. The visitors did little to hide their presence, both in their loud footsteps and carrying voices that echoed through the chamber.

"Damned elf convinced him. I can't believe it!" one of the intruders growled.

The other scoffed with disgust. "Agreed. I thought we would be skinning the orc in the town square for sure—give the men some sense of victory."

The chieftain contemplated the decision to break from his cell. His thoughts raced as the men got closer. Every instinct screamed for him to blast through the thin, stone walls restraining him and flee for his life. But Fangdarr stood in place as two of the guards that had escorted him to his cell came into view.

The closest soldier put his face against the bars. "Here's the scum. It's your lucky day, orc. Your putrid stink won't be poisoning this dungeon any longer."

Fangdarr remained silent, even as the other guard slid his spear through the grating and into Fangdarr's abdomen.

As the man extracted the sharpened tip, he let it reflect off the dim light. "You see? Black. Same as your heart, demon." A devious smile spread across his lips as he turned to his partner. "We should spill it all and say he attacked us in a rage, don't you think?"

"None would question it," the companion responded, forming his own wicked grin toward Fangdarr. "We'll cut you into pieces and throw the chunks over the wall so you can join your kind—at least, until they devour you."

Even in the face of their threats, Fangdarr continued his passive demeanor. He offered no reaction, refusing to grant the men any satisfaction or justification. As the lock to his cell opened, he briefly considered escaping but knew it would be futile. If he acted out, the whole of the city would be against him. And who could blame them? A horde of enemies—including nearly every other orc in Crein—threatened to end the human race at any moment. With no real alternatives, Fangdarr simply stood patiently as the men entered his tiny cell.

"Grab his arms!" one called to the other, brandishing a knife from his belt. His outstretched hand reached up to grip Fangdarr's throat. "Gods! I can't even get my hand around his neck!"

The other guard pulled Fangdarr's arms behind his back and tried to hold his limbs together. "Same with his wrists. This is a big bastard. Just gut the beast!"

"Any last words, filth? A final regret for the babies you've murdered or the women you've raped? Or do orcs rape pigs?" The man pushed the blade against Fangdarr's stomach while laughing. "It's time t—"

"Release him," came a soft voice from behind the men just as the dagger had started to draw blood.

Immediately, the wretched soldiers turned to the unannounced bystander, hiding the dagger behind their back. Fangdarr's eyes met those of the man he had met before, Lucien. A smile found its way to the orc's face, which was returned in slight by the young man.

"Go on, release him," Lucien repeated. "You are relieved of your posts for the day."

The men grumbled in frustration at being denied their ploy before storming off down the corridor. As they left, Fangdarr and Lucien listened to their bickering about delaying too long to kill the orc.

"Are you alright?" Lucien asked, inspecting the wounds that had been inflicted before his arrival.

Fangdarr nodded to his savior. "Thank you."

"Come. It's time you leave this place." The man's smile was genuine as he stepped into the cell and offered his hand to the chieftain. Fangdarr clasped it with his own.

As they made their way through the long corridor, Lucien opened the door leading to the castle's lower level. Fangdarr was forced to shut his eyes in pain from the light shining through the numerous windows. Once his eyes had adjusted, the pair walked out of the room and through another, then another. They passed treasures and paintings of all kinds, the likes of which Fangdarr had never seen. He couldn't help but pause to admire a few along the way. Lucien chuckled as he realized their differences extended far beyond the color of their skin.

"This is it, Fangdarr. The king is through this door. Are you ready?"

Looking down at his torso, the chieftain wiped away the trails of blood with his hand before nodding.

Lucien couldn't hide his admiration as he stared intently at Fangdarr. wishing there was more time to speak with the curious creature. Committing himself to meet with the orc in the future, the prince pressed open the door.

As the orc stepped through, he noticed the door close behind him with Lucien remaining on the other side. He was surprised that his savior hadn't wished to enter the chamber with him, though his curiosity washed away as soon as his friends came into view.

"Fangdarr!" Aesthéa shouted from across the room before sprinting to her companion.

Fangdarr smiled wide as his lover jumped into his arms. They looked into each other's eyes, wishing they could join lips to express their true feelings in that moment. But they knew hateful eyes were upon them. Lightly setting the elf down, Fangdarr greeted Bitrayuul, Cormac, and Elethain—now fully donned in their armor and weapons once more. After their reunion, the half-orc handed Driktarr back to his grateful kin.

Ever reserved, Elethain cleared his throat. "The king is waiting."

Dariel watched it all with high interest. Never had he seen an orc treated as such. So, too, did the king notice Fangdarr's attempt to hide the two fresh cuts on his torso as he approached the throne. Dariel's respect for the orc was growing quickly.

"King Dariel, I present Fangdarr," Elethain said loudly, too accustomed to presenting nobles. He paused, struggling with the habit of addressing feats. ". . . chieftain of the Zharnik Clan."

The king raised an eyebrow. "Chieftain? Your orcs are those outside my city?"

Fangdarr took a step closer, causing the guards in the chamber to grip their weapons more tightly. "I am chieftain. Left village one moon cycle ago. To kill Crepusculus. Avoid war. My people act alone."

Dariel scrutinized the orc. He watched as the pride swelled in Fangdarr at his proclamation of being chieftain, yet contempt and shame at his subordinates acting without his permission. The king's expression was unreadable as he leaned back in his golden chair. "Can I trust you, Fangdarr?"

All in the royal chamber went silent. After many moments, Fangdarr approached the throne and removed Driktarr from his back. Instantly, the guards started charging toward him, though were halted by Dariel's raised hand. The king's eyes remained emotionless as the orc produced the enormous greataxe.

Fangdarr gripped his beloved weapon in his hands. He felt an urge to swing the weapon down through the skull of the man sitting before him—the *king* before him. As the temptation flashed in his mind, it didn't come alone.

Do it. End his life, O' Roaring One. Show the humans' weakness for all to see. Then, when their king lay dead, break open the door for your brothers and relish in the screams of their anguish! You want this. You need this. No orc has ever slain a king before. Be the legend that shall be immortalized through history! Paint yourself in his blood! Carry his head to the wall and throw it into the masses with a roar of victory! For you are Fangdarr, the King Killer!

The weapon in his hands began moving, though Fangdarr didn't notice. He was enthralled by the promising thought of dominating a king. Such a feat his father could never claim, nor any other of his kind through the ages. The chieftain envisioned himself standing atop the walls of Wiston, being witnessed by the hordes of the world's greatest army and claiming it as his own. He couldn't deny the vigor in that image, the pride. He couldn't deny his desires.

Dariel waited, his hand still up for the guards to halt, even as Fangdarr started to lift the axe. The king's depression at the fate that had been brought upon his people had torn away his care for his own safety. All that remained was his hope. Hope that this orc may be the first step toward peace, knowing it was possible for more. That orcs weren't just simple, mindless beasts who only thought of war and bloodshed. Fangdarr was the pinnacle that Dariel thought could steer the barbaric culture toward goodness. He didn't doubt it may be impossible, but if any could accomplish such a feat, he knew it would be *this* orc.

Fangdarr held the axe high above his head. All in the room were on edge. The orc saw Aesthéa step into his peripheral, her gaze pulled him gently from the tantalizing visions Crepusculus had tormented him with. As Fangdarr was reeled back to reality, he lowered Driktarr, knowing what he had almost done. In that moment, the orc questioned his decision to keep his affliction secret. To the others, his actions seemed of his own will—and part of them were. He wanted what was being promised, but not as much as the alternative. The path he had chosen for himself wasn't that of anger and hate. As his eyes locked with Aesthéa, that choice was solidified.

The chieftain fell to his knees and extended Driktarr to the king, his head bowed low in obedience. Even his friends, who knew Fangdarr better than any, couldn't hold back their gasps of surprise as the proud chieftain submitted.

CHAPTER TWENTY

DEPARTURE

King Dariel rose from his throne joyously. All he had wished for from this event had come to pass. His jeweled hand gripped Driktarr's shaft, signifying his acceptance of Fangdarr's offer. However, the wise king did more. Reaching down, Dariel lifted Fangdarr's chin, forcing the orc's eyes to meet his own. The king pulled Fangdarr to his feet and looked up at him with a knowing smile and sorrowful eyes.

Fangdarr had presented his weapon in servitude yet Dariel didn't accept his subjugation. Instead, the chieftain had been accepted as an *equal*. Returning Dariel's smile with pride, Fangdarr clasped the man's forearm with his own. "We will return. Stay strong."

Nodding tearfully, Dariel gripped the orc's arm tighter. The king had made his move.

Turning to his friends, Fangdarr saw each sporting a smile from ear to ear. Even Elethain seemed impressed, both with King Dariel's unexpected attitude and Fangdarr's willingness to cast aside his own pride for the sake of many. The orc was met with warm embraces before turning to seriousness. "What our plan?"

Before any had a chance to respond, the doors to the royal chamber creaked open. A trimmed man outfitted in a fine yet worn suit of armor strode confidently toward them. By his white and blue cloak and his gait, Cormac knew him to be the commander of Wiston's armies. The dwarf extended his arm in greeting. "Ye must be the commander, aye?"

Taking the dwarf's hand in respect, the dutiful soldier responded with the proud and determined voice of a decorated veteran. "I am, Master Dwarf. You summoned me?"

"Sure as stones, lad. Ye and me got some discussin' to do," Cormac explained. "What be yer name, Commander?"

"You may call me Viktor, sir. And yours?"

"Cormac, Captain of the Shield, watchers of the gates of Tarnbar."

Viktor gave a slight nod after casting a cursory glance to his king for approval. "I welcome your experience, Captain. Let us discuss, there is a war room down the hall. Please follow me."

The dwarf started after the commander but halted. He turned to his friends and rushed forward to hug Fangdarr. "Ye be safe, lad. Elves ain't fond of yer kind, don't ye doubt. Stick close to Aesthéa, she'll keep ye out of trouble." Cormac eyed the druid as he spoke, smiling with her stern nod. "Don't ye ever forget who ye are, Fang. Never." With his words spoken—the last that may ever be heard by his friends—Cormac jogged away to catch up to Viktor, fearful any longer of a farewell would force his mind to change.

Bitrayuul watched the pair walk across the room before turning to Fangdarr abruptly. "I'm staying as well."

The chieftain's immediate reaction was to dispute, fearful of the abandonment he had suffered at their last separation, six winters past. But he could see the fire in Bitrayuul's eyes. Though it pained him, Fangdarr extended his arm. "Be safe, Bit." Taking the orc's offering, Bitrayuul responded with a parting nod. No other words needed said. They each felt the pit in their stomach tense uncomfortably as Bitrayuul left to join Cormac, knowing it may be the last they saw of the other.

Elethain cleared his throat, breaking the unpleasant silence. "Shall we depart?"

The orc looked around the extravagant royal chamber once more. If that was to be the last he saw of Wiston, that was the memory he wanted to store in his mind. The lovely canvas paintings lining the walls, the lush carpet beneath his toes, the gleaming, golden throne fit for a king, and the wise man who sat upon it—watching all the pure and deep emotions unfold. Fangdarr bid a final farewell to King Dariel and turned back to Elethain. "To Jesmera."

CHAPTER TWENTY-ONE

STRATEGY

Viktor led the pair down the long hall after leaving the throne room. The lavish decorations became sparser the further they progressed, with naught but an old, large wooden door at the end of the path. Taking the worn metal ring in his hand, the commander tugged open the entry to reveal a lightless room.

Bitrayuul stepped into the void as Viktor struck a torch along the wall. Maps were littered everywhere—the walls, the tables, even the floor held rolled piles—as well as suits of armor, books about tactics, and other military materials. At first, the half-orc had felt right at home, recalling the numerous occasions he and Tormag would sit in the war room with other leaders of the Dwarven Regime. The view brought a sense of homesickness and dread as he realized those memories were all that remained of his father.

"Bothain's beard . . .," Cormac said with a gasp, drawing Bitrayuul's attention.

The commander turned to see the source of their concern. "Oh, that," Viktor said with a sigh. "That is for knowledge. We must learn our enemy—find their weaknesses and exploit them. This war will demand no less. All efforts have been taken."

Cormac let out an uncomfortable groan. "Aye, but . . . this . . . this be barbaric, Commander." He couldn't pull away his gaze. In the center of the room, an orc had been strung up by corded ropes and stretched as far as its limbs could take. It was obvious that the creature had been tortured, with dozens of cuts still fresh on its body. Its skin had been peeled away and its chest cavity cracked open, revealing the organs within. Deep, black blood sat in a pool beneath the suspended orc, slipping through the cracks in the stone at their feet. And on an adjacent table sat its heart—a knife plunged deep into a ventricle.

As if requested, Viktor cut the orc's bindings without any sign of remorse as it dropped to the ground with a lifeless thump. "This is war, Captain. The information I gather here can mean the difference between saving my people and annihilation. Admittedly, we learned little from the beast. However, a troll was brought in last night, which allowed us to learn more about the creatures. You may have fought trolls often within your mountain, dwarf, but they are nearly foreign to us by now. Long has it been since humankind has encountered their stench. We have forgotten much about them and must learn it all anew."

Bitrayuul could only stare at Viktor, who continued to act with nonchalance—dutiful pride, even. The half-orc understood that the life of one could save many, but the humans' savagery wasn't what he had come to expect.

"Let us move on," Viktor said, catching on to Bitrayuul's sustained discomfort.

The half-orc pushed his thoughts away—it wasn't the time or place. "Agreed."

Cormac and Bitrayuul joined the commander at a nearby table. Viktor pushed away all other documents and collected materials to make room for a large, detailed map of Wiston and the surrounding area. "We are here." He pointed to their location before continuing to slide it to the next landmark. "This is the castle. It is surrounded by the different districts and sits within the heart of the city to protect the royal family, of course. There is the Market District, near the docks. The Holy District," his finger slid to the area adjacent the Market District that wrapped around the north-eastern side of the castle.

"Then, there are the three in front," he continued. "The Resource District, in the southwest corner, is where our livestock are contained. Luckily, they are within the city walls, so unless the enemy breaks through, we shouldn't be starved out. Unfortunately, almost all crops are . . . *were* brought in from the outside villages, we keep little on hand—hope you like meat. On the southeast is the Philosophy District, where our library is. It is primarily a place of study and houses the few wizards we have. Though, the need for them to learn offensive magic has been slim. They are all primarily interested in magic for practical uses, so they haven't been of much assistance during the war. Nonetheless, they have all been tasked with aiding at the wall. Their inexperience has nearly gotten all of them killed, however. It seems their books don't teach them the concept of standing in the open while your enemy throws a dozen spears. Over half were killed within the first half-day. The remaining few fled with their tails tucked. Not that I can blame them—they aren't soldiers."

Bitrayuul and Cormac looked to each other, assuming that was the commander's dry sense of humor. Viktor continued, sliding his finger to the front and center, within the wall's gate. "Last is the Military District, where our forces lie. Our entire army resides here, where they can quickly rotate through their shifts, and are entirely in the path of any who break through the gate. Our current strategy is to simply remain vigilant and pick off as many as we can."

"Aye, well, let's get to thinkin'. Ye need anyone else in here?" Cormac asked.

Viktor shook his head. "No, they are all needed at the wall. Right now, our biggest threat isn't the enemy breaking through. It is intimidation. The men are all terrified.

They know such a horde has never been assembled for as long as written history has been known. Already we suffer from the whispers that this campaign will be the end of our kind."

Cormac nodded, understanding that sentiment entirely as Bitrayuul scanned the map more closely. "Commander," the half-orc began, "how much coal or wood do you have?"

The question seemed to catch Viktor off guard. "Uh . . . sir?"

"Coal or wood. Or even oil. How much?"

"We have some coal, a few carts worth. It sits at our blacksmiths in the Market District. Though they are working day and night to produce as many swords, shields, and arrowheads as possible on short notice, so I imagine it will go quickly."

"Stop them," Bitrayuul commanded.

"Sir?"

"We have been fighting trolls for a long time. Steel does not defeat them, *fire* does. It will prove infinitely more useful than the added collection of swords."

Viktor's eyes lit up. "It does? I'm not sure how much coal remains, but I will send for it to be acquired and the blacksmiths halted at once. We don't keep much wood, most of it is harvested by villages and brought by cart into the city. As for oil, we keep a reserve for use at the gate, but there is little."

Cormac rubbed his head. "Aye, it ain't much. Trolls catch fire quick, don't ye doubt, but they need to be wounded first. Their skin be dry, so it burns well, but it don't ignite on contact without the ooze from a wound."

The commander was already nodding. "Our research last night discovered their regenerative capabilities, but we didn't consider burning it in the short time we spent with it. That would explain why it's still alive . . .." Lost in thought, the man returned to reality and changed the subject. "Do you think our supplies will be enough?"

"It likely won't be enough to win the war, but every bit will matter. Most of the enemy is made up of trolls, so anything that can be done to quell the masses is a major advantage." Bitrayuul leaned over the map, committing its layout to memory. "Commander, how many men do you have?"

"Not as many as I would like. But we stand less than ten thousand. Nowhere near the number of the enemy. Let us be thankful that we have a strong wall to hide behind."

Cormac blew a heavy sigh. "Whew, this'll be one for the books."

Bitrayuul moved a finger to each edge of the wall. "Luckily, your ancestors made the wall sheer, so the trolls cannot scale it. They are excellent climbers. Does it extend all the way to the cliff's edge? They may be able to scale the cliff outside the wall and attack from the outskirts."

"It does, but they have been climbing underneath. I have a thousand men on each cliff rotating in four shifts to shoot them down with either rocks or arrows. We were caught unaware at first and lost quite a few men. The trolls nearly made it to our livestock and the library before they we were able to control the situation. Since then, the stream of trolls has slowed considerably as they have realized there is no way to make it past our men. Some have even tried scaling the base of the cliff all the way to the port at the rear of the city. I have moved a small ship to sit in the water and shoot them down.

"I must ask, though," Viktor paused, gathering his thoughts. "Do you believe this war can be won? How are we to defeat such an enemy? Right now, we are struggling just to keep them at bay. If they breach the wall, we are doomed."

Cormac and Bitrayuul looked to one another, knowing the man was searching for their honest opinions. In truth, each were afraid to give it. They both knew the situation was dire, and it was likely their enemy would succeed. The dwarf was the first to speak. "Son, I don't know, Bothain's truth. All I know is that we're goin' to try our best. Our friends be settin' sail right now to Jesmera to request the aid of the elves. If they join . . . maybe. But this won't be an easy brawl. Men will die. We *all* may die. But, I ain't willin' to walk up to me god in his Mines and tell him I went down without a fight."

Viktor turned to Bitrayuul, seeking his feedback. The half-orc removed his helmet slowly, forgetting that the commander wasn't aware of his true nature. Instinctively, Viktor's hand found the pommel of his sword, though he stayed it. With his face revealed, Bitrayuul spoke clearly and with honesty. "As long as the wall holds, we have a chance. Luckily, the enemy does not appear to have any siege equipment, so we should be safe to formulate and execute plans."

As Bitrayuul finished speaking, a loud, booming sound echoed through the walls paired with a small tremor. Immediately, the trio's eyes grew wide.

Cormac groaned in disbelief. "Ye were sayin'?"

CHAPTER TWENTY-TWO

CHANNEL

The guards clutched their spears tightly as Fangdarr passed through the final threshold out of the Market District and into the harbor. Word had travelled quickly, and the men weren't keen that the orc was walking freely.

As Fangdarr and the elves approached the dock, Elethain continued directly onto the ship, eager to leave the distasteful humans behind and return home. Fangdarr paused to look back at the city, desperately hoping it would still be standing upon his return—with Bitrayuul and Cormac in good health to greet him. Already he was regretting his decision to separate from them. He could hardly stomach the thought of a world where they weren't at his side. Aesthéa smiled knowingly at him, unable to offer more in the presence of others.

Together they turned to the ship and continued down the dock. The thick plank groaned under the orc's weight as they slowly trudged up the slope and onto the deck. Before Fangdarr had taken his first step, a pair of human guards slid the plank onto the dock. He felt the boat start to move beneath his feet and thought the soldiers had started to shove them away. Instead, Fangdarr watched in amazement as he realized Elethain's risen kin had slowly kedged the ship out to sea where the wind filled their sails.

As the city started to fade behind them, Fangdarr led Aesthéa to the deck below. There they joined Elethain in the captain's quarters and were surprised to see a man adorned in finely tailored vestments standing next to him.

"Elethain?" Aesthéa asked, expressing her curiosity of the unexpected guest.

The elf looked up from the map he was reviewing. "Yes?"

"Who is he?"

The man stepped forward with a bow while removing his overly large, wide-brimmed hat in a flourish. As the garment swept down, its six extravagant and excessively large feathers of varying species brushed the floor. "Greetings, my lady!"

he began with a level of excitement that rivaled the greatest of festivities. "I am Treager! The captain of the *Eager Treager*, perhaps you have heard it?"

An awkward silence followed.

"None the matter! I have been tasked with aiding your merry band across the channel, of course." His smile was unsettling. Whether by the awkward tilt of his lips from below his long, twisted moustache or the dirty teeth beneath, Fangdarr couldn't be certain.

"Or return the ship if we do not wish to return, I am sure," Elethain added with a smirk.

Treager only smiled wider in return, stretching that odd grin as far as his face would allow.

Fangdarr watched the man with increasing scrutiny, feeling a twist in his gut each time he laid eyes on the captain. "King send you?"

"I was sent to aid, yes."

The chieftain's eyes narrowed more. Now that they were safely away from the ever-watchful guards of Wiston, Fangdarr could speak and act freely. He stepped toward the man, waiting for Treager's hand to slide to the pommel of the thin sword at his belt—or the knife handle peeking out from his left boot.

Once directly in front of the captain, Fangdarr stared down at him with a scowl. "You will betray us?"

"My lord!" Treager placed a hand delicately over his chest with exaggerated pain against his honor. "You don't trust me?"

"No."

"Well, we will have to change that, won't we?" The captain didn't miss a beat.

Fangdarr was certain the man's excessive kindness didn't match his true intentions, despite his words. Nevertheless, he would let it play out. Perhaps he simply wasn't accustomed to humans and this man could be perfectly kind. His gut told him otherwise, but Fangdarr wouldn't dishonor King Dariel by acting on instinct alone. He took Aesthéa by the hand and stormed out of the room, slamming the door behind him.

Retreating to the lowest deck, the pair lay together on one of the cots within the crew's quarters. Aesthéa nestled close to Fangdarr's chest before asking, "Do you believe that man will harm us?"

Running a finger over her arm, the chieftain paused to respond. "Yes."

"So, why not remove him now? Toss him into the water, let him swim back to Wiston."

Fangdarr chuckled, such a thought had already crossed his mind more than once. "Want to. But owe King my honor. Must wait and see."

The elf looked up. "Fangdarr, do not lose who you are at the cost of others. I agree with your decision, but do not disregard your instincts. You are a warrior. Yet, you are kind. You would not harm someone who you knew in your heart did not deserve such a fate."

Fangdarr sat in silence. It was true; he felt that the odd Captain Treager wasn't a welcome guest. From deep in his bones to the cautionary hairs rising on his neck, every instinct begged that the man be cast out. But he couldn't risk breaking the king's trust. Not yet. He sighed, ready to change the subject. "What is Jesmera like?"

"Mostly trees," Aesthéa chuckled. "But it is a magical place, both beautiful and wondrous. There are no fires, nor does the sun shine through the thick leaves above. It's illuminated entirely by fae." She saw her companion's face twist in confusion. "Fae are small, winged creatures about the size of a coin. There are thousands throughout Jesmera."

Genuinely curious, the orc pressed further. "They are bugs?" Aesthéa's let out a soft giggle and shook her head, spurring his next set of questions. "How many elves there? There are magicians? Elves like Elethain? Like you?"

She smiled at the orc's inquisitiveness. "Elves do not number many, despite living for thousands of years. It is not often elves have children. We just always expect there will be time to do so—sometimes we wait too long. Humans produce offspring like beasts because they know their life is just a flicker. They must continue their race. But, to answer your question, yes, there are a few magical elves."

Aesthéa readjusted within Fangdarr's embrace to get her hands free. "Magic is a wide network. There are many different kinds, some more common than others. Elethain is a practitioner of black magic—a rare type. As a druid, I use the magic within nature, granted to me by Cerenos the Forest God. He is the deity that most elves look to." She paused in curiosity. "Do you have a god, Fangdarr?"

"No. Some orcs do, especially shamans. I raised outside of clan, did not follow." He hesitated. "Don't know if gods exist. Never seen one. I my own god. God not give me strength. Not a god that conquered. It me." He looked down to see the elf nodding, expecting such a response. "You said other druids?"

"Yes, two. Unlike other kinds of magic, druids—or even your shamans—are granted their gifts by a god, or so we believe. Some elves perceive we have angered Cerenos, as there has not been a magical elf born in Jesmera since myself, actually."

"Really?"

Aesthéa nodded. "Once it was discovered I held an affinity for nature, I was immediately taken to the other druids. They taught me how to use my gift and the importance of life. I still have much left to learn."

Fangdarr ran his fingers through her black hair, remembering it was the same color as her fur while she was shifted into a bear. "All druids are bears?"

"One can shapeshift into an eagle. I can't imagine what that must feel like, to know what it is to spread your wings and soar on the wind." She seemed to pause in envy at the thought. "The other, the eldest of us, has learned much. She can take the form of over a dozen creatures, including both an eagle and a bear."

"A dozen?!"

Aesthéa nodded before letting out a yawn. Her head fell against Fangdarr's chest and her breathing slowed before turning to the rhythmic metronome of sleep. With his curiosity sated, the orc allowed his companion to rest. He was eager to see Jesmera—less so to be amongst so many who hated his kind. The chieftain would be the first orc to ever set foot in their city, a feat he took great pride in. It seemed almost strange that he wasn't going to be there in conquest, but in diplomacy. Nevertheless, he hoped to earn their trust and bring them to Wiston to save humankind from elimination.

King Dariel needed him.

* * * * *

Elethain let out a muffled gasp against the hand over his mouth. His surprise quickly turned to a scowl as his eyes managed to focus on the dark silhouette of the character leaning over him with a knee planted on his chest. The elf struggled beneath the man's weight, aiming to move but found his arms had been bound.

"Shush, shush, shush, elf," came the familiar, excited voice of Treager—though the man tried his best to whisper. "We're only here for the orc. Stay comfortable in your bed and you'll survive. He's just an orc, after all. You wouldn't die for the black-blooded mongrel, would you?" The captain's twisted smile was hardly visible in the darkened room. Behind him were another ten men that snuck onto the ship in the night, each brandishing their weapons with glee.

Still trapped beneath Treager's hold, Elethain continued to scowl. The man tutted at the elf through his rotten teeth. "Such a shame . . . you are a gorgeous creature." He let out an exaggerated sigh with a shrug of his shoulders before launching a punch squarely against the high cheekbone of his prisoner, then another.

A purple bruise started to form beneath Elethain's bloated skin with a small trickle of blood. Upon seeing the vibrant purple stream on the elf's face, Treager noticed a miniscule speck of blood on his lavish glove. "Ugh! You soiled my favorite glove!" The sheer anger that flooded through the captain's face was intense. Elethain braced for another blow, though none came.

Treager calmed himself by running his hands meticulously over his tailored coat, embracing the feel of the cloth. "As I mentioned," his hand reached up to re-twist his facial hair, "we aren't here for you." Without another word, the captain and his men exited the chamber and shut the door behind them.

Elethain struggled within his bonds but couldn't slip free. His mind reached out to his brothers that had been left on the main deck above. Each stood unmoving with a sack over their head, placed by the unwelcome visitors as they had boarded the ship. After receiving the command, the ghoulish abominations tore through the woven sacks and immediately rushed down the ladder and into the captain's chambers where Elethain remained.

Once his risen kin were present, the necromancer had them cut his bindings. With a groan, the elf jumped to his feet, rubbing the blood from his cheek before stomping out of the room.

* * * * *

Fangdarr woke abruptly as the blade sank deep into his shoulder, just above Aesthéa's sleeping head. He roared ferociously in rage for the unknown assailant coming so close to his lover. Before he could sit up, another sword came down, leaving a deep gash on his forearm. The orc instinctively threw his arms over Aesthéa's small form, protecting her from the men that were slashing away.

"Good morning, orc!" Treager's voice called out from the entryway, bringing a halt to his men's hacking.

Fangdarr peeked up at the man through the stream of blood that was pouring into his eyes from the cuts on his head. He could hardly hear due to his ear dangling by a small piece of skin. "T-Treager?"

"Correct! And *these*," the man said with a wide wave of his hand, "are my men! We are here to kill you, of course." The intruders chuckled at the obvious statement. Treager noticed the small elf druid tucked beneath the orc's arms for the first time and gasped. "My lady! My apologies, we didn't know you would b—" His eyes narrowed with lethal suspicion as the realization hit him. "Why are you here?"

Before the elf could respond, Fangdarr spoke, proving the captain's theory. "Leave her."

"Well, well. You aren't one to be making demands, I would think. This won't do. Oh, no, no, no, it simply will not."

Fangdarr regarded him curiously, though his head started to swoon as the flow of blood continued relentlessly from his wounds.

"You see, the guards of Wiston paid me to bring your head. Something about being a monster and not welcome in their city, blah, blah. It was just you, none of your friends. But this . . . ," the man pondered, tapping his finger against his chin. "Something tells me the guards didn't know about all *this*." Treager motioned to the elf tucked carefully within Fangdarr's embrace. "No, I suppose I may get a few extra coins for bringing *both* your heads. Oh, this is lovely! So much fun, isn't it?"

"Yes, it is." From behind the dastardly captain came Elethain, still donning a hateful scowl. Two man-sized black hands reached forward and grabbed Treager before pulling him toward the elf.

"No, no! Stop! We can work this out! Come now, this is all just a misunde—" Treager's voice turned to a gasp for air as Elethain squeezed the demonic hands tight around his torso, cracking more than a few ribs.

Elethain's ghouls charged toward the men, mowing one down before the nine remaining cutthroats managed to form a defensive position within the small room. With their backs turned to Fangdarr, the chieftain slowly slid from the bed.

Driktarr came into his hand as the nine remaining men watched the ghouls tear apart their ally. With a growl of rage, Fangdarr slammed his axe down through the skull of the nearest vagabond, showering everyone in blood. The orc didn't wait for his wounds to heal before swinging his greataxe in a horizontal swipe through the next in line, bisecting him completely at the waist.

With enemies on each end and their friends' bodies falling into them, the pirates couldn't help but shout in confusion and fear. As if the situation couldn't be any worse, the man nearest Aesthéa screamed in terror as she shapeshifted and mauled him with a heavy claw, rending the vagabond's face open. Like frightened rodents, they continued to shout in fear, unable to get their bearings.

One by one, the pirates were obliterated.

Once the carnage was done, Fangdarr turned to his lover and slid a hand over her bloodied fur. "Good kill, Bear."

Aesthéa nuzzled her face against the orc's leg, only smearing the blood on each of them more. She shifted back into her elven form and looked up at her companion, inspecting his previous wounds. Luckily, Driktarr's healing had surpassed her expectations, as even Fangdarr's ear had stitched itself back together and was perfectly intact. Pleased with her lover's well-being, the elf took his hand and pulled the chieftain out of the room to where Elethain stood—prisoner still in hand, metaphorically.

"Elethain, are you alright?" Aesthéa asked.

"Yes, I am now." The necromancer allowed the abyssal hands to dissipate into nothingness, dropping Treager's lifeless form to the floor with a thud. His abdomen had been squeezed so tightly that he was completely torn in half. From thigh to stomach, the deceased captain's body looked as if it were a wet cloth that had been wrung out, leaving a pool of blood beneath. Elethain looked to Fangdarr. "And yes, I know. You were right. Happy now?"

Fangdarr said nothing, knowing his friend was in no mood for a playful retort. He returned Driktarr to the harness on his back and strode to the captain's corpse. Slowly, he slid the man's upper half forward with his foot before it reached the hatch to the deck below. With a final nudge, the group watched the lavish man disappear with a *thud.* Fangdarr gave a grunt of approval and bent to pick up Treager's flamboyant hat, placing it on his head with a playful smirk.

Elethain simply sighed at the orc's foolishness before turning toward the ladder ascending back to his quarters. "I'm going back to sleep."

CHAPTER TWENTY-THREE

SCARS

Fangdarr and Aesthéa watched their companion storm away before hearing the door slam shut to his chambers above. Covered nearly head to toe in still-dripping splashes of crimson, each looked around to the bloodbath that had now tainted their sleeping quarters. The chieftain slid his arm behind his lover's waist and gently lifted her to his height. With his free hand, Fangdarr brushed away the locks of hair that had matted to her face, leaving a smear of blood in its place. The elf giggled at the pointless act, bringing a smile to the orc as he carried her to their cot, disregarding the swashbucklers' corpses beneath his feet.

After setting the druid down tenderly on the blood-soaked bed, Fangdarr knelt in front of her to inspect for any wounds. Aesthéa waited in silence with a loving smile on her face as her companion slowly slid his hands over her skin. His fingers stopped as they came across a light scratch on her shin. Though fresh, it hadn't cut through her thickened skin. He continued tracing his hand up her leg and didn't slow as her breath quivered upon reaching her smooth thighs.

Fangdarr cast the elf a quick glance to see her biting down on her bottom lip. His hands quickly retracted in fear, thinking he had brought her pain. Aesthéa looked down at him in confusion before seeing his look of concern. She giggled lightly and reached down to replace his hands on their previous path.

Cautiously, the orc continued his examination as his companion's face twisted into foreign expressions. His fingers glided to the top of her thighs, then to her thick leather belt. Seeing that the leather wasn't cut in any way, the oblivious chieftain slid quickly past and continued to the small exposed section of her midriff—not catching Aesthéa's playfully disappointed eye roll.

Fangdarr caught a glimpse of the edge of a marking beneath her jerkin, just above her navel. He lifted the hide, revealing an old scar that went farther than he could see. Rubbing his finger against the raised skin, he looked to Aesthéa.

The elf turned her head to the side. "One of the *benefits* of being royalty," she said sarcastically. Aesthéa could tell the orc didn't understand. How could he? His culture was a completely different world than her own. She exhaled and offered an apologetic smile. "Such occurs when one speaks out of turn in the presence of our king."

Fangdarr scowled. Orcs certainly caused undue pain to each other, but never for speaking their mind. His culture was blunt, simply put. He grew worried that Jesmera may be more difficult for him to understand than he had considered. But the thoughts quickly fled the orc's mind as he focused on the mark once more.

Sliding his fingers beneath the hide, Fangdarr felt yet another scar. His face twisted in concern. The orc tenderly slid his hand out before placing it over the knot keeping the armor in place. He looked up to the elf, silently requesting permission to continue. For a moment, Aesthéa looked away, refusing to show pieces of her skin she wasn't comfortable with. Then, her eyes fell to the orc at her feet, littered in his own scars. The druid closed her eyes and took in a deep breath before nodding to Fangdarr.

Slowly, Fangdarr started untying the knots that kept the vest in place, his thick, clumsy fingers fumbling hopelessly. After a while, he finally managed to get each of the four ties undone. Aesthéa reached down to remove the armor but was halted by Fangdarr's hands falling on her own. The elf looked at him with a questioning stare, wondering why he wouldn't just let her continue and get the endeavor over with. But, once her eyes met his, all resolve fell away. Yellow orbs stared back at her, completely at peace, showing there was nothing to fear. Aesthéa let her arms fall to her sides.

Fangdarr stood and sat on the bed next to her. He tenderly slid his hands beneath her arms and lifted her easily from his side and onto his lap, face-to-face with the chieftain. Then, he slowly began lifting the armor. The bloodied jerkin went up, pulling her black hair with it, before finally being tossed to the floor. Fangdarr felt silly for feeling so awkward and nervous. His heart pounded in his chest as his eyes fell upon his lover's bare torso. Aesthéa kept her visage fixated on him, gaging every expression.

The orc could feel the yearning below his waist as he gawked at Aesthéa's exposed breasts. Blood of their enemies still glistened against her pale skin, reminding Fangdarr of the potent companion he had chosen. His fingers traced over the full extent of her scar, from her navel to beneath her left breast. But there were more. Fangdarr let out a low grumble of grief as he outlined another three of variable sizes. Over twice that number were on her back from what the orc's fingers could tell. He let his fingers scan them all while Aesthéa waited, staring at him with a dead stillness.

Once his inspection was complete, Fangdarr looked to the elf. She sighed and stiffened her lips. "I'm not fond of going unheard." Her gaze finally broke away in shame as her words ended.

The orc gently pulled her chin back to face him. "You have voice." His fingers ran along the largest scar on her stomach once more. "Should never be silent."

Aesthéa smiled at him for his acceptance. Even still, her pain ran deep. The indignity she felt had been built over a long period of time and wouldn't be easily conquered. The elf felt her companion place her hand against his forearm. She didn't need to look to feel the maw-shaped scar from their first encounter. Aesthéa gasped and tried to pull her hand away.

Fangdarr held her hand firmly against the scar until she had settled and looked him in the eye, wondering why he tormented her so. Eyes full of trust, the chieftain calmly whispered, "Scars stories. Some painful. Some beautiful." He looked to his arm where her slender fingers traced the marking of her jaws. "Pages in our book. Remind us where we have been. Not a map to tell us where to go."

Aesthéa instantly broke down at the orc's profound words. Her tears came out in a rush, breaking through the dam she had built to keep the raging waters at bay. She sprung forward and embraced her lover, thankful for all that he had offered her—with nothing expected in return. Fangdarr was more than just a target of her affection—he was a partner. Together, she believed they could accomplish anything. All the pain Aesthéa clung to died away every time she felt his arms wrap around her small frame. The elf wept and squeezed Fangdarr as tight as she could, as if he might slip away. Instead, his own embrace tightened, returning the sentiment.

Tears of joy and relief streamed down Aesthéa's face. There she remained for many moments until a deep sleep took her. And still the orc held her tightly.

CHAPTER TWENTY-FOUR

JESMERA

Elethain started to push open the door to his friends' room, careful to avoid dragging his robe through the dried blood that had soaked into the floor. The door managed to pivot partway before getting stuck on a stubborn corpse from the night's massacre. With an annoyed sigh, the elf stepped away, instead electing for his brothers to push through the barrier.

Within, the couple woke from their slumber just as the door creaked open. The druid was still tightly wrapped in Fangdarr's embrace when she realized that Elethain was entering. But it was too late. Elethain stepped through the threshold and gasped in shock. There was no light in the room, but his eyes didn't need it. His visage turned to a threatening scowl upon seeing his king's niece tucked under the orc's arms, obscuring her exposed and blood-crusted form. The elf couldn't hide his disgust as his mind went to the worst conclusion he could muster. Every thought demanded he shout and curse while eliminating the orc that had poisoned the royal family. An *orc*! Elethain may have had sensitive moments, or even at times cared for Fangdarr in a way he would never freely admit, but this level of intimacy was one he couldn't endure.

"Elethain?" Aesthéa called out with concern.

No response came. Aesthéa could see his lip trembling with pent up rage and his fists clenched at his sides, fingernails digging deep into his palm. Finally, the furious elf broke the silence, surprising even himself as the words came out. "We have arrived." His response was anything but the one he wished to give. Yet, he was bound by duty to obey and advise. The druid had ignored his advice on numerous occasions and there was naught more to do. They had landed in Jesmera and Elethain was confident his king would see to the problem.

Aesthéa and Fangdarr watched with heavy hearts as their friend stormed out of the room, mumbling a stream of curses under his breath. The orc held little care for the necromancer's disgust, though he knew it brought doubt to Aesthéa. In truth, she held no uncertainty that her love for Fangdarr was real and intense. However, now that they had returned to her homeland, a painful twist had turned in her stomach. A part of her knew that facing the king would come someday, but now it had become real.

The druid nearly collapsed as she rose from the bed. Her breaths had changed to quick pants of panic, knowing what lay ahead. Fangdarr rolled off the bed to sit next to her, handing her the leather jerkin she had removed and wrapping her in his arms again. Many moments passed before her breathing finally returned to normal.

Aesthéa sighed deeply and looked to her lover and placed a hand on his jaw. Her eyes welled with tears. "No matter what happens, I'm yours."

Fangdarr couldn't deny his own trepidation at walking into a city full of elves, especially if news of their relationship would take to wind. Nevertheless, he didn't care. He pulled elf closer and hugged her tightly.

Once they composed themselves—and wiped away the crimson paint on their skin—the pair met with Elethain at the ladder to the main deck. His eyes were still full of hate, though he held back mercifully. The necromancer went up the ladder first, followed by Aesthéa. Fangdarr paused as he heard the cheers of a handful of spectators as the elves came into view.

Up the orc went, squeezing his enormous stature through the small opening. As he breached, all cheers instantly fell silent. He watched as the dozen elven guards standing on the shore froze, unsure of how to act. Then the moment of disbelief ended, and all rushed forward, spears raised and bowstrings tense.

Fangdarr let out a heavy sigh. He had expected such a welcome. Though, in that tense moment of inactivity, the orc had hoped against all that it would have gone differently. Slowly, he raised his hands as the agile guards began to surround him, ready to end him on a moment's notice.

Fangdarr looked to Aesthéa, but she quickly turned away. Elethain escorted her away, leaving the orc to his doom. The song in Fangdarr's mind turned to melancholy and rage. He couldn't hide the pain he felt in that moment when Aesthéa abandoned him, despite knowing she had no choice. This was neither the time nor place to make their companionship known, he knew. So, he stifled his desires to act and complied with the forceful warriors as they prodded him with their spears—just as the guards of Wiston had done.

As the orc was ushered past the plant-covered beach and into the deep, vibrant forest, Fangdarr started to notice the drastic differences between their cultures. The path they walked was entirely natural and unblemished. Even the beach in which they had landed held no dock of layered wood or carved stone. Instead, their ship had pulled directly onto the land where luscious and exotic plants sprouted in overlapping bounds.

Even more curious, no light shined through the dense canopies above, giving the darkened forest an eeriness he couldn't shake. While on the shoreline, Fangdarr noticed that Elethain and Aesthéa's pale skin was tanned in comparison to the guards.

After walking for a long while, Fangdarr picked out minute specks of light in the distance. As they got closer, he could them fluttering around aimlessly. Soon, there were dozens. Then hundreds. And as they approached the city's entrance the luminous creatures numbered in the thousands, lighting the area in an ominous multi-colored glow.

It was truly a marvelous sight. From the dusky trunks of the abundant trees that littered the area to the luscious green, purple, and blue vines and leaves that dangled around them, Fangdarr walked with his mouth ajar in awe. The buildings were slender and tall yet made of a substance he couldn't determine.

The chieftain couldn't believe the wondrous city that lay before him. There were tales of the mystical city of the elves, taken from the tortured ramblings of prisoners that previous chieftains had captured. But none had ever described its spectacular beauty. In that moment, witnessing Jesmera in all its splendor, Fangdarr held no regrets that his path of domination had been halted. For if he had ever managed to bring the city to ashes, he was certain he would have taken his own life in remorse.

The procession stopped outside of a twisted gate as Elethain and Aesthéa talked amongst a group of elves who were eager to greet them. Fangdarr's distraction broke as he walked into the guard in front of him. The wicked spear tip cut into his chest, but he paid it no mind. The elf watched as a dark drop of blood rolled down the gleaming edge of his blade—which seemed to be some sort of leaf, though its sharpness gave contradiction—and spat at the orc's feet in disgust.

Soon they were moving again, going deeper into the city. Fangdarr felt his heart beating in his chest with each step. His eagerness to explore more of the exotic culture was matched only by the uneasy feeling that he was walking toward his doom. As more elves came into view, his trepidation only grew. Fangdarr watched as the people of Jesmera shrank back in fear or rallied in instant aggression at the sight of him. The chieftain tried to ignore the constant stares and clamoring shouts that had raised in their wake, but the crowd closed in with each step he took. Had it not been for the guards, the orc held no doubt that he would have been obliterated on the spot without a second thought. He nearly laughed at the barbarism of such clean and serene creatures. They may have maintained their composure for the time, but, beneath the mask, these elves held the fury of orcs.

Fangdarr watched as Elethain and Aesthéa halted at the tall and slender opening of a structure that could only belong to royalty. Its walls emanated a dull yet vibrant and throbbing light and stretched impossibly high, piercing the canopies above. The orc could feel energy permeating from the building, even at his distance. It was an odd feeling, like the tickle of hairs being raised over one's skin. His friends stood at the open entrance at the base of the structure, staring at it expectantly. Then, they stepped forward and vanished completely. Profound confusion struck the orc, but he was pressed forward with no time to ponder.

After approaching the same entryway his friends had disappeared through, Fangdarr attempted to walk through the opening. Immediately, his body was launched back, landing in a trimmed bush next to the path. The orc furrowed his brow and bared his teeth as he rose to his feet, his anger only growing with each moment that the collected elves laughed at his expense. Fangdarr's white-knuckled hands clenched at his side, eager for bloodshed and to end the assault on his pride. But he forced away the seething fury upon seeing the dozens of leaf-bladed weapons pointed in his direction from guards and citizens alike.

Every urge in the chieftain's mind demanded he repay the insult to each spectator personally as they continued their tormenting humiliation. But he couldn't. He *wouldn't*. Fangdarr had to be better. Not for his sake, but for those who were suffering and fighting for their very lives against an impossible enemy. The orc swallowed his wounded pride and began laughing with the elves. The boisterous, grumbling noise that passed through his gaping maw came as a shock to his onlookers. Fangdarr looked at their stunned faces and saw their expressions frozen in only one of two ways: confusion or disgust.

"Don't touch door," the orc offered sarcastically to his gathered crowd. His laughter at his own joke and its effect on the elves had lifted his spirits. Imposing and demanding respect, Fangdarr strode back toward the entryway wearing a smug grin.

The elves muttered amongst each other as they watched the defiant chieftain stomp forward. They couldn't determine if Fangdarr's brutish stupidity or his impressive determination stood superior. None laughed, however. They all watched in trepidation as he approached the repelling threshold.

Fangdarr didn't slow his march as he closed in on the entryway. In the brief moment he had encountered it before, he could tell it was some sort of magical barrier. Though, it couldn't be seen until the moment he made contact. In that fleeting act, the invisible wall had rippled before pushing him away. As the great orc was about to take the last step into the shield once more, he lifted his arms defensively.

The force was enormous! Struggling beneath its power, Fangdarr's planted feet slid back as the unseen magic pressed intensely against his arms. The elves around him gasped in shock as the expected outcome of seeing the orc flying through the air once more didn't come to pass. Instead, their mouths went slack as the orc grit his teeth and held his ground against the constant surge of energy pushing back at him. The guards instinctively stepped closer as the unwelcome guest fought, though even they couldn't hide their awe.

With a roar of defiance, Fangdarr gave a single ferocious push. The previous rippling that could barely be seen formed into a heightened wave rolling out from the epicenter of his thrust. Time seemed to slow as the barrier cracked into a thousand shards before shattering. Each fragment fluttered weightlessly around in the air. Fangdarr gently took hold of a small piece, feeling a soft force still trying to repel him from within his hand. Closing his fist tightly, the shard disintegrated into a fine dust before blowing away. Fangdarr looked at the floating layer of powdered magic—the corpse of his magical foe—and walked through the doorway.

From his rear, the spectators all remained dead silent.

CHAPTER TWENTY-FIVE
NELTHALIUS

"What did you do!?" Elethain shouted, throwing his hands up after watching Fangdarr destroy the barrier. He looked to Aesthéa expectantly as if she needed to control an unruly pet.

Before the druid could act, the guards had regained their resolve and were closing on the orc with their spear blades raised. Despite being forced to the ground, a smile spread across Fangdarr's face.

Aesthéa watched as her secret lover was escorted down the opposing hall, where she knew the dungeon remained. She let out a sigh of hopelessness, though struggled to hide her own smile at the orc's smugness. As Fangdarr and the guards disappeared around a corner, Aesthéa turned her smile to Elethain, who could only roll his eyes before walking toward the king's chamber.

Elethain nodded to the pair of elite guards standing vigilant at the door to the throne room. He remembered the first time he had ever approached the chamber, over a thousand years ago. It had seemed odd that only two guards were stationed to protect the king. However, he had been told that elite pair were of nearly insurmountable skill, both in melee and magic, and were part of an elite bloodline known as Du'Taille.

Using their arcane abilities, the Du'Taille warriors unlocked the door from the outside. Hidden machinations within the magically reinforced wall could be heard clicking and clinking. Then, the wall behind the guards slowly started to retract into the surrounding walls. The moment Elethain and Aesthéa had passed the threshold, the guards closed the walls behind them.

The necromancer's face lit up as he entered the throne room. He always missed the way it made him feel small yet greatly important. The room was vast and tall, expanding above the forest canopy with the pinnacle, exposed to see the sky. A spiral staircase rounded the entire chamber, connecting nearly two dozen platforms that circled the room. Every wall was lined with trinkets, books, potions, and much more.

The expansive collection was what made Elethain always enjoyed being there. It spoke volumes of the superiority of his race. Their long lives granted each individual nearly a hundred human lifetimes, where they could retain and share information within their culture. Tomes of alchemy, other races, and geography were littered in the king's room at his disposal.

Unlike her ally, Aesthéa didn't share the joyous feeling as she entered the room. Rather, her stomach sank with the expectation of the scolding—and likely a new scar—she would receive for defying her instructions to remain in Jesmera instead of pursuing Fangdarr. She looked upon the throne with trepidation. Her uncle sat in the familiar grand piece of furniture that was made entirely of the vibrant bluish-green overlapping vines of the great Eye of Cerenos tree, emitting magical energy.

Elethain bowed. "Your majesty, I have returned with your niece."

King Nelthalius looked up from the immense book in his lap, his old eyes furrowed in a scowl of disappointment. Even though his youth had long passed, the king still struck an intimidating visage. Despite nearing five thousand years of age, his pale skin showed no wrinkles, though seemed dull, matching the blunted glimmer of his white hair.

Aesthéa quickly fell to her knee in a sincere bow, her head tucked low. "Forgive me, Uncle." She kept her eyes on the floor, seeing herself in the reflective, marbled surface even as the king's footsteps grew closer. His silhouette came into view on the mirrored tile before her. Despite the inverted spectacle, Aesthéa could tell his shoulders were tense in stress and his eyes bore holes into her.

"Rise, Aesthéa." The tension in his voice was evident. The druid rose and turned away, unable to bear the weight of his disapproving stare. "You will look at me!" Nelthalius yelled into her face, drawing her eyes once more in fright.

Aesthéa forced her eyes forward. She couldn't stand how weak she felt in that moment. The druid was both brave and fierce in battle. Yet, here she could hardly hold herself up for fear of retribution. Then, she remembered her vulnerable conversation with Fangdarr. No matter how much it pained her, or what scars it brought, she wouldn't be silenced. Aesthéa steeled her resolve and looked to her uncle with renewed determination. "Forgive me, Uncle," she reiterated, this time with a steadied voice.

King Nelthalius scowled once more and, for a sliver of a moment, tensed his lips in displeasure. His nostrils flared as he took in a large breath, then turned back to his throne and sat down slowly. A hundred pounding heartbeats passed as the king stared at Aesthéa and Elethain in deep consideration. Finally, the ancient elf broke the silence. "Did you accomplish what you had hoped, Aesthéa?"

Aesthéa nearly gasped, taken aback at her uncle's willingness to disregard her insubordination. "I-I . . . uh . . . ."

"Out with it, girl!"

"I encountered Fangdarr, yes," she responded in a matter-of-fact tone that drew a raised eyebrow. The king motioned with his hand to elaborate, growing irritated. "He was not the threat we had originally expected. He wa—"

"So he was *more*!? Cerenos bless us, these orcs grow increasingly violent. We must make plans to keep them maintained. Controlled." Nelthalius rubbed his temple at the thought of having to interfere with Crein.

Aesthéa anxiously waited for the right moment to correct the elven king's assumption. "No, Your Majesty."

The king looked up with an angry scowl. "No? You think to question my command?"

"No! I only mean to elaborate," the druid desperately added. She could see the topic wasn't going the way she had planned. Yet the task was proving difficult without revealing her affections. With her uncle's permission, she continued her report. "I attacked Fangdarr, he was alone in the wood. I was bested quickly and expected my death. Instead, he tended my wounds and kept me by his side. At first, my intent was to continue to watch him more closely and report back to you, so that we may make a more informed decision."

"And what did you learn?"

Aesthéa could see Elethain's growing level of disapproval out of her peripheral. "I discovered that he is unlike any other orc. He is a brute, to be sure, but intelligent, calculated, and sympathetic with a good heart."

"A good heart!?" His voice began to amplify with each question. "The same chieftain who has expanded the Orclands to twice their size—in just *two winters*—due to his sheer brutality? The same who continuously raided his neighboring settlements to the point of extinction, forcing the humans to abandon the small communities altogether and retreat further from the forest in safety? It is *this* orc, one who is known for the merciless slaughter, rape, and torture of those he encounters all in the name of domination and conquest!?" Nelthalius stared at his niece incredulously. "You would have me believe *he* is of a kind heart?"

"I would. We return with grave news. News that would be graver still had it not been for Fangdarr's involvement." Aesthéa stepped forward slowly, careful to not press her luck. "Uncle, Crepusculus has assembled an army of unmatchable numbers. Trolls, ogres, and even the Zharnik clan, save for Fangdarr. It was *his* hand that cut down the shadow dragon and gave Crein a small chance of surviving this war. The enemy remain leaderless, yet their number is great enough to keep advantage." She inhaled slowly. "I would ask that we aid them."

At the boldness of her request, Elethain rushed forward. "That is for the king to decide after consideration from the *advisors*. You cannot make such a request!"

Aesthéa turned to regard the necromancer. "Yet, I do."

Elethain started to form his rebuttal before Nelthalius raised a hand while the other tended to the growing pressure in his temple. "Enough!" He breathed a sigh of relief at the silence returning to the room. His eyes closed in thought. Finally, he rose from his throne and stepped to the edge of the room, where he could lay his eyes upon his grand collection. Aesthéa and Elethain waited patiently as the king traversed the chamber slowly.

After many tense and awkwardly silent moments, they could hear Nelthalius' regal voice from across the room. "The orc truly disposed of the dragon, Elethain?"

Elethain's lips tightened but he replied obediently. "Yes, my king."

"Where is the orc now?"

Aesthéa made sure to reply first. "He is in our dungeon, Uncle. He was escorted willingly at his own expense."

Nelthalius turned curiously to her from across the chamber and walked over. "You care for him?"

Aesthéa pondered how best to respond. She knew lying would be pointless, but how much of the truth could she afford to reveal? Would such a claim end in Fangdarr's death, or her own? It didn't matter. The king didn't miss her hesitation.

"You *love* him . . .? You would shame yourself for an orc?" King Nelthalius' shocked expression changed to anger then confusion and despair in quick succession.

Staring ahead, Aesthéa gathered her strength for the fate she expected to come. "I do, as he loves me, Uncle."

Elethain's face contorted in glee, knowing Aesthéa had just condemned the orc, or at the very least their relationship. He could hardly contain himself as the laughter in his chest threatened to break free.

Nelthalius turned away with a resigned sigh. "Such a thing is forbidden, Aesthéa. You know there can be no union. You must end the affection. And never speak of this again."

The druid couldn't control her outburst. She was too far gone and past the point of no return. Her secret was out, and she would give her life to maintain it. "Uncle, no!"

Eyes wide with hostility, the king faced her with sheer anger. "*No*? No!? You seem to forget, as always, that it is *I* who makes the commands! You are but a subject of my will! It is *I* who keeps us safe. You wish to bring our greatest threat to our doorstep with open arms that he may gut us from the inside!" His voice grew larger with each word, booming through the tall chamber.

Aesthéa didn't back down. "Life demands adaptation! I trust in my heart that I have made the right choice. You speak of a world that is dying. Fangdarr is no common orc. He is the pinnacle of his kind, set upon creating alliances with the goodly races and seeking to *end* this war. Even now, he sits in an elven prison of his own will to show his intent, knowing at any moment we may choose to end his life. It is Fangdarr who I put my trust in, as I believe Cerenos has as well."

With the final statement, Nelthalius raised an eyebrow. "You speak not only for kings, but for the gods now as well?" He scoffed at her incessant defiance. "You are but a child, Aesthéa. You do not know what your heart will desire." He took a deep breath. Never in his lifetime did he expect to encounter an issue such as this. No knowledge passed through the ages or scribblings in the thousand tomes on his shelves had ever dealt with an elf—one of royalty, nonetheless—seeking union with an orc. "Cerenos be blessed, the misery of offspring . . .," he muttered before staring at Aesthéa. "Cerenos gives blessing, you suspect?"

Before she could respond, Elethain cut in. "My king, will we truly place the fate of our kind in the biased words of a girl protecting her companion?" Aesthéa shot a scowl back at him.

Nelthalius raised a hand to halt their argument before it began. "Elethain is right." A smirk formed on the necromancer's mouth. "However, I will meet with this orc and determine for myself." After its brief display, Elethain's smugness faded instantly.

CHAPTER TWENTY-SIX
CATAPULT

"Go, go!" Viktor shouted to Bitrayuul and Cormac. The half-orc slid his helmet on, and the trio rushed out of the war room and back toward the throne room. By the time they had arrived, a dozen guards had swarmed King Dariel in protection.

The king watched the group dash into the room. "Viktor! What's happened?"

Sliding to a halt, the commander responded, "Catapult, sir. The trolls must have stolen it from Riveton. They aren't intelligent enough to build one on their own. I apologize, sir, I must go to the wall. Bitrayuul and Cormac will assist." He didn't wait for confirmation from his ruler before taking off once more and exiting the castle.

Passing through the reinforced doors and returning to the courtyard, Bitrayuul gasped in shock. Women and children were screaming as they frantically rushed around in confusion, expecting their doom at any moment. The half-orc's resolve began to dwindle as thoughts of defeat plagued his errant mind. He shook away the nightmarish illusions and followed Viktor and Cormac south toward the wall.

Throughout their sprint, civilians begging for help continued to hinder them. The crazed commoners aimlessly bounced around the streets in fright, shoving each other over in desperation. More than a few mistakenly stumbled into Bitrayuul, only to find themselves cut a dozen times by his rancid, bloodied armor. Each foolish human who sought refuge in his embrace pained the half-orc even more, as he was forced to watch their eyes turn from despair to agony at his sharpened bite. Nevertheless, he was forced to offer whispered apologies as he pushed them aside. There was no time for warmth.

Finally, Viktor rounded the last corner of the Military District to gaze upon the wall. He let out a heavy sigh of relief between labored pants. The wall appeared to be intact, though he couldn't yet examine the damage that may have been done to the other side. As he was about to pass through the tight, spiral stairway that would take him to the top of the wall, a creaking *thuuuuu-wop* sounded, followed by the whistle of a projectile.

"Brace!" Viktor yelled before tucking against the wall. Bitrayuul and Cormac followed suit as the whistling grew louder. They watched as a large boulder crashed against the hardened dirt before rolling to a stop halfway through the district, crushing more than a dozen soldiers. Bitrayuul's mouth fell open in shock as he witnessed the men's bodies disappear beneath the immense boulder, leaving only an explosion of blood and their flattened remnants in its wake.

The commander's face was locked in grim determination, despite seeing his subordinates meet their doom. "Move!" he called, dashing into the staircase. Cormac followed, having no trouble navigating the tight space. Bitrayuul, on the other hand, could hardly squeeze through. As he pressed and wedged his way deeper and deeper into the winding staircase, fear started to sink in. He could no longer move his shoulders.

A bald head peeked down at Bitrayuul from the gap above, glistening with sweat. Cormac's eyes were pressed down by his furrowed brow, further accentuating his eye patch as he looked to his stuck companion. "C'mon, Bit! Yer almost there, lad."

Appreciating the words of comfort—though they did little to calm his panic—the half-orc set his mind to the task. The blades of his armor scraped loudly against the stone walls, screeching in his ears. Finally, he broke through the exit and crashed to the ground. Clasping Cormac's offered hand and returning to even footing, Bitrayuul turned his attention to the enemy beyond the wall.

Countless dark-skinned trolls and orcs—and the occasional ogre—spread from cliff to cliff, covering the land in a sea of darkness. *How?* Bitrayuul thought. *How is such an army possible?* Even in the distance, more could be seen, no larger than specks of blackness. The half-orc's doubts amplified. *There is no escape. No victory can be possible against such a horde!*

Bitrayuul felt Cormac's hand pulling at him. Not realizing Viktor had pressed on, the half-orc followed the dwarf to catch up to the commander as they rushed to the center of the long wall, just above the gate. Already a handful of soldiers lay in a pool of blood, skewered with crude spears.

Donning a grave expression, the Viktor turned to the pair. "The wall has held, though I am not certain how many attacks it can withstand." As if waiting for the words, another boulder soared through the air before smashing into the sheer stone wall beneath them and shattered on impact.

A call came from their rear. "Commander!" As one, Bitrayuul, Cormac, and Viktor turned to see a soldier leading a pair of dirty men wearing leather aprons covered in coal dust and pulling a small cart. Viktor nodded in acknowledgement with a slight sign of hope and moved toward them.

Even Bitrayuul's spirit was lifted as the thick cloth that was draped over the supplies was removed, revealing four barrels of coal. But the half-orc's eyes traced the path to the north, expecting another cart—or ten. None were coming. *This cannot be all . . ..* His previously elevated mood returned to sour thoughts of defeat as Bitrayuul realized their largest advantage against trolls was limited to a single cart of coal.

Cormac, on the other hand, cheered victoriously and was joined in by more than a few of the surrounding men. "Let's light these bastards on fire!" he shouted, drastically improving morale.

After ordering the coal be tucked against the inside of the wall, Viktor ushered Bitrayuul and Cormac into a small room atop the battlements. Bitrayuul stared around the room. It seemed as if it was intended to be used for some sort of command station. Maps were plastered to the walls and a single wooden table sat in the center. However, the half-orc could tell it hadn't been used for its purpose for some time, as storage crates blanketed with dust lined the edges of the room.

Viktor took a seat in one of the stools at the table, extending a hand to his guests to do the same. "So, we have our coal. What is your suggestion?"

Bitrayuul was careful to hide his thoughts of failure with the pitiful amount of coal they had on hand. Though, it didn't matter as Cormac gladly took the reins. The dwarf peered through a thin window facing the south to view the enemy masses once more. "Looks like they've got just the one catapult. That be the biggest threat, don't ye doubt. We need to destroy it. It might take most of the coal, though. Ye got an arcanist, by chance?"

The half-orc raised his eyebrow at the unfamiliar term of 'arcanist'. Viktor, however, seemed to understand the dwarf's question. "There are typically a few within the city. Though most will be useless and finding them may prove to be very difficult. There is another, a powerful mage, but he won't assist."

This time, it was the dwarf who raised his brow. "Won't assist? What do ye mean, he 'won't assist'?! Does he not know what's at stake?!"

Commander Viktor simply looked away, not wishing to employ the same angered reaction as the dwarf—though it was his true desire. "He won't assist. He isn't one to care for such." It was clear there was more the man wished to say, but for some reason he held back.

Cormac looked dumbfounded. He couldn't believe that a man who could prove beneficial would sit idle, twiddling his thumbs, while others protecting the city fell. He waved the thought away, praying to his god that he never meet the man—for both their sakes. "Send a dozen soldiers throughout the city to find whatever arcanists ye can find. It may prove without reward, but I'll not have us disregard the possibility."

Viktor nodded. "And if we find none?"

The dwarf ran his fingers through his beard. "Ye happen to have yer own catapult?"

"No. A hundred years ago there were six within these walls. They were destroyed during the heavy winter four decades ago for firewood."

Cormac nodded, remembering that storm well—though with much less concern due to being within the underbelly of the mountains. He smacked his palms against his bald head, pressuring himself to think harder. Rising from his seat, the dwarf paced around, muttering words to himself, only to shake his head and curse his own thoughts.

Bitrayuul sat watching, feeling a bit helpless. He didn't know what an arcanist was and didn't wish to ask at that moment. However, he knew they needed to eliminate the catapult—which had just landed another attack against the wall. The half-orc joined Cormac in deep thought.

As they each racked their brains, a soldier rushed into the entryway, breaking their concentration. "Commander, the coal has been secured. The oil as well, twelve barrels—we found another eight in storage."

"Good work, soldier," Viktor responded. "We will have execution plans momentarily, see to the men. Make sure no one is growing too tired or hungry. See them fed and that the shifts along the cliffs are still in good standing. Also, send word to the docks, make sure the two ships along each side of the coast fare the same. I won't have our brethren starve as they defend their homeland!"

With a nod, the soldier bowed low and took off to fulfill his commander's orders. Bitrayuul watched the messenger go, his respect for Viktor growing. Even in the most dire of situations, the commander could be counted on to make sure all aspects of war were accounted for, not just the death of their enemies. As the soldier disappeared in the spiraling staircase, the half-orc's eyes drifted upon an object on the battlements in the distance.

"Commander, do you have ballistae?" Bitrayuul asked, as if the answer had been in front of them the entire time.

"Yes, there is one on ea—" Viktor started before his eyes grew large in realization. "Curse this withered mind!"

Cormac looked down the wall, seeing a ballista on the eastern and western end. It seemed odd that soldiers weren't manning the machines, launching bolts into the masses of enemies. Then again, what purpose would it serve? While a hurled boulder from a catapult may bounce and crush a dozen enemies beneath its weight, a single, large bolt could take out two or three at most. "Good thinkin', lad! Commander, bring up a barrel of oil, coal, and a few strips of cloth. We're goin' to dismantle that catapult."

CHAPTER TWENTY-SEVEN

VALOR

The soldiers grunted with effort as they carried the barrels to the command room, sweat dripping down their faces. With the sun quickly descending, time was of the greatest importance. Whether through discipline or ignorance, the defenders had staved off their fear thus far. However, even the most seasoned could feel their stomachs twist at the thought of fighting in darkness. Despite their festering horror, the soldiers trusted Viktor, halting their laborious breaths just long enough to bow before each took their leave.

Viktor hardly paid them any heed as he immediately cracked open the barrels. "Bitrayuul, retrieve as many bolts as you can from the ballista to the east."

The half-orc hesitated. "The east? Would the western not prove closer?"

Furrowing his brow, the commander took a steadying breath that made Bitrayuul question the wisdom of his words. "Yes. The western is closer. And with the sun setting, it will rest behind the weapon, obscuring it from view to the hellish creatures. But the enemy will see you retrieve bolts from the *east* and expect us to fire from there. We shall rely on that stupidity and launch from the west, unsuspected."

Cormac and Bitrayuul looked to one another. Each had heard that humans were often under the impression the evil races of Crein were stupid, mindless beasts that only acted for the drive of whatever blood remain closest. But they knew different. Orcs may be brutish, and ogres even more so, but they weren't without thought. Worse still, trolls were of a sinister mind, both cunning and quick-witted. Such a feeble attempt of misdirection would certainly fall short. Before either could raise an argument, Viktor shouted, "Go!"

The half-orc scowled beneath his helmet but sprinted east along the parapet, nevertheless. His frustration served to benefit as his focus on the corpses of soldiers beneath his feet fell second in his mind. Bitrayuul tried to duck low as he ran to remain beneath the gut-high wall at his side. Carefully picking through bodies, he was forced to slow his advance for fear of stumbling and injuring an ankle. Such a disability would spell his doom quickly in this war.

Spears glanced around him—a few even scraped across his armor—as he continued his path. With a breath of relief, Bitrayuul slid to his knee beneath the final stretch of wall, three paces from the ballista. No blocking wall could be built around the platform, as it would only hinder the turret's scope. He would be out in the open, a prime target for those below.

Spotting a long crate against the wall of the path on the opposing side of the platform, Bitrayuul quickly dashed across. Safely tucked behind the raised wall once more, he looked at the path he had just passed. No less than ten spears had found their way through the gap in the parapets. They had been waiting for him. A smirk appeared beneath his helmet, knowing Viktor should have listened. Their enemies were no simpletons.

Attention returned to the task at hand, Bitrayuul lifted the wooden lid from the case to reveal the missiles within. Immediately he groaned in frustration. It was obvious none had thought to open the crate in ages. For within was naught but spiders and enough dust to etch his name—no bolts. He cursed his luck as he rose to his feet and sprinted back the way he came, disregarding the numerous crude-tipped spears that deflected off his armor.

Inside the command room, Viktor and Cormac looked up as Bitrayuul re-entered, empty-handed and breathing heavily. The half-orc could tell they had just been talking about him, as their voices halted the moment he set foot in their presence. Anger began to brew within him at being disregarded and treated as an errand boy.

Cormac quickly spoke up to break the awkward tension that had filled the room. "Bit, where be the bolts?"

Bitrayuul couldn't keep the frustration from adding venom to his words. "There were none. Just dust and webs."

Viktor turned back to a bundle of tattered cloth on the table. "That is unfortunate. Check the west ballista and pray to your god that our luck changes." His voice once again left no room to be questioned.

Bitrayuul stood motionless, drawing a concerning eye from Cormac and a look of anger from the commander. "Fetch them yourself."

Viktor's hand fell to his sword handle, ready to exchange more than just words. Thankfully, Cormac placed a hand over the man's and his other in front of Bitrayuul. "There be enough enemies out there, lads. We don't need to make more on this side of the wall." The dwarf turned to Viktor first. "Commander, we only mean to help." Pivoting to the half-orc, he added, "Bit, we are here to aid in the city's defense. Viktor takes command here. Ye can fall in line, as I have, or ye can leave. The hostility between ye will only reduce the morale of the men, don't ye doubt. This war will rely on *all* of us."

Bitrayuul let out a long breath, relaxing visibly and offering his hand. Viktor remained resolute in his demanding pose, though finally deflated as well. The man took the half-orc's extended hand and shook it firmly, sealing their unspoken agreement to make the best of their situation—for the sake of Wiston.

"I'll retrieve those bolts," Bitrayuul stated flatly, stepping toward the western door. But he was stopped by a raised hand from the small dwarf once more.

"No, lad. This time it be me. Ye and Viktor prepare the materials." Cormac smashed his shields together in a loud crash before rushing out of the room. Bitrayuul and Viktor watched him go before turning toward one another, their eagerness to uphold their agreement diminished the moment the dwarf was out of sight. Nevertheless, they did as the captain suggested and began working together to prepare for the bolts.

Cormac was already halfway down the long path. His short stature kept only the top of his bald head above the parapet. With a shield raised in cover, the captain easily made it to the crate and kicked it open.

"Bothain's beard . . .." Only two bolts lay within the crate. *Two are better than none.*

Lifting the bolts proved a difficult task; each stood as tall as a man, with a heavy, bladed tip weighing down one end. With his guard lowered to lift the cumbersome missiles, a spear managed to slice across the top of his head. Cormac instantly dropped low, falling to his rear and backing to the wall in safety. His hand slowly slid along his skull to inspect the wound. The dwarf grimaced as he pressed and fingered his way across the gash. He could tell it was a deep cut, possibly even reaching bone, but also knew luck was on his side. Had it been a finger's length lower, the captain would have fallen then and there.

"Bah, second damned cut this week! Next thing ye know, they'll start tellin' me to wear a damned helmet!" Cormac raised his right arm to cover his body and scooped the bolts awkwardly with his left. Slowly, he retreated toward the command room, blood trickling down his back.

"Excellent work, Captain," Viktor commended as Cormac opened the door, ignoring the wound on the dwarf's head. Retrieving the bolts, he set them down on the table with the other materials.

Bitrayuul pulled his friend closer and eyed the gash. "Cormac, are you alright?" The dwarf groaned and gave stubborn protest against the half-orc's prodding yet didn't move away. "It's deep but did not reach your skull. Thank Bothain for the thick heads of dwarves!"

The dwarf cracked a smile with the much-appreciated humor, even managing a brief chuckle. "Aye, were I an air-headed gnome ye would've seen me deflate and blow around the castle! Bahaha!"

Bitrayuul moved away, confident the dwarf was his normal self. They turned to Viktor who had just finished fastening a bundle of oil-soaked coal to the bolt. The man dipped a strip of cloth most of the way into the oil then wrapped it around the missile's shaft, leaving the last bit of cloth that wasn't soiled connected to the bundle of coal.

"Why'd ye leave that last bit unsoiled?" Cormac asked.

Viktor proudly answered in a matter-of-fact tone. "Because otherwise the bundle would ignite the moment we set the pitch to torch. We need it to delay but a moment."

Bitrayuul was impressed with the commander's keen thought toward the flammable materials. He watched closely as the man quickly prepared the other bolt as well. "So, two bolts. Will we fire from east or west, Commander?"

The man's lips tightened in consideration. He looked toward the sun, which sat just barely above the horizon over the Maelstrom Coast. "We no longer have the advantage of the light in the west." Viktor looked out the window to gauge the catapult's position. "The catapult is closer to the eastern ballista. My worry is that the added weight will reduce the range of the ballista. That isn't even considering what it will do to the trueness of its aim."

"East it be," Cormac offered. "We all go. I'll guard. Bit, ye carry the bolts and torch. Make sure they don't touch."

They all acknowledged their agreement and set off down the path, bolts in hand. As they ran along the wall, it was clear that the great stone structure had already suffered over half a dozen shots. A large crack had appeared near the gates where boulders continued to crash. With each impact, more and more rubble fell away as if the wall was slowly trickling away its own lifeblood.

Hearts racing with the weight of desperation, the trio reached the eastern ballista without injury—though not for lack of attempt by the invaders. Thousands below focused all attention on them, launching projectiles at every opportunity. Bitrayuul peered over the wall only to be forced to retreat in cover quickly from the storm of spears the sailed past his head. "We must hurry!"

Cormac walked out from behind the wall first, his large shields raised. Viktor stepped behind the barrier of steel as the pair made it to the large machinery. From behind the dwarf's guard, the commander rotated the lever that cocked back the slot in preparation. Dozens of feeble, wooden spears glanced off Cormac's shields, reflecting in every direction.

Once Viktor had finished, he waved to Bitrayuul to hand him the first bolt. The half-orc quickly passed it over, making the transition as swiftly as possible. Retracting his arm just in time, the commander notched the bolt, then gripped the handles to swing the turret.

In the heat of the moment, Viktor forgot that Cormac was standing adjacent the ballista, knocking the dwarf away as the weapon swung. With the dwarf's shields no longer in place to intercept, the enemy's javelins managed to reach their mark, with three hitting Viktor in quick succession.

The commander yelled out in pain and reactively squeezed the trigger before setting his aim. Cormac and Bitrayuul watched the bolt travel above the masses. With luck, they had proved the bolt could reach the distance of the catapult, though it fell far to the side of its mark, skewering a few unlucky trolls. With the oil unlit, the trolls simply pushed the bolt entirely through their bodies and regenerated the wounds as if they had never occurred.

Bitrayuul felt the familiar pang of hopelessness seep in as the bolt was completely disregarded. That terrible dread pulled at his gut even more once his eyes turned to Commander Viktor coughing out blood as he lay collapsed on the ground.

Cormac slid to the man and put up his shields. Bitrayuul could only watch as the dwarf slowly dragged the commander safely behind the parapet on the opposite side of the gap.

"Ye alright, lad?" the dwarf asked, though he knew the answer. One spear had struck the man square in the chest, collapsing his lung. The dwarf ran his hand over the man's head as soldiers rushed down the path. "Yer men are comin', Viktor. Stay strong."

Viktor's eyes fluttered to the path, where six men were disregarding their own safety for his. He watched as one unsuspecting man was clipped in the neck by a thrown spear, dropping him to the ground in a spray of blood. The man behind tripped over the body and impaled himself with his own sword. The commander growled in frustration at his men's lives being lost simply to aid him. Mustering the last of his strength and will, Viktor looked to the dwarf. "For Wiston . . .." Then, Viktor groaned weakly and rose to his feet before crying out in anger. Cormac quickly followed, placing his shields in front of them once more.

The soldiers had almost joined with them by then, though another fell to a stray missile, leaving only three. Their movement was spurred upon seeing their commander yelling defiantly as he cranked the lever on the ballista, blood pouring from his mouth.

Bitrayuul rose as well, lighting the bolt in the same moment he handed it to Viktor. He watched in admiration as the commander notched the bolt and shoved Cormac out of the way in order to spin the weapon once more. A javelin cut into the man's shoulder instantly. Then another in his thigh, dropping the commander before he could even finish setting the ballista on target, a pool of blood spreading beneath the man's feet.

Watching the last bit of cloth set aflame, Bitrayuul's heart pounded. After another fell, the last pair of soldiers finally reach their commander and tried to drag him back to safety with only a small, round shield raised in defense for each. Cormac and Bitrayuul watched the brave and selfless efforts of the men end futilely as they were both mowed down by the endless stream of missiles. Clutching their wounds, each staggered around the platform in a daze. Disoriented, the men stumbled back before falling from the wall and down to the masses, where they were ripped apart within moments.

Unable to sit idle any longer, Bitrayuul and Cormac rushed from their safe hovels. The dwarf assumed position in front of the half-orc, who grabbed the handles of the weapon, standing over Viktor—a breath from death.

Bitrayuul swung the ballista toward the catapult far in the distance and took aim. He pulled down on the turret, aiming higher to accommodate for the added weight of the bundle that was dangerously close to exploding. The half-orc gave a bestial roar as he launched the missile, pouring all his hope into that single trigger. The constant torrent of javelins was the only reason Bitrayuul and Cormac didn't stand idle to watch the missile as it whistled through the air, a trail of black smoke in its wake.

Viktor raised his head weakly in the last clutches of life, seeing the bolt fly toward its mark. He watched as it crashed into the catapult's launching arm and embedded deep into the wooden beam. The moment it struck, the flames ignited the bundle of oil-soaked coal, bursting in a small explosion. A small smile formed on the commander's lips and his last breath passed with the knowledge that his death hadn't been in vain.

As the catapult exploded in splinters of wood, Bitrayuul and Cormac could hear the triumphant shout of the men along the wall, followed by a much louder cheer as the thousands of soldiers behind realized what had occurred. The men's cries of joy carried loudly, almost drowning out the roars and pounding of the opposing horde.

Cormac quickly dashed past the opening of the platform to sit next to Bitrayuul. They each stared at Viktor's corpse, still pouring blood onto the stones beneath him. "We did it, lad. *Viktor* did it."

Letting out a heavy sigh of relief, Bitrayuul silently thanked the commander in the afterlife for his sacrifice. He turned his head, however, as he realized the men's cheers had stopped. The half-orc peeked over the crenellation at his back and looked out among the sea of black. It was then that he saw it—the reason the soldiers had turned to silence. The reason they were filled with dread instead of hope.

Another catapult was being pulled into view.

CHAPTER TWENTY-EIGHT

FAITH

Fangdarr entered the tall chamber and his mouth fell open in awe. From the stacks of tomes to glittering baubles and even an array of weapons from different cultures, the orc gazed around the room. He nearly gasped as he realized just how high the king's trove went, drawing him in ever more. Never had he seen such a collection. He held no care for books or objects of science, yet the orc couldn't deny the sheer impressiveness of such a wealth of knowledge, no matter how foreign. Fangdarr heard Elethain clear his throat, snapping him out of his admiration.

Upon seeing Aesthéa, Fangdarr nearly called out in joy, but held his tongue. King Nelthalius didn't miss the instant change in demeanor as the orc laid eyes upon his niece—nor her equal reaction—despite their forced efforts. Fangdarr walked toward them, still glancing at every object he could see, curiosity burning inside him. Slowing to a halt, the chieftain stood facing the elven king.

Nelthalius inspected Fangdarr with intense scrutiny. The elf certainly noticed Fangdarr's abnormal size first, followed by the many scars carved into his body. "I see you have consumed the blood of a dragon, orc."

Caught taken aback at the king's ability to discern such a fact, Fangdarr shifted awkwardly. "I always big. Dragon blood make bigger." Like his counterpart, the orc watched for a change in expression as his words found the elf's ear. None came. Fangdarr stared around the room. "You live here?"

Nelthalius nodded, just as curious as the orc. Though, his interest was in the abnormal chieftain himself, rather than the many objects lined upon his walls. Never in his long life had the elf encountered one such as Fangdarr. He wished to glean all he could from the orc and what made him different.

Fangdarr stepped toward the growth-like throne, drawn to its bluish wood and the energy that pulsated from deep within. Elethain reached out to stop the orc, but Nelthalius raised a hand to allow their guest to continue. Aesthéa simply remained silent, careful to avoid triggering any sort of reaction from her uncle.

Bending low, Fangdarr eyed the magical furniture. It almost sounded as if dozens of murmurs could be heard from within the twisted branches. He leaned back with a perplexed face and looked toward Nelthalius. "Your chair whispers?"

The king's eyes went wide. "*You* can hear them?!"

Elethain and Aesthéa looked to each other quizzically. Neither could hear anything. Nor had they ever heard tell of the throne making sound, despite having spent much time at Nelthalius' side. Fangdarr turned to his companions and noted their confounded expressions, realizing only he could hear the near-silent chittering. The chieftain's attention abruptly shifted as the elven king began laughing loudly.

His cackle growing with each passing moment, Nelthalius nearly fell to the floor in his maniacal state. "Oh, Cerenos, you never cease! Ahahaha!" The king's uproar echoed within the chamber for a long while before it began to wane. "I apologize," he started before breaking into a low chuckle once more. "It appears you are right, Aesthéa. Cerenos has plans for this one."

The druid's eyes lit up. "So, does that mean . . .?"

Nelthalius raised a hand, seriousness replacing his amusement and weighing down his brow. "Hold. I have more questions for him." Aesthéa shrank back, not daring to deny the command when she believed she was so close to accomplishing her wishes. Fangdarr nodded with a grunt.

"Do you love Aesthéa?"

Fangdarr rocked back on his heels, glancing at his friends to see if the secret had been revealed. Both just watched him in silence, awaiting his response. The chieftain gave a slow nod.

"How much?"

The orc stared the king in the eye. "Enough to walk into elf city."

Expecting such a response, the elven king nodded. The words alone didn't give credence to the true weight such an action carried. An orc stepping foot in their beloved home was certain death. Yet, Fangdarr stomped in, accepting any fate that be delivered, and even shattered the barrier in front of many spectators. And there he stood, able to hear the whispers of the mystical throne, carved from the Eye of Cerenos itself—a feat denied even most elven kings.

"You are a wonder, Fangdarr. I will grant you a single request. What would you wish?" Nelthalius put the orc to his final test. The king would know the true nature of the orc who stood before him.

Fangdarr crossed his arms and let out a slow exhale. He knew the question was some sort of test, but in which way? Did the king wish for him to ask for Aesthéa's hand, proving his devotion to her? Or for his return to Crein, securing his own safety? Fangdarr couldn't begin to imagine the elf's goal. Nevertheless, he knew his request. "Save Wiston."

A smile formed on Nelthalius' mouth, spreading wide across his dulled, pale skin. "A fine choice, Chieftain. One I shall see granted, on one request in return."

There it was—the caveat. Fangdarr knew something would be taken in return. In truth, he expected it to be a personal request to break the companionship between himself and Aesthéa. As the elf king had allowed him, so too did Fangdarr return the kindness. The orc nodded, signifying the king to make his request.

"We elves are a close-knit people. We are strong and committed to each other, But our numbers are small, despite our ability to live through the ages. I possess less than a thousand capable of war. From what I have heard, those that burned a path through Crein and now pound against the gates of Wiston are exponentially beyond that. I have faith that my warriors can hold their own and take many enemies with them. Yet, the odds are against them. I would not send half of my population to a war that is of no concern to us without certainty they do not all walk to their doom. "However, I shall grant your request on the condition that you travel to Wudhyvn to the west and obtain the favor of the satyrs. If you can enlist their forces, I shall join your cause, orc."

Elethain cut in first, panic on his face. "Your majesty, the satyrs cannot be trusted! They have been sharing Y'thirya with elves for millennia yet have refused to align themselves with us despite our continuous efforts. I *implore* you to reconsider."

The king shot an angry glare at his advisor. "All that you say is correct, Elethain. Nevertheless, they are followers of Cerenos. They may join, they may not. That is for them, Cerenos, and the forest god's supposed 'chosen' to decide."

"'*Chosen*'?" Elethain asked distastefully at the thought of an orc—a *godless* orc—being given the attention of his deity.

"So it would seem. The satyrs will put such a claim to test, I am sure. Either Fangdarr perishes and our people remain here, or Cerenos truly has taken a keen interest in the orc and we follow the desire of our god. Would you request a different path, *advisor*?" King Nelthalius stared directly at Elethain, waiting for the elf to give voice against his king again. Luckily, none came.

Returning to his throne, Nelthalius re-opened the enormous tome he had been reading as if this had been a simple conversation between old friends. As he was flipping through the pages, he stated, "Aesthéa and Fangdarr, go to Wudhyvn and prove the validity of your quest . . . and your companionship."

Aesthéa lifted her head with her uncle's final statement. While not stating it outright, she knew the king had granted her permission to continue her union with Fangdarr, so long as they returned successful. Unable to contain her joy, the rebellious youth jumped into her lover's arms and kissed him deeply. Nelthalius simply rolled his eyes, though didn't miss the sheer disgust evident on his advisor's face.

"Elethain," the king began, staring at the pages in his lap. "You shall accompany them. See that they remain safe. *Both* of them."

The necromancer caught on to his king's intent and cursed his own carelessness, knowing his repulsed expression revealed his thoughts toward the couple's affections. "Your majesty, I am not some errand boy!" The moment the words fell from his mouth, loosened with anger, Elethain regretted his outburst.

In an instant, he was driven to the ground with enormous force, knocking the wind from his lungs and groaning in pain as his body was pressed beneath an unseen weight. Aesthéa and Fangdarr jumped back in shock, thinking some unknown assailant had managed to enter the room. Though they saw nothing.

"You would do well to remember your place, Elethain," Nelthalius said, still reading his book. Fangdarr and Aesthéa realized it was the king who was crushing their friend, though he gave no evidence of such. The king finally looked up from his tome. "You *will* accompany them and do everything to keep them from harm—including giving your own life, should it be necessary." Each phrase came with another shock of force followed by a pained groan from the elf on the floor.

Struggling to breathe, Elethain attempted to break free. He knew Nelthalius was an arcanist, but he had never witnessed his king using the magic aggressively. His muscles grew weary beneath the constant pounding as Nelthalius barraged him with invisible orbs, manipulating force at will with no sign of exertion. The king's mental stamina seemed limitless as he continued to launch powerful assaults that would have expended a common arcanist. After dozens of arcane orbs slammed into the trapped necromancer's chest, Elethain finally managed to hold up his hand in submission.

As quick as it came, the force holding Elethain vanished, leaving him gasping for breath. Fangdarr, wholly unfamiliar with arcane magic, watched the necromancer struggle to his feet. Before he could ask what had happened, Aesthéa tugged on his arm to retreat through the door. "Come, Fangdarr. To Wudhyvn."

The orc followed his lover, casting a glance behind him at the elven king sitting on his emanating throne. A small smile could be seen on Nelthalius' face before it was blocked from view as Elethain fell in line obediently behind them.

CHAPTER TWENTY-NINE

EILFEYN

Fangdarr, Aesthéa, and Elethain rode out of Jesmera on the marvelous mounts they had been offered to aid in their quest—Eilfeyn, the stablemaster had called them. In the orc's mind, they seemed the perfect representation of nature's attempt at an elf in animal form. They pranced through the darkened forest on thin yet strong legs, their pale white skin a vibrant contrast save for the purple etchings on the beasts' fur.

As the group had been leaving the city, dozens of elves all stood in shock at the sight of an orc riding atop their most proud creature. Fangdarr's impressive size made him stand even taller than the enormous branching antlers of the eilfeyn beneath him, only adding to the elves' perspective of the orc's disrespect. Even the beast seemed to share the sentiment, as it continuously reared its head back in subtle attempt to poke at him with its sharp horns. Fangdarr did his best to disregard the insubordinate act, not wishing to provoke the stag-like creature. With luck, the eilfeyn grew bored quickly—having caused only little bloodshed.

As the graceful mounts pounded and bounded through the thick forest, the band made excellent time. When night was upon them—though Fangdarr couldn't tell from the ever-present darkness of the woods—Elethain called out to make camp. Both elves slid easily from their eilfeyn before taking a moment to whisper their gratitude to the prideful creatures. Fangdarr, on the other hand, had never been on such a delicate creature before.

The chieftain looked down at his eilfeyn as it stood waiting in irritation. It cast an eye back at the orc that remained on its exhausted backside. Fangdarr felt an immense amount of judgment from the seemingly sentient animal, as if it thought he were some sort of half-intelligent oaf. Getting up on the steed had been a simple task for one of his size, but, in truth, dismounting seemed an entirely different experience. Fangdarr realized his feet were only a hand-length from the ground, so he tenderly slid to the side. As his foot touched the damp ground beneath, he cracked a smile. It was removed from his face quickly, though, as his eilfeyn bucked harshly toward him with its hip, tossing him to the ground.

Fumbling to his feet, the orc's black-skinned cheeks darkened in embarrassment. Fangdarr scowled at the animal. His furrowed brow lasted only briefly, however, replaced by a guttural chuckle. "Funny Elf-Deer," Fangdarr said, extending a hand in offering. The beast stared at him, obviously displeased, before strutting away smugly.

Aesthéa came by with her mouth spread in a playful grin. "It seems he likes you."

Fangdarr shrugged and raised his voice well enough for the eilfeyn to hear, "Good. Otherwise I eat him." He cast a glance back to the pompous beast and couldn't hold back his laughter as his gaze met the wide-eyed steed staring back at him in terror.

After joining in the hilarity as well, Aesthéa began setting their camp with Elethain. Once they were settled, she handed Fangdarr a piece of bread. "We do not have meat in Jesmera. Though, I imagine it will be available in Wudhyvn. The satyrs do not share our beliefs in that regard, despite being followers of Cerenos." The orc took the food graciously and began chomping down on the soft loaf. His face contorted in disgust as the odd taste of dried plants scraped along his tongue. He looked down to see the inside of the bread held a myriad of crushed herbs.

Fangdarr smiled politely and took another bite, pressing down the bile building in his throat at the foreign morsel. How he longed for meat in that moment. His eyes scanned the camp in hopes of distracting himself from the unfamiliar taste. The chieftain noticed there were neither tents nor fire for the first time. "We are safe here?"

Elethain chimed in, his voice straining from the bruising in his chest. "Yes, this is not the barbaric lands of Crein. The risk of being attacked in the night is nearly non-existent."

"'*Nearly*'," the orc reiterated. Fangdarr didn't know what sort of creatures may be crawling in the darkness around them, lying in wait for them to sleep. But he trusted his friends. This was their homeland, after all. Leaning his back against an ashen tree, the chieftain freed the stress from his shoulders and let out a long exhale before Aesthéa came to sit by his side.

Aesthéa caught a glowing fae as it fluttered around. Fangdarr watched as she whispered softly into her cupped hands as they held the miniscule being before releasing it. The orc blinked in confusion as it faded into the distance, only to return with a dozen others of its kind. The pack fluttered closer and closer, illuminating the area in a soft glow and landing in the center of the encampment. Up close, Fangdarr could see that each resembled a human, apart from wings, a pair of dangling antennae, and four pitch-black eyes that seemed too large for their face. The fae stood and danced amongst each other, as if joined in festivities. Fangdarr gasped in wonder, overwhelmed by the vastly different land he had found himself in.

Aesthéa slid closer to Fangdarr, pulling him from his state of disbelief. She leaned her head against his chest and placed his arm over her. "Aren't they beautiful?"

"They different," the orc began, his thoughts trailing to the familiar memories of his own homeland, "but beautiful in their own way." He finally understood Elethain's eagerness to return to Jesmera during his task in Crein—a land he held no love for. Fangdarr stared over at the necromancer, who was resting on the other side of a large tree to avoid bearing witness to the cuddled embrace of his companions. "As with those," Fangdarr added, pointing to the three eilfeyn sleeping together in a small circle, their heads resting on the rump of the next to keep their antlers off the ground. "Even sleeping, they regal."

"Though they are not the might of the boar, nor the ferocity of the wolf, as you would have it."

"Nor heart of the bear," the orc added with a playful wink. Aesthéa nudged Fangdarr happily and planted a kiss on his hand as he looked on at the marvelous steeds. He truly did find them to be beautiful. Foreign and majestic, though splendid and powerful in their own way. "But, no. They not," the orc finished with a hint of sadness.

Aesthéa embraced the orc more tightly, hoping to squeeze away his growing heartache. The elf quickly fell asleep against Fangdarr, bringing a smile to his face as her gentle snoozes were infinitely more effective at ridding him of his looming thoughts. The chieftain looked around the deep, bluish-green wood shrouded entirely in darkness from the thick canopy blocking the moonlight above. Then to the joyous fae that danced in their camp and the white-skinned, ethereal beasts that had carried them on their journey. And, lastly, to his lover. Her long, pointed ears piercing through a sheet of black hair and her pale skin a stark contrast to his own.

"Just different," the orc said before closing his eyes.

CHAPTER THIRTY
SACRIFICE

Elethain awoke to a hand pressed over his mouth for the second time in the recent days. After his immediate defensive reaction, his eyes turned to anger. The elf looked up, seeing the owner of the pale, white hand sealing his lips.

"Not surprised to see me, Elethain?" the intruder toyed, lifting his hand from the necromancer's mouth. "Go ahead, call out if you must."

Despite the abrupt rouse that had ripped him from slumber, Elethain didn't shout. Instead, he let out a deep and heavy sigh. "I assumed you would come eventually."

"And here I am," came the reply, paired with a sinister grin. One that had been shown to many before they were left bleeding on the grass.

Elethain rose to his feet. "Well, here I am as well," he said with passive dreariness, arms spread wide. "Take your payment of blood, Chakal."

The assassin's smirk was wiped from his face. Chakal was on him in an instant, closing the gap faster than Elethain could see, pressing a curved dagger tight firmly against the necromancer's throat.

Even with the cold blade against his skin, Elethain still didn't flinch. "If you are going to kill me, do so." He took a step forward, forcing the dagger even deeper into his skin, drawing a line of blood.

Chakal's eyes turned to shock, not expecting his victim to press forward. A deep anger took over, though, as the assassin couldn't stand the thought of not playing out his kill in whatever manner he pleased. He withdrew the weapon from Elethain's neck and replaced it with a swift kick of his boot.

Unsuspecting the attack, Elethain fell to the ground. He rose once more, questioning his confidence and rubbing the bruise that was already beginning to form under his skin.

The elven assassin eyed his opponent. "I am not here for you, despite your interference on the ship. I am sure you will never make that mistake again." The wide smile that spread across Chakal's face was disconcerting, as always, even to the one who knew him closer than any other. "I seek the half-blood. Is he here?" the elf asked, though he already knew his answer even before waking Elethain.

Still rubbing his sore cheek, Elethain didn't even hesitate to answer. "He remains in Wiston to aid in the war."

Chakal let out an exaggerated sigh at the thought of backtracking. He had followed the group's movement along the coast, even to Wiston. Though when he discovered Fangdarr was on a ship to Y'thirya, he assumed Bitrayuul had followed, tucked safely beneath the arms of his brother. The elf turned to Elethain and raised his eyebrow in curiosity. "You would betray him so easily?"

"I care naught for the half-orc. Truth be told, he disgusts me. I would not trade my own life—nor even a half-eaten apple—for his."

"Ah, there is the Elethain I know," Chakal said with a boisterous laugh that threatened to wake the others. From around the large tree at Elethain's back, shifting could be heard from his companions.

Elethain stared directly into his old friend's eyes and took another step forward. "We are who we are, my friend."

Chakal smiled. Not the wicked promise of death that was oft upon his face, but a *genuine* smile. The first that had crossed his cheeks in centuries. He clapped a hand on Elethain's shoulder. "Know this, brother. You are the sole one in all the world whose death I would mourn after I have claimed it."

Despite the comment being laced with looming threat and the arrogant thought that victory was guaranteed, Elethain returned the smile with his own. He knew such a statement from the fundamentally monstrous elf wasn't one that would ever be spoken again—to him or anyone else.

The necromancer watched with memories of the past deep in his mind as Chakal turned to leave. As the assassin walked easily away, he stopped next to the proud eilfeyn still deep in slumber. His hand slid over one of the beast's marvelously luminous skin. Chakal closed his eyes as his own memories began to flood back to reality. Images of his youth spent tied at the hip to Elethain came to him as he ran his fingers over the animal's smooth, white fur. A single thought lay more prominent than the rest, where he and Elethain had stolen a pair of eilfeyn and rode off into the night, no care on their minds. Chakal reluctantly pushed the memory away, remembering who he was and all that he had become. "You know," he said softly, clinging to the last remnants of his forgotten youth, "I have always loved these creatures." With that, he continued his walk through the wood, heading southeast toward Wiston.

Elethain fought back his own memories of the same event, unknowingly sharing the scene with his long-lost friend. Once Chakal had faded from view, Elethain heard the elf's voice carry through the darkness of the forest as if right next to him. "And I have always loved you."

CHAPTER THIRTY-ONE

HONESTY

Fangdarr rose first the next morning, though he could hardly tell if it was early in the day or still the night. The orc gently slid himself from his lover's grasp. His fanged smile spread across his cheeks as he watched Aesthéa readjust to regain comfort. Slowly, the orc stepped away, careful to not let the brush of the vivacious nature beneath his feet stir her even more.

"Cerenos bless you, 'Chosen One'," Elethain stated sarcastically from behind the large tree.

The chieftain padded to Elethain with curiosity. A multitude of different questions and urges washed over him. To argue with his newly gained title, explaining that it was unwished and unwarranted. To question why the necromancer hadn't acted on his desires to kill him. They were nearly endless. Yet, one stood above all others. Fangdarr sat down roughly at Elethain's side.

"Why you hate me?" the orc asked plainly. He didn't stare accusingly, nor were his words edged with malice. It was a simple question, asked with genuine curiosity.

Elethain nearly burst with laughter—and most likely expected to. He *wanted* to. But the elf found himself racking his thoughts and coming up empty. For all his intellect, Elethain was caught within his own lies to himself. He had always known it. Hidden deep in the darkened recesses of his heart, the elf knew he didn't hate the orc. Not *this* one.

Fangdarr waited patiently, knowing his question may be simple on its face, but that the answer came with the weight of a lifetime of predetermined perspectives. Many moments had passed before finally Elethain let out a drawn-out sigh.

"Because I must."

With that, Elethain rose to leave, unable to maintain the awkward and harsh exposure of truths between them. The orc remained silent as his hand clasped around Elethain's slender wrist. Fangdarr expected some sort of backlash, though none came. The elf simply stared ahead into the dark and foreboding forest he so loved.

"Elf, you my friend," the chieftain began, keeping his tone calm and honest. "And I not Cerenos' 'chosen'."

Elethain kept his gaze fixated on the woods. "That's the problem, Fangdarr. You probably *are*." He gently pulled his hand free and continued his departure.

Fangdarr took in a deep breath and released it slowly. The morning was already too packed with raw considerations. He felt weary again despite just waking. The orc silently cursed himself for his foolish endeavors. There he sat, questioning the inner workings of an elf while his brother and dearest friend fought for their lives. The people of Wiston needed him. How could he spend precious moments pondering such things when the looming threat of annihilation lingered? Guilt began to twist his stomach as he realized his delay may have costed lives. The time for words was at its end. The task came first.

CHAPTER THIRTY-TWO

WUDHYVN

After waking Aesthéa, the trio were speeding toward Wudhyvn. Fangdarr watched as the dark hues of the forest progressively transitioned into warm shades of orange and green. What had once been a shrouding blanket overhead soon dispersed as the canopies above became sparse. The morning sun hung high and let its warmth breath into the blooming flowers that were sprinkled around the path.

As they approached, Fangdarr could smell the succulence of meat being scorched over a flame as it was carried along the breeze. It was a welcome scent that tickled his nostrils with eagerness. The orc gazed at the village with a sense of familiarity. It was much more closely related to his way of life than the elven community, though it seemed more entwined with nature. Huts made of twisted branches and stretched pelts were scattered through the area with no design in mind.

No guards were stationed, nor were there any walls around the village, allowing the group to approach without threat—until they had been noticed. Once spotted, the sounds of the brutish roars, barbaric yells, and even the pounding of a drum could be heard. Leading the formation, Elethain slowed his steed to a halt.

Dozens of satyrs poured from every direction to surround them. It seemed as if their numbers would never end. Even the young and feeble were among the warriors, showing the strength of their community and its bond. Fangdarr couldn't help but lift the corner of his lips. Such a display of pure kinship put his own village to shame. Even though they were more beast than man, the satyrs stood calm and collected. Orcs, on the other hand, would have ripped apart unwelcome visitors without question.

Fangdarr scanned the crowd. He could feel Aesthéa shift her mount closer to him—and for good reason. The satyrs were tremendously vicious looking, even to the orc. The males stood as tall as Fangdarr and nearly as muscular with thick horns twisted and curved uniquely on each head. Their maws were formed into snarls, baring sharpened teeth that could rend flesh with ease. To the orc, they resembled a cross between a mountain goat and a wolf. Their eyes took to the wolf, giving them a much more imposing visage. If their size alone didn't allow the male satyrs to stand out, the blackened-brown fur covering their entire bodies made it simple enough. Between the males, Fangdarr could pick out each satyress, stern-faced yet beautiful.

While the females shared the same backward-facing leg joints as the males, standing bipedally on large hooves from their back legs, their physique was vastly different. Each satyress stood only half a head taller than female elves and possessed a much softer aesthetic than the beast-like males. Their skin from above the waist—as below was covered in thick fur—was smooth and resembled that of an elf, though lightly brown in tint. Green hair that appeared as if grown from the earth itself flowed down their exposed bodies, with long, thin horns piercing through their grass-like manes on each side of their head just above their pointed ears. Despite their beauty, each satyress wore a grim expression that gave evidence to their confidence in battle.

Fangdarr continued to marvel at the discipline of the community. Though part beast, all waited to strike. Whether for command or prompt, the orc couldn't be certain. He expected his answer would come swiftly as Elethain pressed his eilfeyn deeper into the village.

After a few paces, the necromancer halted. With his voice raised and tone deepened, the elf exclaimed, "I am Elethain, ambassador to King Nelthalius of Jesmera. We wish to speak with Chieftain Thrax'ul."

None of the warriors moved. Each remained fixated on Elethain; sharpened stone weapons in many hands, bowstrings stretched back in others. Their discipline was immeasurable. Fangdarr would never have been able to implement such strict order within his clan. Yet, each satyr around him stood at the ready waiting for their chieftain.

Finally, after a tense delay, an enormous satyr exited the largest hut. He approached slowly with determination, luckily with no weapon in hand—a sign that luck may be in their favor. As the chieftain closed the distance, Fangdarr couldn't help but notice the satyr's size rivaled his own, with bulging muscles that couldn't be hidden even beneath thick fur. Thrax'ul was an intimidating force to say the least. With a maw of ivory blades, sharp and long claws, and the most massive set of twisted horns of the tribe, the creature exuded supreme confidence in his gait.

As Thrax'ul stepped through the crowd, his people silently moved out of his path without breaking eye contact on their unwelcome guests. After he had passed, the circle closed around him. He sized up Elethain first, who remained silent and polite despite his urge to press for haste. Once Thrax'ul had finished inspecting the necromancer, he moved to Aesthéa.

Having been around royal exchanges of emissaries and advisors through most of her life, Aesthéa wasn't unaccustomed to meeting those she was unfamiliar with.

However, it was never done in such an intimate breach of space. Her discomfort showed as Thrax'ul began sniffing her hair with short inhales. The satyr's eyes closed as he took in her scent. His quaking voice resounded like a thunderstorm. "Ah, a shifter." Grinning with satisfaction, the satyr moved to the final member of the party.

Each chieftain made eye contact with the other. Fangdarr slowly slid from his eilfeyn and stood nose-to-nose with Thrax'ul. Sniffing deeply, Thrax'ul took in any scents he could. His face became puzzled with unfamiliarity and he moved closer to Fangdarr to inhale once more. "You are unknown to me, yet you smell of the shifter."

The orc was surprised at the crude beast's articulation. Too long had Fangdarr not used the extensive language and correct enunciation that he was taught, he realized. Nevertheless, his response came in the barbaric tongue of his kind. "As you to me," he started, but gave pause before adding, "Elf is mine. I am hers." He didn't wish to give away such intimate details, but assumed it was known whether he spoke it or not.

"You share your life with an elf? Are you elven yourself? Contorted by wronged magic?"

"I do. You reject us?" Fangdarr replied, disregarding the question of his heritage.

Thrax'ul's throat grumbled as if chuckling. "It is not for me to decide where hearts may lie." He saw the couple visibly relax, bringing another 'chuckle'. The satyr simply shook his head at the thought of elves controlling who one could love—one of many differences between the neighboring cultures. His gaze bore into Fangdarr as he repeated more forcefully, "Are you elven?"

Fangdarr filled his chest with a deep inhale, boasting his pride. "Orc. I am Fangdarr, chieftain of Zharnik clan." He pounded his chest proudly but could see Elethain's shoulders slump in disappointment. A wave of confusion and trepidation washed over the orc, uncertain of what he had just done.

Thrax'ul gave a content groan. "Chieftain?" The satyr turned to his people with his maw spread in a wide grin. "*Chieftain*," he reiterated, drawing an animalistic laugh from his subordinates. Thrax'ul turned to Fangdarr. "Alright, *Chieftain*. Let us have contest. If I am bested, you will have your audience."

The orc looked to Elethain who simply shook his head in hopelessness. There was no turning back now. Fangdarr eyed Thrax'ul with suspicion. "And if *I* am bested?"

The grin pasted on the satyr chieftain's face spread impossibly wider. "Then I take your bear as my seventh mate."

Fangdarr's eyes narrowed dangerously. Contest or not, he didn't like that the chieftain had made such a demand. The orc turned to his lover, seeking her choice. He would never partake in such without her consent. Aesthéa held faith that Fangdarr could defeat his foe, but what of the other possibilities? Would the satyr fight fairly, would his people intervene? The thought of being enslaved tormented her beyond belief.

Before the elf could make her decision, Fangdarr had made it for her. "I refuse." His eyes met hers and in a single moment, her infinite gratitude flashed. Fangdarr turned back to his eilfeyn to prepare to leave, much to Thrax'ul and Elethain's surprise. It wasn't Thrax'ul who halted the orc, but the elf. "Fangdarr, we are here at *your* request. You will let mankind, even Cormac and your brother, fall for a single life? You stupid orc! Why bother seeking the aid of the elves in the first place if you were not willing to do what was necessary?"

Fighting back his growing anger, Fangdarr attempted to ignore Elethain's complaints. Thrax'ul watched curiously, as did all other spectators, as the behavior they had come to expect from elves was exposed.

"Aesthéa would gladly give her life to save thousands! Even *human* lives, yet you disrespect her beca—" Elethain's shouting was cut off as Fangdarr grabbed him by the robes, lifting the elf to his face and letting out a vicious roar.

Elethain scowled. "You would condemn your kin for an elf?"

"I would condemn *all*!" Fangdarr shouted as he threw the necromancer to the ground.

Thrax'ul clapped his clawed hands together and gave a bleated laugh at the spectacle. "Well then, it seems you would have bested me easily, Chieftain." Another laugh came from his followers. In truth, Thrax'ul's interest in the orc had only heightened tremendously at the show of rage. Above all, the bestial chieftain wished to challenge those he respected. It wasn't for power or pride, but for respect. Respect for himself and for those he faced in combat. A simplistic and unwavering need for one to give their all, using only the gifts their god had bestowed upon them.

Fangdarr eyed the satyr angrily at the insult. He knew that Thrax'ul was only attempting to goad him into a fight but couldn't deny its efficacy. The orc stomped forward, ready to demand their contest come without the strings tied to his lover. But he was halted by Aesthéa's hand against his chest. He looked to her with curiosity, his eyes staring directly into hers.

The druid peered back at Fangdarr, then to Thrax'ul. "*I* will fight him."

CHAPTER THIRTY-THREE

PLAN

It was hopeless. How could they win? Thoughts of dread filled Bitrayuul's mind as the next catapult was dragged just past the edge of the Lithe by four ogres. Whether the enemy had been hiding it on purpose or it had simply taken longer to pull the giant mechanical contraption through the dense wood, none could be sure. All that was known was the sacrifice they had made to remove the first, and that no more ballista bolts remained.

The half-orc stared at Viktor's corpse. It was as if the man knew of their failure, as the smile that had previously been frozen on his face had been wiped away. Bitrayuul's eyes stung with tears and his heart sank. *There can be no victory here. Where are you, Fangdarr?*

Bitrayuul felt a rough shake against his shoulder and came to his senses. Cormac was yelling into his face, trying to be heard over the victorious roars of the beasts below. "Lad! We gotta go!" The old dwarf pulled at his friend's arm. Finally, the half-orc shook away his lamenting thoughts enough to follow Cormac down the path, ducking to avoid spears. They rushed into the command room and shut the door behind them.

Removing his stifling helmet, Bitrayuul gasped for breath. It wasn't the sprint that had winded him, rather the crushing weight of despair. His chest felt as if it would burst. Rapid drumbeats of his heart made his ears ring and he began hyperventilating. Meanwhile, Cormac paced around the room, smacking himself on the head in futile attempts to create ideas for their new dilemma.

The dwarf grew irritated at Bitrayuul's lack of composure. "Bah! Keep yerself together, son! This be war! Folks die. There be time to weep at the end, if we make it there. Help me figure out a way to take out that damned catapult!"

Bitrayuul's gasping breaths refused to cease. Between rapid inhales, he asked, "What's . . . the point? What if . . . there are more?"

Cormac looked at him incredulously. "More? Then we break those too! This be war, son! *War*! We ain't poppin' trolls in the caves no more. The men just lost their commander. They're nearly leaderless, save for a few lower rankin' generals, no doubt. We need to find 'em and get a plan goin'."

Before the half-orc could say anything, Cormac stormed out of the room, leaving Bitrayuul to himself. He cried out loud once the dwarf was out of sight, wailing with abandon at all that had transpired in the short time. He regretted not going to Jesmera with Fangdarr. It seemed so impossible that not even a day had passed since his brother's ship had left the docks and already their task seemed a lost cause. Bitrayuul wondered if he even wished for his brother to return at all, for there would only be death waiting for him. The thought brought more woeful sobs to the half-orc as he felt more alone than ever before.

After many moments, Cormac stomped back in, followed by a pair of armored men. Each had a sigil marking their rank on each shoulder. Luckily, Bitrayuul had managed to return his helmet over his head before they noticed him, both to hide his tear-soaked face and heritage. The men could afford to see neither in that moment.

"Bit, these lads are the remaining generals: Koda and Silas," the dwarf captain stated flatly as he peered over a map of the surrounding area. "Alright, lads. We need a plan. Viktor has fallen after taking out the first catapult." Neither he nor Bitrayuul missed the wide-eyed shock on the soldiers' faces with of the news that their leader had fallen so early in the battle. "Ye both are in charge now, and yer needed, don't ye doubt. The men can't be findin' out Viktor's fallen and that another catapult approaches. Or that we be out of ballista bolts and got no way to dismantle it. The wall is already cracked. A few more boulders and we're lookin' at a breach. So, what be yer suggestions, generals?"

Frozen in fear, the men looked to each other. Neither could form words as the influx of such grave information had tied their tongues. It seemed evident that neither had ever been in battle. He exhaled slowly and walked over to them, finger raised and waggling at their faces. "Listen, lads. I know this be yer first war. And I know yer scared it'll be yer last. It'll be the last for many, sure as stones." He could see the apprehension growing in their eyes, so he quickly moved on to his point. "But the men need ye. The people of Wiston *need* ye. And not *just* ye. They need us all. Every man behind this wall be fightin' for those they love. Yer wives and sisters, yer mothers and children. They *need* ye. Some of us may die, aye. But if we don't fight, *all* of us will. We have to try. Failure ends in a fate none should suffer. Now, I need ye both to work with me and stand vigilant. The men need to see that their efforts aren't wasted and their leaders are confident in victory. Can ye do that?"

Koda stepped forward, though his eyes spoke the truth to his hidden feelings. "I will fight, dwarf."

Each of the three sat in silence for Silas to step forward as well. The man was drenched in sweat and the room began to smell of urine. His mouth quivered as if about to speak but couldn't find the words. It seemed as if he had forgotten how, for his eyes darted around to each of them in confusion and fear. Cormac had every desire to shake the man until he spoke but refrained. It needed to be the man's choice.

Tears welled up in Silas' eyes and still his lips trembled. He couldn't do it. He knew he couldn't. With each pounding of the war drums and stomp of the enemies at their gate, he shrank in fear. The debilitating nature of war had sunk too deeply into his heart and swallowed him whole, dragging him to a state of terror he couldn't break. His shame and fear only grew with each passing moment as his comrades continued to look at him in expectation.

Finally, the distraught general managed to form sounds that could hardly be heard. Before any could ask him to speak up, Silas took his sword from its scabbard and thrusted it beneath his chin into his skull. The others in the room jumped back in surprise as blood squirted out vigorously and began to pool at their feet. Bitrayuul and Cormac watched as Koda tried to staunch the flow with futility. Desperately, he pleaded for their help as tears welled in his own eyes as his friend's lifeblood continued to spill onto the floor.

"He-help me!" Koda begged, pressing his hand against the wound. His eyes looked frantic as he realized that neither Bitrayuul nor Cormac were moving to aid him. "Why won't you help!?"

Cormac sighed. "Lad, he's gone."

"No! We can—" the man started to respond, though even he didn't believe his words. Despite the evidence, Koda continued to press his hand tightly against the wound even as it leaked through his fingers. In shock, he finally backed away after setting Silas' head down against the ground gently. Once he had moved away, Koda noticed the vast amount of blood that had poured onto him—the blood of a friend. He frantically tried to wipe it away, though his gauntlets just smeared it more and more.

Cormac walked over with a piece of leftover cloth and began wiping away the blood. "Yer alright, lad." After repeating himself a few times and clearing the crimson stains as best he could, Koda finally settled. The dwarf handed him the cloth. "This. This is what yer fightin' for. To stop the streets from bein' painted this color."

Koda sniffled back his tears. He nodded slowly to Cormac, who nodded back. The man took a breath to steady himself. "What do we do?"

"What are your thoughts, General?" Bitrayuul asked, struggling to keep his voice composed.

The man took another deep breath. "Well, if we have no ballista, it seems impossible for us to break the catapult. Unless we can find an arcanist, perhaps?"

"We've already sent a few soldiers to seek out some mages, but I don't expect them to find any," Cormac replied.

"What about the king's son?" Koda saw the pair's confounded expressions. "Lucien, the prince. He's rumored to be an exceedingly powerful mage for a human. One to rival even elves a thousand years his senior. Have you spoken with him?"

Bitrayuul looked at Cormac, then turned to Koda. "We have spoken to none, save you, Silas, and Viktor. Where can we find this Lucien?"

"I'm not sure, he tends to hide out in odd places, from what I hear—the dungeon, alleyways, cellars. I've only met him a handful of times. He is . . . interesting."

Cormac lifted his eyepatch and rubbed his eyes in weariness. "Send for him, if ye can. It shouldn't be hard to find a prince. In the meantime, what else ye got?"

Koda made a mental note to send a soldier or two for Lucien. "As I said, the catapult is hopeless. An arcanist can launch a flaming barrel of oil at the catapult, at least one as powerful as Lucien can. However, if we cannot find the prince, we should start devoting our efforts to the wall. With another catapult on the horizon, a breach is imminent. We need to start bracing the wall to buy more time."

The dwarf nodded his approval. "Good work, son. Send for Lucien, he's our best hope right now. The catapult is the biggest threat. If they can't break through the wall, then we can slowly whittle down our enemy before we starve. We've sent some friends to Jesmera in the hope that the elves will join—but don't hold yer breath. Do ye know if any have sent word to the dwarves?"

The general shook his head. "We didn't have much warning. An envoy was sent, but his horse returned with his severed head tied to the steed's tail, covered in feces. From more than just the horse."

Cormac ran his hand over his beard, praying to Bothain that his people were safely tucked within their homeland. Bitrayuul, too, shared consideration for the dwarves and hoped that their deity kept them from harm beneath the bosom of the mountain.

"I think," Bitrayuul began slowly, still gathering his thoughts, "we should follow Koda's advice. Let us expect that the catapult cannot be dismantled and plan accordingly. We *must* prepare for a breach. We will need men to brace the wall, as you suggested, Koda. But we should also plan a backup defense. Even through the funneled entry, the sheer force of their number needs to be considered. We only have a few thousand men. They men will not be able to maintain their stamina against the endless masses, even if fighting only twenty at a time."

Koda sighed in agreement. "What do you have in mind?"

"Well, we only have twelve barrels of oil, hardly enough to keep a fire going for long. But we should consider planting a few barrels at the breach with coal lined on the ground behind the wall, placed after the braces are up."

"At that point, why bother? Should we not reserve all the oil we can? And what purpose does the coal serve?"

"Once the wall is breached, the enemy's momentum will be insurmountable. Nothing will stop them from breaking through our ranks, even if it costs them thousands. The fire will slow their advance. Trolls can only be culled by fire; it prevents their regeneration. As such, their fear of fire is one to be used to our advantage."

"And the coal?"

Cormac cut in. "Oil burns hot and fast but dies quick. The coal should take to flame enough to stay burnin' for a bit. It's just to throw 'em off guard. Trolls and orcs don't wear boots," he said, pulling his own armored boot to a stool as if the explanation was necessary. "Ye ever try to fight while standin' on burnin' coals?" Koda shook his head at the rhetorical question.

"Right. Well, sounds like we got a plan for defense," the dwarf continued. "Go ahead and get the wall reinforced and oil and coal in place. Just a few barrels, we need to save some. And don't forget to send for Lucien. We need to be thinkin' about an offensive strategy for that catapult as well." As he finished, Cormac peeked through the small window to view the siege weapon's progress. He cursed and rushed outside to get a better view before coming back in with an angry scowl on his face.

Bitrayuul rose to his feet. "What is it?"

"The damned catapult is already in place. Seems like it's been there for a while, but it be odd we ain't heard any stones crash against the wall yet. Oh, and it's dark out."

With nightfall upon them, Bitrayuul knew the men would be even more anxious. He turned to Koda. "Send those men, quickly. They need to know there is leadership. It's you, Koda. Your presence must be known by the men. Get out and set the preparations. Cormac and I will consider how to deal with the catapult.

With a nod and a salute, the general exited the command room and began shouting orders loudly, bringing a smile to Bitrayuul's face. It was good the man understood the dire importance of hope and his role as a beacon the men could cling to. The half-orc looked to Cormac, who was slowly planting his rear on the stone floor, careful to avoid the pool of blood from Silas' corpse. "What are you doing?"

The dwarf grumbled. "Koda can handle the preparations. We don't know when the wall will break, now that the catapult is in position, and I'm exhausted. If ye think I'm goin' into battle without me strength, ye'd be wrong." Cormac groaned in annoyance, unable to get comfortable. His eyes scanned the surroundings before falling on the deceased general's prone form. With effort, the captain scooched himself the short distance until his head rested against Silas' calf.

Bitrayuul sat in silence, racking his mind for ways to demolish the catapult, but none came. But now that there was a moment of relative silence—save for the dwarf's loud snores and the endless shouts of war around them—he could hardly keep his eyes open. It wasn't long before he leaned against the wall and drifted to sleep.

CHAPTER THIRTY-FOUR
STANDARDS

"Wake up, lad!" Cormac shouted, followed by the sound of weapons clashing.

Bitrayuul rose to his feet on instinct, nearly falling over in dizziness from the abrupt movement. A sudden loud *thunk* resonated within his thick helmet after a blow glanced off his head. Fully awake and panicked, the half-orc's eyes met the glowing orbs of a troll, its rotten smile staring at him past its long nose.

Before Bitrayuul could react, the creature recklessly stabbed forward, thinking to pierce the half-orc's armor. But the feeble stone-bladed dagger fractured on impact against the superior steel and fell harmlessly to the floor. The troll's eyes shifted from deviousness to surprise and fear as its opponent's bladed fist came sailing through the air, impaling its face. Blue-tinted blood sprayed forward, showering the half-orc warrior. Bitrayuul cursed, realizing there was no fire to be found. The long blade of his gauntlet remained embedded deep within the troll's brain, preventing it from fully regenerating. He knew the moment he retracted the blade the beast would heal as if it had never occurred.

"Cormac, we need fire!" the half-orc shouted over the sound of the dwarf's heavy shields slamming into a pair of trolls in the doorway to the west.

Straining to drive back his foes, Cormac grit his teeth. "Check the table, lad!" Already he was covered in the seemingly endless fountain of blood from his opponents. "And hurry, more comin'!" he urged, seeing another pair of trolls rushing up the stairs.

Bitrayuul scanned the table a few paces away. There! Fragments of coal and a bit of spilled oil were left from when they had prepared the bolts with Viktor. Bitrayuul ripped his blade through the side of the troll's head to create a new wound, hoping it would buy him more time. He dashed to the table and grabbed a rolled piece of parchment, uncaring for its contents in that moment. Furiously, he rubbed the paper onto the table where the oil had soaked into the wood, hoping to pull out enough to ignite. Confident it was at least partially sticky, the frantic half-orc smashed the paper onto the coal remnants, sticking them to the oil residue.

Makeshift torch in hand, the half-orc warrior breathed easier, thinking his goal complete. However, he realized he had no flame with which to light his pathetic torch anyway. Before he could even curse his stupidity, the troll behind him latched onto his back and began gnawing at his neck. Though Bitrayuul couldn't see the creature, he knew of its instant regret by the wails its pain as it dismounted.

The half-orc turned toward his foe. Its smile returned as the punctures on its body healed immediately. Bitrayuul could see the reflective oily substance on the troll's skin, wishing he could will fire from nowhere. "Cormac, I need fire!"

From the other side of the room, the captain gave an irritated grumble. He smashed both foes with his shields before quickly turning toward the half-orc. "I got me own damned problems, lad!" Despite his complaint, Cormac closed the distance to Bitrayuul quickly while his opponents were dazed and slammed the blades protruding from his shields together in front of the parchment. The blades clashed harshly, shooting sparks into the air. With luck, a few caught on the oiled paper and burst it into flames. Cormac was already walking away grumpily, muttering under his breath. "Light yer damned torch now!"

Bothain's beard! That's why they don't fight with steel weapons! Bitrayuul fumbled with the torch, dumbfounded at his own ignorance. He thrust it against the oncoming troll's chest and ignited the creature. He rushed to Cormac's side, lighting the pair of trolls in the doorway just in time before the next two had funneled through. Together, Bitrayuul and Cormac were easily able to dispose of the reinforcements, leaving five blazing corpses in their wake. Smoke filled the confined room, paired with the stench of burning flesh, forcing them out.

They looked into the city behind them, expecting to see that the enemy had broken through. Instead, a handful of smoking carcasses could be seen all around—even near the livestock to the west. The pair looked to each other in confusion, wondering how a few trolls had managed to get around the wall. They heard the *thuuuuu-wop* of the catapult in the distance, followed by the sight of a dozen trolls sailing through the air in a wide spray, providing an answer. They watched as the trolls smashed into buildings, rooftops, or the hard ground in a bloody heap, shattering most of the bones in their body, only to rise shortly after.

"Bothain's beard . . .," Cormac whispered in awe.

Bitrayuul was nodding his agreement when he shouted unexpectedly. "The wall!" He took off quickly through the command room, holding his breath through the rotten stench, and coming out the other end. Cormac appeared behind him as the half-orc breathed a sigh of relief. The wall was still intact, with toppled carts, barrels of oil, coal, and other debris planted against it.

"Well, we got good news," the dwarf started, turning his head to the catapult. "This means they might be out of rocks. For now."

The pair turned back to the city, seeing the men quickly close in on the trolls and dispose of them with ease. They picked out General Koda among the ranks and watched him push through to reach the spiral staircase before ascending to stand next to them.

"Glad to see you're still in one piece," Koda said, noticing the black smoke billowing from the structure.

Cormac clasped arms with the man in greeting. "How bad is it?"

The general shrugged. "Not as bad as it could have been. We lost a handful of men, but they managed to stop the trolls from reaching our livestock. Three trolls were caught in the palace, though. They had landed on the castle and made it all the way to the throne room and taken out twelve of the king's guards before being brought down. I was there at the time, speaking with a few of the political advisors—nasty folk."

"How fares the king?" Bitrayuul requested.

Koda sighed heavily. "Not well," he started, though quickly clarified upon seeing his comrades' eyes go wide in fear. "No, no, he suffered no injury. He is furious, though, that such a small number managed to nearly topple us. '*What is three compared to a million?*' he asked the advisors. He wasn't pleased with their inability to respond, either."

Bitrayuul and Cormac nodded. This was a heavy blow. The king needed confidence that they could withstand the attacks that came. Confidence in the men, in himself. But knowing only three—less enemies than they had just disposed of their own—had made it that far would be demoralizing. They hoped that word wouldn't spread through the ranks.

The sound of a troll shrieking to the north broke the air, followed by cheers of men. *Perhaps a morale boost is needed*, Bitrayuul thought. "General, you said the trolls were captured, not killed?"

Koda nodded in response. "Why?"

Already, Cormac had a smile on his face, knowing which Tarabar tradition Bitrayuul had in mind.

* * * * *

A while later, Bitrayuul and Cormac followed behind the growing crowd of cheering soldiers as they carried the trio of live trolls to the wall. Each was skewered, anally to orally, with a long, thick pike and held in the air as a standard. Their regeneration abilities worked against them, as each troll was able to stay alive through the whole ordeal, stuck in excruciating pain.

Upon seeing the tears streaming down each troll's face, Bitrayuul was forced to look away in guilt. Had he never suggested such a brutal display, the creatures would have simply been put to death. Yet, he knew the men needed a sense of victory. This was bigger than him, or the three trolls that had cut down good men who only sought to defend their homes. The half-orc couldn't fathom his sudden weakness, especially facing annihilation. But he couldn't deny it. Perhaps it was his brother's change of perspective, or the losses he had suffered and his own pain he was forced to bear. All he knew was that the barbarism lifted the soldiers' spirits.

So, he watched. He watched and smiled politely, clasping arms with the men who held such joy for the fate they were inflicting on the unfortunate creatures. Bitrayuul even watched as the trolls were carried up to the battlements to face their own army, wriggling in anguish. He watched as the men he considered good and just cut open their bellies and stuck a torch in the gut of each one, holding them on display as they died in torment in front of their kin.

But worse, he listened. Bitrayuul listened to the heart-stopping screeches as their mouths ripped open wide enough to force out screams around the wide pikes that were driven through their bodies. His ears couldn't shut out the subsequent booming cheer of the men as they watched in glee while the trolls died in unfathomable agony. Nor could they hide from the deafening silence that rang through his mind as the trolls stopped their wailing and passed into the afterlife.

CHAPTER THIRTY-FIVE
CONTEST

All fell silent in surprise at Aesthéa's challenge. The satyresses in the crowd were mighty, though none would dare oppose Thrax'ul. She had expected hushed whispers from the female members of the tribe in her support but was met with angry glares and shocked expressions on every face.

Thrax'ul pondered his actions. He expected to win, of course, and with it would come the spoils he wished. However, if he were to lose, his grip on the clan may falter. The satyr took a step forward. "The same rewards are offered." He eyed her closely as he slid a finger along her arm. Thrax'ul gave a low chuckle as Fangdarr shifted angrily on his peripheral.

Aesthéa slapped his hand away. "Agreed. An audience or my enslavement." Her stern gaze showed her seriousness.

"I have no slaves, elf," the satyr said with a wide grin. "All become willing, in time."

"Aesthéa, I must obje—" Elethain cut in, but was halted by the druid's raised hand. He sighed heavily and backed away.

Aesthéa raised her head in pride, defiantly showing she accepted the consequences should she fail. "The terms of engagement?"

The customary grumbling chuckle came from the satyr's throat. Between the excitement of combat with a new adversary and the crude thoughts that came to his mind of the nights to come, his elven prize beneath him, Thrax'ul was beaming with eagerness. "You may use only the gifts bestowed upon you by Cerenos," he replied, flexing his immense physique and bringing cheers from his people.

Over the commotion, Aesthéa shouted, "I accept your challenge!" and turned away. She cast a quick glance at Fangdarr with a reassuring nod. He smiled in response, supporting her decision, though the worry on his face couldn't be hidden.

Elethain and Fangdarr retreated to the edge of the circle with the tribe, granting the pair enough room for their duel. Aesthéa stood at one end, her eyes closed and lips moving slightly in prayer. A dozen paces away was her opponent in all his splendor. His tribe continued to cry out in support of him, growing louder with each flaunted flex of his bulging muscles.

Finally, the onlookers quieted as an aged satyress peddled onto their field of battle, slowed by a limp and leaning heavily on a carved staff. Her fur was hardly able to be seen beneath the overwhelming layer of bone and wooden relics tied to her person. Nearly toppling over in the process, the decrepit creature managed to traverse a few paces before halting. Taking the staff in her hands and planting it into the ground, glowing in a bright, blue light. The shaman gripped the wooden shaft and raised it high into the air, chanting all the while.

"Cerenos!" the ancient satyress started, her voice dry and harsh. "Bless these warriors who seek to prove themselves in your name! Use your guidance to influence the outcome and prove who is just!" With speed that defied her age, the shaman smashed the glowing staff into the grass. On impact, the light from her instrument exploded and seemed to spill to the surrounding area, turning the grass to a dull bluish-green.

Fangdarr heard Elethain scoff and turned to regard him. The necromancer whispered, "It is an ancient spell of shamanism that is believed to demand the presence of your god—if you put stock in such a thing."

The orc was completely puzzled. He didn't hold faith in the gods but was more surprised at Elethain's reluctance to believe the spell's efficacy, being a follower of Cerenos himself. Even more interesting to Fangdarr was the shaman. The orc recalled his own shaman within his clan, who he had left in charge in his stead. And Vrik, the previous chieftain he had bested whom had attempted to use his magic to win the *Ortuk Malid.* From his experience, shamans only held the ability for temporary imbuements and enhancements. Could this shaman differ from orcish shamans, or was Elethain's skepticism well-founded? He couldn't be sure.

Once the shaman called for the fight to begin, Aesthéa expected her brutish opponent to charge her ferociously. But the satyr remained calculated and disciplined, slowly pacing the circle. She pivoted from the center, watching his every move. Despite his muscular physique, the chieftain seemed to move easily.

Finally, Thrax'ul pounded his chest and roared aloud before charging forward. He closed the distance much quicker than Aesthéa anticipated and led with a large open claw. Dipping into a roll, the elf barely avoided the blow.

After her evasion, Aesthéa sought to catch Thrax'ul by surprise at his rear. But he had already spun around with another claw sailing through the air. Her eyes widened, realizing he had expected the maneuver as she tried to duck beneath the swipe but was too late. The satyr's sharp claw sliced open her shoulder and knocked her away.

On all fours, Aesthéa coughed harshly from the wind knocked from her lungs. The sound of hooves stomping closer forced her to look back to her opponent, who refused to relent. Still too dazed to react, she felt his rippled arms close around her torso and lift her into the air, squeezing her as hard as he could.

Struggling to concentrate as her bones threatened to shatter, the druid shifted into her bestial form, breaking the chieftain's grasp. After falling to the ground, Aesthéa immediately got her feet beneath her and launched forward. Her maw clamped down on Thrax'ul's arm, sinking teeth into his flesh. The satyr let out a cry of pain as green blood squirted out, followed by a heavy pummel of his balled fist atop her forehead. Though, it sank the teeth deeper into his arm, the blow disoriented the druid enough for the chieftain to grab the top of her snout. After prying her teeth free, Thrax'ul shoved her back and each stood staring at the other with more respect, breathing heavily.

* * * * *

Fangdarr watched in a series of mixed emotions. Worry, fear, elation, more fear, surprise, joy, then more worry. It was nearly too much for him. He had never been so frightened of a fight before—even against dozens of enemies. The vulnerability he felt tore at him, allowing another to seep in like a festering wound.

End this. He seeks to rid you of what you love most, O' Roaring One. Step forth and claim his life, before the beast ends hers.

The orc's face twisted in confusion. Crepusculus had attempted to coerce him on more than one occasion, but never for the sake of his friends. It was always whispers to push Fangdarr toward domination. The change caught him off-guard, and he couldn't deny the truth to the shadow dragon's words. Thrax'ul stood only a few paces away, his back turned to Fangdarr. It would be so easy . . ..

* * * * *

Thrax'ul and Aesthéa both rushed forward. The satyr lowered his head to ram her with his thick skull, while the shapeshifted elf swiped out with her claws. Each suffered the opponent's blow in the trade. Aesthéa was knocked back but seemed unharmed. Meanwhile, her opponent suffered a deep gash on his hip and was dripping blood down his fur.

Aesthéa charged back in quickly, standing on her hind legs to reach more exposed skin. The satyr grabbed her arms as she attempted to slash at his neck, firmly locked in a stalemate. In response, the druid opened her maw to bite at Thrax'ul's face, forcing him to lean back as far as he could. Hastily, the chieftain ducked his head beneath her chin and pressed up with his sharp and twisted horns, bringing a whimper of pain from the bear as they poked at her neck.

* * * * *

Fangdarr's fear grew immensely as he expected to see his lover's neck get impaled. His weakened resolve only increased the enticement of the cursed whispers that echoed inside his mind.

Now! Kill him! End the beast! Do you not love her, O' Cowardly One? Will you not fight for her? Do you boast to damn all who stand between you only to shy away as she dies in front of your very eyes?!

The orc began sweating profusely as he struggled to maintain control. The whispers refused to cease, playing against his weakness without mercy. He knew Crepusculus sought only to control him, but the words aligned with his fears for Aesthéa. Fangdarr groaned and whimpered, grabbing his skull as he watched Thrax'ul's horns continue to threaten the elf, demanding she yield.

Elethain took note of Fangdarr's state curiously, though expected it was due to the fear he felt at Aesthéa's fate, as he fared little better. The necromancer too watched in tremendous worry, though for selfish reasons. He knew he could never return to his beloved home if Aesthéa fell, even of her own accord. Nelthalius would only offer deaf ears to Elethain's excuses and would cast him out or execute him, and all he had worked for would be lost. Both Fangdarr and Elethain stared on, suppressing their fears and fighting the urge to step in and end the fight knowing it would only start another war between the elves and satyrs.

* * * * *

"Yield!" Thrax'ul shouted to her, gritting his teeth as he struggled to hold her arms back and prevent her from being freed. No response came from the druid apart from whines of pain. "Yield!" he repeated, stretching his legs as high as they could go, pushing harder into her neck.

The elf's mouth was clamped shut from the force of the horn beneath, preventing a response even if she wanted to. It was too late now, she was all in. This was her decision to fight a beast she knew could overpower her. *Do I wish for slavery?* she pondered to herself in that moment, wondering why she would surrender herself to such a challenge. Her eyes could hardly stay open from the pain. Yet, she could make out Fangdarr on the edge of the ring, writhing in anguish. Despite his worries, he still believed in her.

Steeling her resolve, Aesthéa knew she needed to change her tactic. Her mind called out to the roots deep within the earth from the only two trees in the area, though they were far. It took all of her will to pull the twisted tendrils from the ground as she fought through the pain. After a few agonizing moments where she thought her will might break, the roots broke through the ground, shattering the enchantment on the field and returning the grass to its normal color.

Thrax'ul cried out in surprise as the vines entwined themselves around him. Aesthéa collapsed to the ground once the satyr was pulled from beneath her, finally free from the deadly spike beneath her neck. Wearily, she shifted back to her elven form and compelled the roots to pull Thrax'ul away.

Fangdarr and Elethain both cheered over the now-silent crowd as the battle turned in Aesthéa's favor. The orc's renewed excitement and hope shut out the dragon's damning mutterings and returned him to reality. He roared in triumph for his lover. Even Elethain couldn't prevent himself from shouting in support.

The satyr bleated a weak roar filled with anger and defiance. He was so close! His victory was sealed! Thrax'ul could tell by the elf's scent that she could shapeshift, but her ability to control the roots came as a surprise. He pulled against the thick cords with all his might—even managing to break a few—only to be entrapped again. Humiliated in front of his followers, the chieftain continued to bleat in rage.

"Yield," Aesthéa said softly, still trying to catch her breath.

Thrax'ul kept up his rampant bleating, losing all composure at his loss. He thrashed and pulled, refusing to believe his strength couldn't match simple roots of a tree.

Aesthéa retracted the roots toward the ground with the satyr still entwined. Over his outcries, she repeated, "Yield." Still, he wouldn't. Her eyes turned to a scowl, angry that he wouldn't accept he was bested. With undeniable will, she pulled the tendrils deeper into the ground, Thrax'ul with them. "YIELD!"

Even under threat of death, the satyr would still not give voice to her victory. The elf huffed with anger and scanned the eyes of the crowd, their mouths all open in awe. She hated the way they looked at her. She hated the attention. The way they just watched as she was about to claim the life of their chieftain. All the growing frustration—and that incessant bleating! Aesthéa yelled, pressing all her strength into the earth in a final demand.

The spectators watched in fear as the ground around Thrax'ul shot high into the air, trapping him within a tomb of gnarled vines and clumps of dirt. Aesthéa's exhilarating rage pushed her further, forcing her victim to be slowly crushed, praying he would finally submit. The bleating stopped and was replaced by groans of pain, though she continued to squeeze him. She could hardly control herself. In that moment, all she wished for was to break Thrax'ul completely. To make him suffer for the slavery he had demanded of her and the pain she would have suffered had she not been victorious. Finally, the elf could hear the muffled shouts from within, though it took many more moments for her to release him from his prison, dropping him to the ground.

Thrax'ul groaned with the impact, completely beaten. He rolled to his back slowly, embarrassed from the shame he had suffered in front of his tribe. His wolf-like eyes stared at Aesthéa, who still held her scowl of discontent. The satyr spread his mouth into a wide smile before saying, "I am bested, elf."

Aesthéa fell to her knees and cried out in relief as the adrenaline fled her body, leaving her in a heavy state of fatigue. Tears streamed down her face. Tears of joy for her victory, of relief for avoiding enslavement. And of anger for being pushed to such lengths. Fangdarr and Elethain were with her in an instant, offering calming hands on her back. Her lover lifted her in the air and sat the elf on his broad shoulder for all the crowd to see.

At first, there was only silence. But it broke with booming shouts and cheers. A small smile formed on Aesthéa's face, though she still didn't enjoy the attention. The elf felt empowered by their support, especially after defeating their chieftain. She raised her fist proudly and yelled victoriously, only spurring the tribe more in her honor.

As the cheers drowned out all else, the druid closed her eyes. *Thank you, Cerenos,* she prayed silently. *For watching over me and granting me the gifts that allow me to fight for what I believe in.*

CHAPTER THIRTY-SIX
AUDIENCE

A green eyed satyress escorted the trio to the large hut in the center of the village. As she held open the cloth flap, the warrioress placed a hand on Aesthéa's wrist gently and offered a gentle nod of approval. Unsure how to react, the elf politely smiled in return before proceeding into Thrax'ul's abode. Once inside, the smell of crude desires blew Aesthéa in the face. It was as if the hut was used exclusively for carnal recreation—and it very well may have been. Ahead sat Thrax'ul in a throne of wood and fur with his numerous wives at his side, tending his wounds.

"A fine battle, druid," the satyr greeted. Now that the heat of battle was over—and he still seemed to hold control of his tribe—he seemed at ease. In the end, the chieftain got what he wanted most: an opponent who gave their all.

Aesthéa said nothing, still refusing to let go of her anger. Fangdarr—too relieved to care about past insults—sat on a stool across from the tribe's leader before motioning to Aesthéa to do the same. Elethain chose to remain standing, unwilling to touch the barbaric materials within the hut.

The satyr smiled pleasantly after the druid took her seat. All his attention seemed to be fixated on her. "Well, you have won your audience. What brings you to Wudhyvn?"

Fangdarr spoke first as one of the satyr's wives poured a sweet-smelling liquid into four animal skull cups. "We seek ai—" the orc started before being halted by Thrax'ul's raised hand.

"Enough, *orc*. I was speaking to the elf." Extending a hand to Aesthéa and paying no mind to Fangdarr's furrowed brow, the tribe leader waited patiently for her to speak.

Seething in fury at the blatant disrespect he was shown, Fangdarr quieted. Speaking up now would only bring ruin to their quest—and insult his companion as well. He leaned back in his stool and folded his arms. Aesthéa looked at him to ensure he was content before speaking. Fangdarr grunted in frustration but nodded.

The druid settled, not wishing to get involved in the childish contest of masculinity between the two. "We need your assistance, Chieftain. Crein is at war and the humans are on the verge of annihilation. At their gates are trolls, ogres, and," she paused, "Orcs."

Thrax'ul scoffed and raised an eyebrow at that. "An orc and his allies seek aid from his own kind?" He bellowed out a bleated laugh that sparked his conditioned wives to join in the merriment. "The creature is more cowardly than I thought!"

Unable to control his rage any longer, Fangdarr rose to his feet with a snarl. "Come! Let us see who coward!"

Thrax'ul remained unfazed on his throne, sipping his drink. Without breaking eye contact with the boiling orc chieftain on the verge of frenzy, the satyr said, "Continue, elf."

Fangdarr's teeth bared even more at Thrax'ul's ignorance of his challenge. His expression turned to a smug smile, however, as he realized his opponent's dismissal was a concession. "Coward," the orc whispered while returning to his seat. If the satyr heard it, he didn't show it.

Aesthéa had to stop from shaking her head as the two bickered while a task of great importance was at hand. "Fangdarr is one of them, yes. He is the greatest of his kind and does not fall victim to the false promises of a shadow dragon. A shadow dragon which *Fangdarr* felled," she defended.

"*You* conquered Crepusculus?" Thrax'ul asked the orc with skepticism.

Fangdarr's smile spread wide across his face, beaming with pride. Elethain, however, didn't hesitate to steal his thunder. "With the assistance of others, no doubt." The elf cast him a sidelong glance before turning back to the satyr. "You know of Crepusculus?"

Another bleated laugh came from the beast. "Of course. We may not be as long-lived or as notorious in our bookkeeping as you elves, but our kind passes down the stories of our ancestors through each generation. We are a tightly bound tribe and seek to keep knowledge through the ages. We know little of Crein and the rest of the world outside of Y'thirya, in truth. But Crepusculus once resided atop the Eye of Cerenos, long ago."

Elethain seemed deeply intrigued and profoundly confused that he had never heard such an account before. His pursuit of power had led him to extensive research of the living dragons of the world. Yet never had he heard of the shadow dragon residing so near Jesmera. "How long ago was this?"

Thrax'ul pursed his lips together in contemplation. "It is hard to say. We do not keep track of the years, elf, only the events that had occurred. My estimation would be long ago, as Crepusculus' nature led to conflict."

"What you mean?" Fangdarr interjected. His own curiosity was as high as Elethain's due to the unwanted visitor trapped within his mind.

"Crepusculus began attempting to convince the other dragons to wage war on all races, seeking domination of the world. It believed dragons were the rightful rulers and wished to turn all to ash and rot where they may slumber in peace for eternity. Some joined, others refused, leading to a great war between the dragons. There were never many to begin with and no one knows where they came from. But the war wiped out all but a few, according to Aurum, the dragon who threw down Crepusculus and claimed the Eye of Cerenos.

"Aurum befriended our kind and provided us with a wealth of knowledge," Thrax'ul continued. He could see the three were riveted. "Did you know there are creatures known as trolls that can regenerate entire limbs? All because a tribe hunted down one of the remaining dragons—a vicious red—and feasted on its blood. Consuming the blood of the drake gave the tribe the ability to heal immediately, granting them a huge advantage over the rest of their kind. Eventually, they had either eliminated or bred out the non-gifted, leaving only those with the magical enhancement. I have never seen a troll, myself, though such a feat is one I would enjoy seeing."

Elethain was nearly shaking with frustration. All this time the elves had looked down upon the satyrs and considered them unworthy of sharing the island of Y'thirya. And yet, the tribe possessed such knowledge! He could hardly believe it. Once again, his prejudice had blinded him.

The satyr sighed. "None of that matters now. Aurum is gone, as is Crepusculus. Let us pray to Cerenos that the remaining dragons follow the ideologies of the former. Right, Elethain?"

Hardly noticing he was gripping the clear globe on his pendant, Elethain's distraction broke as he realized the implication of Thrax'ul's words. "You . . . you knew?" The elf's expression turned to confusion as the satyr nodded in reply. "And still you did not strike me down?"

Letting out a grumbling chuckle, Thrax'ul responded, "Aurum was told to be a kind spirit who favored *all* races equally. I am confident that no ill will would be held by the drake, and as such none is held by me."

"But how did you know?"

"The Eye is watched at all times by our kind. It is sacred to us. We know all who approach and all who leave. There is a story of an elf and his kin ascending, long ago. When you came to us on behalf of your king in the past, I saw your pendant and the golden beast inside—moving of its own accord. I know not how his fate came to be, nor how you enslaved him. But I see that he is no longer within your pendant, and

Crepusculus remains in his place." Thrax'ul rose to his feet, careful not to spill his drink, or the others that remained untouched on the wooden table.

Elethain clutched his hand more tightly around the pendant as the chieftain held out his hand. The elf knew it wasn't a request, though the greedy instinct in his head screamed to refuse. His shoulders slumped as he handed over the necklace.

Holding the crystalline globe in the air, the satyr watched as the miniature shadow dragon roared in his direction. The reduced stature had done wonders to truncate the dragon's threat, to say the least. Casting a glance to the nervous and sweating necromancer, Thrax'ul slowly handed the orb back to its master. Elethain released the breath he had been holding in with a huge exhale of relief as he slid the cord around his neck once more.

"Now," the satyr said as he returned to his throne, "back to the task. How many strike at the humans?"

Aesthéa sighed. "The enemy number is nearly limitless. We expect a million."

A quick bleat of laughter escaped Thrax'ul as he choked on his drink. "A *million*?! Cerenos be kind, that is not a war. That is an extermination!"

The party couldn't deny the truth to that statement, and their faces showed it. Yet, Fangdarr refused to give up hope. Not while his brother and Cormac stayed to fight. "We have chance. Can beat them. But need help."

Thrax'ul rubbed the base of his horns. "Orc, such a number . . .. How can I damn my own people for a conflict they have no part in? This is not the concern of the satyrs. We are peaceful in our own small corner. These wars are not our doing."

"You speak the truth, Chieftain." Aesthéa's voice revealed her desperation. "But some day it may be. If the humans are eradicated, how long until they cross the channel? How long do you suppose your village of wood and bone can last against an army that shattered the stone walls of a city? This *is* your fight, Thrax'ul. Maybe not today. Maybe not in your lifetime. But someday, this threat will be on our beloved island and the only allies that we may have called upon will be gone from this world. You must join today or know your kind will perish with the rest of us."

A smile spread across both chieftain's lips. Fangdarr was intensely proud of Aesthéa's commanding presence, while Thrax'ul was more inspired by her passion. Thrax'ul eyed Fangdarr intensely. "And what purpose does the orc serve? Are you not afraid he will betray you for his own kind?"

To Fangdarr's surprise, it was Elethain who spoke first. "Fangdarr has proven himself to our cause on numerous occasions. I hold no love for orcs, I can assure you. But our quest would have been lost already had it not been for him."

"And he is chosen by Cerenos," Aesthéa added.

Thrax'ul didn't miss Elethain's eyes rolling in disbelief, despite the druid's conviction. The satyr turned to Fangdarr. "Is that true, orc? You are the subject of my god?"

The orc chieftain looked uneasily at his friends. "I do not follow Cerenos."

Aesthéa rose from her seat hastily, spilling the three drinks on the table. "I believe it! Without any doubt."

After a tense silence, the satyr rose. Slowly, he walked to a small window in the thick cloth, looking at his community happily working together on their day's activities. Thrax'ul closed his eyes and listened to the sounds of his people, taking in their easy chatter as the morning sun shined brightly in their camp's clearing. He knew it was his duty to protect them. But fighting for those he had never met at the cost of many of their lives wasn't a decision he ever wanted to consider.

Thrax'ul turned back to face them with a grim expression. "Alright, druid. I will give you your chance. You and Fangdarr will go to the Eye of Cerenos and prove he is worthy. If what you say is true, the satyrs will go to war."

Aesthéa smiled widely and jumped onto Fangdarr with joy. The orc, unconvinced such proof would be possible, asked the question she wouldn't. "And if I'm not?" The druid's excitement died quickly at Fangdarr's lack of faith in her conviction. She looked at him incredulously before turning to Thrax'ul.

"If you are *not* the chosen of Cerenos, then you will all leave and do as you see fit. There are no strings. You are already forsaken if you seek to fight in this war. Any hostility I add would be cruel."

"And myself?" Elethain asked, not forgetting that he had been left out—a fact that irritated him more than a little.

"You shall remain with me, where I shall pass on knowledge that may aid you in my stead. If you wish."

The necromancer couldn't hide his joyous expression. He was mesmerized by the intellect of the beast-like chieftain. It was as if the creature knew his every thought. Elethain nodded graciously, eager to learn more of Aurum's knowledge—something he had failed to do prior to ridding the world of the benevolent creature.

Fangdarr looked to Aesthéa as she was waiting for him to act, a hint of disappointment still in her eyes at his skepticism. The orc hated that he had made her feel that way, but what did she expect? He was never one to believe in the gods. Why did she expect him to immediately put his faith in Cerenos simply because it was where hers lay? Fangdarr ran his finger through her black hair as he considered what to do. He was certain he would fail the test and disprove Aesthéa's beliefs, which would break her.

Clasping Fangdarr's hand in her own, Aesthéa's eyes spoke for her, letting him know that she was certain he would succeed. With a sigh and a smile, Fangdarr faced Thrax'ul. "Take me to tree."

CHAPTER THIRTY-SEVEN
FODDER

Bitrayuul's eyes remained fixed on the charred corpses long after the fires had subsided. The soldiers had wedged the pikes firmly atop the battlements, leaving the three 'banners' exposed for all the enemy to witness. After witnessing the brutality of the humans, the horde's ferocity had grown exponentially.

Though no friend to trolls, a pair of ogres could no longer bear the taunting. The creatures had grown so enraged that they each ripped a small tree from the forest and dragged the trunk all the way to the wall before hammering against the loose stone. The heavy blows shook the ground, sobering the soldiers' mirth and silencing their laughter. Despite the threat, Bitrayuul couldn't bring himself to raise his great-bow against the beasts who were justified in their outrage. After all, the half-orc knew this was *his* doing. It was he who had suggested such barbarism. He could only close his eyes in regret as he turned away.

Pushing through the men that rushed to the battlements with bows in their hands, Bitrayuul returned to the command room slowly. He knew what would come next and that the blood to be shed was on his hands, even if it was his enemies'. The half-orc heard more than a dozen soldiers pull back on their bowstrings as he shut the door behind him. The thick door shut out the sound of the strings snapping forward, but Bitrayuul didn't miss the halting of the vibrations beneath his feet. Or the booming cheers and resounding laughter of the men once more.

Cormac turned to see his friend's shoulders slumped. "Ye alright, Bit?"

Koda looked up from the bloodied maps he was surveying to greet Bitrayuul as well, not as keen on the subtle body language as the dwarven captain. "Ah, Bitrayuul is it? Please, come sit. We must plan." The man seemed nearly on the brink of insanity. His hand shook nervously as it was extended to the half-orc in the offer to take to a stool. Despite it only being the first morning after the war had come to their gates, the general's eyes were already dark and baggy.

Realizing he hadn't moved, Bitrayuul took a step forward and nodded his thanks before sitting on the small wooden stool. His eyes scanned the room and noticed that the trolls he and Cormac had disposed of previously had been removed, as had Silas' corpse, but the stench and blood remained. He felt nauseous and knew the war would only get worse from there.

"Any word on that mage, General?" Cormac asked, pulling Bitrayuul from his deep trance.

Fidgeting still, Koda tried to speak and act at the same time. He fumbled around with both his words and the maps he was looking through, "Uh, he, umm . . . yes . . . no! No, sorry . . .. No news yet."

Cormac just shook his head. He knew Bitrayuul was probably in a similar state from all the chaos. The thought that he might be the only who could keep a level head, which weighed heavily on the dwarf. Stressed about being the unappointed leader simply due to his resolve, Cormac secretly wished for another to take his place. But he couldn't back down. Despite his lack of interest in taking the helm, the captain knew the war would end quickly if Wiston wasn't led by those who could make hard decisions.

Bitrayuul cleared his throat. "What plan do we have for the trolls being launched over the wall?"

Koda stopped moving altogether and simply stared at the documents. He slumped back into a stool and let his arms hang limp and head dipped low in distress. "I don't know." He let out a heavy sigh. "What *can* we do? We can't reach the catapult, so they can continue to send trolls over as they please. At least until they obtain more rocks from the forest—which should be any day, depending on how many they picked up on their path here." The man removed his gauntlets and tossed them onto the table. Bitrayuul and Cormac noticed his hands were severely burned as they were raised to his weary eyes.

The pair were curious about the man's scars, though it didn't seem the time to ask. They realized they had never given Koda much thought. At first, he appeared to be an unprepared young man who had yet to see thirty winters and was now in a war that would most likely claim his life—and all others. Yet, even in the face of possible annihilation, he was there, trying to make a difference for his people.

Cormac placed a hand on the man's shoulder in comfort and took the last remaining stool. As he sat down, he failed to notice one of the three legs was splintered. Under the dwarf's weight, the leg buckled, and he fell to his side with a loud crash. In an instant, his allies were up to aid him, but Cormac burst into laughter. "Damn the stones, them trolls won't have a chance to get at me if this blasted stool has its way first! Bahaha!"

Pulling the dwarf up to his feet, Koda and Bitrayuul couldn't help but join in Cormac's infectious laughter. They carried on for a long while, just laughing at the absurdity of his comment and how truly dire the situation was—and that it may be avoided by the malicious intentions of a stool. The light-hearted event had lifted the mood tremendously. Nothing had changed. If anything, the dwarf's comment held a truth that all feared to recognize. But even with its deeper meaning, the humor proved effective.

In the final embers of humor, Cormac dragged a small crate toward the table and shook it for good measure, testing its stability before hopping on. He wiggled his rear, checking to be certain it wouldn't spontaneously shatter beneath him. Once content, Cormac smiled. "Right. Now that *that's* settled . . .," he started before he was interrupted by the muffled sound of the catapult swinging its arm through the air. They knew the men could handle the few who came over the wall, so they paid it little mind.

"The trolls ain't much of a problem now that we're ready for them. But ye be right, once they get more stones the wall won't hold much longer." Cormac clapped Koda's shoulder again. "Good job on gettin' it reinforced."

Bitrayuul's eyes fell on Koda. The poor man could hardly stay awake even as Cormac spoke to him. "I think Koda should rest. We can reconvene in the afternoon. The sun is coming up and our enemy has lost the advantage of darkness." The half-orc rested his hand on the general's forearm. "You need rest. The men need to make sure they're resting as well. Send for a man or two and make sure that all soldiers are still rotating shifts through the day. If the wall falls and they are fatigued, we won't hold."

Cormac was nodding his approval even as Koda started to protest. But the man didn't have the energy to even continue. "I'll send for the men, son. Ye rest here, we'll watch over ye, don't ye doubt." A weak smile spread across Koda's face, glad to be in the presence of such formidable and compassionate warriors. Without another word, the man slowly rose from his seat and walked to the corner of the room before lying down on the cold stone.

After sending messengers through the army, Cormac and Bitrayuul pondered their plans, looking over documents and maps of the city for the tenth time. They were unaccustomed to human civilizations. Had this been Tarabar, they would have known much more about the structure of the city and any defensive capabilities that may be in place. Their homeland had numerous tunnels stretching in every direction through the mountains. Unfortunately, such a practice wasn't performed in Wiston.

"These damned humans . . .," Cormac started. "I don't see any contingency plans or escape routes in these pages. Sure, buildin' on a cliff is a great idea! The enemy can only come at ye from one side, but let's be sure to avoid makin' ourselves a way out in case we be cornered!" His sarcastic remarks tickled at the half-orc's heartstrings as he knew his father would have made the same.

Bitrayuul's eyebrow raised as a realization struck him. "Why don't they just leave? Cross Death's Channel and remain on Y'thirya. At least the civilians could be safe."

Cormac was already shaking his head. "Nah, the soldiers won't abandon the city. And the king knows the elves won't let them land. They may trade with one another at times and be at relative peace, but they ain't *that* welcome. And the civilians staying in the city gives the men somethin' to fight for. Ye take that away, and this place won't last long."

The half-orc couldn't deny the logic. "Well, it seems our only option is to repel the enemy then."

"Could always dig our way out. But I'm thinkin' there ain't the time," the captain added. "Plus, where would we dig? Into the water? Anywhere we dig, the enemy is there waitin'. Now we've just made a tunnel for them to access the city."

"We are lucky the enemy does not know how to dig."

"Oh, no. They do," Cormac refuted. "But there ain't no way they can dig either, don't ye doubt." He watched Bitrayuul's face turn to confusion. "If they dig, they either need to dig so deep that the enemies standin' above them don't fall through—which would take a *lot* of diggin', trust me. Or they would need to make sure the enemies don't stand on that path, which would give away that they're diggin'."

Bitrayuul still looked perplexed. "So? What would it matter if we knew where they were digging? We have no catapults or ballistae. We have no way of stopping them from digging."

Cormac nodded. "Aye, that be partly true. We don't need catapults to stop them from diggin'. If we drop rocks on them—which there are plenty around that would do the job—we'd break through the dirt. Then we could drop oil and coal in the hole or shoot them down with arrows. The only problem is that we can only do that once they get to the wall, of course. Then, they'd either try to push through, and most likely wouldn't make it, or would be forced to turn and try to keep diggin' until we run out of rocks."

"I still don't understand. Wouldn't they eventually get through?"

The dwarf sighed. "*Maybe*. But if they do, it would be much easier for us to hold the hole and plug it with their own flaming corpses than it would be for them to breach. And . . .," he started, grabbing a map of the wall. "If they continue to cut across and try to breach while we keep stoppin' them, then they b—"

"Then they break their own line!" Bitrayuul interrupted, bringing a scowl to Cormac's face. The dwarf shoved the map aside in playful irritation.

"Right, lad. If they cut across, then they're shootin' themselves in the foot for when the wall finally breaks. The biggest advantage they have is numbers. If the wall falls, they can pummel us until they break through our frontlines. Ye put a hole in the ground in front of the enemy's one entrance an—" Cormac stopped, just realizing what he said. "Oh. Oh, lad. I think we got ourselves a plan."

Bitrayuul nodded excitedly. "We can dig a deep and wide hole just beyond where the wall is breaking. Then, if the enemy breaches, they'll fall in. At the very least, it should drastically slow their momentum."

As Cormac was looking for the map he had thrown aside, the sound of the catapult swinging could be heard in the distance again. They paid no mind, as usual, except that this time the yells of the men were much more concerning than normal. The pair looked to each other before rising to their feet and rushing out the door. As they exited, they saw the huge, meaty ogre soar through the air just above the wall. It flailed in the air before crashing through a small building.

Even from their distance, they could tell the ogre was already dead prior to the impact. Bitrayuul's eyes went wide and he looked over the wall in concern. Cormac's face twisted with curiosity. "What is it, lad?"

The half-orc scanned the masses for the two ogres that had fallen previously, but they were nowhere to be found. The sound of the catapult's arm swinging through the air came again. Then they saw it, the second ogre's lifeless corpse sailing through the air same as the first, though this time with better aim. The hulking mass connected against the wall only a short distance away from the deep crack before falling to the ground. After it landed, the scattered beasts closed in around the corpse and began dragging it back toward the catapult.

"Seems they found a rock," Cormac said grimly.

CHAPTER THIRTY-EIGHT
OGRES

"Ya missed again, Tod!" the lumbering oaf scolded in his sluggish, guttural voice as he tugged on the mechanism to reload the siege machine.

The other ogre angrily stomped over, leaving giant, flat footprints in the earth. Shoving a finger into the nostril of his ally, Tod replied, "Eh! They brings it back, see? Quit yappin'!" He extracted his finger from his friend's squished nose—a string of slime and snot coming with it—and pointed toward the dozen trolls dragging their dead companion's corpse.

Rubbing his agitated nose, the rope-puller was quick to point out the obvious. "Ya shot Lubnut too high! Now the hoomins got him!" His concern was evident as he worried about what the soldiers would do to his friend's corpse.

"Eh! Lubnut too skinny! He last to eat all the times! How's I supposed to know he fly too high? Trolls was okay when they flew high, Bebbo." Tod crossed his arms stubbornly.

Raising an eyebrow, Bebbo pondered the legitimacy of his ally's words. After many moments lost in thought, he finally raised his head with the spark of knowledge. "Trolls is immortal, Tod! Ya smash 'em and they just squish back togethers."

"So whats?"

"So, Lubnut ain't!" yelled Bebbo with his arms raised in the air, dropping the rope once more and resetting the catapult. As the loading arm fell, two trolls were crushed beneath the counterweight with a bloody squelch. Bebbo and Tod quickly lifted the dense weight off their corpses before watching them reanimate and start raising their voices in anger. Dropping their load and disregarding the string of insults from the revitalized trolls, Bebbo turned to his companion. "Ya sees? Good as new!" Together they laughed and set to work setting the siege weapon once more.

CHAPTER THIRTY-NINE

WEAKNESS

A dozen orcs dragged the ogre's massive corpse through the ranks toward the catapult. Bitrayuul and Cormac looked to the ogre that had fallen behind the wall in their midst, thankful that at least one had been removed.

"Right, let's get a move on that hole, Bit," Cormac instructed, knowing their time may be short. Bitrayuul nodded in agreement and both took off down the spiral staircase. By the time the half-orc had pressed himself through the small entrance on the ground level, Cormac was already speaking with a pair of soldiers.

"—over there. General Koda says we need to make haste and dig deep and wide. At least three men's height wide and ten deep. Then he wants to put the rest of the oil and coal at the bottom. If that wall breaks, he wants to be good and sure that the first damned beasts through that hole go straight into another one!" At first, Bitrayuul was confused by the dwarf's statement that the words came from Koda rather than themselves, but quickly realized the purpose. The men needed to believe in their leader. Their *human* leader. If a small lie got the task done and put more faith in Koda, he cared naught.

Cormac pulled at his friend's arm, dragging him to the side after the soldiers dashed away to retrieve men and digging tools. "Come, lad. I want to speak with the king."

As the pair made their way through the Military District and toward the castle, they heard the sound of the catapult far in the distance. Each turned their head, expecting it was too soon for the ogre to have been dragged back so far already. Their suspicions were confirmed as another dozen trolls flew above the city, followed by warning calls from the men and the sound of clashing weapons and grunts as the trolls were disposed of. Confident the threat would be handled with ease, they continued toward the castle.

Passing through the steel barrier between the Military District and the courtyard, Bitrayuul was surprised to see hundreds of civilians spread everywhere. They slept on the ground, cried beneath cloth blankets, and some even tried to peddle wares. "Aren't these people supposed to be hiding in the northern zones, Cormac?"

The old dwarf grunted in response. "Aye, they should be. They think they're safest in the center, near the king. Truth be told, they're just goin' to end up gettin' themselves and more people killed, don't ye doubt."

Bitrayuul was surprised at Cormac's blunt and negative response. He pondered if the dwarf truly believed that about the people who resided there, looking for hope and safety. But after scanning the crowd, he took note that the soldiers spread through the ranks were surrounded by civilians. If the enemy broke into the courtyard, it would be complete chaos. The people would run rampant, shattering any disciplined attempt to repel the invaders. Cormac was right, these people were just a hindrance.

The thought unsettled the half-orc as they pushed through the ranks to reach the castle. He hated thinking so little of people, even if it was the truth. Bitrayuul's focus shifted, however, as the guards outside the large, intricate doors halted them.

"State your purpose!" the first yelled louder than necessary as he lowered his spear threateningly to Cormac's eyes.

The dwarf held back his desire to respond in anger. "We need to see the king. We have updates on the war at the wall. We're with General Koda, but he's back at the command room seeing to the men and sent us in his stead." At the mention of Koda, the men relaxed and nodded to each other. The second guard banged his fist on the heavy door four times in a discernible pattern: *Bop-bop-BAM-bop*. After a moment's delay, the door slowly creaked open, just wide enough for them to squeeze through.

"Hurry! Go!" a soldier inside shouted, bringing confusion to Bitrayuul and Cormac's faces as they were ushered quickly through the door. As soon as they were through, they looked back to see the soldiers outside pushing back dozens of civilians who were attempting to get inside. Their fearful desperation was etched plainly on their faces. Bitrayuul felt a wave of guilt as the last bit of light disappeared behind the closing doors and the helpless people who only wished for shelter pounded away on the other side.

Even worse, as their attention shifted to the interior of the castle, they saw the room was entirely empty. The half-orc gasped in surprise at seeing the pristine castle unmarred by civilians like the courtyard outside. He had thought those outside were simply the excess, yet none were allowed in. Bitrayuul looked around, completely perplexed as to why the people weren't allowed to reside in at least this portion of the large keep. Just the entrance room alone—which served no purpose other than to host balls or other festivities, it seemed—could easily house double the number that waited outside.

Cormac gave the half-orc a quick jab in his side as they passed through to the next room, mouthing the word, '*Focus*'. In the royal chamber, they were surprised to see that the king wasn't seated on the throne. One of the guards escorting them traversed the great hall and headed down an adjacent hallway. After many moments, he returned and beckoned for the visitors to approach.

"At least he didn't run away, eh?" the dwarf whispered to Bitrayuul. They crossed the room to a small corridor lavishly decorated with fine rugs, a dozen beautiful paintings, and tapestries embroidered with the family lineage. A single plain door lay ahead.

The guard slowly opened the door to allow them inside, followed by four guards to ensure the safety of their king. Cormac and Bitrayuul tiptoed to the bed at the other end of the large room. Bitrayuul stopped and turned to the men. "If the king is sleeping, it would be best not to disturb him."

Each of the soldiers' eyes dropped low. One whispered back, "He isn't sleeping, sir."

Bitrayuul turned to the bed where he could see Cormac already sitting down, whispering to the bundle of blankets. The half-orc looked back to the guards who maintained their downcast expressions. He jogged to the bed, expecting the worst. As he approached, Cormac held out his hand for quiet, listening to the whispers being returned from beneath the heap. Bitrayuul breathed a sigh of relief, glad to know the king hadn't perished.

However, as soon as the half-orc looked upon the king's face, his relief slipped away. The once prideful, compassionate man lay withered as a husk of his former self. The bags beneath his eyes sagged tremendously and the bones within his face could be seen beneath the skin. *How could he fade so quickly?!* Bitrayuul wondered. It had only been a day and already the toll of responsibility had cowed the king. Dariel could hardly keep his eyes open as he struggled weakly to look up at the half-orc. In that moment, Bitrayuul was grateful for the enclosure of his helmet. For if the king could see his expression of hopelessness beneath, he may have passed into the afterlife then and there.

Cormac, however, did well to hide his thoughts as he spoke with the broken man. "We're doin' well out there, yer majesty. Those lads of yers were trained well. We're breaking catapults and only got one left, just a matter of time."

The half-orc was confused. They had come to tell the king of their status and the dire situation they were in. Some of what the dwarf had said rang true, but it was nowhere near the truth that the king needed to hear. Bitrayuul shifted uncomfortably, waiting for a chance to speak. However, Cormac—ever perceptive—latched on to his wrist and squeezed tightly, begging the half-orc to hold back his words.

"Ye just rest up now, aye? The lads will push out them beasts soon enough and all will be as it was. Yer people will rejoice and rebuild to once again thrive." A tear rolled down Dariel's cheek and a mild smile spread across his bony cheeks. "Just hang tight, sir. Cling to hope." Cormac laid a hand on the king's shoulder above the thick blankets in reassurance before rising to his feet. As the dwarf stepped away to leave the room, each of the guards looked to him with profound gratitude and tears rolling down their own faces for doing what they couldn't. Cormac nodded in return before exiting and closing the door behind him.

Bitrayuul looked to the guards, then the king. Every desire in him begged to tell Dariel the truth and remain honest. But at what cost? For what purpose? The man was dwindling on the brink of death, clearly starving himself as some sort of self-punishment for the predicament they were in. His despair ran so deep that he seemed to no longer care if he lived or died, despite the thousands looking to him for guidance. With a heavy sigh, the half-orc turned toward the door with the guards following behind him.

Upon opening the door, they could see Cormac slumped on the floor with his back to the wall, sobbing profusely in his first real display of emotion since the war had started. The proud dwarf looked up, tears and snot dripping down his face, noticing they were watching him and rose quickly to his feet. He wiped away the mess from his face with his long beard as best he could, leaving a web of snot between the thick hairs and cleared his throat. "R-right," he started, his voice breaking. "Let's get back to the wall." Before any could argue, the dwarf turned away and started trotting back toward the throne room at a brisk pace, trying to hide his muffled cries and sniffles.

Bitrayuul watched him go, uncertain of how to act. He had no idea the dwarf was even struggling in the first place, let alone why his encounter with the king was the event that set him off. The half-orc felt completely at a loss. Having no alternative in mind, he fell in line behind Cormac and began the trudge back toward the wall.

CHAPTER FORTY

SELFLESS

Bitrayuul had followed Cormac back to the Military District without either uttering a word. The dwarf trudged to the large hole the men had started to dig and put his hands on his hips, nodding with approval. Though only mid-day, the hole was already the correct width and a man's height in depth. At that rate, they may have the pit completed within two days, it seemed.

After inspecting the work and commending the men on their efforts, Cormac went to re-count the inventory of coal and oil. Bitrayuul followed behind but cast a glance toward the gloomy sky as the sound of trolls hissing and screeching came above. He tried to trace the trajectory of the living projectiles, but it was impossible to track all dozen of the creatures. His quick check had served him well, however, as Bitrayuul caught a glimpse of one of the trolls smashing against the western battlements just beyond the command room. *Koda*!

Unfortunately, one unlucky troll landed squarely next to Bitrayuul, catching him by surprise and pulling him from his distraction. The creature's body shattered against the ground with the sound of bones fracturing. As soon as it had landed, its body immediately began mending back to form. Bitrayuul hacked away at its corpse while calling for a torch. In short time, a young soldier had retrieved a flame and set the troll ablaze. Without pausing to check his work, the half-orc sprinted toward the wall, yelling for his dwarven companion as he departed.

Cormac eyed him curiously before understanding where Bitrayuul was headed. Propelling his stubby legs forward, he charged after his friend, each praying to Bothain that the last remaining human leader awoke in time.

After finally squeezing through the unforgiving spiral staircase, Bitrayuul kicked open the eastern door of the command room. He let out an immediate sigh of relief as his eyes fell upon Koda's back, standing victoriously over a flaming corpse, blue blood dripping from his sword. "Koda, thank Bothain you're alright," the half-orc said as Cormac came up behind him.

Still facing away from them and staring down at the troll that sought to end him, the general slowly turned to face the pair. Their hearts sank as they saw Koda's eyes closing and blood pouring from the side of his neck where an artery had been severed. The man fell to his knees, unable to even form a weak smile. Bitrayuul dashed forward to catch the wounded soldier as he started to fall.

"Koda? Koda! Come on, Koda. Stay with us. You'll be alright, Koda. You got it. The troll is gone. You got it. Just open your eyes, Koda. Keep them open," Bitrayuul begged, his voice breaking as he tried to pry open the man's eyelids to no avail. The half-orc could feel Cormac's hand on his shoulder. "No! Not yet! He'll be fine! Get that fire, Cormac! We need to seal the wound!"

With his voice barely a whisper, the dwarf choked out, "It's over, lad."

Bitrayuul shook Koda's lifeless form harshly. "No! It's not! It can't be!" He sobbed painfully when the man didn't respond. Bitrayuul knew the blow this was to their cause. In that moment, it seemed the final bit of light they had in hopes of victory—even survival—fell with Koda. He continued to shake the corpse, only spilling more blood onto himself and the floor.

Sighing deeply, Cormac sat down on the crate at the table, placing his bald head in his hands. The dwarf's mind was racing. *Do we tell the men? Do we hide his body, throw it over the wall? Will they listen to me? Bitrayuul? What choice do they have?* Dozens of questions rushed through him, each only serving to overwhelm his already high stress level.

As if the pain they were suffering wasn't enough, the sound of that damned catapult continued in the distance, launching more and more trolls over their walls and killing unsuspecting men as they slept. Cormac put his hands over his ears, hoping to shut out the customary *thuuuuu-wop* of the arm swinging through the air. But he couldn't get it out. *Thuuuuu-wop. Thuuuuu-wop*! *Thuuuuu-wop*! It was driving him mad, knowing each repetition of that groaning, foreboding sound brought more death.

Finally, the irritated dwarf rose to his feet and stomped hastily over to Bitrayuul. Cormac couldn't look at Koda's body any longer. He tugged at the man's leg, but Bitrayuul resisted.

"Wh-what are you doing?"

Cormac remained silent and continued to pull but was no match for Bitrayuul's strength. Retracting Koda, the half-orc dragged the fallen soldier to the corner of the room, a profound expression of disgust hidden beneath his helm. "What are you doing?!" he repeated.

The dwarf looked up at his friend, tears streaming down his face. He crawled toward Bitrayuul and weakly tried to grab Koda's leg once more. "We got no . . . no choice, lad. They can't . . . can't see him like this." The moment he finished the cracking words, Cormac let his head drop low against the cold stone and wept openly.

Bitrayuul remained on the defensive, clutching Koda as if he were a defenseless child. Though, the half-orc sobered as he watched Cormac weep. Bitrayuul understood what the captain aimed to do. The dwarf wasn't wrong; if the men saw their last in command fall, what hope did they have? But what did Cormac plan to do, throw the general over the wall? Where his memory would be desecrated by being torn to shreds? Did it matter?

Cormac slowly tugged on Koda's leg as he sobbed, not expecting him to move at all. But once he felt the man's lifeless form shift closer as he pulled, the captain looked up to see the half-orc had relinquished his hold. That act alone brought the dwarf greater anguish than even the man's death. In the act of Bitrayuul letting go, Cormac knew that his steel-hearted determination had infected the half-orc. It was clear that Bitrayuul was letting Koda go for the good of the people and sacrificing his own wishes to do so. In theory, such a selfless act was sound. But the deeper meaning, the distraught captain knew, was that the first piece of Bitrayuul's honorable heart had just been chipped away—the rest would fall easily from there on.

Even still, it was best for the fate of Wiston. So, the dwarf—joined shortly after by Bitrayuul—drove away their sorrow for the sake of duty. Together, they lifted the general and carried him discreetly out the western door. Their need for stealth fled, however, as they noticed the handful of guards stationed atop the western wall all lay dead. It was a sight that was hard to bear in that moment. Determined to see it through, they clung to their task—for what else could be done?

Slowly, the pair lifted Koda to a crenel in the parapet. A javelin whizzed by and the man slipped from their grasp. Every instinct begged them to watch his descent, but they couldn't bring themselves to do it. Instead, they shut their eyes and cowered behind the wall. Even after clamping their hands over their ears, they could hear Koda's body being torn apart.

A lifetime worth of grief seemed to pass before the sound of flesh tearing and bones cracking had finally ended. Feeling almost numb, Bitrayuul and Cormac trudged back to the command room and shut the door behind them. They sat next to each other, trying futilely to erase the memory of what they had just done. Bitrayuul, hardly able to form words, tried to speak first. "Wh-what," he paused, clearing his throat and mustering his will, "do we do now?"

Cormac took in a deep, steadying breath. "Don't know, son. All we can do is try to keep diggin' and survive, I suppose."

"Do you think Fangdarr is coming back? With the elves?"

"Ain't nothin' would stop Fang from comin' back but his death. But, seein' as how he went to an island full of stinkin' elves, he may already be dead." The dwarf's attempted humor felt dry, even to him. "All I know is that your brother be the most honorable person I know. If he's alive, he's comin'. It's only been two days since he left, so he would've landed this morning, judgin' by the maps."

Two days . . .. Bitrayuul could hardly believe it. There was yet to be a breach and already every leader of the human army had fallen. "So, unless he turned around the moment he stepped foot on Y'thirya, he won't return for at least another day?"

Cormac was nodding his head in confirmation. "Aye, lad. And convincin' an elf to meddle in human affairs is goin' to be a hard sell, don't ye doubt. I been prayin' to Bothain every time I close my eye that he lends his strength."

The half-orc closed his own, realizing it had been a while since he had last begged his deity for support. He prayed in silence for Fangdarr's swift return—with an army in tow—and that Wiston would survive. It felt pointless in that moment, but he clung to hope that his god would see them through. Once his prayer was finished, he rose to his feet. "We need to determine our next course of action. We cannot inform the men that their last in command has fallen, but we must give the appearance of leadership. *We* must be their leaders."

A half-hearted smile crossed the old dwarf's face. In truth, he was joyed that Bitrayuul was stepping up, even in the odds they faced. But after all they had endured already, it almost seemed pointless. Cormac silently scolded himself for the negativity. Bitrayuul was right, it was up to them. He groaned as he got to his feet. "Right, well let's get through the night, aye?"

CHAPTER FORTY-ONE
UNPREDICTABLE

Bitrayuul and Cormac pushed through the ranks, shouting commands and offering support and reassurances that victory was possible. Those digging the pit, to the guards defending the livestock, and to the ships manning the cliffs, they reached as many men as they could. Each time they barked orders, they were met with looks of confusion and disbelief. But the half-orc and dwarf exuded confidence and allowed no dispute that they were in charge. Whether the men knew it or liked it, the pair had assumed command.

By nightfall, Bitrayuul and Cormac were too exhausted to continue and retreated to the command room. As they shut the door behind them, they failed to notice a soldier standing in the room waiting. Startled, Cormac had to stop himself from attacking the lone man. "Bah! What ye doin' sneakin' up on someone in the middle of a war, lad?!"

"Apologies, sir. I bring news. Where is Commander Viktor?"

Bitrayuul cast a sidelong glance to his companion. "Uhh . . . Viktor is ou—"

"He's gone," the dwarf interrupted. "Viktor is dead, lad." His icy tone was made more severe by the stern gaze he wore. In that moment, with only a single soldier in his midst, Cormac's tolerance for keeping up the charade had faded.

"Oh. That's extremely unfortunate, are the men aware? What about the next in command, Silas and Koda?"

Cormac sighed as he slid to his rear against the wall. "All gone. The men don't know." He eyed the soldier's expression intently. "And we need to keep it that way."

A look of confusion crossed the man's face. "B-but this is drastic news! How long have they been gone? The wall hasn't even fallen!"

Bitrayuul raised a hand to silence the soldier, seeing Cormac's frustration growing. "Your reaction just now is exactly why none have been informed. If word spreads through the ranks, this war will be forfeit long before the enemy breaks through. They need to have hope. Cormac and I have assumed command for now—a fact we are both not happy with," he added, seeing the man's eyes narrow in distrust. "So far, the men have been listening to us as they believe we are relaying messages from Viktor or Koda. But Viktor fell yesterday, taking the first catapult with him. Koda fell earlier today. Trolls ambushed him in here while he slept."

Breathing heavily, the man seemed ready to scream in outrage. "General Koda was left *unguarded* while he slept? Where were the soldiers stationed up here? Where were *you*?!"

"Lad, shoutin' won't do anybody any good. We were ordered to set the men to task on digging the pit. By Koda," Cormac lied. "Then he asked us to speak with the king on his behalf for a status report. On our return, we found him—and all his guards—dead."

Steadying himself from the shock, the man sat down and took deep breaths. Bitrayuul slid onto the stool next to him. "So, you see the predicament we are in. We are doing all we can to keep the men in high hopes. In truth, we are terrified. But losing hope means the death of us all. Will you help us?"

The soldier stared at Bitrayuul, then Cormac, distrust still present in his gaze. But his eyes fell to the floor and he nodded. "Alright. Well, since you two seem to have taken lead, I have news." He produced a small piece of parchment and unrolled it, revealing a small yet intricately detailed map of Wiston. "You've been looking for the prince, right? We found him. He's been hiding out here." He placed his finger on the map at the rear of the castle. "In the dungeons."

"The dungeon?" Bitrayuul questioned. "Is he a prisoner?"

"No, he supposedly likes to . . . sit in there," the man replied, not hiding his own opinion of Lucien's odd behavior.

Cormac breathed a sigh of relief. "Right. Well, we know where he is now, the stinkin' coward. We need to rest, though. We'll seek him out in the mornin'. Maybe *he* can be convinced to lead his people." Rising to his feet and finding an open slab of stone on the floor to rest on, the dwarf muttered loud enough for all to hear, "Probably not."

Bitrayuul smiled at the messenger. "Thank you, sir, for understanding the dire situation we face."

As the half-orc started heading toward his own section of floor to sleep the man nodded. "Rest well. I will remain here and watch over you both. Can't have our two newest Commanders be cut down in their sleep, can we?"

Bitrayuul chuckled politely before drifting to sleep with the sounds of Cormac's heavy snores echoing in the room.

* * * * *

Waking to the sound of cheers the next morning, Cormac and Bitrayuul ran out in a hurry, past the messenger, who slept face-down in a pool of his own drool on the table. As the pair exited, they saw the reason for the men's jubilation. Stuck on top of the wall was the ogre corpse—unable to be used as ammunition for the catapult any longer.

"Bahaha! Bothain's beard, our prayers be answered, Bit!" Cormac shouted with joy as he ran over to the meaty carcass and gave it a kick for good measure.

Bitrayuul smiled and thanked his god for answering his prayers. He walked up behind his friend and gave a cheer of relief, raising his fist high in the air to the men below. Their uproar nearly brought him to tears as he could tell their hope was renewed. Riding the high, the soldiers went back to digging the pit. Already it was half the depth they had planned with no signs of failing to reach their goal. Their spirits restored their vigor with the threat of the wall crashing down on them at any moment halted—at least until the enemy had finished their search for more boulders. It seemed as if luck was finally on their side, spreading its warmth through every man.

Then came the rain.

CHAPTER FORTY-TWO

GUB

"Now lookit what ya did, Tod!" Bebbo yelled to his companion after watching their kin's corpse get stuck on the battlements.

"Eh! It was the wind, it was! Or he sneezed, yeh?" The pair continued to argue between themselves over whose fault it was that their last available ammunition was now wasted. They immediately fell silent, however, at the sight of their leader, Gub, trundling toward them through the masses. Gub passively swatted away trolls in his path with his large club, a leafless tree he had ripped from the earth. As he closed the distance to Tod and Bebbo, they lowered their eyes to avoid his gaze.

Though a head shorter, Gub stared daggers up at them, nearly losing his makeshift crown of twigs and a single plain leaf. He enjoyed their cowering. It reminded him of his power and the brutal way he had earned it. Years ago, the ogre had been one of a kind heart and dopey charm, blissfully living in solitude within the Lithe. It wasn't until he had been taken in by a small tribe of ogres that his vicious brutality had taken form. At first, they had taken pity on him, thinking his droll dumbness was a defect from birth. But, eventually, playful taunts grew to insults and insults sparked rage. One too many tormenting words had been seared into the altruistic ogre, evolving him into something much more terrible.

The young oaf that had enjoyed walks through the woods to collect useless trinkets had perished with his transformation. In response to their abrasive behavior, Gub had murdered the tribe's leader by pressing his fingers deep into his predecessor's eyes whilst he slept. Once his tormentor had fallen dead, Gub ate him—one bite at a time until he had consumed the entire corpse. Since that incident, the other ogres' fear of Gub had allowed him to assume the self-appointed mantle of their leader.

"What this? Where Geed?" Gub asked through gritting teeth.

When no response came from either Tod or Bebbo, their leader slammed his tree into the ground. They each yelped in fright and began whimpering their response. "H-he there . . .." Bebbo slowly pointed toward the wall.

Gub followed his finger to Wiston to see the soldiers raising their spears and swords in victory at the hulking corpse that lay sprawled atop the wall. He shot his subordinates a bone-chilling glare. "Ya got him stuckeds?! We needed hims!" In truth, Gub cared little about the loss. All the brutal leader cared for was his dominant status. Though, to be dominant, he needed underlings and only a handful of ogres remained. Tod and Bebbo had stayed to man the catapult and launch trolls over the wall while Gub had sent out the remaining few to search for rocks in the forest.

Before turning to leave, the ogre shouted at the pair, "Keep sending trollsies! Rocks soon!" As he walked away, Gub grew irritated with the sheer number of trolls in his path. No matter how many he swatted aside, they always seemed to come back and swarm him once again. Yet the trolls never lashed back in retaliation. They knew the need for the enormous brutes was paramount in breaking down the wall. So, they stuck to just insults. For now.

Slumping to the ground against a tree he had claimed as 'Gub's Throne' to anyone who would listen, Gub tried to parse through his memory and recall why he had bothered to join this campaign and deal with the frustration of countless trolls and stinky orcs. He remembered a voice had crept into his head many moons ago and promised the chance to sit atop a throne worthy of his name. '*Gub the Conqueror*' it had called him. The grand visions of thousands dead at his feet and him chewing the corpses of any he wished while sitting on the human throne in Wiston had certainly accomplished the task of driving Gub to war.

"Gub the Conqueror," the ogre whispered to himself with glee as he could still see the fear on Tod and Bebbo's faces as they frantically cranked the catapult once more.

CHAPTER FORTY-THREE

CHOSEN

Traveling behind the same satyress that had escorted them to Thrax'ul's tent, Fangdarr and Aesthéa were led to the southern edge of the village. Eyeing their guide curiously, the orc noticed only two of the eilfeyn were waiting. "You not riding?"

Before the satyress could respond, Thrax'ul appeared from behind a nearby tent, a handful of bright orange berries in hand. "Satyrs do not ride," the chieftain stated proudly as he lowered the fruit to the pair of eilfeyn. "We respect the creatures and do not subject them to such."

"How she keep up?"

Thrax'ul chuckled. "Do not worry, orc. Brea'la is more than able."

Fangdarr eyed the satyress, who only smiled mischievously in return. In truth, the orc held little doubt of her prowess—judging by the well-used stone spear and wooden longbow across her back. Though, skilled or not, he wasn't sure how she would be able to maintain a good pace on foot. After he and Aesthéa mounted their steeds, Brea'la nodded to her chieftain in assurance. Then, proving Thrax'ul's words, she kicked off hard with her hooves and sprinted ahead. Taken aback by her sudden speed, Fangdarr spurred his eilfeyn to follow—the superior chuckle of the satyr chieftain sounding at his back.

Maintaining a hastened pace for the journey, it wasn't long before they reached the edge of Y'thirya and could see the Eye of Cerenos ahead. Fangdarr's jaw fell slack in awe at the sight, as the mid-day sun's light reflected off the enormous tree. The growth stood taller than the castle of Wiston and any peak of the Tusk mountains. He had seen the magnificent structure far in the distance on their travels but couldn't fathom the true magnitude until he was up close. Fangdarr tilted his head up, hoping to see the apex, but it pierced even the clouds.

"Beautiful, is it not?" Brea'la asked. Her eyes looked upon the tree as if for the first time, shining with the same marveled expression of amazement that remained in

Fangdarr's gaze. Though she had looked upon the Eye many times before, she always felt the same sense of joy with each visit.

At a loss, Fangdarr nodded. He realized it was the first time he had heard the satyress speak. The orc expected her dialect to be similar to the males, with rough, resounding voices and bleated mannerisms. Instead, Brea'la spoke more akin to an elf—clear and sweet.

"How high does it go?" Aesthéa asked in equal admiration. Being a member of the royal family, it wasn't the first time she had seen the Eye but was certainly the closest she had been. The elves were so concerned with avoiding conflict with the satyrs that they no longer visited their most sacred structure.

"It is hard to say. It shrinks and grows through time. We are uncertain as to why, but we do not climb the tree often. Hooves do not make climbing easy," Brea'la replied with a wink. "It is no matter. We will not be climbing today."

Fangdarr looked to their guide curiously. "No climb? What we doing?" He continued to scan the great tree. It's bluish-green bark was mystifying and calming, as if emanating both joy and sadness at once. A thick blanket of purple and blue leaves covered much of the Eye, reflecting the sun with dazzling sparkles. One didn't need to stretch their imagination far to assume a deep magic remain twisted within.

As he looked up at the clouds, Fangdarr cast a quick glance to the east. Dark and ominous storm clouds could be seen hovering thickly over Wiston, with the occasional flash of lightning. Cursing himself for taking the time to look upon things of beauty while his brother and friend fought desperately to keep the war at bay, Fangdarr turned to Brea'la. "How we cross water?"

"Normally, we swim. However, I had something *else* in mind." Brea'la looked to Aesthéa, "If you do not mind."

The elf raised her eyebrow curiously. She knew what was being asked. "I have vowed not to use my gifts for mundane tasks, only in the defense of life." Aesthéa's words sang out with pride, though she was concerned her defiance would anger the satyress.

Contrarily, Brea'la's face lit up and her eyes shined with admiration. "You truly are a wonder, druid. It is rare to find one who would not use the gifts bestowed upon them for any opportunity." Her smile remained fixed on her face as she stepped into the water. "Come, there is a hidden path."

Fangdarr and Aesthéa looked to each other. The elf couldn't help but show her excitement at approaching the Eye and becoming closer to her god. Her companion, however, continued to mask his guilt and apprehension, knowing she may soon crumble in his failure. They each dismounted and fell in line behind Brea'la, careful to step on a shallow path of stones beneath the water.

With each step they took, the energy they felt pulsating from the tree grew. It seeped into their bodies and minds, tingling their skin and causing them to feel the profound sense of both joy and sorrow. As the water deepened, the emotions became stronger, clashing together intensely. Every moment passed with pure bliss only to be constantly overtaken by a deep and overwhelming wave of despair in a vicious cycle. By the time the group was only a few more tip-toed hops away from the Eye's shore, they all had tears streaming down raised cheeks on smiling faces. Fangdarr tried to resist but it was futile. It was as if he felt commanded by his own undeniable voice, demanding he simply *feel*. Then, as the three pulled themselves up to the floating island made entirely of the tree's mystical roots, entwined in an overlapping lattice, the emotions ceased, and they were left feeling empty like never before.

Brea'la smiled to her new companions, seeing the streams of tears that had rolled down their confused faces. "You have passed the first test. Some have drowned on the path to the Eye—even satyrs. It is by no means treacherous, but it forces you to feel emotion in its most bare form. There are those who cannot handle such passion. I am glad to know neither of you fell."

Fangdarr and Aesthéa made eye contact once more. Had the orc known the possibility of death by some sort of magical judgment, he might have chosen to abandon their quest. It irked him that such a test would be put upon him without his knowledge. His anger slowly boiled at the thought of falling to a magical path through the sea rather than in battle, but he held back his emotions.

They walked onward, leaving a trail of shining wetness in their wake. As soon as each drop of water touched the ground, a miniscule flower instantly blossomed, piercing through the thick bark of the tree's roots. Not stopping for more questions, Brea'la led them toward the base of the tree. A large, flat stone could be seen embedded into the wood.

Brea'la stopped a few paces from the stone and waited silently. Fangdarr and Aesthéa stood by, expecting her to do something, but she remained motionless. After many moments, the satyress impatiently commanded Fangdarr, "Approach the stone."

Fangdarr released a low growl in his throat but moved to the slab anyway. Aesthéa stepped back with expectant eyes, waiting for something marvelous to occur. The orc stood a pace away from the large rock. His eyes danced around, looking for some sort of indication of magic or the presence of Cerenos. Time slipped by and Fangdarr grew impatient. His brother needed him. Cormac needed him. And yet he stood upon a supposed magical tree to be deemed 'Chosen' by a god he put no faith in.

The orc growled and turned toward Brea'la. "This stupid. Let's go back."

Shooting him an angry scowl, the satyress' hands quickly pulled out her spear. "You go nowhere. Not until you have proven you are Chosen, as was promised."

Fangdarr returned her glare but didn't pull Driktarr from its harness. Instead, he stepped closer to Aesthéa. As he looked upon her face, the chieftain couldn't hold onto his anger. His eyes turned soft as he relaxed once more with a long exhale before turning back toward the stone.

Brea'la continued to hold out her spear defensively. But her guard lowered quickly as she watched the large orc stand squarely in front of the smoothed stone, arms spread wide.

Fangdarr stood silent and waited in his vulnerable pose. Not for himself. Not for Brea'la. Not even to expedite the frustrating process so that he may hasten his return to Wiston and aid those in need. No, it was all for her, the elf that had stolen his heart, against all likelihood. It was the look in her eye as his gaze locked into hers that compelled the great orc chieftain to stand resolute in front of a stone that he considered just that—a simple stone. But he would do everything he could to make her wishes come true. In his mind, it only added to the pain she would feel when the truth was revealed. But, if that came to pass, it would be her god to blame and not he.

Aesthéa and Brea'la stood next to one another waiting for something grand to occur. In truth, Brea'la had never seen anyone interact with the great tree. She had only been told stories of such. While Fangdarr waited motionless, a tinge of doubt crept into her own mind. The satyress pushed the thought away, deeming any possibility of lack of divine interaction to be the orc's fault.

Time dragged on slowly before Fangdarr finally turned his head to Aesthéa. His concerned expression was full of sadness as he lowered his arms to his sides. She watched him curiously, not understanding at first. Then it hit her—the realization that all the druid thought to be true was false. Fangdarr wasn't Chosen, and Cerenos had either disregarded them or never existed at all. Her eyes widened at such a harsh reality and she ran to the stone herself.

"Wait!" Brea'la called to the elf before rushing after her. "You must not interfere!" The satyress charged with her spear locked in her grip. Brea'la didn't wish to cause the elf harm, far from it. But she couldn't allow Aesthéa to disrespect her beliefs.

Aesthéa pounded on the stone with her fists. Tears welled in her eyes at the thought of being abandoned by the deity she so cherished. As she launched blow after blow against the immovable stone, Brea'la closed in. The satyress thrust her lethal spear forward toward the elf's spine, but it was caught by Fangdarr. Looking at him wildly, Brea'la tugged on the weapon's shaft. But the orc's strength dwarfed her own ten times over.

Jumping back and relinquishing her weapon, the satyress pulled her wooden bow from her shoulder and launched an arrow instinctively. In the moment it released, Brea'la's eyes widened in shock. In that single moment the missile cut through the air, she wondered if she was truly about to kill innocent people on the sacred ground. It didn't matter. The arrow had already hit its mark by the time the concerned satyress had finished the thought. She watched as the sharpened stone tip dug deep into Fangdarr's chest above his right pectoral.

Brea'la fell to her knees and threw her bow aside, scared to even touch it. She looked up, expecting Fangdarr to be closing in on her in retaliation. Instead, he simply glared at her, blood trickling down his torso. Behind him, Aesthéa continued her hopeless assault against the sheer stone, pounding away with abandon and bloodied fists. Brea'la was stunned that the orc would just remain motionless—even in the threat of death—just to ensure that the elf could play out her frustration.

Low sobs started to come from the prone satyress. Her anger at Cerenos was being directed at the foreign creature that stood defiantly in front of her. "Why do you not strike? Are you a coward as Thrax'ul says?"

Fangdarr scowled at the insult but remained immobile. His hand closed around the arrow buried deep into his chest before ripping it out without even a wince. Dropping the projectile to the ground, the orc began walking toward Brea'la.

This is it, the satyress thought. *Cerenos forgive me.* Her eyes closed as Fangdarr approached. Brea'la waited in torment for the quick inhale of breath that she knew would come. Instead, she gasped in surprise as the orc's strong hands clasped around her arms and lifted her to her hooves. Opening her eyes slowly, her gaze met Fangdarr's and saw only forgiveness. He smiled to her once it seemed evident she would stand on her own, then turned back to Aesthéa, who had worn herself out and was slumped against the bloodied stone.

Brea'la was at a loss by Fangdarr's devotion to his companion and his choice to spare the satyress' life, even after she had attempted to kill him. She started to approach them but halted upon seeing Aesthéa's blood being slowly absorbed into the stone.

"Look!" Brea'la called out, extending a finger. Fangdarr and Aesthéa followed it to the tablet and caught the last glimpse of purple blood before it disappeared. Curious, Brea'la stared down at the bloodied arrow the orc had extracted and saw that the blood had been completely removed.

Fangdarr tapped them both on their shoulders as he looked down at his bleeding chest. They all watched as the wound began stitching itself closed, without even leaving a scar behind. Brea'la and Aesthéa stared wide-eyed in pure joy. "Cerenos is here!" Aesthéa blurted out with excitement, hugging herself tightly against her lover's arm. "He has accepted you, Fangdarr! Isn't this wonderful?"

The orc saw the look of wonder in her eyes as she waited for him to reply. His cheeks cracked a small smile, which seemed to be enough as she took Brea'la's hands in her own and jumped around in joy. A wave of guilt ripped through the orc as he watched them. In truth, despite his wound healing, Fangdarr held no belief that his companion's Forest God was the cause though he couldn't deny the possibility.

Brea'la turned to Fangdarr, happiness still spread across her thin face. "You have been Chosen, Fangdarr. This is wondrous! We must return swiftly to Wudhyvn and inform Thrax'ul." She turned back to Aesthéa once more and kissed the elf deeply on the lips—bringing a shocked look to Fangdarr and the elf alike—before continuing her elated dance.

Ignoring the awkwardness of the kiss, they headed back toward the northern edge of the island, following the path of tiny flowers that had bloomed on their initial trek. Aesthéa and Brea'la skipped ahead merrily as Fangdarr trudged on, his thoughts heavy. He watched as the pair of female warriors entered the water and began making their way back on the path to Y'thirya. The orc cast a final glance behind him to the Eye of Cerenos wondering if he truly was Chosen. The great tree in the distance stood motionless, offering no proof to such a claim. Though enormous and mystical, it stood just a tree. Fangdarr smiled as he once again witnessed the happiness in his companion and her newfound friend. Did it matter?

CHAPTER FORTY-FOUR

MUD

"Bah! Can we never get a break?!" Cormac yelled toward the sky as the rain clinked against his armor. As he peered upward, cursing the gods for their sense of humor, a drop fell into his one good eye. "BAH! Curse the piss from the heavens!"

Bitrayuul watched his companion and would have laughed at his misfortune had the doom of the rain not sobered his mood. Soldiers in the pit were looking up at the darkened sky with equally defeated perspectives, searching for their commanders to guide them. "Come, Cormac. We are needed."

Falling in line, the dwarf muttered a stream of curses under his breath at their luck. Driving away his frustration and donning a mask of irrefutable confidence, Cormac assumed control as they reached the edge of the pit. "Right, lads! Just a wee bit of water. Nothin' to be afraid of, don't ye doubt! We need to get some canvas cloths and set up a canopy so the pit don't fill too much. Rest of ye, start scoopin' out the pooled water. If we can get that canopy up swiftly, we shouldn't lose too much time. Move, move, move!"

Looks of suspicion were thrown at Cormac from all directions. Men tired of being ordered around by an outsider while they wondered where their *real* leaders were. A few even called out from the crowd in request to speak with General Koda or Commander Viktor. Bitrayuul shifted uneasily as scrutiny of their ploy began to come to light, but the dwarf didn't miss a beat. His sheer confidence and persistence stomped out their pressing questions and distrust. Repeating his orders once more, the dwarven captain refused to show concern with their growing insubordination.

Eventually, the men gave up trying to dispute, knowing the tasks they were set to were sound and would increase their chance of survival. However, it didn't stop the soldiers from grumbling as they worked. Cormac could see the anger on their faces. Their growing discontent was an obstacle he needed to clear before it threatened all.

Bitrayuul turned to his companion who seemed to be silently locked up from stress. "I think we should seek out Lucien, the arcanist."

Cormac nodded his agreement. The pair departed toward the castle, feeling the defender's icy stares at their backs. Before they had even left the area, the dwarf could hear disgruntled comments being made at his expense between the men. He begged Bothain that they would find the prince to lead the people of Wiston, as it was obvious it couldn't be him.

As they pushed through the large door between the Military District and the courtyard in the center of Wiston, Bitrayuul gasped in shock. The number of civilians that had been packed into the gardens had more than doubled since their last visit. "Bothain's beard . . .."

"Aye, ye ain't jokin', lad. It's only been a day since we last stepped foot here. Now look . . .." The civilians numbered more than a thousand by then and were pressed together too tight for comfort. Fights were breaking out everywhere as stress ran high in the unfavorable conditions. Women and children were often huddled in fear—not from the enemy outside the walls, but the aggression held within. It was chaos. All the guards that had been stationed throughout the courtyard were gone, most likely hiding in the castle for their own safety. The rain only made it all worse. Mud splashed in every direction, drenching even those who sought to avoid conflict. The few possessions the frightened civilians had brought were being ruined as the heavy rains continued to pour.

Bitrayuul couldn't believe that such animosity lay within the heart of the city, especially so close to the building that was meant to serve as a beacon of hope. He wished the king would muster the strength to at least come and speak to the people—*his* people—to restore their faith. Instead, a crowd constantly pounded on the castle's heavy doors to no avail, their wails of despair giving voice to their feelings of abandonment.

"Come, lad. The dungeon is around back, hopefully it's clear," Cormac said as he tugged at Bitrayuul's arm. It took them a long while to circle around to the back of the castle, pushing their way through the crowd. At first, Bitrayuul continuously apologized as his sharpened armor cut into those who strayed too close—a common occurrence. However, after more than a dozen victims were shoved into him, the half-orc gave up on his politeness and simply pushed through, letting his armor clear the path for them. By the time they neared the dungeon entrance, the spines on Bitrayuul's armor were painted crimson.

"Bah, they're everywhere!" Cormac growled. The entrance to the dungeon was open, with no less than ten civilians trying to squeeze themselves into the doorway.

"Step aside, Cormac, I'll try to get us through."

Cormac put a hand on the half-orc's shoulder. "Don't bother, son. Even if we could get in there, it ain't likely the mage is sittin' comfortably in there anymore. And there ain't no guarantee we'd get out without havin' to cleave some civilians, sure as stones."

Bitrayuul's shoulders slumped. He stared once more at the crowd and the frantic expressions on most of their faces. *This situation has gotten out of control,* he thought. *It has only been three days!* His eyes fell upon a young girl with blonde hair standing near the castle wall. Her drenched hair matted to her face, nearly covering her eyes as they were fixated on one woman being assaulted by three others a few paces away. Immediately, a wave of despair rushed through Bitrayuul as his mind played over the scene of Lilyana's death at Chakal's hand. All went silent as his sole focus fell on that little girl as she watched her mother get beaten.

Then, as the mother fell limp to the mud, the trio of women removed any possessions from her person before moving over to the little girl. Immobilized by his own fear, Bitrayuul stared at the child's confused expression as the women closed in on her. They ripped off her clothing in search of any possessions the mother may have hidden but found nothing but the dirty doll the girl clutched in her grasp. Then, for no other reason than because they could, one of the desperate and merciless women struck the girl against the temple while another pulled the doll free. They laughed in unison at how little of a challenge the child posed and walked away in search of their next victim, leaving the girl bloodied and face down in the muck.

"Bit! What are ye doin'?!" Cormac yelled up at him, breaking the half-orc's trance. The dwarf's eyes were wild with frustration and anger, giving evidence that it wasn't the first time he had called to Bitrayuul. "Move your feet, son!"

Bitrayuul remained motionless, looking back to the little girl. She had gotten to her knees, dripping blood and mud from her hair and face, and was crawling over to her mother whom had remained motionless even as a dozen others had stomped over her body. Before Bitrayuul could even consider acting, Cormac was roughly pulling him through the crowd toward the northern exit. The half-orc couldn't pull his gaze away as he watched the girl simply lay down next to her mother before being trampled deep into the mud herself.

Finally, after pressing through the crowd with dreadful speed, Cormac pushed open the steel door to the Market District just to be free of the overcrowded courtyard. As the door swung open, a similar crowd piled in the streets of the market was revealed. "Damn the stones! There's no escape, Bit!"

The half-orc said nothing. He was still locked in silent anguish over the scene he had just witnessed and its reminder of his half-sister. Bitrayuul felt the wind get knocked out of him as he fell to his knees with a sudden pain in his groin. With the immense flash of pain, his stupor ended and his vision turned to the dwarf, hands on hips in irritation. "Wh-why did you do that?" Bitrayuul coughed out.

"Because ye need to focus. I know the courtyard was chaotic. But ye need to focus. Stop lockin' yerself in." The captain's face was grim and stern. He needed Bitrayuul at his best and couldn't allow the half-orc to lose hope due to the atrocities he had witnessed before the battle had even begun. "Now, do ye want to search for the arcanist or head back to the frontlines where we're needed most?"

Bitrayuul pondered as he rose to his feet nursing his aching groin. The crowd in the market was still packed, but calmer. They could traverse the streets more easily but finding a man that they had never seen among an endless sea of unknown faces seemed impossible. "Let's get back to the wall," he replied with reluctance.

Cormac nodded and began leading them southwest through the Market District, rather than back through the courtyard. "We'll go around to the Resource District, then back to the wall. I'd like to check our food stock while we're out. Judgin' by the state of civilians in the courtyard, we might not have as much food as we'd hoped. Plus, I ain't steppin' in that courtyard again. Not without riskin' me shields smackin' a few around, don't ye doubt."

As they pressed through the market, scanning faces in hopes of finding Lucien, they only encountered the hopeless stares of every civilian watching them pass. Bitrayuul tried to shut his eyes against their vacant visages of defeat, knowing their gazes would affect him. With luck, he managed to keep his composure until they made it to the gate leading to the Resource District. Thankfully, four soldiers were stationed outside, ensuring none entered without permission.

The dwarf smiled widely at the sight of guards manning the food source. If the townspeople had forced their way in there, the stocks would be depleted within days. "Aye, lads. We're passin' through, want to check the current stock levels." Each guard looked to each other with caution, reminding Cormac that he wasn't known by all. Before they could dispute, he added, "I'm Cormac Shield-Arms, Captain of the Shield in Tarabar. Me and me friend here are workin' under Commander Viktor and General Koda. They've tasked us with checkin' stock."

Bitrayuul's heart pounded in his chest. He had no desire to come to bloodshed with the soldiers, especially in view of so many civilians. Luckily, the men seemed to ease upon hearing the name of their officers. "You may pass," one man stated, slowly pushing open the steel door.

"Many thanks, son," Cormac replied as he stepped through the portal. Bitrayuul was quick on his heels.

Immediately, the smell of animal excrements and blood filled their nostrils, along with the rotten stench of burning troll corpses. They started to walk forward on the path along the wall, inspecting the fields to their right. All seemed well. Over one hundred bovines and thrice that many fowls grazed in their respective pastures.

Cormac and Bitrayuul approached the entrance to the enclosures where two guards and a man in a wide-brimmed hat made of straw and holding a muddy pitchfork stood talking. "Greetin's to ye. Name's Cormac. I'm with Commander Viktor and General Koda and here to check on livestock. How we doin' on supply?"

The man that could be none other than the farmer in charge of the animals spit some of his chewed barley at the dwarf's feet. "Stock's fine."

Quickly becoming irritated, Cormac stepped forward. "How many bovine ye got left?" His voice was slow and threatening.

Not backing down, the man stared down at the dwarf and slowly spit once more at his feet, letting it drag down before breaking off and being sucked back into his foul-smelling mouth. "Enough."

Seeing he wouldn't get any real answers from the man, Cormac turned his gaze toward the large pile of troll corpses that were still burning. "Ye lose any men over here, soldier?"

The farmer eyed the soldier, as if expecting him not to answer. However, the man couldn't refuse, as he was under the impression that Cormac was under direct orders from his commanding officer. "A few, sir. Five in total since the first launch, though only one in the past day. We are growing more aware and have plans of action in place now."

Cormac nodded and turned his head to the other guard. "Soldier, ye think there be enough food? How long do ye think supplies will last from what ye've seen here?" The dwarf ignored the angry scowl from the nearly fuming farmer at being circumvented.

"Uh, I'm not sure, sir. I would guess at least a week, as long as the trolls don't come in mass or the wall breaks." Sweat trickled down the man's brow as he was forced to bear the farmer's accusatory gaze.

"Good man. Right, farmer, keep up the good work. The people of Wiston are countin' on ye, don't ye doubt!" Cormac said, walking away before he even finished. Bitrayuul walked past the group to catch up to the dwarf, fully expecting the man to lower the pitchfork in his hand and attempt to skewer Cormac. But no threat came, and the farmer stomped back to his pasture and began shoveling hay for the bovines with vigorous fury.

Bitrayuul didn't say a word as they pushed through the final doorway back into the Military District. They reached the pit and saw that the canopy had already been constructed and was diverting rain away from the hole while a few dozen men used ropes and buckets to scoop out the water and mud.

"Keep up the good work, lads!" Cormac shouted, getting naught but distasteful glares from the men as they powered through their exhaustion. The dwarf looked up, seeing that the dark clouds were still thick and stretched for many leagues, promising more rain or worse. Though the sun couldn't be seen, he estimated that it had to be past mid-day. He stared around at all the soldiers working hard in the muck to secure their defenses.

The dwarf began unbuckling his shields from his forearms and turned to Bitrayuul. "Lad, I need ye to hold onto these for a bit, if ye please. Don't lose 'em." The half-orc hesitantly took them with a look of confusion hidden beneath his helm. Once the dwarf had handed over his cumbersome and heavy shields, he walked toward the pit and slid down the slick wall to the bottom. Once in the muddy pool, Cormac asked one of the men for his bucket. The soldier—and those around him—stared blankly at the dwarf but did as instructed.

"Me thanks, son." Cormac scooped the pail into the brown water and called out for it to be pulled up to the ground level where it was emptied to the side. Once it came back down, the dwarf scooped another load and let it ascend once more to the soldier above. The men watched Cormac with a newfound respect as his worn, steel armor was slathered in mud in the trenches with them, slaving at a task many in command would consider below them.

Bitrayuul watched from above, smiling all the while after realizing Cormac's intention. He didn't believe the men would question him any longer.

CHAPTER FORTY-FIVE
POTENTIAL

Bitrayuul decided to return to the command room to take a short break. The trek took him nearly twice as long with Cormac's shields further slowing the large half-orc's progress through the tight, winding staircase. As his frustration grew, so, too, did his stress. He sighed as visions of the chaos in the courtyard played in his mind, threatening to push him past the brink of control.

Within the suffocating passage, Bitrayuul resisted the urge to just break down and weep then and there. He forced himself to press on—if only to free himself of those cursed stairs! After finally squeezing himself out into the open air, the half-orc gasped desperately. For many moments, he simply lay on his back atop the battlements and stared up at the sky as the rain poured over him. For a brief moment, there was no haunting memories of his loved ones who had perished. No horrific scene of the little girl in the courtyard as she was trampled to death. No war. There was only the rain.

Realizing he couldn't simply lay there forever—and getting odd looks from the few guards stationed atop the wall—Bitrayuul pulled himself to his feet and headed toward the command room. As he pushed open the sturdy wooden door, the half-orc immediately noticed a man sitting at the table in the center of the room. He had to reject every instinct to shift into a defensive stance. "Who are you?"

"I noticed you've been looking for me. You're easy to spot in a crowd, to say the least," the man said with a smile. His feet swung up to the table and he leaned back on his stool. "So, what do you want?"

Bitrayuul inspected the unexpected visitor further, from the man's plain and muddied boots to his short, unkempt brown hair. By all intentions, the man looked like a common civilian. "You must be Lucien." The quick lift of the corner of the prince's lips proved the half-orc's assumptions.

Taking the stool across from the prince, Bitrayuul set Cormac's shields quietly on the ground and sat down with a sigh. "Well, I'm tired so I'll get right to it. We need you to aid with the war efforts." Lucien remained silent. Bitrayuul watched him impatiently for many moments, unable to bear the miserable silence. "Your Highness, this is important. Do you not care for your people?"

As soon as Bitrayuul had finished his question, Cormac pushed in the door covered nearly head to toe in mud. He took a moment to inspect the visitor before stepping inside. Without saying a word, he looked around the room to find his shields and went to retrieve them. Slowly, he buckled them to his forearms before sitting on the crate next to Bitrayuul, ignoring the trail of muck in his wake.

Seeing Lucien's amused smile, the half-orc continued. "You will watch your people die? For what purpose?"

The prince let out a heavy blow of air. "This is not my war."

Before Bitrayuul could retort, Cormac turned to him with a face as still as stone. "Take off your helmet, Bit." The half-orc looked at his companion with confusion, but obliged. Lucien didn't react to seeing the orcish heritage of the warrior sitting across from him. "Now, ye sit across from a *dwarf* and an *orcblood*, and ye be trying to tell us that the war in *Wiston* that threatens the eradication of all *humans* is not yer war? Ye want to rethink that, son?"

Lucien's grin fell from his face, replaced by irritation. "I wouldn't expect you to understand. I appreciate your efforts in Wiston's defense, but, in this war, I am no more than a commoner."

Cormac smashed his hand on the table. "We know yer a mage, boy! Good men are dying to protect the city, and ye have the strength to aid, yet ye sit in the muck and play with the scum between yer toes?!" His incredulous stare was only matched by the intensity of his voice. It took all he had not to leap over the table and bash the man into sense.

"I never wanted to be this!" Lucien shouted in reply, growing to anger himself. "You think I asked for this '*gift*'? This is a *curse*! I am forever damned to be whatever my father, or my *people* need me to be. Never given the opportunity to be nothing more than myself! I hold no desire to be what is expected of me, dwarf. My father forced me to train as a mage since I was a child simply because I possessed a strength that surpassed the norm. None have ever stopped to ask what I want or how I feel. So, no, I would rather watch Wiston burn than aid it. I can make no difference anyways. Wiston will fall, and all will perish. Every effort the men make only delays the inevitable. Life holds no purpose. We are just struggling on borrowed time until sinking into the mud beneath our feet!"

Bitrayuul's eyes just stared at the man's retaliation in awe. Living with dwarves, he had rarely come across those reluctant to fight, but he could at least understand the sentiment. However, he never encountered someone with such a negative perspective on life itself.

Cormac, on the other hand, had met a few who had shared such a nihilistic outlook. His fists clenched tightly in anger as he struggled to keep himself calm. The captain cared little about the man's viewpoint, until Lucien brought up the men's futile efforts and their inability to succeed. Such words were infectious and would spread through the ranks like a plague, poisoning the resolve of those who have worked so hard to survive—especially if coming from the lips of the prince. The dwarf couldn't hold back any longer. Not after spending time deep in the man-made pit with the soldiers to strengthen their bond. Red with rage, he leapt over the table.

Lucien was expecting such a hostile reaction after watching the dwarf's expression boil. Quickly raising his hand between himself and Cormac, he mentally called forth an invisible orb of force that sent the dwarf tumbling backwards into the wall. Rising to his feet, Lucien said, "I don't wish to fight you. I only came here out of curiosity. Let me go. You may fight your war, just leave me out of it."

Bitrayuul was unsure of how to act. He had never encountered an arcanist before and wasn't aware of what they could do. Cormac, on the other hand, was briefly familiar, and rose from his prone position with even more anger. "No! Yer goin' to fight, whether ye want to or not! They *need* ye, Lucien! Don't turn away from them!" The dwarf charged forward once more, this time keeping his feet planted sturdily on the floor and his shields in front of him.

Lucien's hands moved in quick flicks, throwing out multiple orbs toward the dwarf. But this time Cormac was ready. Each of the orbs crashed into his shields, dissipating on impact and slowing the dwarf's advance. But the fierce veteran closed the gap between himself and Lucien and pushed the man into the wall with his shields. Each of the blades were only a finger-length from the prince's neck. "Ye *will* help us!"

The prince grit his teeth in frustration. He only wished to be left alone. Yet at every turn he was forced onto the path of others, simply because of his magical prowess. Lucien hated his abilities and what they had required of him. In most cases, he rarely ever used magic simply due to his reluctance to give credence to the very thing he couldn't stand. But now it was time to show just what kind of monster they had bred. Straining beneath the dwarf's heavy shields, Lucien conjured a wave of force that propelled the dwarf—and the perplexed Bitrayuul—harshly across the room and kept them pressed against the wall.

Cormac and Bitrayuul groaned in pain as their bodies were pushed harder and harder into the wall. They could see Lucien standing in the center of the room with both arms extended forward as if he were channeling the forcefield through his body. Beads of sweat dripped down his face as his magical stamina rapidly depleted. The man knew he was capable of much more, but it had been a long while since he had exerted himself with such vigor.

Finally, the prince dispelled the forcefield, dropping the pair to the floor. They inhaled a large breath of air to refill what had been squeezed from their lungs and slowly tried to rise. By the time they had gotten their feet beneath them, Lucien was already gone.

CHAPTER FORTY-SIX

MOBILIZE

Fangdarr slowed his eilfeyn to a trot behind Brea'la and Aesthéa as they approached Wudhyvn. The sun had descended far past the horizon, leaving only the dim light of the moon to illuminate the village. It amazed the orc how different the western half of Y'thirya seemed than the east. Where the elves resided, the forest seemed to be most vibrant in the moonlight, while here was the opposite. The community had been so full of vitality and joy in the rays of the sun earlier. But in the darkness of night only the calming sound of a low breeze and light bleating could be heard.

Fangdarr noticed there were no guards stationed. Anywhere. Nearly every member of the tribe slept peacefully within their small tents. It seemed absurd that the satyrs could rest without fear of assault.

They halted their steeds just outside of Thrax'ul's dwelling. Brea'la turned to face Fangdarr and Aesthéa, her smile still wide across her cheeks. "I shall see if the chieftain slumbers." They nodded politely in reply as she disappeared beneath the cloth flap of the large tent.

While they waited, Aesthéa took the time to quickly turn to Fangdarr and finally express the happiness she had felt on their journey. She jumped into his arms and kissed him passionately through her smile. Fangdarr could taste the salt of tears on her lips and pulled her away, thinking she may be in sorrow. But he knew instantly they were tears of joy—brought on by her faith being taken as unmistakable truth. The elf couldn't bear the distance any longer. She pushed through his light hold and kissed him once more.

"Should I wait a moment?" came the amused whisper from Brea'la poking her head through the tent. Aesthéa let out a childish giggle to match her feelings of just being caught in the act. Keeping the orc's hand in her own, the elf led her companion toward Thrax'ul's abode. As they were about to enter, Elethain stepped out from around the corner.

"You have returned." The necromancer's expression seemed an odd mix of surprise and discontentedness. "It appears Cerenos did not strike you down, orc. Perhaps he mistook you for an ogre and pitied you." Elethain's smile and playful insult blew harmlessly past Fangdarr, though received a scowl from Aesthéa. Before the druid could raise her voice, Elethain lifted a hand. "Apologies, my lady. I meant no offense. This is good news, we should rejoice." Despite his flat tone, Aesthéa backed down. She clutched Fangdarr's hand more tightly and pulled him into the tent.

As they entered the dark dwelling, they could see Thrax'ul sitting on his throne. The satyr appeared to be glistening in sweat, as did three of his doting brides. The chieftain took notice of his guests stares and offered a smug grin. "Brea'la tells me you have news, orc. She would not say, but her excitement provided the answer. You are Chosen, then?"

Fangdarr's stomach sank. He knew his answer would be a lie, if only to himself. His mouth opened to speak, to offer some ploy that would allow the satyr to put faith in him. But his mouth closed as soon as it had opened, unable to form the words. Thrax'ul watched him curiously with those wolf-like eyes. Fangdarr dared not turn to Aesthéa's expectant expression. He knew she would be there, eagerly waiting for his recounting of Cerenos' blessing being bestowed upon him. It would only make it infinitely worse should Fangdarr speak the truth he believed.

Finally, with every urge repelling him, Fangdarr responded, "It is true. Cerenos give blessing." He paused, building up the courage to tell the final lie. "I am Chosen." From the moment the words had begun falling from his mouth, the orc felt sick to his stomach. He could feel the bile rising in his throat as every part of his pride cursed himself for lying—to himself, to the satyrs, and to Aesthéa. Fangdarr glanced to his lover and saw the stretched expression of happiness on her beautiful face. It was almost enough to push him over the brink and take back his words. He hated himself for knowing the only reason Aesthéa held such joy was because she had been told what she wanted to hear, not the truth. But there was so much more at stake. This was beyond Fangdarr and his pride. This lie, though heavy on his heart, would be the words that made the difference in the war. It would save countless lives, including his brother and his most trusted friend. How could he not make the sacrifice?

Thrax'ul remained silent, staring daggers directly into Fangdarr's eyes. The satyr knew there was more behind the orc's words that weren't spoken. Yet, he could also see the struggle the orc had forced himself through. With a low grumble, the satyr chieftain rose to his full height and motioned for Fangdarr to do the same.

Each stood facing one another, considering all that would come to pass from their choices. Slowly, Thrax'ul extended his hand. "We are with you, Fangdarr, as Cerenos my witness. To the end."

Fangdarr took Thrax'ul's hand in his own and formed the bond. The orc nodded in thanks, truly appreciative of the beast-like creature's aid and thankful for being trusted—though he didn't feel it was deserved. "When do we move?"

"First light. I shall inform the village now and oversee preparations. Our number is small but should rival the elves due to their . . . reluctance to reproduce." The chieftain smiled at Elethain who politely returned the gesture as he took the minor insult. Like Fangdarr, the elf knew too much relied on the alliance with the satyrs. Then again, without the satyrs, the elves wouldn't go to war—sparing the death of many of his kin—and the humans would be eradicated. The thought certainly amused the prejudiced elf. Though, despite his desires, he held his tongue. Above all, he wouldn't bring shame to his king.

Elethain rose to his feet. "What is your number, exactly? I imagine you do not have ships to carry your warriors across the channel. The elves will need to transport you." Elethain relished sweetly in the reliance the crude beasts would have on his kind.

Thrax'ul didn't miss the elf's intent but accepted the lash in response to his own. "Three thousand will heed the call." The chieftain turned his back on Elethain and directed his conversation to Fangdarr. "We follow you, Fangdarr. See that my people do not die in vain—and that some may return home to tell the tale." The orc nodded, though both knew such a promise was impossible. "Go now. Rest. I will prepare the army. You should reach Jesmera tomorrow mid-day. See to it that King Nelthalius aids in your quest. For if he does not, send my warriors home." Elethain scoffed at the notion.

Brea'la escorted the three guests out of the tent and toward a nearby dwelling. "So, to war?" she asked with a smile as she held open the flap for them to enter.

Aesthéa went in first while Fangdarr responded, "To war." He crouched inside behind the druid and laid down next to her to rest. Outside, Elethain refused to enter for fear of letting his pristine elven skin touch the animal skin that covered the hovel. Instead, he conjured a small, horizontal wall of black magic and lay himself atop with a smug grin that only grew upon seeing Brea'la's astonished face.

Within the tent, Fangdarr clutched Aesthéa tightly. The nausea in his gut had finally simmered with the knowledge that, despite not giving voice to his own thoughts, Wiston may be saved.

CHAPTER FORTY-SEVEN
REDIRECTION

"What was that?!" Bitrayuul cried out between coughs as he crawled to his knees. Cormac simply lay on his back to take advantage of the moment's rest. The half-orc groaned as he rose, struggling to breathe.

Still staring at the plain stone ceiling, the old dwarf nonchalantly grumbled, "I hate mages. Hate 'em." With a resigned sigh, Cormac too rolled to his knees and crawled to the nearest barrel to pull himself to his feet. "Well, guess that's that. He won't be helping anytime soon."

Bitrayuul placed his helmet over his head as he eased himself onto a stool cautiously, as if at any moment his legs would give out beneath him. He wished the captain's words didn't ring true but knew otherwise. After the encounter, it seemed obvious that the prince cared more about the right to his own choice than the lives of his people—hardly a noble worthy of his esteemed title.

After Cormac joined his friend at the table, they sat together in silence unsure how to react to Lucien's assault. Despite nearly crushing them, the harshest wound came from the prince's words. There was no hope in his voice. Not a shred of belief in the men risking all to defend the city. Such thoughts were infectious as their deepest doubts had been given voice for the first time.

Time passed on with naught but the muffled sounds of the catapult slinging endless loads of trolls over their walls that slowly chipped away at their resolve. They couldn't rest, for sleep would risk all should they be awoken by foe over friend. All that could be done was wait and survive for however long was needed for Fangdarr to return. Soon the pit would be complete, and the storm would pass. So too would the enemy have finally retrieved enough stones to break through their defense and shatter their ranks. It was all just a matter of time.

Stretching as he stood, Bitrayuul stepped toward the door. Cormac lifted an eyebrow curiously. "Where ye goin', lad?"

"Just to stretch my legs. I'll check on the diggers while I'm out." The half-orc didn't bother turning to face the dwarf as he spoke. He exited the room to clear his head and get some fresh air, walking into the darkness softened by the moon. As he walked outside, the 'fresh air' that surged into his nose was the ever-present foul stench of the enemies below the wall. Bitrayuul scrunched his nose in disgust and made his way down the stairs to the ground level.

Absentmindedly, his legs carried him north through the city before reaching the interior gate separating the Military District from the courtyard. Bitrayuul shook his head to regain his focus, not realizing his legs carried him so far. He stared at the barricade before him, knowing what remained on the other side. Odd looks came from the pair of stationed soldiers as the half-orc simply stood in silence.

One of the guards tapped the butt of his spear impatiently on the ground. "Are you going in?" When no response came, he scoffed in annoyance. "Listen, you either need to go in or press on, we don't have all day."

It didn't matter, the half-orc hardly even heard the man's irked voice. He was too lost in his own thoughts as the flashes of that little girl and her trampled mother paralyzed him. Finally, Bitrayuul slowly turned and walked east along the wall toward the Philosophy District. *Perhaps some solitude,* he thought. *Anything but that forsaken courtyard.*

During the trek, Bitrayuul passed dozens of soldiers. After the fourth or fifth, he noticed that he was no longer getting uncomfortable stares as he passed. Instead he was met with nods of respect. *Would they react the same if they knew what I am?* How he wished to remove his helmet and let his comrades see him for who he truly was.

Travelling down an alley along the wall outside the courtyard, the half-orc finally encountered the wall to the Philosophy District. He worked his way inward, following the stacked stones until he reached the gate. Thankfully, no guards were outside to greet him with frustration. Bitrayuul pushed on the heavy door and immediately let out a gasp in shock. He could hardly even open the door wide enough to poke his head through as the crowd of civilians were pressed so tightly inside that it would budge no further. They were everywhere! In the small glance he could steal, Bitrayuul failed to notice a single exposed section of ground between the mass amount of people.

He couldn't take it. The number of clustered people made even the courtyard seem small—though arguably less chaotic. Bitrayuul could feel the disgruntled civilians pushing the door closed on his helmet as they were shoved from their seats. Without a second thought, the surprised half-orc pulled his head back out and let the steel door slam shut with a resounding boom. He dashed back to the darkened alley, ready to scream. *Where do they come from?! Why do they hide here instead of their homes?* Dwarves were a tight-knit community, but this hive-like behavior of the humans seemed completely irrational to Bitrayuul. He couldn't understand why they all flooded to wherever they could in the miniscule chance of safety, even when it offered nothing but a new kind of danger.

Slumping against the wall, Bitrayuul's armor screeched against the stone as he slid to the ground. He didn't know whether to sob or shout. His frustration only amplified the painful memories he had tried to shut out and the foreboding anticipation of doom that lie ahead. *Lucien is such a coward! Taking the easy way out to avoid the harsh realities and difficult decisions that are expected of a leader,* he thought. The redirection of anger helped assuage the other more painful emotions he was feeling. *How easy it would be to simply walk away right now and never return. I could easily say this is not my fight—and it isn't! But what of the greater good? What of the innocents stacked inside the walls of your city, Lucien? What of the children who are orphaned and crushed into the mud simply because you are not there to guide them? Where are you?!*

As he played out his anger, Bitrayuul realized that the words he shouted internally weren't only directed at the negligent prince, but Fangdarr as well. The thought shook him to his core. He had never considered Fangdarr a coward, nor did he have any conscious desire to hold his brother's departure over the orc's head. How could he? Fangdarr left in order to bring aid to their cause. The knowledge that his anger had been cast to his undeserving kin tore apart the final thread holding the half-orc together. He wept openly in the secreted alleyway, hoping none would find him and see the true weight on his shoulders in his most vulnerable moment.

"Are you alright?"

Bitrayuul quickly tried to recuperate and slid a hand beneath his helmet to wipe away the mess that had formed inside. "I-I'm fine," he began, cursing his ever-rotten luck. "Who goes there?"

No response came. Instead, the sound of boots lightly padding against the ground came from down the alley. Bitrayuul waited as the steps grew louder and louder in his right ear, expecting a passerby to have discovered his hiding place. His mind had already started formulating fabrications of the cause of his dismay—anything to keep the truth hidden. Finally, when the footsteps seemed terribly close, he could sense a presence to his left. As he turned, a dagger pressed against his throat between the plates of his armor.

"I must say, this armor is exquisite, orcblood. Is it dwarven?" Chakal's eyes danced around the steel, glowing with curiosity. He seemed completely at ease, leaning against the wall as if it were a bright summer day and he had just awoken from a long-needed rest. Immobilized in panic and rage at coming face-to-face with his father's murderer, Bitrayuul tried to slide away but felt the blade against his neck press deeper. "Now, now. Where are you going? Surely it can wait." A sinister smile spread across the assassin's lips as lust filled his eyes. He had the half-orc pinned and completely under his control—exactly as he liked.

Thankful for his concealing helmet, Bitrayuul was relieved the imposing killer couldn't see the fear in his eyes. With the dagger's edge tight against his jugular, his voice came in a raspy whisper. "What do you want?"

Chakal seemed to ponder for a moment in feigned ignorance. "That's right! I almost forgot. I'm here to kill you, if I recall correctly. So, what is your morning like? Are you free right now, or should we reschedule?" The ensuing laughter that came from the elf wasn't share by his victim.

With a flick of his wrist, Chakal retracted the blade from Bitrayuul's throat to allow him to speak. The elf waited for the half-orc to respond to his humor. His bright eyes shined with the excitement of a young dwarf on Bothain's Day, eagerly lying in wait.

Bitrayuul didn't know how to act or respond. Anything he said or did—or didn't do—could easily push the assassin over the edge. He recalled Elethain's advice of doing nothing, but something seemed off with Chakal this time. It was as if simply rejecting the assassin of his game wouldn't be enough. There was too much enthusiasm in the elf's expressions, as if he already knew the outcome of their conversation no matter Bitrayuul's input. The half-orc could see the elf's face quickly turning to anger at his silence. He needed to act now.

"Why are you here, Chakal?"

The building irritation on the elf's face disappeared immediately at the odd question. However, as soon as the confusion had replaced the anger, an enraged visage returned tenfold. "W-why am I here? *Why am I here?!* Do not act ignorant, Bitrayuul. You know the reason you sit at the edge of my blade!"

Daring to risk it all, Bitrayuul simply shrugged in response. The elf's angled eyes grew ever more narrow. It seemed feigning ignorance was a one-way road between the two.

"I am here because *you* could not leave well enough alone! Do not think I have forgotten your interference in my duel with your mother, orcblood. Nor your brutish brother's frustrating desire to throw people into the ocean!" Chakal's dagger was out in a flash and pressing against Bitrayuul's neck once more.

The half-orc questioned his decision at that point but decided to play it out to the fullest. If he was to die in this alley, he would do so with the brief satisfaction of knowing he had irritated the elf beyond reason. He visibly relaxed despite the screaming sensations to flee or avenge his father pounding in his head. "You do know there is a war going on? This is the largest war in history, Chakal. One that will most likely annihilate the humans and everyone here defending Wiston—myself included." A thought came to Bitrayuul and he quickly put it to words before the elf had a chance to cut him off. "Why don't *you* aid in the war? Then you can kill and murder as you please." It destroyed him to ask for the elf to aid in their endeavors, even in a desperate attempt to save his own life. Beneath his enclosed helmet, tears rimmed his eyes as the memory of his father's corpse being thrown into the fire played in the back of his mind.

An explosive and seemingly genuine outburst of laughter came from Chakal. "You want me to help you survive this war, just to kill you after? And save the pathetic humans from the result of their greed?" His laughter continued, echoing off the narrow alley. The expression on his face shifted to a wicked and fierce scowl as his words turned more sinister. "No. I lost Malice to the dragon when I should have ended her myself beforehand! I shall not allow you to escape my blade at the hands of a stray arrow in a war between factions!"

This was it. Bitrayuul closed his eyes and waited for the dagger to sink deep into his neck and spray his lifeblood over the stones. To his surprise, he was at peace with the notion. A great burden seemed to have slipped from his shoulders knowing his doom would relieve the stress he was under. Waiting. Waiting. And yet, it never came. Bitrayuul cracked open an eye to see Chakal staring emptily at the wall in front of him.

Curiosity got the better of the half-orc, forcing him to pry. "What stays your hand?" He could hardly believe the words as they escaped him. *Are you a fool?!* he berated himself.

A smile spread across Chakal's lips. "You know, I am a creative elf. I truly am. There are nearly an infinite number of ways to end a life. A duel between warriors is my favorite by far, but such a method can become bland. I seek new ways to bring thrill into my hunting. You wish for my help in this war? I will need something in return."

Bitrayuul hated that he even considered asking, but he couldn't stop himself. "And what is that?"

The wicked and terrifying grin painted on the elf's face grew impossibly wide with glee. "There is one I have never been able to kill. He adds complications, you see, and has been elusive to my desires to end his miserable life. I will aid in this filthy war for you. I will spare your life, and even your brother's, as this is a prize I have sought for hundreds of years. Should you fail, I will come for you. And your brother. And the dwarf. And every small child I've witnessed you fawn over like an overprotective matron. *Everyone* you care about will die should you fail to hold up your end of the bargain. I will kill trolls, orcs, and ogres, all in return for this *one* simple task." His voice had grown exponentially in eagerness at the thought of savoring the meal to come, clenching down on that final bite that had escaped him for so long.

Torn between selfishly saving himself and Fangdarr at the cost of another, Bitrayuul contemplated desperately. If he refused, his life would most likely be forfeit then and there. But did he lack the honor of sacrificing himself to save another, or would he stay true to the morals Tormag had instilled in him, he wondered. Guilt and self-loathing were all Bitrayuul could feel in that moment. He knew his answer long before he had even considered it. The shame that coursed through him made him wish for death, but the half-orc's weakness was too great. His shoulders slumped as the thought of Tormag's disappointment weighed on him. "What task?"

Chakal's maniacal laughter hardly allowed the words to pass between his open lips. "Kill Elethain!"

CHAPTER FORTY-EIGHT

HOME

Fangdarr watched as the hateful and incredulous stares directed at him quickly shifted to a mix of awe and discomfort as the elves of Jesmera witnessed the orc lead three thousand bestial warriors through the streets. Unlike his last visit, Fangdarr wasn't apprehended on his entry into the beautiful city. Instead, he sat atop his eilfeyn with Aesthéa and Elethain riding in line behind him, followed by Brea'la and her kin.

As they approached the king's tower, Fangdarr slid himself from his steed. Aesthéa and Elethain followed suit and pursued the orc to the narrow portal at its base. With a steadying breath and bracing for the impact from the unseen magical barrier, Fangdarr stepped forward. He exhaled with relief as his body passed through without being rejected. Shortly after, Elethain came through behind him.

To their surprise, Aesthéa was thrown from the portal and rejected entry. They watched in confusion as she called out angrily as if her uncle could hear her. Fangdarr and Elethain attempted to pass through the magical barrier once more and help her through, but they were repelled from the inside. Getting to their feet with painful groans, they slowly stepped toward the invisible wall. Fangdarr didn't know what to do. He didn't want to anger or insult her by continuing without her. Nor did he want to risk the king's wrath.

"It's okay, Fangdarr. Go on. I'll be waiting for you out here," Aesthéa said softly, though she couldn't see him due to the arcane wall.

Pleading with his eyes, the orc waited as if he expected the barrier to be dispelled any moment, as a cruel joke played by the king. He knew it to be false, though, and shared the druid's trepidation.

"Come, Fangdarr. We must meet with the king," Elethain urged. His dutiful service remained his highest priority. If the king didn't wish for his niece to join them then he held faith in a sound reason.

With the necromancer's footsteps growing quieter as he walked down the hall, Fangdarr watched the worried look on Aesthéa's face grow more and more. "I love you, Bear," he muttered before turning away. He knew she had managed to hear his muffled words by the small smile that had spread across her face. Aesthéa didn't respond, however, as she wished to see his face when the words fell upon his ears. The elf turned back toward the envoy of satyrs—she would wait.

Fangdarr caught up to Elethain outside the king's chamber. Without any exchange of words, the pair of elite guards granted them entry. Though it had only been a few days since last they set foot in the room, the orc was again floored by the marvelous collection of trinkets that scaled the walls.

"Greetings, Fangdarr," Nelthalius said as he rose from his twisted throne. "And to you, Elethain." The necromancer bowed his head, watching with irritation as Fangdarr remained erect. The king paid little mind to the orc's unyielding stature. "I hear whispers that you are indeed chosen by Cerenos. Is that true?"

The orc cursed his luck. He knew he should have expected the perceptive elf to put him on the spot immediately. Lying to one of his prowess wouldn't be easy. Fangdarr sucked in his breath. "Some believe."

A smile spread across the king's pale face. "But not you?"

Fangdarr was immeasurably thankful that Aesthéa hadn't been permitted entry in that moment. *Perhaps this is the reason? Unhindered honesty?* He shook his thoughts away and nodded in reply, earning a scoff and chuckle from Elethain.

"Now, now, Elethain. Do not blame the orc. You too are a hard one to convince of the unseen workings of our god, are you not?" Nelthalius glanced to his advisor. Fangdarr was surprised to see the king had come to his rescue against the minor hatred that Elethain still harbored. "No. He has been honest. A trait I'm sure you would not expect from one of his kind."

Pride swelled in the chieftain's chest. Such praise from the leader of a race that hated orcs more than all others wasn't what he had expected. "You honor me, King."

Disregarding the orc's polite words, Nelthalius turned away from the pair and strode around the room. Moments passed in awkward silence as he slowly paced, searching for the words he wished. Finally, the king halted. "Might I ask, Fangdarr, why do you fight your own kind? The humans have driven out orcs for as long as history has been written. The trolls and ogres have received the same treatment—even from the dwarves. Those known to be 'good' are no more than murderers on a path of endless slaughter of those they deem monstrous. Is this war not just the reciprocation? A fair reprisal in response to the treatment your kind has been forced to endure for millennia. Do you not believe that humans and dwarves should be eradicated for the acts they have committed?" His eyes bore into Fangdarr with much more intensity. "So, I ask you, why do you not join them?"

Another intense question. It seemed Fangdarr would be forced to answer quite a few hard truths today—some even he had never put into words before. He tensed at the thought of having to expose his inner thoughts. In truth, it brought him pain to turn against his kind. Yet, such an answer may completely unravel all that he had worked for. Fangdarr didn't know whether to remain honest or hide behind more lies.

Honesty. He knew the elf had swayed his decision with the previous praises that were offered, yet Fangdarr didn't care. He would have wished to follow the same course anyway. What purpose was there in fighting for a good cause if he couldn't be truthful about his intent?

The orc took in a long breath and lifted his chin. "I wanted my people seen as equal. Peace between us and other races. But . . . they have done things. *I* have done things. Bad things. To feel I belonged. Pain I cannot take back. Horrors I cannot erase. To people who should not forgive. Orcs can never be equal. They single-minded. Lusting. Only consume. Even now, they seek to feed that lust. To rape. To kill. I cannot stop them. It their way and, in their mind, their right. We are cursed. Destined to destroy. I thought to change that. Change who we are. But I cannot. We are what we are. Beasts. I see differently. It is *my* curse. To know how monstrous we are and fail to bring us to humanity. All I wanted was for orcs to be equals. To feel breeze without sniffing for blood. To not count our triumphs by notches on our blades or tears of those we have defiled. I cannot change who we are," he slowed, finally realizing the truth himself. "But I can stop us."

After his long, truth-bearing speech, Fangdarr looked up to see the ever-present scowl on Elethain's face had been replaced in awe. The king turned toward the orc and walked forward, stopping a few paces away. "A fine answer, Fangdarr. You are one of a kind, to be sure."

The orc's body deflated. He knew what came next.

"But . . .," Nelthalius continued, confirming the orc's fears. "While I commend you and your noteworthy wisdom, it is *your* people, under *your* command, who now strike at Wiston. And it is they who will strike down *my* people should I send them to war. Yes?"

Elethain stepped in. "Your majesty, the orcs in the enemy's army are nearly a negligible number. Even if the orcs were on *our* side, it is the trolls who are the real threat." Fangdarr offered a smile to the necromancer, who returned it in kind—though the elf's expression dissipated as he met the king's scowl.

"I will get to the point, Fangdarr," Nelthalius began in a commanding tone. "I no longer wish to sacrifice the lives of my kind."

Fangdarr stepped forward wide-eyed. "What of our agreement?! Satyrs with us. We ready to defend Wiston! Four days. Four days since we left! They need us now!"

Seeing the orc press forward, the king drove him back forcefully with magic in warning. Fangdarr had nearly forgotten the king was a powerful arcanist, but he didn't back down. Once more Nelthalius repelled him, this time with more power. Fangdarr resisted but slid across the smooth floor. "Enough, orc! Our agreement is at an end! You will have no aid from the elves. Take your filthy beastmen and their sharpened sticks and go aid those who brought this upon themselves! Had the pathetic humans not wiped out their own kind a thousand years ago, they would not need to beg for the aid of those they spit upon in secret!"

Once more, Elethain interjected to come to Fangdarr's aid. "My king! We cannot break the agreement. If Wiston survives the war they will know of our betrayal. Some day they may strike back at us! I urge you to reconsider."

Nelthalius turned an even more furious glare toward his subordinate. "You forget your place!" he shouted as he blasted Elethain across the room. "You would march our own to their deaths for the sake of *humans*?! They are but a blink to us! We witness a hundred of their generations in our lifetime. They are bugs by comparison! They are the pets we keep beneath our shadow to serve our own purposes. Now they have wrought destruction upon themselves and you, *orcs*, and *dwarves*," he spat in disgust, "have already spared them instant annihilation with the fall of Crepusculus! Where were the humans when the great shadow dragon loomed in his cave, plotting their demise? Nowhere! They sat in their cities and worked their fingers to the bone to bring in enough coins to line their coffers while their children starve! They are naught but greed and consumption, surpassing even the wild lust of the orcs. The only difference is they rape for coins rather than power—then have the audacity to call the actions of others '*unjust*'. I will not keep the disease of man aflame. They are on their own!"

Completely astounded, Elethain pulled himself to his knees. He knew that his own prejudiced views could be harsh, but in all the years he had served his king, Nelthalius had never once shown any such beliefs. The necromancer had only ever known the elven leader to be kind, compassionate, and good. Despite agreeing with Nelthalius in part, Elethain couldn't deny his conviction to his king had wavered tremendously.

Elethain looked up to see Fangdarr's extended hand. He took it and was pulled to his feet by the expressionless orc. There was no sadness in Fangdarr's face. No anger or disbelief. There was only acceptance. The orc knew he couldn't change anything, so what purpose was there in trying? They could only press on. Together, they began walking out of the chamber, ignoring the tumultuous string of insults the king spat regarding humans and their faults. Perhaps it was just the ramblings of an ancient elf nearing the end of his life. Or, more likely, the king had kept his true nature hidden for so long that once the secrets had become uncorked, they couldn't be stopped. It mattered not.

The pair stood at the portal, still hidden from view from those outside. Before passing through, Elethain halted the orc with a hand on his arm. Fangdarr stared at the elf patiently, waiting to hear what he had to say. "Fangdarr, I did not know he held such beliefs. Nor that he would renege on your agreement. He was a kind elf. One full of heart and passion. I share in his beliefs; you know I do. But you have shown me that there is more than just hatred in this world. We must strive to be better, for the benefit of others." Fangdarr laid his own hand over Elethain's shoulder in thanks. "I am with you," Elethain continued, "to Wiston and beyond." With a final smile and a wave of happiness at knowing he had finally chosen to do the right thing and not simply pursue his own ambitions, the elf passed through the barrier.

Fangdarr sighed heavily. Even the strengthened bond between him and the powerful necromancer wasn't enough to pull him from the underlying despair that he would be forced to endure from the king's decision. "To Wiston . . .," he said to himself with reluctance before stepping through the arcane wall.

CHAPTER FORTY-NINE

TRUST

Under cover of darkness, Bitrayuul led Chakal through the city to the command room, taking care to avoid as many soldiers as he could. Luckily, the elf had little trouble going unnoticed, as the last thing the men needed was the false hope that the elves had arrived. After passing the last sentry, the half-orc stepped into the room and was greeted by Cormac who appeared to have just stirred from a short rest.

"Where ye been, lad? Bothain's beard, is it night already?" He rubbed his temple awkwardly to avoid stabbing himself in the head with the blades on his shields, still strapped to his arms. "I must've dozed off. Want to look for some fo—" Cormac's words caught in his throat as Chakal entered the room.

The captain was up in an instant, shouting a warning to Bitrayuul and charging the elf. The half-orc caught him mid-stride and restrained him with difficulty. "Cormac, no! He has come to aid us!"

Cormac stared at Bitrayuul like he had gone mad. "*Aid* us?! Ye remember the last time he '*aided*' us? This damned pretty boy cut down yer father and threw him in a fire! Kill him, son!"

Bitrayuul struggled to push aside the painful memories at the mention of his father. "No! We need him, Cormac! And besides, we cannot defeat him. He could have killed me, yet he hasn't." He could see the anger that still burned in the dwarf's eyes.

Walking up to the assassin, Cormac stared up at the elf with intense scrutiny before slamming a shield across his face, drawing blood. The purple droplets rolled past Chakal's wicked grin and onto the floor. "Well," the dwarf started, "at least we know the demon can bleed." He continued to wait for the elf to lash out and kill him. Even if it meant his life, Cormac needed to prove to Bitrayuul that the elf was playing them. Yet, no reaction came. Just that sinister smile and the promise of retaliation in Chakal's eyes. He couldn't know that Chakal would endure far worse at a chance to accomplish his greatest goal, his sweetest kill. Nor that it was Bitrayuul who was indentured to that service.

The captain continued to glare suspiciously at the elf with his one good eye. With a grunt of disapproval, he shoved past Chakal and stormed out of the room, mumbling about checking the progress of the pit. Once the dwarf was out of earshot, Chakal turned his smile on Bitrayuul. "That went well enough, I would think."

Every word that spilled from the assassin's mouth was an assault to the half-orc's memories. He couldn't stand the certain hint of victory latched onto every sentence. It was as if Chakal knew he had already won. The extreme confidence only served to remind Bitrayuul of the beast he had tethered himself to, completely powerless. It tore at him. He wondered if he would ever have the strength to defeat the elf. Perhaps with Fangdarr and the others at his side, the half-orc could find a way to rid himself of the lingering infection and break his agreement. A hundred plans tried to take root in his thoughts, all ending in lives lost—a trade he didn't want to make.

Driving away the hopeless strategies, Bitrayuul took a seat. "Well enough." He removed his helmet, setting it on the wooden table and re-tied his hair, drawing a surprised look from Chakal.

"I didn't know you had hair, orcblood." The elf's eyes fixed more closely as he slid onto a stool. To Bitrayuul's surprise, he seemed genuinely curious about such a menial feature. Chakal's eyebrows raised as he leaned back on a single foot of the stool—anything to prove his abilities at every turn. He turned his attention to the large, bladed helmet and swiped it deftly. "This is fine work. The dwarves always astound me with their skill."

Bitrayuul raised his own brow in curiosity. He didn't expect Chakal to praise dwarves. The assassin picked up on his expression, however, and pulled out his dagger. "I'll let you in on a secret, orcblood, because I know you're *dying* to know." His pale hand lifted the curved dagger for Bitrayuul to see. "I imagine you do not know much of elves, but they use a kind of leaf for their blades. It's a process, you see. They dip the leaves in a solution that hardens them, leaving them light in weight yet granting the strength of steel. Elves discovered the formula thousands of years ago, though only a rare few are given the privilege of its knowledge."

Bitrayuul watched the dagger turn over effortlessly in Chakal's hands, reflecting the torchlight against the blade. The elf continued, "I refuse to use them anymore, the leaf-bladed weapons. I was cast out from my kind and am no longer welcome—much like I can imagine you feel in both of your worlds." His eyes glanced up at the half-orc, making sure to note Bitrayuul's gaze turn away. "Besides," Chakal slid the dagger back into its sheath, "I much prefer the ring of steel anyway."

"Are your weapons enchanted?" the half-orc asked, exposing his curiosity

Chakal laughed aloud with abnormal intensity. "Gods, no! I am not one for such tricks."

Remembering their previous encounters, Bitrayuul couldn't deny the truth of that statement. That is, until he fell upon a consideration that had irked him during their journey. "What about for travel? You were able to catch up to us even as we escaped on horseback. And your wounds seemed to heal rather quickly after your first duel with Malice. Magic?"

The assassin's face turned grim at the accusation, rocking Bitrayuul back on his heels. Through gritted teeth, Chakal responded, "I've told you, *orcblood*, I am not one for such tricks." Feeling his heart beat more quickly as the elf's eyes bore into him, Bitrayuul remained silent. Chakal's visage instantly reverted to passiveness. "In any case, my skills are not limited to combat."

Bitrayuul wasn't satisfied with that answer but had to accept it, nonetheless. They sat in silence, simply staring at one another. Bitrayuul felt terribly uncomfortable as the expressions on the elf's face continuously changed, even without provocation.

After a prolonged silence, Cormac came through the door once more and gave a helpless, "Bah!" upon seeing Chakal still present, breaking the pair's awkward staring. Choosing to ignore the elf, the dwarf turned to Bitrayuul. "Pit be nearly done, the lads are doin' good work."

"Good, it is almost morning. With luck the storm will pass tomorrow, and they should be finished before the day is at an end." Bitrayuul ran his hand over his head. "With even more luck, Fangdarr should have returned by then."

"It is possible," Chakal chimed in, drawing a scoff from Cormac. "I encountered them in the forest on Y'thirya. They sh—"

Cormac rushed forward with his nostrils flared. "Ye what?! Did ye kill them, ye dog?"

"Cormac! Let him finish, please," Bitrayuul begged. The dwarf halted his advance but still fumed in silence. With an exaggerated wave of his hands, Cormac offered for Chakal to proceed.

A smile formed on the elf's face—it's only purpose to further enrage the stout warrior. "As I was saying, they were headed west, most likely to Wudhyvn to seek the aid of the satyrs. And no," Chakal added, turning to Cormac, "I did not harm them. I was looking for Bitrayuul. Elethain informed me that you were here, so *here* I am." Bitrayuul gasped at the knowledge that Elethain had offered him on a platter to the notoriously vicious assassin. It certainly made his task of killing the necromancer more palatable—a fact Chakal knew well.

"Bah! Tricky words from the trickster himself!" Cormac refuted. "Bothain's truth, there be no love between Elethain and Bitrayuul, don't ye doubt, but handin' him over for ye to do as ye please . . . even Elethain ain't that heartless."

Chakal spread a wide grin once more, directly at Bitrayuul. He never pulled his gaze away as he responded to the dwarf's argument. "I assure you; he is that and more."

All fell silent as none were willing to continue the point or change their opinions. After he could no longer bear it, Chakal asked, "What exactly would you like me to aid with, Bitrayuul?"

The half-orc perked up at the question, realizing he hadn't considered the part the assassin would play in this war. After all, what could one elf do? "Any chance you can dismantle the enemy's catapult?"

"Unfortunately, there *are* things that my skills cannot perform. Wading through an unending ocean of enemies to chop apart a mechanism is one such limitation."

Cormac laughed. "Hah! So, he *ain't* perfect!"

Chakal smiled and winked back at the dwarf. "No, but I can see over the parapets."

The dwarf grumbled and muttered curses under his breath before slumping to a seat on the floor. ". . . that's why they got embrasures . . .." He continued to mumble words under his breath before his face lit up with an idea. "Hey! I know somethin' ye can do. Go and find us the prince and convince the bastard to lead his people!"

Raising his brow in confusion, Chakal seemed reluctant. "You want me to find a spoiled snob and tell him to stop hiding?" He turned to Bitrayuul. "Is that what you want?"

Bitrayuul looked at Cormac. Neither were interested in dealing with the young man again and both knew that Chakal was more versed in matters of forced persuasion. With a shrug of his shoulders, the half-orc said, "It works for me. He's a stubborn one, perhaps you'll have more luck."

Despite the insult of being sent on such a low task, Chakal couldn't argue with how simple of a trade it would be. It certainly beat the prospect of swimming through the host of trolls to cut apart the catapult. With a resigned sigh, the assassin rose from his seat to leave. "Don't expect me tonight."

CHAPTER FIFTY

RETRIBUTION

Chakal pulled up his hood to shadow his features from the soldiers lining the walls. It hardly mattered as each was locked in distraction, watching out anxiously over the massive army. The elf could see the fear in their eyes. The constant expectation of threat had broken them down at their core. Even safely atop the battlements, the soldiers would watch the monsters beneath cut each other apart at the slightest transgression, only to regenerate anew. As the assassin crept past each sentry, he had to stop himself from scoffing at their weakness and pushing them to the beasts below.

Amused by the thought, Chakal's mood lightened. But he pushed the devious desire from his mind and pressed on, eager to find somewhere to rest in privacy for the night. He scolded himself for being sent on such a trivial task by the half-orc. Nonetheless, if that was the cost of finally ridding himself of Elethain, so be it.

From his vantage point on the wall, Chakal scanned the area in search for a peaceful place to sleep. He wasn't fond of the idea of waking up to that damned dwarf's shield-blades sinking deep into his chest. A dimly lit window at the top of a tall tower in the Philosophy District caught the elf's eye. He sneered in disgust as the ground level was swarming with hapless peasants and townspeople. Thankfully, the tower appeared somewhat close to the wall, perhaps enough to make the jump.

It took the elf a while to traverse the stretching path toward the eastern section of the city. He was stopped for questioning by a pair of curious guards who took the moment's effort to realize the dark-leather garb Chakal donned was terribly out of place. The elf had considered simply ignoring them, but he was too annoyed at being treated as a dog sent to fetch and his principals fled. Unfortunately, these guards—the only ones trying to do their duty, really—would be the ones to suffer for it. Before throwing them over the wall, Chakal sliced through their throats to sever their windpipes. He didn't even bother to watch as they fell silently into the waiting jaws of the horde below, still clutching their necks. The assassin was unable to hide his smile as he heard the excited howls and vigorous ripping of flesh.

Thanks to the negligence of the other nearby sentries, no alarms were raised and Chakal managed to reach the wall lining the Philosophy District unhindered. He stared up at the tower where the softly glowing room high at the top still flickered with candlelight. Backpedaling a few steps, the elf sucked in his breath in preparation for the leap. It was long, nearly four times his height. Sprinting forward, Chakal planted his foot atop the parapets and launched himself with all his might into the air. With his legs and arms tucked tightly against his body, the elf managed to connect against the tower. His face smashed against the stone, drawing a frustrated scowl, but his fingertips managed to catch hold of the stacked stones that lined the structure. Staring upward, he discovered he was nearly halfway up. *Could have been worse.*

Chakal's agile form began scaling the stones toward the summit. Each window he passed the elf made sure to peek in and see what would lay beneath him once inside. Luckily, the building consisted of only old men, typically reading or enjoying the forced pleasures of their house workers. Despite his distorted morality, Chakal looked away in revulsion as the young women—and one miserable sodomized man—were forced to endure the hot breath of ragged men on their necks simply due to the difference in their social status. Such acts were in poor taste to the assassin, forcing him to carry on quickly.

Grunting with the effort, the elf pulled himself into the narrow window and slipped into the highest room. Instantly, he realized he wasn't alone as a startled gasp came upon his entry. He was up in arms in a moment and already charging forward with a snarl painted across his visage. The elf didn't expect the room to be empty but planned to deal with whomever he found upon arrival. Instead, nearly a dozen frightened women were packed into the small room, staring at him in terror.

Though the look in their eyes brought him exhilaration, Chakal slid his blades back into their scabbards and took another step forward. The women all backed away instinctively from the shadowy figure that had come into their room unannounced. Each was battered and bruised. Judging by the darkness, their wounds were recent. *It seems this war has already brought spoils*, Chakal realized. It didn't take much to make the connection, especially with the scenes had witnessed on his ascent. These women had traded their bodies to the abuse of the scholarly men who resided in this tower, most likely with the thought that what they would suffer here was the lesser punishment than what they would be subjected to piled up outside with the rest of the commoners.

Scanning the room, Chakal noticed one bed and half a dozen blankets spread on the floor. *Gods, I am too kind.* He slowly approached the nearest woman, who whimpered and tried to back away. None had seen an elf before, especially one jumping through their window in the dead of night in the middle of a war. The elf patted the air with his hand. "It is alright. I will not harm you."

They remained unconvinced. It was as if they could sense the underlying wickedness beneath his calm demeanor. Nevertheless, the assassin bent to a knee and produced a knife from his belt. Once more, they all gasped in trepidation upon seeing the blade. Moving the blade closer to the woman, Chakal grabbed her wrist forcefully and put the handle in her hand. Her eyes went wide in confusion, begging for an explanation.

"The men below have allowed this war to present them opportunities. It is time you do the same. Take your lump of flesh and repay their hospitality. This is a war. It is brutal on all fronts, as you all have now realized. Claim this tower for yourselves and rid the world of those you hate." His hand closed the frightened girl's fingers around the shaft of the knife.

For many moments, there was only silence. The girl with the blade looked at him, then the knife, then back at him. "W-what if we are caught? The guards will strike us down."

Chakal smiled at her and ran a slender finger through her greasy and disheveled hair. "My dear girl, there are trolls being flung into the city without relent. Surely one could have entered through a window." He winked, then rose to his feet and stood watching them.

They all looked to each other with the confounded look of caged animals who had just discovered the gate had always been unlocked, chattering amongst themselves. Chakal expected there to be more naysayers, yet they surprised him. It didn't take long for the rest to pull candleholders and other objects that could be used as clubs and line up at the door. The girl with the knife stepped over to the elf and looked at him with tear-filled eyes. "Thank you," she whispered, pulling a slipped strap of her gown back up to her shoulder—as if modesty were suddenly relevant. Chakal nodded in reply and watched them funnel out the door, tiptoeing their way down the spiral staircase.

As he padded to the entrance, the elf saw the girl clutching the blade give him one final look. Her eyes met his as a wicked grin spread across his face just before the door was shut. Despite the elf's look—and the dread it had spread through her—she continued down the stairs. It was too late to go back now.

On the other side, Chakal's smile remained etched into his cheeks and his eyes went wild at the thought of the women carrying out their vicious task. He wedged two chairs into the doorway to prevent being disturbed and began removing his equipment. With an exhale of relief, he fell to the bed and embraced the soft sheets of cloth beneath his exposed skin. It wasn't long before the sounds of men crying out in pain to be reach him, paired with the vengeful screams from the women. Chakal's smile spread even wider as he passed into sleep with the wails of anguish filling his ears.

CHAPTER FIFTY-ONE

HUNTING

The sun piercing through the small window stung the elf's eyes and broke his sleep. Chakal stretched his body and let out a content sigh. Sliding to the edge of the bed, he reached for his armor. As his arm extended, the light in the room made his pale skin seem more akin to the shade of humans'—a displeasing thought, to say the least. He retracted his arm back into the shade.

With his attire donned once more, Chakal removed the wedged chairs from the door. He had considered simply slipping back out the window, but he was too curious of the night's events. As soon as he opened the door, the assassin was met with the huddled form of the same girl he had given his knife to. Every instinct in his merciless mind commanded her immediate death, yet he paused.

Chakal bent low to inspect the girl. He could tell she was still asleep and had spent the night on the cold and uncomfortable stone steps waiting for him to open his door. A wide bruise covered the left half of her face, though the blackness did little to obscure her features. In addition to the beating she had taken, a deep cut ran the length of her forearm and was still seeping with a slow stream of blood. The elf almost pulled out his dagger to put an end to her. But stayed his hand as her right hand still clung tightly to the borrowed knife—the blade she had used to win back her freedom. Chakal's face turned to a smile as he realized she had succeeded in her vengeance.

Sliding an arm cautiously beneath her sleeping form, the elf lifted her from the unforgiving stone and carried her gently to the bed. He placed her down with care, making sure her sleep wasn't disturbed. Once she was in place on the cushioned furniture, Chakal opened a small pouch on his belt and pulled out a pinch of an odd-smelling green paste. Gently, he lathered it over the cut on the girl's arm, confident it would speed the mending. Then, he slid a light blanket over her and turned away without a word. The assassin gave one last look to the injured girl, proud of her achievement. With a tender smile, the elf pulled himself through the small window and back out into the sun.

* * * * *

Chakal crept past the final guard and into the vast and empty room. It wasn't the first time he had been in the throne room of Wiston, though admittedly it had nearly been a thousand years since his last visit—always unrequested, of course.

It seemed odd how few guards remained in the castle. He supposed it was due to the war or perhaps the raging mob he had to slip through to get inside. Their lack of presence gave him the freedom to walk about the decorative chamber as he pleased on his search. The assassin scanned the walls for the item he was looking for and was surprised further still that it hadn't been an easy object to find. Chakal continued through the castle before coming to a hallway where six guards were seated. Only one remained awake and seemed distracted by the loose stitches on his leather belt. The elf nearly let out a burst of laughter at the pitiful level of security. It almost removed the fun of his little hunt. Almost.

Eyeing the hallway in hopes it contained what he needed, Chakal let out a sigh of frustration. The item remained directly above the lone awakened guard, taunting the elf with its presence. Every desire in the assassin begged him to simply kill all six guards and be done with it. A fair trade for their hindrance, in his mind. But, doing so would only put the city on alarm and worse would require he also kill the king he knew rested beyond the door. The prospect of killing the king amused Chakal, yet it quickly passed. Though he killed on occasion to avoid detection, he wouldn't end the life of a king without greater purpose.

With another stifled and exasperated sigh, Chakal tied his cloak tightly around his body to secure it before pulling himself up the stone walls outside the corridor. Once he was higher in the air, the elf rounded the corner and began scaling the wall as close to the ceiling as he could. The stone ceiling was much lower in the hallway, however, leaving him just a spear-length above the guards. Cautiously, he crept along the wall, careful to avoid the numerous paintings and tapestries that littered the hall. Despite the short length of the path, it proved much more difficult than anticipated, causing the assassin to regret his decision to not simply end the guards' lives. But he was too close to back out. Another few pulls and he would reach the item he sought.

The guard below stirred slightly at the sound of twine sliding free from the thick nail in the wall as Chakal began extracting the object. Whining as the relatively large item came free, the nail nearly fell from its hole in the stone. He eyed it with the intensity of every bit of hatred in his body, willing it not to fall and make all his effort for naught. An eternity of anxiousness passed as the small bit of iron continued to creep out at a dreadful pace. The elf wanted to scream in frustration but could only maintain his menacing stare, promising an excruciating death to the nail should it fall. With luck, the iron held in place and he nearly burst out triumphantly.

With the item in hand and the guard resuming his distracted picking of his seams, Chakal began the even more difficult task of backtracking with one arm encumbered. The object was nearly half his height, causing his movement to be dreadfully slow and tedious. Sweat dripped down the elf's brow as he put great effort into silently moving back toward the main room and out of the hallway.

Only a bit more. Twenty pulls. Nineteen. Eighteen. The regret Chakal felt earlier for not simply killing his way to what he wanted was amplified tenfold. He even considered killing the guards after his task was complete just for making him go through the trouble. Twelve. Eleven. *Almost there* . . . he emboldened himself. *All this for that degenerate half-orc. No* . . ., his gritted teeth spread into a smile through the taxing strain. *For Elethain.* Done! As he finally reached the corner once more, Chakal pulled himself around it in a final heave and leapt to the floor, landing in a roll. He wasn't sure if the guard had heard him or not and he wasn't about to stay and find out.

Chakal tucked himself into another hallway just as the lazy guard peeked out from his post. Sweating, panting, and cursing, the elf looked to his prize and rolled his eyes. The item wouldn't make his task any easier, but at least he now had some sort of semblance of who he was looking for. Chakal stared at the painting before removing his dagger and cutting out the prince's face and stuffing the extracted piece into his tunic.

Now I know what you look like, Prince Lucien.

* * * * *

Over half the day had passed and Chakal was growing irritated. Normally, the assassin would enjoy the thrill of the hunt and even be willing to spend months or years in search of his target. But this was different. This was some meaningless assignment given to him as part of Bitrayuul's agreement, not a joyous hunt to prove himself worthy. The elf had questioned civilians, interrogated guards, and even visited the harlots in the few inns that had continued service during the war asking for more information on Lucien's whereabouts. He was growing tired of the man's seemingly nonexistent trail, forcing the elf's task to not be as simple as he had hoped.

Luckily, the last guard had finally given him some sort of a lead—though with a knife shoved into the man's eye, how truthful might it be? Between shouts of agony, the man offered the prince's known hideouts: the castle dungeons and the docks. Chakal had already searched the dungeons to no avail and was headed toward the docks at the northern edge of the city, frustration adding weight to each pounding stomp.

The guards stationed at the large gate between the Market District and the port looked uneasy as the elf headed their way. Chakal didn't have his weapons out, but it must have been the disgruntled look on his face and the way in which he pressed forward. His scowl wasn't even meant for them, yet it shook the men to their core. They each looked to the other as the assassin approached, silently acknowledging their fears. Without saying a word or asking his purpose, one of the guards began opening the gate. The other quickly followed suit, expediting the spread of the large door and allowing Chakal entry. Not even a glance came from the elf as he passed through, for he was too trapped in his own irritation to even bother with them. As the door closed behind him, Chakal began scanning every direction frantically in search of the elusive prince.

His gaze landed on a few notable landmarks where the man could be hiding. There were a handful of ships, a wharfmaster's shack, three large warehouses, and plenty of spots where one could evade discovery if that were their aim. Chakal pressed on, heading down the path toward the wharfmaster first. As he kicked open the door forcefully, the men inside jumped up in a start. None made a move and were immobilized in confusion and fear at the sight of the angry elf standing in the doorway. These were simple sailors, Chakal knew. Hardly men who would dare raise a weapon to him.

Chakal raised a finger to the man he assumed was the wharfmaster and watched the man's face drain of color. Slowly, the officer tip-toed toward the elf, nearly staining his trousers in fright. Chakal slid an arm around the man, increasing his fear a hundred times over. All the other sailors in the room watched as the elf whispered into the man's ear. They waited, unsure of how to act, and witnessed the man's face contort from fear to confusion then back to fear once more. Shaking his head, the wharfmaster screwed his eyes shut, expecting his lack of information to bring his doom. Instead, he felt the elf pat him twice on the back and walk away slowly. Once Chakal was out of sight, the wharfmaster fainted from the stress.

Chakal eyed the warehouses and the boats, wondering which the prince would prefer. By the few accounts he had received, the man was one for seclusion, leaving him to believe the warehouses would certainly be a wasted effort.

Face grim with hatred, the elf continued his hunt toward the ships.

CHAPTER FIFTY-TWO

MORTALITY

Chakal ignored the shouts of the sailors stampeding down the dock as he climbed aboard the first vessel. His disgruntled walk hastened as he kicked through each cabin door in search of Lucien. *It should not be this hard to find the son of the king!* His fury grew with each barrier he powered through, as if he were being taunted at every corner. By the time the sailors had descended the ladder to interject Chakal had searched half the ship.

"You there! What are you doing? Halt! *Halt!*" Their joined shouts amplified when the elf disregarded them. A few brandished swords, others clubs, and one a slimy, bug-eyed fish dripping oily ooze. Growing annoyed at Chakal's incessant searching, the largest of the group stepped forward, pointing his sword threateningly.

At that, Chakal finally stopped. He turned to regard the man and his colleagues, a world of hate in his sneer. Without uttering a word, the assassin stepped forward until his nose nearly met its opponent. The other sailors stared at their friend with confusion, wondering why he hadn't struck out against the elf. They couldn't fathom the paralyzing fear that afflicted the man, rooting him in place and making his heart pound.

Hardly audible, Chakal responded with his own command. "Leave. Or die." No more was needed. The elf saw the color slip away from the burly man's face and knew he had won. Before the sailor had even begun his retreat, the elf turned and continued his search through the few remaining rooms. While he was in a storage room at the rear of the ship, Chakal heard the frantic scuffling of boots and confused questions from the other sailors before ascending the ladder behind their terrified comrade. The footsteps kept their pace even as they rushed along the main deck and across the docks. Normally, the assassin would smile at his prowess, but not this time.

A loud groan escaped the elf as he kicked the door he had just smashed open, blowing a hole through the wood. That was the last room, and he was growing more restless. His pace increased, refusing to accept that he wouldn't have his prey by nightfall. As Chakal returned to the main deck, he noticed the sailors were rushing toward the city—most likely to retrieve guards. It wouldn't matter, none would come. This was a war, and the city itself was just as dangerous as the horde that remained outside the wall. The guards wouldn't risk chaos for the sake of one angered deviant. Chakal walked to the rail and saw that the sailors had kicked down the ramp in a final act of defiance. An amused chuckle almost broke free from his mouth. Gripping the rail tightly, the elf flipped himself over and somersaulted through the air before landing on his feet on the wooden platform below.

It didn't take Chakal long to reach the second ship. He noticed that this one, too, had its ramp kicked down. He lamented for not simply killing the sailors on the other ship. *I've grown soft*, he thought, realizing this was not the first time—nor even second—he had allowed some who stood in his path to live that day. The thought was just another tally to the score of his ever-growing frustration. Tensing his legs, Chakal sprang upward toward the rail. It stood twice his height, but he managed to get a few fingers hooked around. After pulling himself up, he made his way down to the deck below.

The first room was empty, as he expected. Then the second. As he kicked open the third, Chakal barely even looked inside, expecting to find little more than packed goods or rats within. He had already walked two steps away before the glimpse his eyes had caught registered in his mind. *That wasn't empty!*

Chakal peeked his head back around the corner to see a young man with raven hair sitting on one of the barrels, despite the door to the room just having been splintered. The elf stepped in and shifted his shoulder to allow the dim light from the lantern in the main room to catch the man's face. The assassin pulled out the folded portion of the painting he had taken and held it up to the light. He looked between the artwork and the man—nearly a boy, Chakal realized—and confirmed the match before tucking it away.

"You are *extremely* annoying," Chakal stated with an exhausted sigh.

Dumbfounded, Lucien stared up at him with his round, brown eyes, raising a hand to shield against the light. "What? Who are you?" He rose to his feet and looked closer at the man—no, *elf*—standing in the doorway. "An elf?"

Chakal finally seemed to calm from the built-up rage that had been stoking since taking on this quest. "I have been searching for you all day!" His eyes turned to rage once more at the thought of his efforts. Though, they quickly diminished, and his expression returned to happiness. "I am glad I found you!"

After waiting for the prince to speak, the elf's smile began to fade. *Why does he not speak?!* Chakal forced a smile once more, though the devious luster in his eyes gave his true feelings away. "I need you to come with me, please."

"Why?"

A burst of laughter came from the assassin. "'*Why*'? Why, indeed? I know not, nor do I care. I was tasked with collecting you, and so here I am. My day has been wasted searching for you, and now here you finally are. So, please, come with me, as I grow weary." With each phrase, Chakal's eyes and smile grew wider, stretching to their limit.

Lucien could tell the elf in front of him was one of severe threat—and instability. Nevertheless, he sat back down atop his barrel nonchalantly. "Who sent for me?"

Chakal laughed once more and began talking to himself in a frantic voice. "Of course, he would want to know. I suppose I would. Why wouldn't I? Just being summoned out of the air, no details of who, where, from, how, why?!" He stopped his outward thoughts abruptly and maintained that frightening smile. "You were summoned by Bitrayuul and Cormac. A pair nearly equal in annoyance as you, Prince Lucien. Now, please, come with me." The elf turned to walk away, expecting the young man to follow him.

After a few paces, Chakal stopped and turned to see the prince had remained motionless. "Why do you not move?!" The assassin's eyes were red with anger as he stared at the man leaning easily against the wall. "You *must* come!"

"Why?"

"Ahaha! Why? *Why?!* I know not, child. All I know is you are expected to come, so come! Come, come, come, COME!" Chakal kicked his boot into the door with each command, shattering through what had remained. The prince's nonchalance had him teetering on the brink of insanity and the deep nagging inside him that compelled he put an end to the whelpling was growing exponentially more difficult to ignore.

Lucien sighed and shifted to be more comfortable on the unforgiving barrel. "They want me to fight in the war and I don't want to. We're all going to die anyway, what does it matter?"

"It *matters* because you can either die here and now or atop the wall! At least have the decency to claim a few trolls before you perish!" Chakal stomped forward and grabbed Lucien by the neck. Before the prince could react, the elf lifted him into the air and slammed him into the wall with as much force as he could muster, wetting the wood with blood. "So, which is it, boy?" Chakal crazed eyes stared deep into Lucien's as they turned bloodshot from the assassin's fingers clamped tightly around the prince's throat. Refusing to wait for a response that would never come, the elf snapped. "Die now," Chakal said, smashing Lucien's head into the wall, "on this", another slam, "forsaken," *slam*, "and miserable," *slam*, "ship!" The blood on the wall grew with each thrust.

After the final assault, Chakal threw the man through the doorway and into the main room then quickly pursued. He felt so alive! All the day's stress and pent-up rage had now finally been given voice—and the prince would suffer it all. Lucien coughed out a mouthful of blood and tried to roll to his knees, but Chakal was there with his foot already reared back. Another large mouthful of blood splattered to the floor as the elf's boot connected against the prince's gut.

Looking down at the man's huddled form, Chakal spat in disgust. "Now, you *will* come with me, you putrid, withered, useless, lowly, degener—" The elf was interrupted by an intense burst of force against his chest, throwing him back a great distance before crashing against a wall. He groaned from the surprising blow but managed to pull himself to his feet. The smile on his face seemed to grow even more. It looked as if his face would tear at any moment from being stretched so far. "Ahaha! You are an arcanist! Oh, the gods and their humor!"

Despite knocking the elf back, Lucien hardly had enough time to pull himself to his feet before he heard Chakal's rushed footsteps grow closer. The haziness in his eyes made it difficult to see more than the rough silhouette of his target. Raising his hands up simultaneously, Lucien heard the hard *thud* of the elf smashing face-first into the invisible wall he had formed.

"Ahahahahaha! This will be exquisite!" Chakal shouted in response, spitting out blood that had spilled from his nose and over his lips. He dashed around the room, pivoting with each step to take advantage of Lucien's dazed sight. With each deft turn, he could sense the forcefields that he had avoided where the prince had tried to anticipate his movements.

Lucien tried to keep a level head but was growing more frantic as the elf made steady progress toward him. He could see only the glimmer of blades and their stark contrast to the darkened room. How he wished he could rub his eyes to clear his vision! His hands worked as fast as they could to throw up the continuous walls, hoping to catch the elf once more. But it was no use, his opponent was too skilled. *How can he sense where the walls are?!*

Chakal continued his maniacal laughter as he dashed every which way to avoid the barriers. The oncoming elf had stopped the fearful prince from thinking clearly. It wasn't the first time the assassin had faced an arcanist—far from it. He had sought out every type of opponent he could in order to improve his skills. Arcanists, shamans, enchanters, conjurers, druids, clerics, necromancers, every school of magic. Each using magic in different ways that had taught Chakal how to best all opponents.

Finally realizing his mistake, Lucien shouted as his hands clapped together harshly. He watched and listened as the elf let out a pained groan as the enormous walls to his sides closed in on him. Taking the precious moment, the prince rubbed his eyes. Too long. By the time he had opened them, Chakal was already back up and only two paces away. In his desperation, Lucien tried something new. An application of force magic that he had dabbled with long ago, before he had tried to give up on magic.

His hands twisted together quickly and ascended. As Chakal closed in, dagger aimed for his heart, Lucien slammed both hands toward the ground.

A shout of pain came from the assassin as he was pressed against the floor in an instant. It felt as if a thick, wet cloth had been draped over him—though weighing as much as an ogre. His eyes burned with hatred as he tried to pry himself free, wiggling beneath the invisible layer of force that continued to press him down into the planks. "No! This is not the end!" Chakal growled as he continued to twist and writhe. The elf watched as Lucien considered ending him then and there, a hand raised in front of his face. "Do it! You will not get another chance! I will hunt you to the ends of the world unless you kill me now!"

Surprise crept through Lucien at Chakal's disregard. The prince felt an uncomfortable resemblance rumble deep in his core. He knew that the assassin would hunt him forever—it was clear in Chakal's eyes. There would be no relent to the elf's pursuit. Lucien's hand steadied as it sat a finger-length away from Chakal's forehead. The prince had never taken a life before. Even now, after barely surviving the assassin's assault, he didn't know if he could bear the weight of such a burden for the remainder of his days. Such a thought was one of the reasons he wished to avoid the war.

Chakal continued to spit insults and commands for his own demise from the floor. In truth, a small piece of him wished the prince would end him. But the majority was filled with overwhelming thoughts of vengeance and the desire to repay Lucien for the insult he had inflicted. The worst kind to Chakal—making him bleed. With each taste of the purple ichor that wet his tongue, the elf was reminded of his own mortality and the thought that even he was fallible. He had lost this time and he knew it.

Head spinning with the thought of defeat and his wounded pride, Chakal could hardly contain the rambling thoughts about what a disgrace he was to himself. A thousand copies of his own mentality shamed itself, pointing and laughing at his fate. But all turned dark once Lucien let out the blast of force from his hand.

CHAPTER FIFTY-THREE

RETURN

Fangdarr clutched the rail anxiously as Wiston came into view—still standing, thankfully. Torches lit the city and the moon's fading light reflected off the castle walls. The orc's racing heart settled upon knowing the city hadn't yet been overrun. Still, he was startled as he felt Aesthéa's hand against his back.

Sliding her hand into Fangdarr's, Aesthéa turned the orc to face her and could see his trepidation. "We are almost there, Fangdarr. The city has not yet fallen. We can help."

Offering a weak smile in appreciation, the orc turned his gaze back toward the city. *Can we, though?* It had been almost five days since they had departed, who knew what may have been lost. And for what? They were nearly in the same state in which they had left, thanks to King Nelthalius' betrayal. Despite the elf's dishonor, the orc wouldn't sink to the same lowness. As agreed with Thrax'ul, Fangdarr sent the satyr army back to Wudhyvn—save for Brea'la, who demanded she stay of her own accord.

As if she could sense his thoughts, Brea'la approached Fangdarr and Aesthéa at the rail. The orc knew that her assistance may be minor in the grand scheme of the war, but his respect for her had grown immensely with her decision to remain with them. While her kin marched home, the satyress had chosen to put her life in Fangdarr's hands—all to aid those who meant nothing to her. It couldn't have been an easy decision, he knew. Brea'la smiled at the pair and placed her arms around them.

No words were spoken. They weren't needed. Each knew the wind carried them closer and closer to their likely doom. Even Elethain strode over to them with a smile on his face. Returning it in kind, Fangdarr was genuinely happy that the powerful necromancer—his friend—had stuck by their side.

All four warriors stood by each other until the very moment Elethain's reanimated kin pulled the vessel to the docks from beneath the water. Once berthed, they walked down the ramp and onto the groaning wooden planks toward the city's rear.

Walking toward the city, the group peered around cautiously. The port seemed entirely devoid of life. What was once bustling and full of merchants and guards alike had become an abandoned shadow of its former self.

"What is that?" Elethain asked, pointing ahead to a darkened lump in the middle of the dirt path halfway to the rear gate. They quickly jogged closer but remained on the defensive.

Approaching first, Fangdarr determined it was a man lying face-down in the dirt. The man's clothes appeared to be in dirty commoner's clothes, with a bloodstained hood. Against the warnings of his friends, the orc rolled the man over for his own curiosity. Fangdarr gasped as he realized who the man was.

"You know this creature, Fangdarr?" Brea'la asked as the orc scooped the man up. He didn't need to respond, however, as Elethain also discovered the subject's identity.

"That is the prince!" The elf threw his hands in the air. "What is he doing out here all alone?!"

Fangdarr adjusted Lucien within his arms, cradling him carefully. He ran a finger over the prince's cheek, feeling for warmth. A fraction remained, though the cold of night may have obscured the truth. The orc's finger slid to Lucien's neck and felt for a pulse. It was weak, but present. Fangdarr turned to the others. "We go to castle. He need help."

Elethain's mouth opened in argument. Not for the aid of the prince, but that Fangdarr couldn't simply walk into the city that was at war with his kind—the prince on the edge of life in his arms—without being cut down. But he said nothing. Fangdarr had proven on more than one occasion that he could be trusted. It was time for the humans to learn of the orc who had risked all in their name.

Together the group rushed toward the city's rear gate but found it was locked. Ever resourceful, Elethain willed his corpses to scale the wall and release the mechanism from the other side. Frightened screams echoed from beyond the door. As the gate opened, a pair of guards stared in bewilderment at the trio of ghouls that simply stared back at them lifelessly.

"Halt! Wh-who goes there?!" one of the men shouted as the group passed through the gateway, his spear in shaking hands. The other guard stood next to him, equally terrified, but rooted firmly. Their eyes went wide as they realized what the open gate had revealed. The orc in front of them stood nearly twice their height and holding what they could only assume was the corpse of an unlucky man. After finally tearing their horrified gaze from the giant creature, they saw the pair of elves and another beast-like woman of the likes they had never witnessed before.

“Pl-please, don’t kill us!” cried the second man, dropping his spear and raising his arms in surrender. The first guard stared at the man in disbelief for abandoning his duty, though couldn’t blame him.

Fangdarr slowly approached and bent to his knee, revealing the prince’s unconscious form. “He need help. Please.” He could tell the guards saw the concern in his eyes and heard the compassion in his voice as they slowly stepped forward to see who was in the orc’s embrace.

“The prince!” Immediately, they were back up in arms with their resolve reinforced upon seeing the prince’s prone form. “What have you done to him?!”

The elves rushed in front of Fangdarr and spread their arms wide. “Enough!” Elethain shouted. “He did nothing. *We* did nothing. We had just returned from Y’thirya and saw him lying on the ground. He was attacked, but not by us. Please, we must get him to the castle immediately or he will die.”

Both soldiers stared at each other, then to Lucien, then back to the uncommon intruders—their spines still quivering in fear at the sight of Elethain’s kin. Despite their distrust and uneasiness, the men nodded in agreement for the prince’s sake and offered to escort them through the city. Elethain put a reassuring hand on Fangdarr and the companions followed behind the soldiers as they departed, making sure to lock the gate once more.

After pushing through the chaotic masses of civilians in the courtyard, they finally made it into the castle. Luckily, the humans gave Fangdarr and his friends plenty of space out of fear, though their increased panic upon seeing an orc had only riled them tenfold. As the heavy doors closed behind them, the terrified shouts of the crowd muffled to a dull hum. One of the escorts rushed off deeper into the castle to fetch others to aid the prince while the remaining soldier stayed at the group’s side, eyeing them with his hand tight around the shaft of his spear.

It wasn’t long before a dozen guards and a pair of maidens dressed in pure white gowns were seen rushing toward them. Fangdarr instinctively tensed, expecting them to be coming for him. His muscles pressed against the prince and the young man stirred in his arms.

“F-Fangdarr?” Lucien asked weakly with half an eye open. The orc smiled at him but looked up as the entourage came. The guards demanded that he hand the prince over to them. After complying, the orc watched half the guards and the two nurses rush him back in the direction they came. As Lucien faded from view, Fangdarr realized all attention was on him.

The orc rose to his full height, causing the men to tilt their heads back to glare at him. Their eyes shifted between Fangdarr, his axe, and his friends in rapid succession. He could tell they were waiting for him to give them any reason to act. “Lucien will be alright?” he asked lightly.

The soldiers continued to watch him with suspicion. They knew that this was all a ploy to enter the castle. Their minds were made up. One man, the youngest in the rear of the pile, approached bravely. Unbeknownst to Fangdarr, it was the messenger who had spoken with Bitrayuul previously. "I hope so. Who are you?" The young man's comrades stared at him as if he were inviting a beast into their den to serve up their own slaughter. But he pushed them away with reassurance that his trust was well-placed.

Bending to his knee once more to seem less imposing, Fangdarr replied, "Fangdarr. You see Bitrayuul or Cormac? They are well?"

"Yes, they are at the wall, last I saw. They are friends of yours?"

Fangdarr nodded. "Brothers." He rose once more. "We send for them?"

Despite the arguments of his companions, the young messenger agreed without hesitation. He pointed to two of the men and asked them to inform the pair at the wall that their friends had arrived. No matter how much they disputed, or how many years they held over the young soldier, the pair of guards he had pointed out eventually went on the task assigned. As the messenger turned to Fangdarr, the orc could see the surprised look on his face as if even he didn't expect the outcome that had occurred.

Elethain stepped forward, rolling his eyes at how pitifully the guards reactively pointed their spears at him. "Where is the king? We were sent to Y'thirya with his permission."

At that, every man—even the brave messenger—let their heads sink low. The elf pursed his lips upon realizing the man was either dead or dying by their reactions. One of the other guards, a much older man judging by the white tints speckling his beard, came forward. "The king cannot be seen right now. He rests."

Elethain nodded in thanks and sighed quietly. He was surprised the city hadn't fallen with the king's presence lacking. The deep-rooted prejudice within the elf wanted to claim that such a reluctance to lead would never have occurred in the elven kingdom. But after his own king's most recent actions, even the loyal advisor began to doubt that claim.

CHAPTER FIFTY-FOUR
AMMUNITION

Guttural howls of excitement forced Tod and Bebbo to turn before releasing the packed group of trolls sitting in the cradle of the catapult.

"Eh? You hear dat, Bebbo?" Tod asked with an eyebrow raised.

Bebbo bopped his friend over the head with a meaty fist. "'Course I hear dat! What ya fink, I'm stoopid?"

Tod pondered for a moment, unable to comprehend the rhetorical question. Just as he was about to answer, the sound of crudely built wheels squeaked and creaked over the commotion of the army's cheers. From the southeast came one of their kin, pulling a large wooden cart. Though the transportation vessel was terribly constructed, it had managed to hold together long enough to complete the task. Within its rickety walls sat four large boulders that the ogre had proudly collected. The giant creature closed the distance to his comrades waving his arms triumphantly with a wide and toothless smile.

"Tod, Tod! Go gets da boss, quick!" Bebbo shouted as he patted their friend on the back. "Me and Wort here gotta get da stones ready!"

Normally, Tod would have been disgruntled to be sent on such an errand—especially when being forced to interact with their horrific leader—but this time they had good news. *Great* news, even. As a result, the ogre nodded happily and lumbered toward Gub's makeshift throne to the east.

By the time Tod had returned with Gub in tow, Bebbo and Wort had already shooed away the waiting batch of trolls and loaded in the first boulder and placed the remaining three to the side. Gub walked up to Wort with an eye of disapproval. He tilted his crown of twigs so his underlings could see it better as he spoke in a slow and condescending grunt. "Only four? Ya been gone for days!"

Wort eyed the small tree trunk in his barbaric leader's hand and shifted uncomfortably. "Al-all I could finds, boss. The rest was cleared out," he started, nodding uncontrollably. "Yeah, yeah! These was all I could finds . . .." Wort's gaze fell to the ground in shame as Gub stuck his nose as close to Wort's face as possible.

After giving a good sniff, Gub grunted. "Beh, four better than none. Where da rest of the rock-getters?" After tense silence, Gub repeated himself with anger that made the three ogres cower.

"No see dem, boss. We separated like you asked, we did! Ain't seen dem in a few days." Wort tensed his muscles as he spoke, expecting a heavy blow to come at any time.

The trio of ogres waited while their ringleader considered what to do. Even the nearby trolls and orcs who anxiously awaited the fall of the wall didn't press Gub as word of his 'exploits' had passed through the army over the campaign. Finally, a wicked grin appeared on the ogre's face and he licked the few teeth he had remaining. "Bring down da wall!"

Every creature within earshot roared triumphantly with renewed vigor that spread like a virus through the entire horde. With stones to launch, it was only a matter of time before they all would have what they came for. Too long had they been sitting in the stomped earth, waiting for the barrier that held them at bay to come crashing down.

Gub watched as Tod and Bebbo excitedly released the first boulder into the air. As it travelled, the hollering shouts beneath it intensified to earth-shattering rumbles. A million pairs of eyes traced the stone's path as it soared toward Wiston with the weight of their anticipation in tow. Soldiers atop the battlements shouted warnings and blew horns to raise alarm. The expected fight was about to come.

Unfortunately, every roar and cheer from the trolls and orcs transitioned immediately to dismayed groans as the boulder flew just above the wall. Gub turned an angry eye to his subordinates at wasting one of the few stones they had managed to acquire and stomped over. Tod and Bebbo were already fighting by the time he had arrived.

"Bebbo, you forgots to change da aim!" Tod exclaimed, shoving his companion.

Not seeing Gub directly behind him, Bebbo retaliated and pushed Tod back. "Nuh-uh, it was your job! You da spot-picker! Always was and always is!"

Tod quickly bit his tongue as their leader bore down on them with a spine-twisting glare. Without a word, Gub wrapped his thick fingers around Bebbo's throat and squeezed with all his might.

As the life was being pressed out of poor Bebbo's writhing form, kicking and clawing desperately, the ogre's eyes turned bloodshot and filled with tears. He could hardly see the dark silhouette standing over him as Gub leaned in. But Bebbo didn't need his sight to feel the immense agony surge through his face as their cannibalistic leader bit off his nose. The stranglehold around Bebbo's neck prevented him from screaming in pain, yet Gub watched in glee as the soundless screams formed on the creature's face.

Each of the spectators in the area, including Tod and Wort, watched in disbelief as Gub chewed his underling's nose as the final bit of life was drained beneath his crushing grip. After dropping Bebbo's lifeless body to the ground, Gub swallowed the chunk of flesh and dragged the corpse to the remaining three boulders, "You miss rock, you become rock!" Tod and Wort nodded a dozen times in fear of meeting the same fate as their friend before working to reset the catapult. Gub watched them with a grim expression that showed no room for error. Not now. They were too close. Eyes narrowed in a lethal glare, he spoke with the promise of death. "Launch again."

* * * * *

A horn blasted in alarm before the stone flew over the wall, crashing into a nearby building. From within the pit, Bitrayuul and Cormac stared at each other with grave concern. They knew what that sound meant. Immediately the pair called for the men above to pull them and the remaining diggers out.

As they climbed over the lip of the hole, their eyes fell upon the nearby building where the first boulder had struck. Cormac turned to the half-orc. "Looks like it be time, lad. Ye ready for this?"

Bitrayuul let out a drawn-out sigh and a lighthearted chuckle. "No, but that doesn't matter much, does it?" He felt the dwarf clap a hand against his back, splattering his already muddied armor with even more wet earth.

"Aye, lad, it really don't. Bahaha!"

Together the pair started shouting orders to the men to make the final preparations. Despite their fear at what was to come, the soldiers listened obediently. Cormac helped with pulling the rest of the diggers from the pit and had them throw all the remaining coal and oil down to the bottom. For a moment, the dwarf had also considered throwing in the small bit of coal and barrels of oil they had lined along the wall but decided against it. Better to not put all faith in a single trap, he knew.

Bitrayuul, on the other hand, set out preparing the men. As he was gathering them into defensive formations, a second boulder crashed against the wall. "Where did it hit?!" he called out to the sentries atop the battlements.

"The crack!"

The half-orc grit his teeth in concern. "Will it hold?"

The sentry leaned over the parapets once more to further inspect the damaged wall. After reappearing, he called back, "It should for now! The stone shattered like the others as well!"

Bitrayuul nodded to the man in confirmation. The temporary elation he felt with the news of the boulder breaking was short lived, knowing others remained. Unless the gods had decided to spare them, the half-orc knew the wall would soon fall.

After completing their preparations, Bitrayuul and Cormac waited side by side at the edge of the pit. They continued to call out commands, informing the men to keep to their shifts and not panic if the wall came down. Thankfully, only a single breach point was expected, meaning the enemy's numbers would be irrelevant. Their greatest chance of defeat was fatigue. Ten thousand standing against an army a hundred times greater would need to rely on tactics, not strength.

Now, with only three thousand men at their side, Bitrayuul and Cormac waited. Their traps were in place. The men were ready. The sound of the catapult's arm was heard once more, and a boulder whistled through the air before crashing soundly against the weakest point in the wall. By some manner of luck—or a cruel joke of the gods—the cracked stones in the wall shook violently and fissured ever more but held tight.

Cormac turned to Bitrayuul. "I wish Fangdarr was here?" The half-orc nodded in response, thinking the same. As if another cruel joke, a guard tapped Bitrayuul lightly after pushing his way through the soldiers. The look of fear on the man's face showed he hadn't spent much time near the wall. That suspicion was solidified as the man took off running back the way he came as soon as his message was delivered.

"What is it?" the dwarf asked. "Seems a bit of an inconvenient time to be gettin' invited to the ball, don't ye doubt. Bahaha!" Cormac's humor was short-lived, however, as Bitrayuul excitedly handed him the note.

Despite giving the letter to the dwarf, Bitrayuul stated its contents. "Fangdarr is here! He's in the castle." His words abruptly ended there, leaving out the rest of the note's contents for the dwarf to read himself.

"What?!" Cormac shouted as his eyes finished scanning the parchment. "I told ye not to trust that elf, Bit. I *told* you!" He continued his grumbling and shoved the message into his pocket to prevent anyone from reading it. The last thing the men needed was news that an assassin was loose in the city and had nearly killed the prince.

Bitrayuul hung his head, knowing the words of his friend rang true. But what choice did he have? Anything to keep Chakal at bay, and the task seemed easy enough. He didn't know why he expected the remorseless elf who had mutilated his sister in front of her own mother, to show any sort of restraint. Did it matter, though? The prince had refused to even aid in their struggle. Instead, he just wanted to sit back and watch Wiston turn to ash. While Bitrayuul cared little for the prince's outcome, Cormac was right. Lucien's fate carried enough weight to wipe all hope from the men.

The half-orc watched his friend shaking his head and muttering under his breath. The captain made eye contact with Bitrayuul. "The next time ye see that damned elf, kill him."

CHAPTER FIFTY-FIVE
REPRIORITIZE

The pain in his temple pounded as he came to. Groaning with every miniscule movement, Chakal blinked open his eyes but saw naught but hazed blurriness. *Gods, my head hurts.* Keeping his eyes clamped shut, the elf wearily raised a hand to wipe away the drool that had stuck to his face. *What happened?*

It had been nearly a thousand years since the assassin had felt pain like this. The burning sensation that stabbed at his muscles as he tried to pull himself to an upright position seemed foreign due to its prolonged absence. With a grunt of pain, Chakal forced his eyes open and rubbed out the crust that had taken root. After his vision cleared, he scanned the room. No, not a room. *A ship?* he wondered. *Gods, my head!* His pale fingers slid along his throbbing temples. For each move he made, his head responded with brutal retaliation. Trying to make sense of everything, the elf simply sat still in the center of the ship's lower deck.

The soft light coming through the ladder hole above proved that it was morning, though he couldn't remember when he came on the vessel or even why. Chakal groaned in mental anguish as another wave of pain washed over him. "I'm not even doing anything!" As if in response, his skull let out another pulse of agony to silence him. Growling with frustration, Chakal jumped to his feet. *I am in charge! Me!* As soon as he had put his feet beneath him, the elf's legs gave out and he crumbled to the floor in a jolt of pain. After the sensations subsided, he found himself laughing at his fate.

"Hahaha!" His laughter grew in intensity. "HAHAHAHA!" If there was anyone else there, he assumed they must have been ignoring him. His laughter refused to cease, no matter the agony it brought him. It was a battle of wits against his mind and his own stubbornness and he refused to lose. His eyes began to water, and his laughter evolved into maniacal cackling. Faster and faster he pushed out the exclamations, refusing to relent. His outbursts stopped him from thinking about the pain and shut out all thought. There was only the battle. Finally, Chakal rose to his feet once more. And still he cackled, even as his wobbling knees threatened to buckle again.

Standing at full height and pleased with himself, the assassin's cackling turned to amused laughter. In truth, his head was in twice the pain, but Chakal was standing on his feet and in complete control once more. With a long inhale, he ceased his outburst and turned all his emotion into a wide and wicked smile. It grew even wider as his foot took a step forward and he didn't falter. Then another. And another. Chakal let out the trapped air in his lungs, confident he had returned to his former self—save for the hammering in his head.

Even without the stomping in his brain, the elf couldn't remember how he had come to be on the ship. Slowly, he stalked around the room searching for any evidence. He noticed the door to one of the cabins had been blown apart and stepped past the wreckage. The tiny cubby was hardly visible in the dim light from the single lantern hanging in the main room where he had been unconscious, though he could see well in the dark. Yet, there was enough flickering light to cast a reflection from the blood against the wall.

Chakal leaned closer. His finger scraped the wooden planks, chipping off the dried crimson stain. *Half a day old. And human.* Flicking away the flecks of blood from his finger, he glanced around. It was obvious a scuffle took place in the small, darkened room. The pain in his head was beginning to subside, but still he couldn't remember all the details. It was obvious he must have been involved in the dispute here. Chakal raised his hands up and began tracing his body. They slid against his arms, his chest, and even up to his head. No blood. Just an enormous bruise on his forehead.

The elf returned to the main room and scanned his surroundings. Bits of memory were creeping back as his eyes met the familiar scene, though he could never make out the face of his opponent. By the fact that no blood came from the bruise on his head, yet he had been knocked unconscious, he had determined his opponent to be some sort of wielder of magic. The most likely candidate being an arcanist, or perhaps even a conjurer, but why? Why would he be fighting someone on this ship?

A groan of frustration came out and he kicked apart a door to the next room. Then the next door. There was no benefit, save to play out his frustration in the best way he knew. After every wooden door lay splintered in ruin, Chakal sat against a large crate in the corner of the room and rubbed his head. *Think, think! Why can't you remember*!?

As the assassin sat wallowing in his withering confidence and defeated by his own mind, he started fumbling through his pockets. *Gods, I'm hungry. How long has it been since I last ate?* Rummaging through the many folds of his tunic without luck, he felt an odd piece of canvas tucked near his breast. He extracted it with confusion and held it out in front of him beneath the light.

You! His eyes scanned the material as his fingers smoothed the creases that had formed. As he inspected further, his memories came flooding back to fill in the blanks. No longer was his opponent some shrouded, black mist. It was *this* man! "Prince Lucien," he whispered as the missing details fell into place. Chakal started cackling once more as he realized that he had come upon the man to bring him to that damned half-orc.

"Oh, Elethain, my friend . . .," the assassin started, his eyes tracing the painting with viciousness. "It seems you are no longer at the top of my list."

CHAPTER FIFTY-SIX

BREACH

Fangdarr turned to the guards after hearing a dull sound to the southeast. "What was that?"

"Catapult. The enemy seems to have obtained more stones."

The orc eyed the soldiers. "I go to wall to defend." It was clear he wasn't asking their permission. When no argument came, Fangdarr turned toward his friends. "You ready?"

As one, each of the orc's companions nodded in reply. Together, they pushed open the large, steel doors. The moment the portal had opened, the panicked crowd of civilians tried to push their way in. They would have easily overwhelmed the meager wall of soldiers had Fangdarr not been standing in their path. The hope that had illuminated every civilian's face upon the doors opening was replaced with terror when they were instead met by the large orc. Instead of rushing past through the open gates, every desperate person turned on their heels in fear. Fangdarr simply shook his head in disbelief and descended the stairs as the door closed.

With his friends in tow, Fangdarr barreled through the rushing crowd in the courtyard. Finally, he reached the gate that led to the Military District. The pair of soldiers standing at the barrier nearly fled their post as they saw the unlikely band approach. To their credit, the men stayed and demanded they halt. Fangdarr, however, continued forward without a word and pressed open the gate. Both guards, immobilized in their terror, let him and the others pass without dispute and nearly fell to their knees in relief when the large door closed behind them. Once they had gathered themselves, they chuckled in disbelief at one another then resumed their duty as if it had never occurred.

Once out into the empty streets, Fangdarr and his allies started to jog. It was still a fair distance to the wall, and they knew the fighting could start at any moment. The group slowed to a stop after hearing the release of the catapult far in the distance, followed by the monstrous cheers of enemies and the alarmed shouts of Wiston's soldiers. Then, with undeniable certainty, they heard it. Their stomachs sank as the rumbling vibrations pulsed through the ground beneath their feet. The wall had fallen.

* * * * *

This is it, Father. I wish you were here with me. Bitrayuul watched as the boulder sailed through the air and crashed against the wall. With luck, most of the wall had collapsed outward rather than in, otherwise their traps may have been rendered useless by the heavy debris. After the fallen rocks crushed a few dozen trolls, dust flew into the air and shrouded the opening.

"Hold!" Bitrayuul shouted in confidence. He, and every other man there, waited in anxious fear. It took everything the half-orc had to not turn and flee. He couldn't. Not in the final moment. He would make his father proud. How many times had Tormag stood defiantly in the mines of Tarabar as their enemy breached, he wondered? Whether it was once or even a hundred times, Bitrayuul was certain that Tormag would have stood firm.

"Hoooold!" the half-orc called out once more. It was coming. He knew it, the men knew it. Soon, behind the screen of dust their enemy would come. *What are they waiting for?* In truth, it had only been a mere moment since the wall fell but it seemed to stretch forever. *Bothain, bless us.* Bitrayuul gripped his father's hammers for support. In the madness, he had nearly forgotten they were there. As his fingers closed around the shafts, a sense of relief came to him. *Are you watching, Father?*

Bitrayuul looked to Cormac. The dwarf's remaining eye stared grimly ahead from behind his raised shields. The half-orc gave one final look to his surroundings. Everything was in place. The traps were set. The men were ready. A hundred archers lined the wall and on rooftops, all waiting for the first sign of their enemy. This was it. Wiston's last hope.

Through the thick cloud of dust came their enemy. First one, then ten, then a hundred. The trolls and orcs rushed through that small opening with reckless abandon and hatred in their eyes. Bloodlust carried them forward even more than the thought of domination. In the moment of their advance, the enemy cared little for the grand scheme. It all came down to blood.

"Now!" Bitrayuul shouted as he witnessed the surprised expression form on the first troll's face as it fell into the pit. The half-orc ignored the oil and coal near the wall. He needed the enemy to face the pit first. A handful of flaming arrows came from the wall and down into the pit below, instantly igniting the oil that coated the bottom.

Already almost a hundred of the monstrous invaders had fallen into the hole and screamed in agony as the flames immolated their living bodies. The men held their cheers as the endless stream of monstrous foes followed the predicted path. One by one, hundreds poured into the inferno, blinded by their lust.

Bitrayuul looked to Cormac again. Their plan was working! He had been skeptical that the brutes would be so easily tricked. Eventually they would catch on, he thought. But his doubt proved false as the tide continued to push forward without relent. Those behind the front line couldn't see what fate lay ahead, only that the prospect of blood was beyond the ally in their path.

The smell of burning beasts wafted through the district. That rotten stench came in such a strong wave that it nearly made a few men collapse despite their best attempts to cover their nostrils. The putrid smell was worth it, though. Wiston's defenders' spirits were high as the pit of hell itself staunched the flow of the monsters that had come to take their homeland.

Within the deep pit, the pillar of fire continued to grow, as did the shrieks from those dying below. The men had dug wide and deep to make sure the trap would claim as many as possible. But their victory seemed to be short-lived as the pit was already half full in a short time. Over a thousand corpses must have been burning within the trench, yet still the horde pressed on. The realization that soon the pit would be filled ran through every man like a plague.

Bitrayuul heard a man behind him whisper, "By the gods, is there no end to them?!" Mutterings of agreement were exchanged as doubt crept in. The inhumanity of their foes was a heavy blow to the goodly men of Wiston, as they watched a thousand beasts unwillingly sacrifice themselves to the pit so that soon those behind them may pass unhindered. No matter the efficacy of the trap, there were just too many. Every man watched in blank horror, all with the same thought poisoning their minds. *There can be no victory here.*

CHAPTER FIFTY-SEVEN

BLOCKAGE

Bitrayuul tried to ignore the men's growing doubt and concerned mutterings. They needed him to be strong, now more than ever. He couldn't deny his own like-minded feelings as the flaming pit's voracious hunger had finally taken in its fill. The inferno raged high in the air but the corpses within had piled past even ground level.

Though the pit was still doing an excellent job of preventing their enemies from entering, the defenders knew it wouldn't last. The fire would die out quickly in the open air after it had consumed their enemy. It was time for a new plan and Cormac was prepared. With his short arm raised in the air, the dwarf yelled at the top of his lungs. "NOW, LADS!"

The archers lined on the rooftops lifted their bows and pointed them at the gap. Each iron tip dripped with oil as the men pulled back on their strings and took aim. Cormac tossed a wink to Bitrayuul, as if apologizing for taking a small portion of their dwindling stock of oil for his defensive plans. Before the half-orc could even react, the sound of bowstrings snapping forward came. A hundred missiles whistled overhead, passing through the pillar of fire and into the breach point, igniting the oil-dipped heads along the way.

Though it was hard to see through the large fire in their path, guttural cries of anguish filled the air and the monsters fell where they stood—right in the hole in the wall. Cormac raised his voice once more, calling for another shot to keep up the momentum. Arrows whizzed past again, catching fire and setting aflame trolls on the other side. After another two volleys, the breach was sealed with the flaming corpses of their victims. The men cheered as their emotions were back on high.

Bitrayuul looked to Cormac who was happily joining the men in their excitement at quelling their enemies again. He clasped his hand against the dwarf's back and laughed.

"Aye, bet ye didn't think yer ol' pal Cormac had a trick or two up his sleeve, did ye? Bahahah!" The captain continued to cheer and holler, ramping the men up with hope.

The whole of the collected army watched as their enemies were once again held at by—this time by a wall of their own kind. After many moments of waiting, the immolated corpses began to die down. Those stacked in the gap diminished much sooner than the churning pit that refused to relent.

As Bitrayuul and Cormac watched the last flicker of flame wisp away in a small trail of smoke in the makeshift wall of corpses, they heard a commotion at their rear. Men began shouting in shock and pleas of halting their attack came in reply. Standing over half a man's height above the fearful soldiers, Fangdarr approached, his friends at his side.

"Fang!" Cormac shouted, breaking his formation temporarily to retrieve the orc. "Hold on, boys, he's with us! They're all with us!"

Bitrayuul watched his brother proudly push through the remaining soldiers in his path, disregarding their hateful stares. Never did the half-orc ever feel such a surge of emotions upon seeing Fangdarr. He couldn't find words, instead he was immobilized with joy and renewed hope.

Fangdarr smiled as Cormac hopped toward him, laughing heartily all the while. Once together, they clasped arms openly, showing the men that the orc wasn't to be feared. Thanks to their newly acquired respect and trust in the dwarf, none questioned the bond. "Where ye been, son? We been waitin' for ye. The fun's just about to start, don't ye doubt!" He continued to grip tightly onto the orc's large forearm as a tear trickled down each cheek.

Looking down at his small friend, Fangdarr replied, "Elf lands, Satyr lands. But now I have returned. Ready to fight." His eyes connected with Bitrayuul, causing his face to light up. The orc was glad to know both of those he considered kin were safe. He waved his brother over, beckoning him closer.

As Bitrayuul forced himself to swallow his emotions and walk forward, Cormac spoke once more. "We're glad to have ye, Fang. We been holdin' 'em off, but there sure be a lot of them. Even Bothain's mighty hammer wouldn't make a dent in their numbers."

Fangdarr only nodded in reply. He was too concerned with Bitrayuul's slow approach to listen. When his brother finally closed the distance, the orc extended his hand in greeting.

Bitrayuul had nearly forgotten how big the dragon's blood had made Fangdarr, especially due to their separation over the last five days. It became evident, though, as the half-orc was forced to clasp his arm against the orc's at nearly chest height. The paralyzing emotions he had felt before crept up once again, stilling his tongue. All he could do was shake his arm quickly, as if it expressed how greatly he had missed his brother.

Bending his head low toward Bitrayuul's ear, Fangdarr whispered, "Thank you for keeping Wiston alive."

The half-orc nearly fell to his knees. It took everything he had to hold himself upright beneath the weight of that statement. The stress of the past week had been such an overwhelming burden, growing heavier and heavier as he continued to grit his teeth through it, losing pieces of himself along the way. Hearing such acknowledgement from Fangdarr was like hearing it from his mother herself. His brother was proud of him. Proud of the struggle he had powered through to keep those who needed him lifted. All Bitrayuul wished for in that moment was to openly weep and relinquish the stress for good.

Breaking the tension, Cormac asked, "Say, who's this one? She with you?" Bitrayuul and Fangdarr turned to see the dwarf eyeing Brea'la curiously—as were all the men around her, though they were gawking at her exotic beauty and exposed form.

Fangdarr opened his mouth to reply, but it wasn't needed. Brea'la had already stooped low to meet the dwarf at eye level. She caught the dwarf looking at her vibrant green hair and thin, twisted horns. "I am with Fangdarr," she started before slipping the tip of her spear against the dwarf's chin to push his face down to look at hers. "And Wiston."

"Bahaha! Oh, lad, this one's fierce!" He laughed even more as he watched each of the men that were inspecting her naked torso retreat and pretend to not be staring as she rose. "Aye, fierce indeed." Next, Cormac strode over to Elethain and Aesthéa. "Bothain's beard, elf," he started, eyeing Elethain. "I thought ye'd have stayed behind on yer island."

Glaring yet grinning, Elethain nodded in reply, holding back the comment he had in mind regarding never missing an opportunity to watch humans die.

Finally, the dwarf came up to Aesthéa. His eyes turned to a smile and he leaned forward to kiss her hand. "Thank ye, lass, truly. Thank ye for keepin' him safe." The druid bowed her head and slid closer to Fangdarr.

Bitrayuul eyed his friends, glad that they were all together once more. Then, he came upon a dire realization. He leaned in to whisper to Fangdarr. "Where are the elves? Are they preparing to set sail?" The orc's instant scowl provided all the answer he needed. Though he felt his stomach sink once more, Bitrayuul nodded to Fangdarr. "Well, we're together now. We *will* survive this war." Eyes bright with eagerness, his brother returned the nod.

After moving past Fangdarr, Bitrayuul also offered his thanks to Aesthéa. However, upon seeing Elethain, he had to stop himself from gasping as he remembered Chakal's arrangement. Trying to recover for his awkward reaction, the half-orc turned to Fangdarr. He had already opened his mouth to speak before realizing the men could hear him. "How is the prince?"

Cormac's eyes opened wide, hoping the men didn't overhear. The dwarf desperately motioned with his face and eyes to try to get Fangdarr to halt his reply. But the orc didn't catch on.

"Lucien fine. Resting," Fangdarr responded, drawing a relieved sigh from Cormac.

Bitrayuul nodded. Thankfully Chakal hadn't killed the prince. But the half-orc wondered if his deal with the assassin still needed to be upheld. He glanced at Elethain once more with mixed emotions. On one hand, he didn't wish to kill the necromancer—especially not during the war. Contrarily, Elethain had given him up to Chakal without so much as a thought of hesitation. Why should Bitrayuul not return the favor?

Fangdarr stepped toward the frontline while his companions finished their introductions and greetings. As his gaze fell upon the tactics Bitrayuul and Cormac had utilized—strategies the orc had never considered—he couldn't help but feel proud.

Though the orc could see the smoldering trails of smoke rising from the charred corpses in the breach point and the withering flames within the pit, he knew eventually the war would continue. Whether it was today, tomorrow, or in a week, he would be forced to face his own kind for the greater good. The prospect brought him great sorrow, but Fangdarr knew it was the just path. The excited chattering and laughter behind him by his companions had only solidified that thought.

It's coming, O' Roaring One. Fangdarr growled in contempt as the familiar voice crept into his mind. *Your destiny awaits on the other end of that wall of corpses. It is coming now. You have made the wrong choice, Blood-drinker. All you love will fall to ruin and the throne of bones shall remain empty. Rid yourself of those who betrayed you. Humans. Elves. Dwarves. All will fall to the shadow. It comes now.*

After the poisonous words ended, Fangdarr sat in silence with his teeth bared. The jarring discomfort of Crepusculus' essence lingering within him and corrupting his thoughts always brought a scowl to his face. He wondered at what the shadow dragon had meant, though. *What is coming? The horde? Death?*

A barely audible *thud* came. Fangdarr looked around and saw that no one else seemed to notice.

Thud.

It came from the wall. The orc looked toward the pile of corpses stacked in the breach with suspicion.

Thud.

It moved?! He could've sworn that the charred carcasses had shifted slightly.

Thud.

He was certain. The seal had moved with the dull pounding. Others were taking notice by then. Each of his companions had stopped their laughing and easy conversation by the fourth thud. They stepped forward, taking position next to Fangdarr and watched the wall with grim expressions.

Thud.

There was no denying it, whatever it was. Elethain turned to the rest of the group. "I'm going to take a vantage point atop the battlements. I will be of little use in the fray." Before any could dispute, the necromancer took off at a light jog toward the wall with his brothers in tow.

"I shall go as well," Brea'la offered, pulling her wooden longbow from her shoulder. She turned to Aesthéa and Fangdarr. "Do not die, my friends. But if you must, I shall meet you in the Garden." Fangdarr gave his customary nod while Aesthéa hugged the satyress in fond farewell. With that, Brea'la rushed toward the wall on the side opposite of Elethain.

For a moment, Bitrayuul considered retrieving his own bow from the command room and firing arrows into the masses, but he was needed on the frontlines. In truth, what would he achieve? A dozen arrows would do little against the host they faced. Instead, his feet remained planted firmly where they belonged.

Fangdarr turned to Aesthéa. "You should go. Safer atop wall." Though all the soldiers that were stationed on the battlements had been recalled, it was nearly impossible for the enemy to reach the top of the wall without first breaking through the defender's flanks.

The druid smiled and pulled the orc down to give him a kiss, drawing disgusted and confused looks from the soldiers. "My place is by your side. If we are to die, it will be as one."

Thud.

Thud.

Thud.

The men all stood waiting with their hands tight around their weapons. Their hearts pounded in their chests, though they did their best to keep their faces stern and determined. Fear gripped them all. Fear of death, fear of pain, and worst the fear of failure. Wiston was relying on them. Many would die, perhaps even most. But no matter what, it couldn't be *all.*

Thud.

Fangdarr watched as the carcasses shifted with each assumed blow. His teeth bared once more as he felt the mental link re-open. *It comes now, Roaring One. Meet your doom.*

With a final thud, the top half of the pile of smoldering corpses fell forward, covering part of the flaming pit. In the opening stood a single, twisted-twig crowned ogre wielding a tree, sporting a menacing scowl and toothy smile.

CHAPTER FIFTY-EIGHT
DEFEND

Once the seal broke, a tide of orcs and trolls rushed through. This time, they cautiously avoided the pit, slowing their advance in order to flank the sides of the wide hole and its hungering flames.

"This is it, lads!" Cormac shouted over the roaring of the monstrous beasts that were only a dozen strides away. "For Wiston!" Each of the soldiers uniformly let out a burst of cheer, steeling themselves as the enemy approached. Though horror remained an undeniable plague in every man, they held their ground, for what choice remained?

Elethain and Brea'la were already in place on the battlements and putting their skill to work. In truth, the satyress had simply wanted to loose her arrows so she could leave her bow and empty quiver off her person to avoid their awkward detriment. By the time the horde broke through, she had already launched two arrows, aiming for the few ogres in the ranks. Her targets were far but slow and clumsy, making for easy targets as they timidly stumbled toward the wall.

The pair of arrows the satyress had released missed their mark, but she didn't mind as they were only meant to gauge the pull of the wind. With the third missile loosed, Brea'la watched as it soared over the thousands below before sticking into one of the ogre's shoulders. A smile spread on her lip as the beast halted its advance and looked at the new wound in confusion. The brute was much less intelligent than she had anticipated, as it looked around and pointed at trolls with an accusatory finger as if blaming them for the arrow. A tinge of humor spread the smile on her face even more, but there was no time to hold thoughts of smiles and laughter. Her expression quickly sobered as she let her next arrow fly.

On the other side of the command room, Elethain was less interested in the ogres. He knew that their cowardice may very well turn them from battle with enough of Brea'la's arrows finding their mark—unless they became enraged. Instead, the necromancer focused his efforts on slowing the tide. Conjuring brief walls of black magic in front of the breach, he temporarily repelled the oncoming forces, breaking their momentum. After halting enemies with the magical wall, Elethain would dispel his conjuration and the pressing horde would instantly surge forward—typically falling prone as they did so and trampling those who fell.

While Elethain's tactics did wonders for stemming the tide, his companions and the soldiers defending inside the wall still found themselves hard-pressed against the growing numbers. Cormac and Bitrayuul remained in the center of the defensive formation in order to be seen by as many soldiers as possible to keep hope. However, they soon realized that their flanks were taking the brunt of the attack. Without a word, they looked to each other and took off in opposite directions to assist with the flanks near the wall and leaving Fangdarr and Aesthéa to defend the center.

Fangdarr watched the half orc and dwarf depart and felt a deep sinking in his stomach. Every instinct begged him to follow one or the other. But he stayed. The men needed him in the center. Even if they feared his presence, the soldiers could easily see him, a towering titan, and take hope—even if only in the ironic gratitude that the orc fought *for* them and not against them.

Even with the dwarven captain on the left flank and the half-orc general on the right, the enemy's number was still too overwhelming. The horde spilled past the flanks and spread to the center, filling what little space remained. Roars of triumph and anguish were constantly being shouted from both sides. The fire that had barely survived in the pit was now vivacious once more as new bodies—from both factions alike—were kicked in.

Elethain noticed the number of enemies inside the wall were beginning to grow. With a frustrated sigh, the elf kept a magical barrier up longer than usual to allow the troops within to regain their ground. Already he could feel the drain on his energy begin to take its toll. The warlock cursed himself for not leaving the defenders to their own fate as it had costed him dearly. He would need to conserve as much of his energy as possible.

On the opposing battlement, Elethain heard Brea'la cheer in ecstasy and traced her gaze to one of the ogres falling to its knees, clutching its eye. Impressed that a satyr could perform such a feat, the elf offered a nod. He watched as the other ogre dragged its friend hastily away from the battlefield in cowardice. Brea'la let loose the last arrow in her quiver toward the brutes in good measure, clipping the other ogre in the leg and spurring its frantic retreat. With her quiver empty, she threw it and her longbow to the ground and picked up her spear. Her blade ready, she kicked off the wall with her powerful hooves and leapt into the fray next to Cormac—impaling a particularly resilient orc that wouldn't relent against the dwarf.

Staring wide-eyed at the sudden blade piercing through the orc's skull—and the furry pair of legs landing on top of it—Cormac laughed aloud. "Bahahah! What an entrance!" His amusement was quickly subdued, however, as a nearby troll sliced at him with its sharpened stone daggers. "Bah! Ye smelly rat," he said as he raised his shields to intercept the blows. The superior dwarven steel caused the troll's weapons to fracture, bringing a surprised and frightened expression to the creature's face which never ceased to amuse Cormac. He countered, driving the blade of his right shield up through his foe's neck. Blue blood spilled out, covering the captain's arm in gore. As he kicked the troll back into the flaming hole, another instantly took its place.

On the opposite flank, Bitrayuul was under equal duress. Wielding his father's magical hammers, Bitrayuul was a whirlwind of steel. Even the soldiers surrounding him were forced to give him space as the half-orc's deadly armor, covered in blood and tattered skin, threatened anything in range. Though he inflicted pain to his foes endlessly by slicing with his bladed gauntlets or throwing the pair of crushing magical war hammers, Bitrayuul was struggling to bring down any foes permanently without fire.

Remembering the ambush that had led to Tormag's death, Bitrayuul grabbed a nearby troll. The half-orc quickly rubbed the hammers against a wound to coat them in the oily substance that had seeped out. Confident that the weapons held enough of the flammable ichor, he shoved the troll into the pit and threw the hammers into the dancing flames where they ignited before returning to his hands.

In the center, Fangdarr's chest pounded with excitement as their enemies spilled from the flanks. The thrill felt out of place in such a horrendous scenario, yet the orc couldn't deny his pleasure at the blood to be spilled. As he brought his beloved axe down onto the head of a troll in a spray of blue, he roared in ecstasy. Flinging the troll's broken form into the pit's growing pile of bodies, Fangdarr immediately shifted to his next target. How he had missed that feeling! The splatter of blood against his skin, the horrified expressions on his victims' faces as they met their doom in a single blow. Of not knowing if the day would be his last. The sensation was exhilarating, reminding him of what it was to be an orc. All thoughts were on those in his path, cutting them down and kicking their bodies into the flames. With each kill his bloodlust grew and his eyes glowed with a hunger that couldn't be sated.

The men around him began stepping back in fear as Fangdarr's lusting swings continued to whistle through the air. Despite the orc's seemingly reckless abandon, Aesthéa remained at his side, confident that he would bring her no harm. She had shifted into her animal form as soon as the enemies closed in. At her companion's side, she swatted away their enemies with heavy blows and submerged herself into the heat of battle.

Together, Fangdarr and Aesthéa had quickly decimated any that were foolish enough to approach, leaving them briefly unhindered. Fangdarr scanned the battlefield. Cormac and Brea'la seemed to have their flank under control but were still pressed against the overwhelming numbers. Across the gap, Bitrayuul was making quick work of any trolls who approached now that his weapons were able to immolate trolls as they made contact. However, due to the soldiers' fear of getting too close, he was slowly being surrounded. With a quick glance upward, the orc watched Elethain launch spears of conjured black magic into the masses beyond the wall. Fangdarr could only assume the elf was singling out as many orcs as possible, as trolls would simply regenerate the wounds he had inflicted.

Turning to his lover, Fangdarr rubbed her ear affectionately. One of them needed to remain in the center while the other helped Bitrayuul. He bent down to her, knowing she wouldn't wish to split apart. "You stay? Need to help Bit."

Aesthéa cast a glance to the half-orc and saw that he was in dire need of aid. She let out a meek whine, her eyes tilted in concern. With a huff of dispute, the elf-bear patted her paw against the ground.

Fangdarr couldn't help but smile as he remembered their playful encounters before he had discovered she was more than just a bear. He rubbed her ears once more and winked. "Okay, Bear. You come with me."

Rushing to Bitrayuul's aid, Fangdarr and Aesthéa intervened as a pair of orcs had circled to his back. The half-orc nearly spun and attacked his friends after hearing the conflict behind him but stopped just in time. He would have gladly thanked them for their assistance save for the immediate need to turn around and deflect three more incoming attacks.

Together, the trio pressed back their enemies. But for each they slew, the pile of bodies grew wider and wider, forcing them back to avoid the stinging flames. They watched as the crowned ogre who had cleared the first blockage lifted his enormous club once more while standing at the towering pile. With a heavy swing, the ogre launched a handful of flaming carcasses toward the soldiers. The men shouted in panic as their flesh burned. Their pain forced them to push the lifeless limbs off themselves—typically into other soldiers.

Another swing came from the monstrous beast, knocking bodies toward the other flank. The ogre's thick skin made negligible the bite of the flames, allowing him to swing with abandon. After another few hits, half of the corpses that were piled above ground level had been spread among the ranks and creating chaos. This time, instead of sitting back and letting the orcs and trolls charge the frontline, the crowned ogre walked through the pillar of flame and came out on the other end directly in front of the center of the formation. To the men's credit, none turned and fled at the sight of the creature that was nearly thrice their height. Instead, they raised their swords and charged headlong toward the menacing foe.

Gub held no expression as the soldiers came at him with their gleaming weapons. His hatred for humans had been so absolute that it had become normal. In his mind, they were nothing more than common insects to be swatted away. With tremendous strength, the ogre swiped his tree-club in a wide arc in front of him, clipping every man and sending them flying. Before the men could even register the sheer strength of the beast, Gub slammed his club onto a pair of prone soldiers. As the trunk peeled away, their bodies stuck to the bark, dripping gore over their comrades. Then, the men turned to flee.

CHAPTER FIFTY-NINE

DUEL

Hearing shouting to his left, Fangdarr turned to see the large ogre crushing soldiers with every swing. He spun back to Aesthéa. "Stay." The elf looked at him with the same expression as before, but it quickly faded as she saw the conviction in her lover's eyes. With a quick flick of her tongue against his hand, Aesthéa returned to the fray as Fangdarr rushed toward the monstrous ringleader.

As the orc fought his way around the formation, cutting down trolls and pushing them into the flames with every hindered step, he kept a concerned eye on the horrific creature that was obliterating soldiers without relent. Fangdarr had only managed to close half the distance due to the unending flow of enemies before a sharp pain in his side broke his focus. Furrowing his brow, Fangdarr regarded his assailant and came face-to-face with an orc.

Pushing his crude sword deeper into Fangdarr, the opposing orc's expression turned to glee as gleaming black blood trickled down his blade. As their gazes met, Fangdarr expected him to cower in fear and intimidation. Instead, the invader continued to push his iron sword to the hilt with a grin spread ear to ear. "You not fit to lead!"

Fangdarr bared his teeth in rage. This unnamed orc truly thought he could be his downfall. The chieftain wrapped his hand beneath the orc's chin. Mimicking his foe's grin, Fangdarr's eyes were nearly hidden beneath his scowl. With all the malice he could muster, the chieftain forced the invader's face closer and growled. "You are nameless! You will die the same!"

The orc showed no fear as Fangdarr brought Driktarr's hook down, piercing his foe's heart. With the last few moments of the unrecognized brute's life, Fangdarr pulled its dying corpse in line with his side to see how the wound it inflicted had stitched itself closed, leaving a scar in its wake.

As the light faded from the orc's eyes, he let out a weak string of words that the chieftain could hardly hear. "I am . . . another story." With that, his eyes closed forever.

Fangdarr looked at his foe and felt an intense sense of guilt for what he had done. He had slain more than a few orcs since the battle had started, but this was the first he had actually interacted with. It was much more difficult to ignore the sense of betrayal he felt running through him as he still clutched the carcass of one of his own. A young orc who simply wanted to carve his tale into the legacy of their greatest chieftain—the one who had betrayed them.

Now, you see what you have done? Crepusculus slithered back in. This time, Fangdarr didn't immediately shift to anger or attempt to mentally repel the dragon's plaguing essence. *All you worked for, your legacy, has fallen to ruin. You are no longer Fangdarr, the greatest chieftain of the Zharnik clan. You are The Betrayer. Kinslayer. You have turned from your own repressed and shackled people for the sake of those who would continue to see them wiped from their lands or worse. You are not the greatest orc, Kinslayer. You are the weakest.*

Every rational thought that Fangdarr could have rebutted with escaped him. *Am I weak?* He had never considered that his actions not only defined his future but reshaped his past. The legacy he had built among his people was once a legend that would be passed down through the generations. His tales would be told with grand recounting, immortalizing him forever. Yet, all would be unmade. His legacy would become one told through gritted teeth as warning to his kind. 'Do not stray from your people. Do not abandon us, for that is the path of The Betrayer'.

Fangdarr clutched his head in frustration and let out a ferocious growl. Sorrow turned to blind fury as he realized that he still held the orc's jaw in his hand. The chieftain gently laid the dead orc at his feet. *You do not deserve to burn, brother. You shall be remembered.* His finger ran over the new scar on his side, committing it to memory.

The chieftain watched as more of his kind were being killed. They fought for what they believed in and charged in to earn their place in the world—just as the orc Fangdarr had just slain attempted to do. *Perhaps King Nelthalius was right . . .. Is this path truly just? Will I let my people fade to the histories?* Each thought only made Fangdarr more confused and even more angry. His gaze fell upon his companions, those he loved even more than his own kind and had stood by him through everything.

Could he abandon *them*? If one thing was certain to Fangdarr, it was that they would never consider abandoning him. Never. How could he even consider turning his back on them? *Perhaps I <u>am</u> a weak orc . . ..*

No. I am not.

Roaring loud enough for all to hear, Fangdarr cut down the nearest troll. Then the next. Blood sprayed in every direction as Driktarr sailed through the air, cutting through flesh and bone alike. He carved a direct path toward the ogre, who had become aware of his presence. Finally, covered head-to-toe in the gore of his victims, Fangdarr rushed toward Gub. The ogre lifted his massive club as the orc charged, ready to intersect the wicked axe that would surely be leading. Fangdarr should have easily seen his foe's intention but rage had blinded him.

Fangdarr leapt into the air in the last moment with Driktarr raised high above his head. Gub nearly laughed aloud as the orc took the expected route and held the tree firmly in his path. Despite Fangdarr's improved strength, his axe's blade wedged deep into the wood and became rooted in place. He continued to hold the shaft of his weapon tightly, nearly on the tips of his toes due to the ogre's towering height. In his enraged state, he failed to notice as the brute's foot retracted before slamming into him.

Leaving his weapon buried, Fangdarr took the brunt of the blow straight to the chest, knocking the wind from his lungs and launching toward the flaming pit. Luckily, the littered corpses slowed his approach as he slid along the ground. Too angry to recognize pain, the chieftain was on his feet and rushing forward once again—unarmed and unafraid.

Gub stomped toward him with both meaty arms cocked back to swing the club. As it travelled through the air, Fangdarr tried to absorb the impact with his arm tucked against his body. But the ogre's strength was too great and, again, the orc was knocked away.

This time, Fangdarr crashed into a group of soldiers and trolls who were fighting nearby. The men shouted in frustration as the orc's interference allowed the more agile trolls to gain advantage over them. Fangdarr couldn't have cared less in that moment; he was too concerned with the crowned ogre that stomped toward him. He orc eyed Driktarr, still embedded in the tree. As Gub closed in, weapon cocked back, Fangdarr scooped up a crude iron sword from a nearby corpse and rushed to meet the menacing brute.

The tree passed through the air headed straight for Fangdarr's charging form. This time, the orc fell to his stomach as it soared barely overheard. Once it had passed, the chieftain sprang to his feet and lunged forward with the sword, piercing Gub's stomach. Howling in pain, the ogre launched a swift backhand, driving Fangdarr away.

Gub looked down at the wound in his fattened gut. Black trails of liquid spilled down under his belly and dripped to the ground in a steady stream. With a shout of anger at being shown his own mortality, the ogre dropped his weapon to the ground and straightened his makeshift crown. Once pleased with its position, he grabbed a pair of soldiers' corpses from the ground and launched them at Fangdarr.

Wincing as the armored projectiles bruised his raised arms, Fangdarr hardly noticed the next pair of soldiers being thrown at him—these two alive and screaming.

One wielded a sword, accidentally slashing Fangdarr across the arm as they connected. But he wouldn't wait as more missiles were launched in his direction. Forced to change his tactics due to the nonstop barrage of bodies, Fangdarr took to dodging, rolling, and deflecting any way he could. Gub's rolling laughter as the chieftain danced out of the way boomed through the area.

"Face me!" Gub taunted between laughs. After nearly two dozen bodies had been flung, none remained near enough to grab. Both factions had seen the ogre not discriminating in its fodder and steered clear to avoid being scooped up. "Eh?" The ogre paused, looking around at those who had scooted away. "Gah! Quit ya scramblin'!" he yelled, stepping toward the nearest fighters.

Fangdarr took the window of opportunity. As Gub trundled toward the warriors, who were pushing and shoving each other to get out of the ogre's path, the orc rushed toward the enormous club where his axe was rooted. He pulled with all his might but Driktarr remained wedged into the wood. Fangdarr pulled again, trying to wiggle it free and pushing on the trunk with his foot. His whole body tensed, and his muscles threatened to burst. He could feel the wood start to release its embrace and took in a large breath of air and tugged once more, straining his muscles to their limit. Just as his weapon was about to slip free, the orc was hit by another unlucky defender who had been caught.

The soldier yelped in surprise as his armor crashed against the side of Fangdarr's head, leaving the orc dazed as they both hit the ground. "No touch, orc!" Gub shouted.

Fangdarr could hear the ogre's heavy footsteps growing closer. His right eye was blurry from the blow, but he could feel his hand holding tight to a familiar object—his axe! His foe was almost upon him. *Get up, get up!* Fangdarr commanded himself. As he rolled to his side, he heard the bone-chilling scream of a soldier in Gub's hand just before the man's skull smashed against the earth in an explosion of gore. Still holding the dripping human flail, the ogre swung the corpse toward Fangdarr once more.

Half on luck and half instincts, the chieftain had barely managed to roll out of the way just as the lifeless man smacked against the ground where he had been, leaving a body-shaped blood print. After rising to his feet, Fangdarr stood facing Gub where they eyed each other viciously. The ogre leader's eyes turned toward his club, which lay a few paces away. When he turned his gaze back to Fangdarr, his eyes grew wide as he realized his mistake. The orc had already closed half the distance, axe held above his head.

Gub bared his few remaining teeth in frustration. He didn't have enough time to reach his weapon and was left with only the shattered soldier in his hand. With a roar of defiance, he charged toward the orc, swinging the man's mutilated corpse through the air.

Just as Fangdarr was about to take the final two paces to his enemy, he planted his left foot hard against the ground and reversed his momentum. Gub, anticipating a blind charge, swung wildly at the position where he had expected Fangdarr to be. Due to the orc's redirect, the ogre missed entirely and stumbled forward.

As Fangdarr completed his full spin, the blade of his axe connected against Gub's right arm and cut clean through the bone, reaching his torso. Before the ogre could even cry out in agony, Fangdarr had once again reversed his swing, extracting Driktarr. He swung it in a wide arc behind his head to accelerate before bringing it down in a devastating cut through Gub's neck. Fangdarr's eyes glowed with fury as the ogre's head rolled along the ground, dislodging the twisted twig crown.

A few onlookers were watching by then, distracted by the battle between the two colossal warriors. They watched as Fangdarr huffed with exhaustion before his axe's enchantment restored his vitality in a surge of energy.

Bending low, Fangdarr pushed his fingers through the greasy strands of hair on Gub's head. Once he had a handful, the chieftain lifted it high into the air and roared victoriously for all to hear. Every spectator watched with stunned expressions as Gub's drooped face stared back at them with lifeless eyes beneath sagged lids. Fangdarr's mountainous outcry rumbled through all with a heavy weight of fear and intimidation—even the soldiers, until they saw the ogre's dripping head in his grasp. The spectacle renewed their morale, knowing the greatest enemy had been culled.

Fangdarr kept Gub's head tightly in his hand. In that moment, he cared little about the overall effect it had on the war. This was *his* fight and victory had been necessary. A wave of relief washed over him as he came to terms with what that meant. *I am no longer the chieftain of the Zharnik clan*, he thought, knowing he had made his choice. *Just Fangdarr the orc.*

As the fighting around him picked back up, Fangdarr looked down at Gub's corpse with disgust. In part, he was thankful for what the ogre had given him. The menacing brute was the final threshold that brought Fangdarr to acceptance that he had turned his back on his people for what he considered the greater good. The orc watched as blood continued to spill from Gub's severed neck, saturating the dirt below.

Continuing his inspection, Fangdarr noticed an odd object peeking out from beneath a fold of Gub's stomach. It was hardly noticeable but still caught the orc's eye. He reached down and lifted the edge of the dead ogre's belly. Once the object was free from its entrapment, it rolled to the ground where Fangdarr could see it more clearly. As soon as he realized what it was, the orc dropped Gub's head and his face contorted in shock.

It was the small, round rock he had given to an ogre he had met years ago. A gift for a friend.

CHAPTER SIXTY

REPRIEVE

Fangdarr's heart gave way to the sinking feeling of despair. Eyes wet with sorrow, he picked the bloodied stone up from the ground. Memories of his past came flooding back like a wave of anguish as he rolled it between his fingers. The pebble had been given to a friendly ogre who had taken him in when he was lost and weary after his mother's death. The brute could have ended his life the moment he stepped into its cave. Instead, the creature showed him compassion and companionship. Fangdarr recalled their short time together and its sour ending. The pair had encountered a group of ogres in the forest who had agreed to take Gub in—but not Fangdarr. The orc was left alone in the empty woodlands as he watched his only friend leave him behind. From that day, he had changed and set off to carve his own path—the true beginning to Fangdarr's legacy.

With the simple trinket in his hand, Fangdarr couldn't determine whether he felt angry or hurt. The painful abandonment he had suffered from Gub's departure had plagued him in those early days of his solitude. But he had since forgotten its sting. With a slow exhale, Fangdarr slid the stone into his belt. Then, like years ago, he hid his feelings away behind an insatiable lust for bloodshed. Looking back to Aesthéa and Bitrayuul for strength, he growled in frustration and kicked Gub's head into the nearby flames.

Cutting his way through enemies, Fangdarr reached Bitrayuul and Aesthéa. Both resembled the splashed canvas of an artist as blues and blacks dripped down their skin. The orc could tell they were growing weary.

"We need to rotate the next shift!" Bitrayuul called out over the loud clashing of metal between assaults from a trio of trolls. With a heavy sweep of both hammers that had since been extinguished, the half-orc momentarily disabled his attackers by shattering their skulls. He tried to scan the opposite flank for Cormac but couldn't see the stout warrior beneath the sea of gray and black.

Straining his lungs, Bitrayuul called out to the captain. "Cormac!" No response. The half-orc deflected a lunging stab by a troll behind the three he had crippled. "CORMAC!" he shouted again with everything he had. Nothing. A sinking feeling came with the implication of that silence. Unfortunately, his opponents recovered, and his slight window of opportunity perished.

Fangdarr continued to look out over the ranks in search of his friend in between the crushing slashes of his axe. He listened for the sound of shields smashing against foes but couldn't pick out anything from the endless combination of sounds that rang in all directions. Roars of triumph, shouts of anger, wails of agony, and the clashing of steel, all fought for dominance and drowned out the others in rapid succession. "CORMAC!" Fangdarr yelled.

It wasn't Cormac that heard his call, however. As Fangdarr and his friends continued to cut down enemies and kick them into the drastically widespread flames, a large black wall formed. It stretched from where they stood to the opposite side of the gap in an opaque, magical barrier. Slowly, it began dragging toward the gap, pulling dozens of trolls and orcs with it. They knew right away that Elethain was granting them time to regain ground that had been lost. As the monstrous beasts were repelled, the path between Fangdarr and Cormac became clear, and their beloved dwarf stood on the opposite end.

"Cormac!" Bitrayuul and Fangdarr shouted as they rushed forward, Aesthéa close behind. Simultaneously, the dwarf called out to them in glee as his own worries were washed away. Brea'la followed the captain and all five companions met in front of the breach as soldiers regrouped behind them. Cormac and Brea'la were both covered in blood as well as their companions—some their own. The dwarf was bleeding from more than a few cuts on his head, soiling his bandage. Likewise, the satyress' body gleamed with sweat and a dozen trickles of vibrant green.

Bitrayuul looked at Elethain's wall as it began to wobble and crack. "We only have a moment. Cormac, we need to rotate defenders. Can you send for someone? I will send a man from my end as well to ensure the task is complete."

"Aye, lad, it'll be done."

"We will need to rest as well," Brea'la chimed in. Thankfully, Aesthéa tilted her maw down in agreement as none of the men wished to admit their own need for respite. Bitrayuul and Cormac agreed, but felt a deep sensation of guilt at the thought. These were *their* men now. How could they expect them to fight without their presence?

Fangdarr watched the magical barrier threaten to shatter at any moment. "You send for soldiers. I help Elethain." Before he had even finished, the orc was already turning toward the elf's location but was stopped by Bitrayuul.

"No!" All eyes were upon the half-orc waiting for an explanation. Bitrayuul could feel the sweat forming on his brow as he searched for a reason for his interruption. "I will go. You cannot fit in the staircase."

"Then I shall go instead," Aesthéa offered after shifting back to her elven form. "Brea'la will join me. We will rest in the room above, even for just a moment. Then we shall rejoin the fight." Everyone was nodding their acceptance—except for Bitrayuul.

The half-orc cursed himself for the predicament he had gotten into. *Do I even need to kill Elethain? Will Chakal still come for me?* A dozen questions formulated as Bitrayuul began to stress. It didn't matter, the druid and satyress were already half-way to the stairs by then.

Cormac and Bitrayuul each quickly sent a soldier to fetch the next shift. Though the fighting hadn't been going on for very long, exhaustion was rife through the men. Bitrayuul knew they would soon be at their limit and needed to rest. In addition, Cormac's defensive tactics had drastically consumed the supply of arrows by then, if any were left at all.

At least two hundred men lay dead after valiantly giving their all. Bitrayuul forced himself to look away from the hollow eyes of each fallen soldier. While they had suffered losses, the enemy's casualties were far greater. No less than five thousand trolls had been culled and most of the orcs. But it seemed a pittance against the near endless sea that still awaited them. What hope did they have to quell an army that dwarfed their own by over a hundredfold? Such thoughts were meaningless, Bitrayuul knew. Whether a hundred thousand or a million it mattered naught, for every enemy that charged toward them may be the blade that cuts too deep.

With the raging inferno at their backs, the defenders prepared themselves as Elethain's barrier dissipated and their enemy closed the distance. Both sides clashed together violently, swinging and stabbing at any in their reach. The chaos made nearly all disciplined action flee in place of recklessness and fearful actions. Men who had been trained for years for exactly this purpose broke their ranks and slashed away desperately, only to only to be overwhelmed by the horde. Orcs led by their blind lust charged into the fray to be cut down before they could even let the first swing of their sword whistle through the air. This was war. This was chaos.

* * * * *

From above, Elethain offered his smug smile as Aesthéa and Brea'la breached the staircase. Despite his expression, the necromancer nearly collapsed into their arms from exhaustion.

Seeing the satyress stare at her with a questioning gaze, Aesthéa said, "It is his magic. It consumes his life force as it is used. He needs to rest."

Together, they dragged his limp form toward the command room and kicked open the door. The thick stench of troll blood wafted out, but they entered with their noses scrunched and set Elethain on the ground. Brea'la glanced to the necromancer's ghouls standing motionless. "Will he be alright?" she asked, inspecting the slow-moving black markings beneath Elethain's skin.

"He just needs to rest. I am glad he aided us, but it could have killed him."

Brea'la could hear the sadness in the druid's voice. She calmly put a comforting hand on the elf's shoulder before sliding to the ground with a sigh of relief. Her eyes remained closed in bliss despite the unstoppable pounding of her heart. The muffled sounds of the war raging beneath them permeated through the stone.

Opening her eyes to the soft scuffle of boots dragging against the floor, Brea'la watched Aesthéa slide down next to her. Both were covered in the gore of their enemies and a few wounds of their own but offered no complaint. Instead, they took comfort in the other's presence and rested their head against one another. Though their minds raced, each fell asleep as the stress in their bodies began to slip away.

* * * * *

Cormac smashed the nearest troll with his shield making it more difficult to hear the soldier behind him trying to relay a message. "Ye what?" the dwarf called out, dipping beneath a high slice and retaliating with his own. "Speak up, lad!"

The man repeated himself, informing the captain that the second shift was in place and ready to take over. Barely hearing him, Cormac just nodded in reply and continued to push back against his opponents. Adjacent to the dwarf, Fangdarr was making short work of all in his path. The fear that the trolls had for Gub was nothing compared to what they felt for the one who had slain the menacing brute.

Following his brother's example, Fangdarr smeared troll oil over the head of his axe before igniting it in the flames behind him. With each powerful swing of Driktarr, he hacked down and immolated trolls simultaneously, sometimes two or three at a time. His greataxe's enchantment kept the orc's vitality peaked almost constantly, allowing him to barrel through the horde without ever feeling the tug of fatigue. Instead, his speed only accelerated as more and more fell to his blade and the lust for battle filled his heart.

A horizontal swipe clipped a pair of trolls and their bodies set fire. A vertical chop and another fell in a blaze, screaming in agony. As the countless enemies surrounding the orc managed to cut into his flesh, their ecstatic expressions quickly changed to horror as Fangdarr's wounds mended immediately and nullified their progress.

Cormac and Bitrayuul took advantage of Fangdarr's endless supply of energy and began organizing the shift change. With luck, the men on the second shift didn't hesitate to do their duty and join in the fray. Contrarily, between the fatigue that pulled at them and the sight of their friends dying at their side, every man that had survived the initial assault was ready to let those behind take their place.

The new soldiers watched in fear as Fangdarr continued to hold nearly a dozen trolls at bay, covering half of the hole of the wall singlehandedly. Their trepidation only grew as the orc started moving *forward* through the breach. Cormac noticed their frightful expressions and let out a loud howl of laughter. "Bahaha! Just be glad he's on our side, lads!"

Every man nodded in agreement as Fangdarr worked his enormous axe furiously. His roars of triumph rang out viciously over the crowd, interrupted only by the agonizing screams of his opponents.

By the time the men had rotated, nearly a hundred bodies were burning around Fangdarr. Every time his axe had consumed the oily substance, he would press his blade deep into another troll to replenish its supply before continuing his brutal massacre. Dozens of new scars had formed on his body. Small cuts, large slices, it didn't matter. Each wound stitched itself as quickly as it came, leaving only a white mark in its place.

Seeing that the men behind him were now ready, Fangdarr began backpedaling. In truth, he felt he could have continued for half the day, but the risk was unnecessary. While his mystical greataxe healed him with each enemy it culled, the orc was only ever one heavy blow away from suffering a wound from which he couldn't recover.

Bitrayuul and Cormac were off to the side in brief conversation before Fangdarr had returned to the ranks. Upon the orc's arrival, they informed him that they were going to rest in the command room with the others. They didn't need to tell Fangdarr that it was up to him to keep the men inspired to continue.

After climbing the stairs, the half-orc and dwarf looked out beyond the wall. "Bothain's beard, lad . . .." Cormac's mouth fell open in disbelief. "We ain't even made a dent!"

Bitrayuul scanned the masses. It was true, it didn't look as if they had made any difference at all. The enemy still stretched for as far as their eyes could see, just waiting for their chance. "True, but I see no ogres. Nor any orcs." A smile spread beneath his helmet. "We are winning."

Cormac let his own smile shine. They slowly opened the door to the command room, careful to not alarm their friends. Once the pair stepped inside, they realized all three were sleeping peacefully and moved to join them, laying against the cold stone and letting their stress dissipate with slow exhales.

Eyeing Elethain, Bitrayuul rolled away to avoid dealing with that mental conflict. Instead, he forced his thoughts to be more optimistic. His previous words repeated in his head as if they were a lullaby rocking him to sleep. *We are winning* . . .. *We are winning.*

CHAPTER SIXTY-ONE

DOOM

"Wake up, wake up!" Cormac shouted as he snapped to his feet after the door flew open and trolls started to pour in. His alarm was unneeded, however, as each of his companions were already making desperate attempt to repel the intruders. A roar of pain came from Aesthéa, followed by a retaliatory growl as her maw clamped around a troll's face.

Bitrayuul was struck hard in the shoulder as he got to his feet, knocking him off balance and toppling him back to his rear. The troll that had landed the blow was on him in a heartbeat, slashing relentlessly. Arms raised defensively, Bitrayuul's thick armor prevented the beast's cuts from doing any harm. Until one lucky slice found a small opening between the plates and cut his arm just above the elbow. Grimacing in pain, the half-orc kicked out with his boot to knock the troll away. He could feel the warmth of blood trickling toward his wrist, though there was no time to pause as his foe rushed toward him once more.

On the other end of the room, Elethain expertly repelled the mass of trolls pushing into the room by blasting them back with barriers and the occasional conjured abyssal spear he launched through the doorway. "We need fire!" Already beginning to feel his energy depleting by driving back the constant stream of invaders, he let a few slip past to be met by his risen defenders.

Cormac, guarding the opposing door to stop more trolls from entering, grumbled a response. "Bothain's beard . . .. Ye accidentally sleep through the night and wake up to a gray-faced bastard!" Though no one had heard him over the sound of weapons clashing and hissing trolls.

Brea'la stabbed forward with her spear a dozen times, keeping a troll out of reach. But each time she stabbed through its flesh the wound simply regenerated by the time the next strike landed. In between her lunges, the satyress glanced around the room in search of some way to start a fire. She dipped her shoulder back to avoid a lunging slice, cursing herself for her distraction.

Cormac ducked beneath a swiping dagger only to be forced to take a step back further into the room as another troll launched itself at him with both weapons leading. The stone blades shattered against the dwarf's shields before he retaliated with a heavy slam against both trolls, stunning them. In the moment he had purchased, Cormac created a pair of sparks by slashing his blades together. The embers quickly faded without reaching the oily residue on the trolls, causing the captain to groan in frustration as his foes pressed again.

* * * * *

Fangdarr shouted orders to the men around him, hoping to achieve some semblance of structured formation. But it was pointless. The chaotic battle raged on with drastically renewed vigor as the trolls started coming over the wall in a stream. He was uncertain how they had managed to scale the wall, but their method mattered little in that moment. Cutting down every foe he faced, Fangdarr watched in horror as the overwhelming wave of trolls surrounded the command room above. It was obvious that his friends had taken a longer rest than anticipated, as it was already nightfall. He had already been forced to rotate the defenders, bringing in the last round of soldiers to defend the city. The orc was rife with regret for not waking his friends during the last shift as he had considered.

With darkness on their side, the trolls came with all they had. The aggression they had shown before was nothing compared to the way the monstrous creatures acted in the dead of night with their numbers no longer being restricted. The odds had turned, and the beasts knew it.

As soon as Fangdarr had taken note that the trolls were somehow coming over the wall, he sent a man to fetch all soldiers—even those who had just been rotated out. This was no longer a containment. Trolls clambered over the battlements and jumped to the ground below in the front of the city, even outside the Military District. Fangdarr could only watch helplessly as hundreds traversed the wall and launched themselves into the Resource and Philosophy Districts, where only civilians remained.

Despite the horde rampaging through the adjacent districts, all Fangdarr's thoughts were on the command room. His concern only continued to grow as the entire structure was nearly hidden beneath a layer of trolls. They were even standing on top of the building and attempting to stomp through the stone roof. A tumultuous torrent of fear and rage gripped Fangdarr and he charged through the ranks recklessly toward the wall. Dozens of blades sliced through his flesh as he sprinted, but he couldn't stop. Not with his dearest companions trapped against such unfavorable odds.

Unable to squeeze his enormous body through the spiral staircase, Fangdarr ran along the base of the wall in search of a way up. In his blind desperation, the orc failed to notice as a pair of trolls leapt simultaneously from the wall and plunged their daggers deep into his neck, shoulder, and back. Fangdarr growled in pain. He immediately felt his legs go weak. His eyes turned hazy and the thick smell of iron filled his nostrils as his blood poured onto the ground.

Fangdarr growled weakly and tried to lift Driktarr to cut into one of the beasts. If he could just get one . . .. But it was impossible. The trolls' daggers were lodged deep into his shoulders and locked them in place. Their wicked grins stretched wider than ever as their victim fell to his knees with a whimper of agony.

This is the end, Kinslayer. The path you chose was false and you will die by an unnamed foe. You shall wither to dust among the humans you so cherish. Rest now, for your doom beckons.

The orc glanced up at the command room once more, hoping to instill enough rage into his heart to blind himself to the crippling pain. But he could hardly make out the building anymore. All he saw in the darkness was the gray forms crawling over the structure like a swarm of giant bugs. Fangdarr's hand gripped his greataxe tightly, clinging to his reliable heirloom desperately as his eyelids became heavy. For a moment, the orc thought he could see a tall and regal creature ahead, though its silhouette was blurry from his fading vision. It stood twice his height and seemed a mix of vibrant green and wooded brown. But as he blinked weakly, the vision faded and there was naught but stone and trolls.

* * * * *

"We can't hold them!" Brea'la shouted after wincing in pain from another cut. It was moments such as this the satyress was envious of the males of her kind, for their thick fur covered their entire body and not just their lower half. She growled in reply, pushing her spear with all her might through the troll's face and into a crevice in the stone wall behind it. Without hesitation, Brea'la reached forward and ripped the stone daggers from her temporarily incapacitated foe's grasp. Leaving her foe impaled, the satyress quickly began striking the stone blades against one another.

Brea'la cursed herself as her blood on the troll's dagger prevented any friction between the blades. "Come on, come on!" she panicked, wiping the weapon on her furry thigh. She looked up to see the troll sliding forward, pushing its face along the shaft of her spear. *Clash, clash, clash.* No sparks came as the blades slid along each other and the satyress was on the verge of tears. Not for fear of her opponent, but for letting her friends down. Lifting her gaze once more, she could see the troll was nearly at the end of the shaft.

From Brea'la's side, Cormac caught a glimpse of the weapons in her hand. "Ye need steel!"

Blinking in confusion, the satyress looked down at the daggers in her hands, realizing they were stone. With a groan of disappointment for her carelessness, she peered around the room in desperation. But her foe fell to the ground in front of her, blood dripping from its face. It met her horrified expression with a separated scowl as the gaping wound began to mend.

"No!" Brea'la shouted, kicking out with her hooves and driving the troll back. In the few precious moments she had, the satyress quickly turned toward Bitrayuul and ripped his father's hammers from his belt. She knew this was her only chance, both for her and her friends. Spinning back to her lunging foe, the heads of the hammers crashed together, releasing a shower of sparks just above the troll's head. She watched in trepidation, begging her deity to let the cinders remain full of life as they fell. Time seemed to slow, and the once-bright embers were dwindling quickly with the cool air. But a few stayed hot and fell onto the troll's face and immediately ignited the abundant supply of the flammable substance that shined against its skin. With an exclamation of surprise and relief, Brea'la jumped back as the immolated troll lashed out with its flailing arms, screaming in pain.

The room lit up as the intense inferno spread around the troll's body. Cormac's laughter echoed between the wails of agony. With a swift smack of a shield, the dwarf grabbed hold of one of the intruder's wrists and pulled it behind him into the other burning troll where it joined in its screams of pain. Aesthéa and Bitrayuul followed suit, taking advantage of the moment of fear in their foe's eyes as the thought of an excruciating death became real. Each launched their opponents into the fire and pungent smoke began to fill the room.

* * * * *

Fangdarr whimpered in agony as he felt the trolls pull their bloody weapons from his body. His eyes opened from the rush of pain for the briefest moment. In that single glance, the orc witnessed the bright light coming from the small window of the command room. *They're alive!* With the daggers no longer in his shoulders, Fangdarr growled in debilitating anguish as he put the last of his strength into lifting his axe. Blood poured from his wounds as his severed muscles strained. Thanks to his hulking form, there was still enough muscle to lift his weapon from the ground one last time. Shouting in defiance, Fangdarr plunged Driktarr's hooked end into one of the troll's abdomen. Reacting quickly, the other troll sank its daggers deep into Fangdarr's neck.

The orc's strength faded and his grip on his beloved axe fled with it. Driktarr dropped to the ground with a heavy thud. Fangdarr's body went limp and he slid forward, freeing himself from the troll's blades before crashing face-first into the ground.

CHAPTER SIXTY-TWO

DESPAIR

With a fire started, the group was able to quickly regain control. Despite their progress, they were still trapped within the room with the unending masses still pushing to get in and the blaze's thick smoke was starting to fill their lungs. At the first opportunity, Brea'la returned Bitrayuul's hammers with a grateful smile before dislodging her spear from the wall as the others maintained their defense at the entry points.

Cormac and Bitrayuul held the eastern door, while Elethain and his brothers held the west. Aesthéa and Brea'la were trying to fan the smoke out of the nearest window with little luck. Unable to stand the suffocating vapors anymore, the druid was forced to rush to the southern window to catch her breath. After coughing out the smog in her lungs, she opened her burning eyes and gasped. The trolls had formed a ramp out of corpses—and even a few hundred living trolls—to reach the top of the wall. One stood on each side of the command room and dozens of trolls were spilling into the city with each moment. The druid rushed to the other side of the room and poked her head out of the window to see how the city fared. Immediately, she cried out in despair, forcing her companions to turn their eyes to her.

"What is it?" Elethain called out. When no response came, he pressed further. "Aesthéa, what happened?!"

She couldn't speak. There were no words that could express the weight of her emotions. The druid fell to the floor and began sobbing uncontrollably with her head in her hands. Her companions stared at her in confusion before Brea'la crept anxiously to the window.

A look of shock formed on the satyress' face when she saw the reason for Aesthéa's sorrow. Somberly, she turned to her friends. "Fang . . .," her voice broke. "Fangdarr is dead."

* * * * *

The troll shouted in ecstasy, hoisting its blades in the air as if showing off the black blood dripping from them. Its companion, clutching its stomach in pain as it regenerated, joined in the triumphant uproar from the surrounding trolls as they stared at Fangdarr's corpse.

In response to the exciting chatter, the pair of trolls who had culled the enormous orc put their hands under his arm to flip him. They wished to show all the orc who had betrayed his kind and threatened to end their campaign—and claim Driktarr as their prize. Straining in effort, the trolls rolled Fangdarr to his back. They each jumped up and down in eagerness upon seeing the marvelous greataxe in all its splendor. Together, the trolls lifted the weapon into the air. Soldiers that were still fighting watched the spectacle and felt their hope vanish. If Fangdarr had fallen, they too would soon follow.

Bringing the axe back down due to its weight, the trolls began laughing to one another and clapping each other on the back. In their joy, they failed to notice the yellow orbs that were staring up at them with a scowl. The small bit of vitality that had been restored after piercing the troll's stomach had finally finished mending the most grievous of Fangdarr's wounds, offering him just enough strength to survive. He reached for Driktarr and felt his hand close around its familiar shaft before punching forward with the weapon. The blade cut into the one of his assailants and it let out a squeal of shock. By the time the second troll had noticed, Fangdarr had already pulled the axe from the first and let it swing forward, clipping the other in the thigh.

With each small attack, Driktarr drank the blood of its enemies and continued to heal Fangdarr's wounds. The second cut was enough to allow the orc to pull himself back to his feet. He raised his axe high and slammed it down through the first troll's meager forearm and continued deep into its shoulder. A surge of energy rushed through Fangdarr, restoring him completely.

Fangdarr eyed the crowd and a smile spread on his face. Every onlooker watched him in profound amazement. *He truly is immortal!* they thought as his wounds sealed themselves. The orc's blood still reflected in the dim moonlight, proving that he had indeed suffered the wounds that should have killed him. The masses waited for Fangdarr to make the next move, as they didn't know whether to fight him or bow to him in that moment.

Now, see how they fear you, conqueror. Respect you. Lead them, and they shall follow you to the end. Crepusculus' voice sweetly whispered in Fangdarr's mind once more with the promise of the world at his feet. His smile was still wide as he roared loudly, drawing confused looks from the trolls. But the outcry wasn't for them. The orc was waiting for a response that he knew would come. Like a rumbling echo, every soldier of

Wiston cheered at the sound of Fangdarr's roar. An *orc's* roar. One that gave them hope, despite their hatred of his kind. One that gave proof of his existence and his fealty to their cause.

With a final glance to what he was turning from, Fangdarr spun around and jumped high into the air before grabbing hold of the rough stone of the wall. One hand above the other, the orc scaled his way to the top as the trolls below just watched him dumbfounded. Fangdarr roared vigorously, pointing with his axe at a group of trolls standing between him and the command room where his friends remained. His smile remained pasted on his face in eagerness for the bloodshed to come.

* * * * *

Everyone nearly froze in shock at Brea'la's words. They would have each crumbled in despair, as Aesthéa had done, were it not for the desperate situation they were in. Bitrayuul, however, abandoned his position next to Cormac and rushed to the northern window.

"Lad, h-hey! Where ye goin'?!"

Brea'la faithfully stepped in behind Cormac without a word. The satyress' spear slipped past the dwarf and impaled foes as he hacked away with abandon, tears streaming down his face.

On the other end, Elethain was huffing with rage. His emotions were a storm inside him as he thought of all that Fangdarr had been to him. Hatred for the orc, hatred for himself, and a deep respect that had bloomed into admiration. The elf's magical tattoos danced wildly beneath his skin and his tear-filled eyes went wide in a frenzy. Launching a barrage of spears at the trolls in the doorway with a crazed outburst, he drove them back. Then, conjuring a pair of large demonic hands, Elethain grabbed a flaming troll corpse from behind him before flinging it out the door. Half a dozen of the trolls he had impaled with conjured spears burst into flames and howled in pain. He didn't hear any of it. All Elethain could hear in his mind was the repetitive string of words: '*Fangdarr is dead*'.

"Where is he?" Bitrayuul asked in a whisper as he searched through the masses below with no sign of his brother. "Where is he?!" When none came to his aid, the half-orc bent low and shook Aesthéa violently. "Where is my brother?! Show me!" The elf refused to budge. Growling in frustration, Bitrayuul lifted her from the ground and held her face against the window. "LOOK! WHERE IS FANGDARR?!"

Aesthéa's eyes were clamped tight, refusing to look at her lover's again. But Bitrayuul refused to relent. The elf whimpered in pain as his fingers pulled up on her brows to force her lids open. She fought back with all her might, but the half-orc and his magical gauntlets were too strong. Giving way from the pain, her eyes were pried all the way open and Aesthéa was forced to face the sight of Fangdarr's lifeless form once more. But he wasn't there. Her eyes opened of their own accord as she lunged her head forward in surprise.

"Well?!" Bitrayuul pressed as he watched Aesthéa scan the battle below.

"H-he's . . . he's not there . . .." Her gaze continued to skirt around. She didn't know whether to be terrified or hopeful. "I don't see him, Bitrayuul. He was just there." Aesthéa peered out the window then turned to the half-orc. "Hold my legs." Before he could register what she had said, the elf slid her slender form out the narrow opening as far as she could go. On instinct, Bitrayuul grabbed her ankles to stop her from falling.

Looking up at the trolls stomping on the roof, Aesthéa remained as quiet as possible to avoid detection. But in order to see she needed to stick her body out far. It was only a matter of time before a troll would spot her and she was completely defenseless. It didn't matter—she needed to know.

She scanned the masses along the battlements. *Cerenos help us, there are so many!* Thousands covered the entire wall in a blanket of black. The front half of the city was already overrun and soon the horde would be able scale the gates to the next districts where most civilians were hiding. *Come on, Fangdarr, be there . . ..* Aesthéa scrutinized every spot on the western battlement, expecting to see her giant companion sweeping away trolls with his axe. But she saw nothing but trolls.

A hissed roar came from above her as a troll lunged down at her with its blades leading. With barely any time to react, the druid shapeshifted into her bestial form. The pain she felt as the troll's daggers glanced off her fur-covered arms before the creature fell to the ground below was little compared to the agonizing squeeze around her midsection from the tight window. While shifting had spared her from the troll's lethal leap, her enlarged form nearly broke her bones within the stone embrace of the window. As soon as the troll fell past her, Aesthéa returned to her elven form and let out a yelp of pain as Bitrayuul pulled her inside. Her hand trembled as it pulled down the waistline of her pants, revealing a bruise quickly spreading around her entire midsection.

Bitrayuul knelt at the druid's side and began inspecting the wound, pressing it gently with his steel fingers. She yelped in pain and begged him to stop, but he continued. "This may be the only chance we get. We need to see if it's broken."

Tears lined her eyes as the half-orc continued his brief inspection, pressing deeper and deeper with his hand in search of bone. Aesthéa bit her lip to avoid crying out but it did little to mute her whimpers. Finally, Bitrayuul looked up at her, "It isn't broken, thank the gods. But I need to drain the bruise to relieve the pressure. Hold still."

The half-orc slowly slid a blade across Aesthéa's pale skin. She let out a sharp wince as the amplified pain became excruciating. But as the blood that had been trapped beneath her hip was pressed through the incision she exhaled in relief. Once it was drained, Bitrayuul stood and offered her a hand. "Can you move?"

Taking the half-orc's arm, Aesthéa tested putting weight on her injured leg and rotated her hips. She nodded in confirmation with a slight smile, forgiving Bitrayuul for his previous aggressiveness toward her. Before they could return to the window in search of Fangdarr, Elethain called out, "He's coming!"

As quickly as it had come, the necromancer's frenzied state had diminished as Fangdarr came into view—slashing and chopping all in his path. The orc was nearly to the door but with every encumbered step, a dozen trolls slashed at him from all directions, leaving a trail of black blood in his wake. Yet his axe always found a mark and restored him with each swing. Seeing Elethain's face through the flames of a pile of trolls in the doorway only ten paces away, Fangdarr planted his foot hard and swung his axe in a full circle around him, knocking away his foes. With the momentary respite, he sprinted for the door.

Behind the flames, Elethain watched the orc barrel through the host of trolls, suffering harsh wounds. Stretching his arms to each side, the elf slapped them together with a loud *clap*! All the trolls between the door and Fangdarr wore surprised expressions as an opaque black wall closed in from both sides with blazing speed—scooping up the pile of flaming corpses as well. The sound of bones crunching muffled the pained squeals as the creatures were crushed between the two barriers. When the magical walls dissipated, only a stack of burning corpses was left in its place, clearing most of the way for Fangdarr.

Raising Driktarr to his side, the orc chopped the last remaining troll, which had barely avoided the necromancer's walls and jumped through the fire. His grievous wounds began healing as he passed through the doorway—a thousand trolls on his tail. Once inside, Elethain returned to his task of repelling the invaders while Aesthéa and Bitrayuul embraced their companion. The druid looked up at him with tears in her eyes and saw a hundred new scars on his body. She whimpered at the thought of the pain he must have needed to endure to reach them.

"What happened, Fangdarr? I thought I saw you . . .. I saw you die." Aesthéa's arms clamped tightly around her lover as she cried, remembering the sight of his lifeless body.

Fangdarr pulled the elf's chin up gently to gaze into his blazing yellow eyes. "It take more than thousand trolls to keep me from you."

CHAPTER SIXTY-THREE

MADNESS

"Glad to see yer still kickin', son!" Cormac excitedly called out over the slams of his shields. "Now, could ye help us keep these trolls out?"

Fangdarr bent low to pick up a burning troll from the floor and walked to the eastern door to Cormac and Brea'la. "I hold. Go." They rotated positions as Fangdarr blasted the pair of trolls that tried to press into the doorway with the flaming corpse of their kin. As the trolls panicked and rolled on the floor, the orc fell to his knees to avoid the low ceiling. While his mobility was restricted, his axe wasn't. With a quick, sidelong chop of his weapon, both trolls ceased their spasms and caught fire.

Seeing that the other side had rotated, Elethain called out for Bitrayuul to take his place as well. The half-orc rose to his feet but paused, recalling his deal with Chakal. His mind raced as the internal conflict returned to the forefront. In that moment, he trusted Elethain's ability to help them survive the war more than Chakal's promises. *But what if I'm wrong? What if Chakal is out there helping right now? Or what if he kills me? What if he kills me even if I kill Elethain? Agh! Damn that wicked elf!* He stepped closer to Elethain. *It would be easy, though. If I just kicked him out into the trolls, he would be dead in an instant and none would know it was me . . .. No! We will not survive this war in either case. I will not die knowing I was a coward to the end.* Bitrayuul's grip tightened around his war hammers. *I will not disgrace my father.*

Solidifying his decision, the half-orc threw his hammers past Elethain's head, clipping the next pair of trolls. "Go! I will hold!" Bitrayuul's heart pounded as his weapons flew back to his grip and ignited in the wall of fire along the way. *I hope I made the right choice.*

Elethain let out an exhale as he sat next to the others while the orcish brothers kept the tide at bay. Thankfully, the smoke in the room had been nearly entirely expelled so they could catch their breath. Already their bodies ached from exhaustion and the sun had yet to come up. "We need a plan; we can't keep this up—even with Fangdarr."

Cormac nodded, rubbing the sore muscles in his shoulders. "Aye, ye ain't kiddin', elf. Never thought I'd see the day me arms were too tired of smashin' trolls, don't ye doubt."

Remaining silent, Aesthéa still tried to collect herself from her emotional distress and refused to take her eyes off Fangdarr. Seeing that the druid wasn't going to speak, Brea'la asked, "Do you have anything in mind?"

"Eh, there be too many of the beasts. By now the trolls must be at the walls to the next districts. Civilians, lass. We be holdin' our own here, but soon they"ll wash through the city and burn it to the ground. Won't be no one left." The dwarf stood with a groan and looked out the window. "Our lads are still kickin' below, but not many—perhaps about a third be left. Won't be long now . . .."

The mood grew somber at the realization that the war seemed unwinnable. Brea'la raised her head curiously. "Did anyone determine how they were scaling the walls? If they could do so all this time, why wait?"

"They couldn't," Elethain began. "Well, they *could.* The wall is sheer, they cannot scale it on their own. But they piled the corpses and formed a ramp. After a while, they realized they could just use the living as well. A few thousand would suffer the pain of getting trampled for a whole day to allow them to take the city. Ingenious, really. Since they regenerate, none would even need to sacrifice their lives for such an act. Though, the pain would be unimaginable. We are lucky they did not consider such an act immediately or this war would have ended before the first day. They are, apparently, not the dull cretins that we originally thought. This is their first war in open field, they typically rely on mountains. I am surprised they even came to this strategy at all, as they are leaderless."

Cormac scoffed at the elf's admiration of the trolls' tactics. Ignoring the dwarf, Elethain added, "The orcs are all dead and the ogres have fled, at least. But none of that matters. Trolls have been the major threat all along."

Brea'la looked around. "So . . . no plan then?" The subsequent silence was enough of a response.

Elethain's face turned into a smirk. "Well, there is *one.*" Each of his friends turned to regard him with a look of curiosity, reminding the elf of what it felt like to feel superior. His noble voice started slowly, "We have a way, but it's dangerous."

Cormac laughed. "Bahaha! *Dangerous*? Look around, lad!" Elethain's smirk only grew at the sarcasm.

"So, what is it, Elethain?" Aesthéa chimed in, finally pulling her gaze from her lover.

"Crepusculus." The necromancer pulled the clear orb from beneath his robes, revealing the miniscule shadow dragon imprisoned inside. He watched in relish as their eyes went wide.

"Crep— CREPUSCULUS?! ARE YE MAD?!" Arms out wide, the dwarf was shaking his head in disbelief.

Elethain rose to his feet, disregarding the dwarf's concerns. Aesthéa stood and put a hand on his arm. "Elethain, no. We cannot risk it. We should at least confer with Fangdarr and Bitrayuul first."

The necromancer tugged his arm away. "There is no time. We must do this now or all is lost." In truth, Elethain cared little in that moment for the sake of Wiston. All thoughts were on the power in his hand. He remembered the day he had enslaved the shadow dragon, and the day he had claimed Aurum, long ago. *God, the power!* It had been such a short time since the shadow dragon's soul was locked away that Elethain was certain that the beast would still fight for control. *I can do it,* he assured himself. *I can control it. I must, or we all will perish.* Despite the bickering of his friends, Elethain rushed to the window and smashed the orb against the stone. "Go, my minion! Go and seal my victory!"

As soon as the prison was shattered, Fangdarr howled in blind agony. The dragon's voice that had been poisoning his mind since the day of its doom resonated a hundredfold within him.

Free at last! Join me, Roaring One, and we shall claim the throne of Wiston then all of Crein! Come! Destroy our enemies. Shroud yourself in their blood and shatter their bones beneath your grip! KILL! Let them suffer your strength and know their weakness. KILL! Maim and mutilate as you please. KILL! Ravage their women and fill the land with your offspring to spread your legacy. KILL!

KILL! KILL! KILL!

Turn on those who would see you fall to obedience. KILL! The humans who imprisoned you for the color of your skin. KILL! The dwarves who took your true father. KILL! The elves who betrayed you in your time of need. KILL! The satyrs who did not believe in your strength without the blessings of a false idol. KILL!

KILL! KILL! KILL!

You are a conqueror. KILL! It was you who has earned the right to lead. KILL! You who shall eradicate the humans. KILL! The dwarves. KILL! The elves. KILL! Your friends. KILL!

Now is the time, Fangdarr. Kill your friends. KILL YOUR FRIENDS. ***KILL YOUR FRIENDS!***

Within a single moment since Crepusculus was freed, Fangdarr turned into the room and swung Driktarr toward Cormac. The dwarf let out a yelp of surprise as the orc's hunched form looked down at him with an intense viciousness that he had never seen. Luckily, in the orc's blind rage, his axe was embedded deep into the stone ceiling above. "What are ye doin', son?!"

Elethain quickly placed a magical barrier into the doorway to prevent the advancing trolls from entering where Fangdarr had left. "Crepusculus has changed him somehow! Someone hold the door, I have to control the dragon!"

Brea'la hurried over and began pushing back the trolls, allowing Elethain to return to the window. Though she worked her spear as fast as she could, the trolls' aggression increased drastically at the sight of their deity. The beasts came with reckless abandon, pressing the satyress back and landing multiple cuts on her in quick succession. At the western door, Bitrayuul too struggled against the amplified assault.

"Fangdarr, stop!" Aesthéa begged, trying to stare into her lover's enraged eyes. For a moment, she thought the orc would calm, but instead she was met with a heavy backhanded slap that knocked her across the room. Cormac leapt in, slamming a shield hard against their friend's face. The dwarf had hoped to daze Fangdarr enough to shatter whatever madness the orc had been afflicted with, but it was no use. Completely unfazed by the heavy blow, Fangdarr grabbed the dwarf and lifted him off the ground.

"No, no, no, Fang!" Cormac wiggled as much as he could beneath the impossible grip to no avail. Holding the dwarf tightly, Fangdarr's mouth opened wide and bit down on the dwarf's armored shoulder. "Bah! Get off, lad!" Locked in place, Cormac continued to slam his shield half a dozen times into Fangdarr's face.

Forced to ignore the orc's rampage, Elethain had both hands extended out through the northern window toward Crepusculus. Already he was sweating tremendously as he struggled to maintain control of the dragon as it rapidly grew to the size of a castle. He willed his brothers to aid his allies in defending the doors. A pair went to aid Brea'la while the third went to Bitrayuul, leaving Cormac and Aesthéa to deal with Fangdarr.

I own you, slave! Elethain communicated to Crepusculus as it flew over Wiston, roaring in all its grand splendor and leaving trails of blackness in the sky. The men below stared up in awe and fear, only to be cut down where they stood by their foes in the distraction. The presence of their idol put the beasts in a frenzy, spurring them forward with more quickness, more aggression, and more bloodlust. Pulling with all his might, the necromancer commanded the drake to come toward him. In the air, Crepusculus shook its head violently as if trying to break free of the mental chains. Yet, it finally complied and turned back to its master.

As the dragon flew past, Elethain saw that the light in its eyes hadn't been replaced by the dull blue to show that he had complete control. Nevertheless, he rushed to the opposing window facing outside the city—dodging a swipe from the orc—as he commanded his pet to strike out at the horde of trolls below. A torrent of purple liquid shot out from the dragon's mouth, covering nearly a thousand trolls in the first swipe. Their bodies instantly conflagrated from the acidic breath and started to spread like wildfire as the trolls writhed in pain and flung the burning ichor every which way. Another pass left a blazing glow of purple through the heart of the swarm, melting all it touched.

After Fangdarr swiped at Elethain, Cormac was able to break free from the orc's one-handed grip and fall to the floor. As he rolled out of the way, Fangdarr's crushing fist came slamming down where he had been. The dwarf called out to Aesthéa.

The druid rubbed the back of her head and looked at the purple blood on her fingers. Groaning in pain, Aesthéa watched Fangdarr attempt to slam his fist down onto the dwarf through hazy eyes. Looking around the room, the elf saw each of their allies too entangled to aid Cormac. It was up to her. Aesthéa considered shifting to her bear form, but what could she do? Even unarmed, Fangdarr was still strong enough to defeat her and she wouldn't risk injuring her companion. The druid came up with an idea just as Fangdarr began tugging on Driktarr's handle and rushed to the window.

With Elethain's ghoulish kin aiding them, Bitrayuul and Brea'la regained the ground they had lost and were effectively repelling the invaders. Elethain, however, was struggling immensely with the battle of wills between himself and Crepusculus. Sweating profusely, the elf cursed having spent so much energy defending their position. Flying over the trolls once more, the beast vomited a thick layer of acid directly in front of the wall, cutting off the rest of the army's advance. Confused by their idol's betrayal, the trolls started to run around in panic.

Elethain's muscles swelled with so much pressure that he could feel vessels bursting in his arms and head. With all he had, the elf strained against the mighty will of Crepusculus but couldn't hold on any longer. With an expulsion of breath, the necromancer was forced to relinquish control over the dragon and crashed to the floor. Nearly fainting from the severe fatigue, Elethain's bloodshot eyes screwed shut in agony as the dragon's victorious roar resonated in the distance. The elf tried to pull himself up but fell back in exhaustion, listening to the sounds of wingbeats coming closer—the drums of defeat.

CHAPTER SIXTY-FOUR

CONTROL

Cormac kicked out at the back of Fangdarr's knee, hoping to buckle it. But the orc withstood the blow without so much as a flinch and continued to pull on the axe still buried deep into the stone ceiling. With a final tug, Driktarr came free and Fangdarr turned to face Cormac. The dwarf stared back with grim determination, wondering just how far this fight would go.

Aesthéa looked back into the room with the sound of the greataxe coming free. She needed to hurry. Her hand extended out the window and the druid called to the roots hidden deep under the ground far below. Hearing Fangdarr roaring behind her only made her call out louder, ushering the growths as fast as she could. Desperation and fear amplified her abilities, granting her the strength to rip the plants from deep in the ground where they had shied away from the humans' reach. With a burst of dirt, a dozen thin roots surged from the earth toward Aesthéa. She directed them into the room where they quickly twisted around Fangdarr's limbs.

Restricted, the orc growled at Cormac and turned his attention to the plants that ensnared him. He pulled forward with his arms, snapping a few of the thin vines. The dwarf watched as the thicker roots strained and threatened to snap. Instinctively, Cormac jumped onto Fangdarr's back and began pulling with the plants. Aesthéa focused all her mental strength on restricting Fangdarr. "Elethain! Release the dragon!"

Elethain blinked rapidly as his eyes rolled in every direction. The pounding in his head was unbearable. Crepusculus roared as it soared overhead and into Wiston, a looming specter of death casting a shadow over the necromancer's eyes as he realized his failure. Soldiers and trolls alike could be heard screaming in agony as they melted beneath the drake's unforgiving and unprejudiced sprays. With the last bit of strength he could muster, the elf pulled himself to his feet before stepping toward the window—completely oblivious to the conflict in the room.

As soon as Elethain had managed to complete the taxing journey of a few paces, he witnessed Crepusculus lay another thick beam of acid across the battlefield. He shut his eyes to force back tears at his own weakness. *Why could I not hold it? A-am I so weak?* Stretching his hand out the window with laboring breaths, Elethain attempted to command Crepusculus once more. He could feel his legs give out beneath him, forcing the withered elf to hold himself up with his remaining arm. *No, I . . . must . . ..* He begged himself to continue as his eyesight began to fade. The black magic was draining his lifeforce to near depletion. Elethain tried to disregard the blood that was pouring freely from his eyes, ears, and nose. Finally, he slid to the ground in a groan and ended his feeble attempt.

Nearly devoid of life, the elf could only see splashes of white in his vision. His ears couldn't hear the struggle his friends were enduring hardly an arm's length away. And, worst of all, Elethain could no longer hear even his own thoughts. He sat an empty shell, siphoned away and consumed by his own magic. All he knew in that moment was the wicked and confident chuckle of the thunderous beast in his mind.

Elethain, your worst moment is upon you, Crepusculus communicated in its ultimate tone, condescending and triumphant. *It is not your death, elf. No, you have never feared death. You have lost, Caller of Shadows. Your greed. Your lust. Your ambition. You are but a human with pointed ears and pale skin, no better than those you hate. Now, you have fallen because of your lack of restraint. Your endless need to consume stretched too far and now you sit consumed in return. You have failed, Shadowspear. You have failed your friends, your people, and most of all yourself. Die now in horror of what you have become.*

Despite the harshness of the drake's words, Elethain couldn't register his emotions. Nor could he feel the sting of defeat or the shattering weight of his own failure in its gravity. There was only a white emptiness, both in mind and vision.

"Elethain!" Aesthéa cried out for the third time, though she knew it to be meaningless. She watched him crumble to the floor, distracted by his eyes staring straight at her but seeing nothing. The sound of a vine snapping brought her back to the task at hand, cursing her lack of attention. All her efforts returned to keeping Fangdarr restrained. But the druid became distracted once more as a large vine fell to the ground lifelessly. Aesthéa stared at it in blank confusion. *How?! It did not snap!* Her mind raced as Fangdarr started making progress with the reduced strength holding him back. Another vine fell to the ground. *What?! How is this happening?!*

Aesthéa scanned the room in search of some unseen force that was cutting apart the plants that barely held the ferocious and maddened orc at bay. A moment of clarity struck her as she remembered where the vines had come from. Staring out over the window ledge, a dozen trolls on the ground were hacking away at the roots to shut out the life within them. Another vine fell to the ground and Cormac groaned with all his might as Fangdarr snapped the remaining few entwining his limbs and regained his freedom.

From the window, Aesthéa watched as Crepusculus continued to lay waste to the soldiers and trolls below. She could only gaze in horror as the drake continued its onslaught and the trolls were already climbing over the next wall into the courtyard near the castle.

"Cerenos help us . . .."

CHAPTER SIXTY-FIVE

REALITY

Lucien rose abruptly, clutching his head in agony from the sudden movement. Muffled banging and screams had managed to find their way into his room within the castle, breaking his slumber. He pushed aside the lavish, silk blanket and revealed bandages wrapped around his exposed torso. The prince felt a tingle crawl up his spine as flickers of memories came to him of his encounter with that sinister elf came to him. Such thoughts fled quickly, however, as the screams and pounding refused to cease.

After donning the first tunic he could find—the bloodstained and dirty piece of cloth he wore the previous day—Lucien slowly walked toward the castle's entry chamber where a pair of guards argued. Before he could ask what the source of their dispute was, the answer became evident. The large door to the castle shook violently as helpless civilians outside smashed against it with all their might.

The scenes that filled the prince's mind upon hearing the peoples' screams struck a profound chord in his heart. For all his nihilistic talk of life's lack of meaning, Lucien found a sinking weight in his chest as wails of terror echoed beyond the portal. His mouth quivered. It was obvious people were being slaughtered like livestock. Men shouted as swords cut through them. Women screamed as their huddled forms sought to protect the babes at their breasts, only to be obliterated as they stood helpless against the horde of trolls that surged through the courtyard. Worst was the dying screams of children—that high-pitched squeal of horror before ending abruptly. Lucien's entire perspective of the world was brought to reality in that single moment with the annihilation of his people.

One of the guards took notice to the prince's presence after being shoved back by the other. "P-Prince Lucien! Your majesty, we didn't know you were awake!"

Lucien just stood in silence, tears streaming down his face as his focus remained on the sounds beyond the door. The guards stared at one another before calling for him again. "My lord, please, what do we do?" No response came. "My lord?"

Lucien couldn't hear the man as he was too lost in thought. *So, this is the depth of leadership? This is what my father wished to prepare me for? The harsh decisions that would define our kingdom for years to come.* Lucien clamped his eyes shut in sorrow. *THIS?! I was never prepared for this!* The prince wrapped his hands around a rail to steady himself. *Was I so selfish to ignore this? Could I have made a difference?* His perspective was shattering at the height of conflict, leaving him to pick up the shards of his identity at the worst possible moment.

The prince looked up to see one of the guards walking toward the door and muttering about the cowardice of the royal family. "Stop!" he yelled as the man's hands had wrapped around the door's locking mechanism.

Standing still but huffing angrily at the commanding call of a boy too scared to lead, the guard stopped. The man didn't know if he waited due to the order or his own fear. His knuckles were white as they gripped the lock.

"Walk away, soldier," Lucien commanded, hiding the immense shame he felt. "There is nothing we can do."

The guard spun on his heel. "You would sit here and cower?! Those are *your* people, Prince Lucien! You and your father have been absent from this war since its inception!" Stepping forward, the other guard attempted to stop the man from saying things he would regret but was pushed aside. "We have given our lives for *you.* This cursed family! And for what? So you can turn your back on us? Outsiders are leading Wiston right now. *Outsiders*! A damned *orc* is out fighting for Wiston and the men follow him. That should be *you*, Lucien! Instead you hide around the city and spout falsehoods about how life is meaningless to any who will listen. Your father sleeps away his sorrow on the edge of death instead of rallying and fortifying the men's morale. You aren't worthy to lead!"

Lucien took it all in. Even as the soldier approached him and began stabbing an accusatory finger into his shoulder, the prince absorbed every beratement that was slung. His eyes fell to the floor in shame as tears dripped from his chin. As the man continued to unleash rampant insults, the prince whispered, "You're right."

"What was that?"

"You're right," Lucien repeated, bringing his glazed face back up to meet the man's scowl. "I am weak. *We* are weak. You are right." A smile spread across the soldier's face—and an incredulous look formed on the other guard's—as his words seemed to finally resonate with the prince. The soldier nodded victoriously until Lucien added, "But the door stays closed." Unable to stand against his subordinate's wide-eyed stare, the prince turned back toward his room as the man shouted insults of his cowardice at his back. Lucien couldn't contain his emotions as he walked away, knowing he had just abandoned his people again. He wept from within the safety of the castle, promising himself he would be a changed man. An endless stream of curses came from the lone guard that sought to tell the world of Lucien's weakness.

But the soldier's feet remained planted and the door didn't open.

CHAPTER SIXTY-SIX

LINK

With each passing moment, more soldiers fell. Disciplined tactics fled in place of desperate thoughts of survival as the swarm of monstrous trolls overwhelmed their prey—soldiers, civilians, it mattered naught. Soon the city would be overrun, and mankind would be erased from history. The usurpation that had been orchestrated by Crepusculus, after years of whispering into the ears of prominent beasts. The trolls held no care that their deity of shadow killed thousands of their kind with each swoop of its lethal breath. Sacrifice was necessary. Under the drake's command, trolls would supplant mankind and seal their position within Crein—as was promised.

Aesthéa knew that failure was upon them as she watched the events unfold from the window of the command room. There was no chance of escape, nor even survival. She turned slowly to Fangdarr, squared off against Cormac, his most trusted friend. The elf knew they would all die that day. But she refused to allow her lover to die as a puppet and would do all she could to ensure that the orc would travel to the afterlife without claiming the lives of his friends—no matter the cost.

Shifting to her bestial form, the druid rushed forward and swiped a heavy claw across Fangdarr's back. The deep gash spilled blackened blood to the floor, but Aesthéa didn't relent. Though it tore her apart, she let another slash cut through his flesh. The orc's roar of pain nearly stopped Aesthéa dead, knowing she was the source. She cried out in anguish as another claw swung through the air—this time caught by the orc.

As Fangdarr held the druid's furry paw in place, their gazes met. For a moment, Aesthéa thought that perhaps the connection would be enough to break the affliction. But the orc's yellow orbs narrowed in a scowl and Driktarr rose.

Cormac cried out in protest and latched onto the orc's raised arm. "Lad, ye've got to stop! We're yer friends!"

Fangdarr's blind madness heard no words, compelled by the irresistible will of Crepusculus. A thousand whispers of conquest rampaged in his head, painted red by the blood of his allies. The orc grunted in annoyance at the dwarf's persistent tugging. Growling vigorously, the orc's arm began slowly moving toward his lover.

The elf's sorrow-filled eyes did nothing to slow the orc. She didn't even attempt to break free. Her will to live had drained the moment Fangdarr looked her in the eyes and chose to end her life, maddened or not. Aesthéa waited for the axe as it edged closer and closer.

From the side of the room, Bitrayuul called out to Fangdarr. The half-orc knew that Crepusculus must have been the source of his madness, but how could they possibly kill the drake? He glanced around the room and saw the pair of ghouls and Brea'la managing to hold back the tide at the other end. Then his eyes fell upon Elethain who lay motionless on the floor, eyes open but unseeing.

"Brea'la!" the half-orc shouted over the commotion of roaring trolls. "Be prepared to defend!"

"What?! What do you think I've been doing?"

Her words fell on deaf ears as Bitrayuul rushed across the room. Standing over Elethain's unconscious form, the half-orc hesitated. *Is this the right decision?* He stared back at the door he had left where one of the elf's ghouls fought tirelessly. "You're alive, Elethain," Bitrayuul said in a harsh whisper, lifting the elf by his robes. "But I need you not to be." The half-orc let out a small whimper as he stared into the elf's face. "I know you're fighting still. I know you're using the last of your energy to keep your brothers here to protect us." He wept in between words, hardly able to continue. Everything relied on this moment. Bitrayuul's voice fell to just a slow murmur. "You need to release Crepusculus. If you cannot, or will not, then I must end your life. Please don't make me, Elethain. We need you. You *must* break the link. Damn your pride, Elethain. Break the link!"

Bitrayuul waited in silence as his heart pounded, expecting the necromancer to shrug off all ailments and do as requested. The half-orc turned his head to regard the entryway he had abandoned. Trolls were pushing the ghoul back by sheer overwhelming numbers and would soon pour into the room. And Fangdarr's axe was only a hand's length from Aesthéa's sorrowful eye. "Come on!" He shook Elethain roughly, begging the elf to make the decision for him. "Please . . .."

But Elethain heard nothing. He saw nothing. What dwindling spark of his consciousness remained was simply maintaining the link to keep his reanimated kin—and Crepusculus—alive.

Sucking in his breath to steady himself, Bitrayuul slid the blade of his gauntlet deep into the elf's heart. The half-orc let out a whimper as a purple stain began to spread through Elethain's robes, overtaking all other hues. He was forced to turn away as the last flicker of life in the elf's eyes diminished.

As soon as the necromancer was no more, the bond that granted the three ghouls life expired. Bitrayuul was already on the move toward the western doorway as the reanimated corpse withered to dust, stopping the trolls from entering the room.

Every troll stopped and turned to their deity in concern as Crepusculus let out an odd roar as if in great pain. They watched as the immense shadow dragon began falling toward the ground. Then, their idol that had made their glory possible withered to dust with no explanation. It was simply gone. The burning frenzy that had coursed through their veins turned to ice and froze them in place as they stared expectantly at the spot in the sky where the dragon had perished.

Returning to their cowardice, every troll began screeching in terror. If their deity could inexplicably fall, so too could they—all of them. In their irrational minds, the chance of victory had been eliminated with their god. Only a tenth of their massive army had fallen, still outnumbering the remaining human soldiers a thousand to one. Yet all turned and fled, believing they would soon follow Crepusculus to the afterlife.

As the squealing creatures clambered over the wall in fright, Bitrayuul turned upon hearing a familiar voice behind him. "What happened?" Fangdarr's eyes scanned the scene and met his lover's defeated expression from a hair's breadth beneath the blade of his axe. "Aesthéa?!" Driktarr fell to the floor, with Cormac following shortly in an exhausted sigh of relief.

"Bothain's beard, lad. Ye need to eat a wee bit less meat!" The dwarf lay on his back, letting the cool stone chill the sweat that drenched him. He lifted his head slightly to look up and over his beard to see Fangdarr clutching Aesthéa tightly and sobbing. Cormac rotated his neck to Bitrayuul, then to Brea'la, each huffing with fatigue. "What happened to the trolls?"

Bitrayuul moved out of the doorway to let the dwarf see the endless stampede of trolls scrambling back over the wall. "They are retreating in fear with the fall of Crepusculus. Just like when we were ambushed in the Tusks. Once Raz'ja fell, their fear overcame rationality." Even the half-orc was surprised at their neglect of the party, though their cowardly pack mentality was consistent. It seemed all they cared about then was their own survival.

Brea'la approached Fangdarr and Aesthéa with a smile on her face, but quickly gasped in surprise upon seeing Elethain's crumbled and blood-stained form against the wall. "Elethain!"

Fangdarr and Aesthéa halted their embrace and rushed to the elf. The orc watched in grief as the satyress shook the limp necromancer gently and pulled open his eyes. "D-did I do this . . .?" He fell to his knees and pulled Elethain closer as he joined Brea'la and Aesthéa.

"No," Bitrayuul said softly. "I did."

CHAPTER SIXTY-SEVEN

STAINED

All eyes were on Bitrayuul. Fangdarr's expression was twisted deep in sorrow, searching for an explanation. "Why?"

"I had no choice, Fangdarr. He needed to break the link to Crepusculus."

Fangdarr glared at Bitrayuul. Before the boiling rage in the orc could be formed into words, Aesthéa put her hand on Fangdarr's shoulder. "You were afflicted by Crepusculus and attacking us. The trolls were spurred on by the dragon's presence as well. There was no chance of victory without the drake falling. It was the only way."

Bitrayuul was surprised that the druid had come to his defense. He removed his helmet to reveal the pain on his face. "I didn't want this, Fangdarr. I begged him to break the link, but he was too far gone."

The grief in his brother's voice seemed real enough to Fangdarr. His shoulders slumped and he turned to face Elethain once more and scooped the elf into his arms gently. Feeling the necromancer's slender form limp in his embrace only caused another wave of sorrow to surge through him. Staring directly into his friend's unseeing eyes, the orc closed them with his fingers.

They all waited as the remaining trolls charged by. Realizing his back was still torn from the deep rends of Aesthéa's claws, Fangdarr passed Elethain to Aesthéa and Brea'la. Without a word, the orc bent to retrieve his axe and walked toward the nearest door. No explanation was necessary for his friends, especially once cries of pain and terror could be heard after the squelching chops of his axe. It wasn't long before the orc re-entered the room with his back fully healed and fresh blood dripping from his weapon.

Once the straggling trolls all seemed to have passed, the companions exited the command room and looked out beyond the wall. The dark sea of monstrous creatures continued to flee, tripping over each other in their hysteric cowardice. A few hundred died even in their escape as they foolishly stepped through the trails of acid left by their idol, a final reminder of their mortality. Fangdarr leaned over the parapet to see the pile of corpses that had been stacked against the base of the wall. He couldn't help but acknowledge just how close he and his friends had come to being wiped out. Yet, somehow, they had survived. His downtrodden eyes glanced to Elethain. *Well, most of us . . ..*

As one, Fangdarr and his allies turned toward Wiston. Bitrayuul and Cormac both gasped at the sight that lay ahead. Thousands upon thousands of corpses—humans, trolls, and orcs alike—were littered among the Military District. Fires continued to thrive, including the hellish pit that seemed to be insatiable in its lust. The number of bodies was astounding. Below, they could see a few remaining soldiers struggling to step over the layered carcasses in search of survivors.

"So few . . .," Bitrayuul whispered louder than he had intended. Not even a thousand men were left.

The dwarf rested his hand against the half-orc's back. "Aye, lad. But there'd be nothin' left if it weren't for ye."

Bitrayuul stared down at the purple blood that had nearly dried completely on his blade. Despite the truth behind Cormac's statement, he felt a deep sense of guilt. No matter how much troll or orcish blood had been spilled by his gauntlets, it was Elethain's blood that coated the blade. The metaphor seemed fitting to Bitrayuul, as he knew the action he took would weigh far heavier on his heart.

With Elethain back in Fangdarr's gentle and cradling arms, Bitrayuul and Cormac led the party through the city. Their movement was slow, hindered greatly by the corpses they had to step over. Thousands of lifeless eyes stared up at them. Fangdarr met the hollowed gaze of many of his kind, but, for the first time, he didn't shy away. He no longer considered them kin. Neither did he feel responsible for their deaths. The orc may have turned his back on his people and their barbaric ways, but it was they who had turned their back on what was right.

Slowly, the group picked a path through the Military District. The few remaining soldiers each nodded to them in respect as they passed, some even shaking their hands in tearful gratitude. Grim expressions still seemed to be on most of the defender's faces as the thought of the war being at its end seemed too surreal. As the realization slowly set in, some fell to their knees and wept—in thanks or in sorrow—while others kept their sternness and carried on, refusing to show emotion.

After a long while, the party had finally reached the gate to the courtyard. To Bitrayuul's surprise, the doors were slightly ajar. He gasped and rushed ahead, pushing them open with haste. The door only shifted a short distance before getting stuck—not enough for him to even stick his head through. With his imbued gauntlets granting him more strength, the half-orc pushed harder and began scraping the obstruction aside with the heavy door. But as soon as he looked up to walk through, he froze in his tracks.

"What is it, Bit?" Fangdarr asked.

After no response came, Cormac jogged ahead to join Bitrayuul. The dwarf had a good idea as to what may have entranced the half-orc, and when he poked his head into the doorway as well, his suspicions were confirmed. He pulled his head out with a heavy sigh, only adding to the others' curiosity. Cormac grabbed Bitrayuul's wrist in reassurance. "C'mon, son. It'll be alright."

Light whimpers echoed from inside Bitrayuul's helmet as he took a small step forward. It took all he had to make that step and it was even harder to take the next. His boots dragged with an immense weight as he willed himself to walk through the entryway, knowing what was on the other end.

After Cormac and Bitrayuul disappeared behind the partially open door, Fangdarr could hear his brother's sobbing lamentations. Concern ripped through the orc as those woeful cries pierced his ears with a profound sadness. "Bit, what's wr—" Fangdarr passed through the door to console his brother but halted immediately upon meeting the source of Bitrayuul's sorrow.

Standing wide-eyed with his mouth ajar, Fangdarr scanned the courtyard and saw naught but the mutilated bodies of civilians. Thousands. Mothers, elders, children—none had been spared. The silence that rang through the once beautiful garden was deafening. From behind the orc, Aesthéa and Brea'la each gasped upon passing through the door before quickly turning to sobs. Though none of the group had any attachment to these people, the brutal massacre shook each of them to their core.

"Were we too late?" Brea'la asked between cries. She looked around and saw no form of life. Even wails of pain would've been welcome. Instead, there was only the still silence of death.

Cormac continued to pull Bitrayuul forward and the rest followed. As they took care to avoid stepping on the victims—as much as one could—Fangdarr noticed that not a single troll was seen among the dead. This was more than just a massacre. This was eradication, the attempted annihilation of the human race. He looked to Elethain in his arms and understood Bitrayuul's actions. At the time, his brother hadn't even known about the fate of those beneath their feet. Fangdarr realized that if it had been *he* who had needed to make the decision, he would have done the same as Bitrayuul after seeing the horrors they walked through now. Despite the rationality, it didn't dispel the guilt the orc felt for thinking he would have killed his friend for the greater good.

As they reached the steps leading up to the castle's doors, Bitrayuul cried out in sorrow again. The pile of corpses at the door stood three bodies high. Together, Bitrayuul and Cormac gently lifted the lifeless forms out of their path. By then, even the resilient dwarf had tears in his eyes as he was forced to lift the broken bodies of children that had been trampled beneath their own people and place them to the side.

Bitrayuul, sobbing profusely without relent, placed a hand on the giant door of the castle and fell to his knees. Though he had been showing his emotions, the half-orc had been restraining the true level of grief he felt in his heart. Until that moment. As his hand slid across the door slowly, feeling the hundreds of scratch marks left by the terrified people trying to get in, he wailed in anguish. His mind created the illusionary scene of helpless women and children clawing at the door before being cut down without hesitation. He felt stained by the horrors in this courtyard. This day would live with him forever—every part of it. From the light weight of dead children in his arms to the thin indentations of the scratches beneath his fingertips, Bitrayuul would never be the same. None of them would.

Fangdarr placed a hand on Bitrayuul, followed by Aesthéa and Brea'la who then turned to embrace Cormac as well. The half-orc continued to weep despite their comfort, even as the doors began to open.

CHAPTER SIXTY-EIGHT
HEROES

The giant doors groaned as they swung inward, revealing a pair of guards cautiously peeking through the gap. Bitrayuul looked up at them and immediately charged forward, pushing through the opening. Before they could react, the half-orc had a hand tight around both of their throats.

"W-wai— st-sto—" one man gargled, unable to form words beneath the powerful squeeze crushing his windpipe. They each kicked out with flailing legs, hoping to break Bitrayuul's hold, but it was hopeless. Fueled by rage, he refused to relent. Cormac tugged on his arm and begged him to stop, but Bitrayuul couldn't hear him. All he saw was the vision in his mind of the people who begged for salvation but were met with the unyielding presence of a sealed door. The guards' faces turned purple and their heartbeats began to fade yet Bitrayuul still squeezed.

"Why ain't ye helpin' me?!" the dwarf shouted to his motionless friends. "Fang?" Cormac glanced to Fangdarr, then to Brea'la and Aesthéa. Each dipped their head low in dejection, despite the heinous act the half-orc was committing. "We just *saved* the humans! Now ye want to kill 'em!?"

No matter how much the honorable captain pleaded, Bitrayuul pressed with all his might until the light faded from the men's eyes. Blood trickled from their sockets and still he refused to release them. Finally, with a wailing sob, Bitrayuul dropped their corpses and screamed in anger.

The sound of quick footsteps echoed through the expansive room. "What have you done?!" Bitrayuul looked up to see Lucien staring at him incredulously from the top of the small set of stairs further in. He knew the prince was the reason the guards didn't open the castle during the invasion, even if it had meant protecting thousands. Bitrayuul stomped forward, this time *all* his companions attempted to stop him—a pair of guards was an atrocity, but a prince would unravel all that had happened.

Lucien saw the determined half-orc and began backpedaling. "Wait, I can explain," he started, but Bitrayuul kept coming. "You were right!" The angered half-orc halted a few paces away but was still tense, as if expecting Lucien to elaborate. The prince steadied himself with a breath and spoke more slowly. "You were right. I should have helped you in the war. I was a fool."

Bitrayuul visibly relaxed and let out the shaky breath he was holding in. "Why?"

"Because it was necessary for Wiston's preservation. There were too few left in the castle. Opening the door would have served only my conscience—and with it the death of the last leaders of Wi—"

"LEADERS?! What *leaders* are those, Lucien?" Bitrayuul took a step forward, his fiery anger refueled. "If I recall, the '*leaders*' of Wiston cowered in fear or hid with the civilians while *we* led your people. *Your* people. The people who died outside that door in the hopes that their '*leaders*' would provide salvation."

Lucien had his hands in the air defensively and was continuing to backpedal as the half-orc advanced on him threateningly. The prince's service workers watched in curiosity from the far corners of the room, listening intently to the scolding. In truth, they agreed with all the half-orc was saying, but could never voice such an opinion. "Alright, alright! Yes! You are right! I abandoned them. *I* demanded the door remained closed. And I would do so again, if needed. *That* is what it is to lead. Hard decisions must be made for the greater good!"

By then, Bitrayuul was laughing at the irony of the prince's statement. A flux of emotions plagued him, distorting his thoughts. He drowned out the prince's continued rant of justification and listened to the dozens of thoughts in his head. Then, without a word, Bitrayuul launched a fist into Lucien's stomach before walking toward the side hallway where King Dariel waited.

Doubled over and coughing, Lucien called out to Bitrayuul. "H-hey! Wait!" Grimacing in pain, the prince hobbled after him. "Stop!" The rest of the party followed to ensure the furious warrior didn't turn his aggression to the king.

Bitrayuul approached the king's door and slowly turned the handle. As he stepped inside, he was shocked to see Dariel standing with a smile. Already the man looked much livelier than the last time Bitrayuul had seen him. The king's skin was starting to return to a normal color, though was still stretched as if drained. "Ah! Master Bitrayuul!" The old man reached out and put a hand on each of the half-orc's arms, careful to avoid the bloodied spines. "So good to see you." Lucien stepped into the room and started protesting as Fangdarr and the others entered close behind. The king paid Lucien no mind, however, and lit up upon seeing the large orc. "Fangdarr!"

"It is goo—" Dariel started before realizing Elethain lay in the orc's arms. His expression turned somber. "Oh. I'm sorry for your loss, my friend." The king offered his hand in comfort and took a moment of silence in respect. Then, his eyes turned to happiness once more and filled with tears. In truth, the king was happy, but his cheeks became lined with streaks of wetness as he looked upon the bloodied and battered group in his chamber.

"My friends . . . I can't begin to thank you for what you have done. Truly. You are heroes, all of you. I heard your shouting from here, Master Bitrayuul. You are right. We *did* abandon Wiston. It shall be my greatest shame. I know not whether our people will trust us ever again. But," he smiled, "I do know that it is only in thanks to you all that we have a chance to win back their faith. Without you, Wiston would have burned to ash and man erased from history."

Bitrayuul, still nearest to the king, didn't know what to say. All the anger he felt before was muted with Dariel's renewed vitality. The half-orc removed his helmet to let Dariel see the conflicted expression on his face—a mix of despair and hope. "Your majesty . . . the war is over. Many were lost. Some that could have been avoided," Bitrayuul turned a glare toward Lucien. "Others not."

Dariel caught the accusatory scowl toward his son. "But it *is* over, yes? Wiston is safe, thanks to you. To *all* of you!" The smile returned to his face as ignorance over Bitrayuul's words fell on deaf ears.

"We are not here for recognition or heroic tales. We only did what we thought was right."

"Of course, of course. Pray tell me, what is it I can provide to show my gratitude? Ask anything of me and you shall have it."

Bitrayuul, secretly wishing for nothing more than to see Lucien punished for his cowardice, remained silent. Instead, he turned toward his companions.

Fangdarr stepped forward first. "Elethain sent to Jesmera. Be buried with his people." The king nodded his acceptance and waited for the next request.

Next, Aesthéa approached with a grim expression and was greeted by Dariel. "And you, miss?"

"All I wish is for a life with Fangdarr, and you to be granted the knowledge that we sought the aid of my people at the risk of his life. We were promised their assistance, yet it was revoked when the time came due to their hatred of you. I wish no ill will or war between our nations, but it is wrong for me to hide such a fact from you. King Nelthalius is not one to be trusted." With her words of wisdom offered, the elf retreated to the group and was met with a smile from her lover.

Dariel frowned with the news. "I see. That is unfortunate. Thank you for informing me." He seemed to contemplate the implications of the elves' betrayal for a moment before shaking his thoughts away. "Anything else?"

Bitrayuul turned to Brea'la who simply shook her head. Then he looked to Cormac who did the same. With a sigh, the half-orc smiled at Dariel. "I just want to go home, to Tarabar."

* * * * *

After staying in town for two more days, the companions were riding slowly away from the city on horses gifted by the king. Each turned and waved at the large group of people atop the wall that wished to see them off. The soldiers would never forget what the unlikely group of outsiders did for them and waved with tears in their eyes. Bitrayuul looked at his friends and smiled as the cool breeze blew through his armor, glad to finally be out in the open again and heading for Tarabar. They had all decided to join Bitrayuul on his return to ensure the road was safe—and to get away from the suffocating coddling by the people of Wiston.

Bitrayuul looked to the edge of the forest—or what remained of it—and saw the death that had swept through the once lush woodlands, a heavy reminder of what had just transpired. Yet, against all hope, they had succeeded. Though he was plagued by visions that would torment him for the remainder of his days, the half-orc breathed easy. He was eager to go home.

Fangdarr happily looked to his content brother, glad that Bitrayuul didn't shatter from ending Elethain's life. Perhaps it was due to being a necessary act for the greater good, the orc wondered. Nevertheless, Fangdarr knew it must not have been easy to claim the life of a friend, even given their mutual distaste. His hand slipped into his belt and retrieved the small pebble that had escaped from beneath Gub's stomach. He rolled the stone between his fingers, remembering the day they had met with fondness—though the memory had faded with time. *No, killing a friend isn't easy.*

"What's that?" Aesthéa asked, noticing Fangdarr staring intently at his trinket.

The orc quickly clamped his hand around the rock and placed it back into his belt. "Memories."

CHAPTER SIXTY-NINE

INESCAPABLE

Lucien stared out the window as the band of heroes departed Wiston. He couldn't bear to bring himself to their departure. Instead, he elected to watch in secret from the high vantage point of a tower within the Philosophy District. As his gaze traced their movement, the prince felt the longing sensation to take to the wind with them and see what the world had in store. But he couldn't, for his own crippling doubt of himself forced him to remain immobile. How he wished he had chosen to act differently . . .. Perhaps things could have been different—had he not been such a coward.

That was the truth of it, after all. And Lucien knew it. For all his ramblings and deep inner thoughts reflecting on the futility of joining the war, it wasn't some profound speculation that kept him hiding on the outskirts, shying himself from its terrifying view. Far from it. It was fear, masked by fancy words and a glorified perspective that even he had started to believe. The prince hated himself for not rising to the challenge when he was needed most. In part, he blamed the high expectations placed on him. They had worn him thin before his time was ready, leaving naught but a hollow shell—at least that's what he told himself. But as he watched those who selflessly risked all for his people fade along the horizon, all the lies he told himself were laid bare and Lucien could do nothing but sigh at his weakness and wallow with regret.

The prince forced his chin up, promising himself that things would be different. Wiston would be made strong once again. And he would be strong. For himself, for his people. No longer would he hide from the horrors of the world as others acted as a shield in his stead. He would become a beacon of hope for his people. Lucien's lips curled into a small smile. "Thank you," he muttered toward Fangdarr and his friends.

"Oh, I wouldn't do that just yet, little prince."

Shocked, Lucien turned around and immediately let out a blast of force from his extended palm at the vaguely familiar voice. His eyes shot in every direction as the room seemed to fill with cackled laughter. *Where is he? Where is it coming from?!* Preparing himself, the prince slowly pivoted from the center of the room with great caution.

"Your heart gives you away, Lucien," the voice taunted. "Your body moves slowly, but your heart pounds. It thumps deep within your chest, for it wishes to run in fear. But it cannot. And neither can you."

Lucien spun quickly, expecting the intruder to attack with his last word. He immediately threw up magical barriers to prevent any assault that may have been coming but was left sweating anxiously as none came.

Another cackle of that maniacal laughter came—this time from directly in front of him where the barrier stood. "You are so undisciplined! You could have been quite the little warrior, you know. One to rival even the elven elders. But you lack refinement."

"Who are you?!" Lucien shouted in frustration. He could feel the drips of sweat on his forehead sliding down toward his brow.

Once more from every direction, his assailant responded, "Me? I am just a simple elf, really. I have my passions like any other, killing just happens to be my favorite. I saw you gawking out the window at your city's saviors. Lucky for you, their convictions are strong. Much stronger than yours, at least . . .."

Lucien growled in anger. "Just tell me what you want!"

The prince could feel the hair rise on the back of his neck. Spinning around forcefully, Lucien's eyes met Chakal's and the prince's heart sank. In that merciless grin Lucien could see the elf's intent clearly. Only one of them would be leaving the room.

CHAPTER SEVENTY

ONWARD

Approaching the tree line for the Lithe, each of the companions silently lamented at the sight of the forest stripped of its greenery. The forest seemed a corpse for as far as the eye could see. The vivacious soil had been trampled beneath the stomps of hundreds of thousands, depleting it of life and leaving it scarred. Every tree in the woods was bare and charred, resembling a carcass left to rot in the sun.

They had kept to what remained of the road on their journey east to Tarabar. The group had even passed through Beast's Teeth—or the pile of ashes that once was—along the way, not even bothering to stop and search for survivors. The war had wiped out nearly all of mankind. From their brief discussions with King Dariel before departing, less than a quarter the population had survived—and very few able-bodied men. Thankfully, winter was still many moons away, but it would certainly prove to be difficult, nonetheless.

After three days of steady riding, Tarabar came into view. Cormac and Bitrayuul immediately brightened at the familiar sight of the enormous and intricate steel doors at the base of the mountains.

"Ah, there it be," the dwarf chirped with a smile. "Home."

Bitrayuul put his hand on Cormac's shoulder. "We made it."

They decided to take a short rest before continuing the last spread of path to the city. Aesthéa and Fangdarr rested easily against a tree, laughing at each other's whispered jokes. Taking a seat next to the pair, Brea'la began to join in on their humor. Bitrayuul caught Cormac eyeing the satyress' bare torso and flicked the dwarf's ear with a playful grin.

"Eh?!" the dwarf squeaked in startlement. As his eyes met the half-orc's, he knew he had been caught. "I, uh, I . . .. Oh, to hell with ye! I was just noticin' that her hair be the greenest thing in these damned woods now, that's all!"

Bitrayuul couldn't help but smile as Cormac's cheeks turned red from embarrassment. The half-orc cast a quick glance at Brea'la, skipping over the bareness of her skin and staring at her vibrant green hair. It saddened him to realize the truth behind the dwarf's statement. With the Lithe stripped of color, the satyress truly did stand out.

Cormac flicked Bitrayuul's ear in reciprocated playfulness as the half-orc's gaze lingered too long. "It be the hair, right?" They both laughed loudly. Once their comedy had come to an end, the dwarf looked up at Bitrayuul. "I heard ye went to see Lucien before we left."

Caught slightly off-guard, the half-orc gave a light sigh. He didn't want anyone else to know that he had sought out Lucien. In truth, he had wanted to make amends. Though, he would never apologize for the actions he took. "I did. Well, I tried to, at least."

"And?"

"And he wouldn't see me. He just hid in the room with the door locked. He didn't answer me as I called through the door—nor when I may or may not have pounded on it in frustration." His eyes slowly turned away, knowing he had acted childishly.

Cormac chuckled. "Not that the brat didn't deserve a stern talkin' to, of course. How'd ye know he was there if he didn't answer?"

"I saw his shadow beneath the door. He was standing right in front of it. Probably waiting to see if I would kick it down so he could blast me away." They each let out a howl of laughter once more, lightening the mood. "More likely, I think he just didn't know what to do. It was obvious that he was conflicted. I think he hates himself for his cowardice and doesn't want people to see. I suppose I can understand. It doesn't make me any more forgiving, though."

"Aye, lad. That's rough, don't ye doubt. I ain't no prince, so I can't say what might've pushed him away from reality. All I can say is let the past stay where it belongs and look to the future. Wiston is safe and will rebuild. We survived the war and can live to tell the tale over our next pint back in the comfort of our own homes." Cormac patted the half-orc on the shoulder. "It'll be good to be home. Ye won't forget the war, son—ye never will—but bein' home will help."

* * * * *

As the group approached the partially open gate, Cormac spurred his horse forward, eager to see his old friends atop the entry. He called out to them eagerly, a look of excitement on his face. He had so much to tell them. Stories of his travels with Fangdarr, the tale of taking on Crepusculus, and much more were ready in his mind to be shared over a dozen tankards of ale. But after calling out for a third time with no response, the captain grew worried.

"What is it?" Bitrayuul asked as he and the others pulled up their horses. Cormac's grim expression gave the half-orc an unsettling twist in his stomach.

"Somethin' ain't right. There be no one here."

Fangdarr stated the obvious with a foreboding tone. "Gate open."

They all dismounted from their steeds and approached the gate with caution, their weapons drawn. Slowly, they slipped through the gap and entered the tunnel. As they made their way deeper, the light that came through the gate started to diminish. "How can you see in here?" Brea'la whispered, causing the group to stop and look at one another.

"Can you not see in the dark?" Bitrayuul asked. The confused look he received was all the answer he needed. He exhaled and pondered for a moment, staring at his friends for feedback. All he got in return was silence. "Alright, umm . . . we don't know what's down here, so we can't light a torch. Can you wait here and watch our backs?"

Brea'la seemed dejected at the prospect of being left alone but nodded in agreement. Bitrayuul and Cormac continued their slow steps toward the city. Fangdarr put a reassuring hand on the satyress' shoulder and smiled before following the pair down the tunnel. Aesthéa grabbed Brea'la's hand and squeezed tightly. As the elf was about to depart, the satyress pulled back on her hand. When Aesthéa turned toward her friend, Brea'la planted an intense kiss on her lips. Disregarding the druid's shocked expression, the satyress smiled and released her hand. "Be safe, Aesthéa."

The elf slowly turned and walked away, still coming to terms with what had just occurred. She cast a glance back to Brea'la, who stood smiling at her, before rushing to catch up to Fangdarr. Aesthéa opened her mouth to relay what had just occurred, but clamped it shut. It wasn't the time to have a rampaging orc attacking his friends again.

All four of them crept forward, coming up to the end of the tunnel where it opened into the vast, cavernous city. Cormac peeked out, unsure of what he might see, Bitrayuul close behind. As soon as the dwarf got his head past the tunnel wall, he clamped his hand over his mouth and shut his eyes to muffle his startled outcry. Confused, Bitrayuul poked his head out as well and gasped aloud before falling backward and couldn't stop from crying out.

Growing worried, Fangdarr and Aesthéa looked at what had caused their companions to collapse in despair. They each stared at the scene and understood immediately, for the entire city was littered with thousands upon thousands of corpses, both dwarves and trolls. As the orc took a few steps forward, the smell of rotting bodies assaulted his nose. His eyes scanned every direction yet were always met with the same outcome—more bodies. Listening intently, he tried to shut out the distracting sobs of his brother and friend but heard nothing. No clashing of steel, no shouting, nothing.

Taking another few steps, Fangdarr approached the first dwarven carcass he saw. Blood stained the stout warrior's tunic and was caked to his armor and skin. The dwarf's open eyes stared up at him in their hollow lifelessness. Fangdarr lowered his fingers to close the warrior's lids in respect before moving his hand to the dwarf's cheeks. The body was dreadfully cold, giving evidence that he had fallen days ago.

Fangdarr turned at the sound of Aesthéa approaching. She looked up at him and whispered, "What should we do?"

"Nothing we can do."

They returned to the tunnel where Bitrayuul and Cormac had nearly collected themselves. They saw the downtrodden expression on the orc's face and nearly fell victim to another round of sobs. Fangdarr waited patiently as they each remained immobilized in their sorrow. Finally, Bitrayuul rose and pulled Cormac to his feet. "W-we need to look for survivors," the half-orc muttered.

Fangdarr was already shaking his head, but his dwarven ally was nodding. All three started whispering in argument over the risk involved. As their whispers turned to hushed shouts of disagreement, Aesthéa turned her head back to the city. She perked her pointed ears and tried to drown out their commotion. "Shh!"

They each turned to face her and saw the elf cautiously listening. "Do you hear it?" she asked.

Listening in silence, they all waited for any sign of noise and for many moments they heard nothing. Then, a faint noise started to resonate. It slowly grew louder, but still they were unable to determine the source. Aesthéa's eyes shot open as her heightened hearing caught on. "Run!"

None argued with the elf. They trusted her judgement, turned on their heels, and retreated up the tunnel. The sound of hollering and hissing started to grow louder from deep within the city, resonating off the walls and bouncing through the corridor. They sprinted up the path and could see it grow lighter as they approached the entrance. Brea'la stood with her back to the wall as they sprinted toward her. Her surprised look turned to determination as she turned and started to run up the ramp before they even reached her.

Each slid through the gap in the gate once more and pondered what to do as the light of the sun blinded them. They wondered if they should close the doors to seal the trolls in or simply run away. As their eyes readjusted to the light, they could see a small army rushing toward them in formation. Bitrayuul placed a shielding hand over his eyes. "It's King Dariel! We can repel the trolls with his aid!"

Cormac looked toward the humans as they approached. The king was riding in a horse-drawn cart that was marvelously decorated and wearing a gleaming suit of armor. There must have been at least five hundred soldiers at his rear, each on horseback. "How does he know the trolls are here?"

Bitrayuul didn't hear him. He was already waving excitedly in greeting as the men closed the distance. Fangdarr and Cormac shared a glance in concern. The soldiers of Wiston halted a spear's throw away, drawing a confused look from Bitrayuul.

The half-orc stepped forward. "Your Majesty, thank Bothain you're here! There are trolls in th—"

"You will hold your tongue, demon!" Dariel's eyes were red with rage. He seemed to be struggling with even getting the words out of his mouth. "You . . . You will pay for what you have done!"

Bitrayuul looked around at his friends before returning a perplexed look back to the king. "What? Done what?"

The response only seemed to anger Dariel more. Tears streamed down his face and he appeared to be ready to collapse. "You. Killed. MY. SON! ATTACK!" All five hundred soldiers obediently followed their king's command—though they hated to do so. Every man knew that it was Bitrayuul and his allies who had saved Wiston, not King Dariel. Yet, as far as they knew, Bitrayuul was accused of killing the prince. They had no choice.

As the men charged toward them, Fangdarr drew his weapon. However, Cormac pulled on his arm in restraint. "No, lad. We can't. Not after all we did to keep the miserable whelps alive in Wiston." The sound of muffled hissing was still barely audible from the gate at their backs. "C'mon, we've only got one choice."

One by one, they each turned and slipped back into Tarabar, despite the looming threat that still lingered in the city. After they passed through the gate, Cormac disappeared into a secret tunnel to the side and pulled on a latch. As the enormous gate began to close, the dwarf hoped he had made the right choice. For the mechanism was irreversible, trapping them in the city.

As the light in the tunnel faded with the groaning of the doors, King Dariel's grieving shouts of outrage could be heard. His pained sobs were joined by the pounding of his fists on the steel door, screaming curse upon curse at the half-orc and his friends. Outside, Dariel fell to the ground and wept in sorrow before his men carefully dragged him away.

With the door sealed behind the party, the hissing of the wicked trolls was amplified. Aesthéa gripped both Fangdarr and Brea'la's hands tightly as they realized the severity of the situation they had found themselves in yet again.

Cormac nodded his head and steeled his resolve. "Only one choice," he repeated as he started walking down the path toward his homeland.

www.ingramcontent.com/pod-product-compliance
Lightning Source LLC
Chambersburg PA
CBHW030623310726
48979CB00003B/849

* 9 7 8 1 7 3 2 7 6 0 7 5 2 *